T0065471

THE CASE OF THE BEAR

A Bertrand McAbee Mystery

Joseph A. McCaffrey

authorHOUSE®

AuthorHouse™
1663 Liberty Drive
Bloomington, IN 47403
www.authorhouse.com
Phone: 833-262-8899

Published by AuthorHouse 06/16/2021

ISBN: 978-1-6655-2871-9 (sc)
ISBN: 978-1-6655-2870-2 (e)

Cover Picture: The bear tamed by St. Sergius of Radonezh.
Photo taken at the St. Sergius Monastic Complex, Russia.
Photo by Joseph A. McCaffrey

LIST OF BOOKS BY AUTHOR

OTHER McABEE MYSTERIES

All of the above titles are also available in audiobooks. Please refer to Audible.com.

REVIEWS OF EARLIER MCABEE MYSTERIES

Cassies Ruler

If you love mysteries, you have plenty here to keep you glued to your book until it unravels at the end. While a violent account, it reflects the subject at hand and makes for a good read.

- Illinois Standardbred

Confessional Matters

The good guys and bad guys in the religious hierarchy and other disciplines are wonderfully characterized, and the action seems very much like what you read in the newspapers nowadays.

- The Leader

The Pony Circus Wagon

The pre-WWI historical background and international intrigue distinguish this gripping and at times addictive mystery from the standard whodunits.

- Kirkus Reviews

DEDICATION

In memory of my dear brother Jack (February 16, 2021) and his stalwart wife Martha

PART ONE

RUSSIA: FROM AFAR

CHAPTER ONE

Joanna Goodkind drove up Gaines Street, a treacherous and steep hill in winter. The plows had moved most of the snow to the curbs but there were the inevitable chunks clinging to the pavement. Given that her Mercedes 550 had Nazi DNA in it, the pieces were of no consequence to the four wheeled beast. She turned left at Eighth Street at the crest of the hill, and proceeded west. Most of the 100 year plus mansions that she now passed had been restored to their original 19th century condition. These structures pointing south had a commanding view of the Mississippi River that served as the border between Iowa and Illinois. She was in the city of Davenport, Iowa, and across the river stood Rock Island in Illinois. It was the Quad City area completed eastward in Illinois by Moline and Bettendorf in Iowa.

Joanna was in a hurry. An ugly Iowa winter had dismantled her, depression draining her. Tears would burst from her eyes without warning as darkness and cold grabbed at her. Historically, she would have escaped to her place in Naples, Florida, right after Thanksgiving, usually just before winter's onset would stab at her stability. But her mother's physical and mental condition had worsened, taking her from assisted care to skilled care. Joanna had no real choice – she was stuck, first time in 13 years. Yes, winter would have its way with her this year as her mother coped with the terror of realization that she wasn't going to get better. And the way that Joanna felt right now, neither was she. Thank God for Alexandra. As she headed west, she could feel the pull of this most important person in her life.

Eighth Street, west of Gaines, had a serrated ridgeline. Some of the mansions sat precariously on the edge of a steep bluff, as close as fifteen feet from a plummet. Others had generous amounts of land.. Alexandra had the best of it all including extraordinary views of the Mississippi Valley and its centerpiece the third longest river in the world.

Four ancient oaks were spaced perfectly behind a four foot stone wall. A steel gate was positioned under an arch as Joanna pulled up to a voice activated receiver. She pressed the red button, waited, and to a "Yes?" she gave her name. The gate slid to the right of her Mercedes and allowed entry. She drove in and wove into a circular drive that allowed three parking spaces pointing north. She knew these spots were meant for clients. All three were vacant. She parked in the rightward slot, looking in her sun visor's lit mirror to make sure that the dread that was in her did not compromise her face. Alexandra could be quite stern about these things.

Joanna rang the bell and the front door was opened by Maria, the maid. They exchanged greetings as Joanna went to the room, to the left of the entryway, in which Lady Alexandra displayed her prodigious skills. Joanna sat. It was a small room, no more than nine by twelve, given the otherwise huge size of the whole dwelling. The carpet was laid to an almost exact fit to the floor. On occasion, she studied it. It was hand-woven, Iranian by her estimation, and probably a 19th century heirloom. Its reds, blues, and tans, patterned so beautifully, captured her eyes. A round table stood close to the center of the room. It was of a rich mahogany with sturdy legs that curled into fists. Two cushioned seats were positioned on either side of it. A low wattage lamp was alit and stood to the right of a heavily curtained window. The walls of the room were painted a dark grey. She sat, experiencing a nervous expectation while she awaited Alexandra's entry.

She came into the room from behind Joanna, with her usual silence, except for the slightest of tinkles from her silver wrist bracelet. Joanna looked up at her and said, "Thank you so much for seeing me I…"

Alexandra raised her right hand and stopped her mid-sentence. She complied immediately as she looked into the intense black eyes of this gaunt, tall woman whom she estimated to be in her mid-50s.

She sat and in her Russian accent said, "Close your eyes and give me your hands."

Joanna did so and for what seemed an eternity there was dead silence in the room. This was not uncommon but today's stillness seemed longer than ever.

"Your husband, Joanna. You are so fearful. Please speak with me I have never felt this much fear in you before. Dread is a more appropriate word, yes?"

Joanna's spent-up self broke as tears poured from her eyes. Only the tight grip of Alexandra held her from collapsing to the floor.

At the very same time in downtown Davenport,

Bertrand McAbee arose from his desk chair, paced seven steps and stood in front of his large office window. What he saw was a bleakness that had an eerie beauty. River Road, AKA Iowa 67, railroad tracks, a snow covered plain and the Mississippi River – not frozen over, but movement slight and turgid. To his left he observed the Rock Island Arsenal, a mega federal facility reached on the Davenport side by the famed rotating Arsenal or Government Bridge under which Lock and Dam Number 15 was located. Number 15 was part of the elaborate mechanical process that allowed barge traffic to and from Minnesota to Louisiana along the great river. Directly across from his gaze was the city of Rock Island in Illinois.

He had been urged by his friends to go south for the winter. He went for a few weeks in January but for reasons he was not sure of he tired of Pompano Beach in southeast Florida and he came back to Iowa's wintry ways.

He was adrift in many ways as he speculated about his future. He still had his investigation agency, ACJ, but like the Mississippi River it too was moving slowly. When he hit his mid 70s he decided to put brakes on the enterprise. In doing so he cut his caseload by 80%. New cases were rarely accepted by him. When they were, they had to have a quality that enticed him by their singularity. Recently he had three such. One, in particular, continued to bother him even though it had been somewhat successfully resolved. It was about a high school club that was started 50 years ago called the Demosthenes Club. As it turned out it brought McAbee into contact with some vile characters, ultimately, the case leaving a bittersweet taste in his mouth.

He turned and saw Pat Trump at his office door. She

had been with him from the beginnings of his altered career course from classics professor at St. Anselm College to the world of private investigations. No Pat Trump, no successful agency, he knew. She had red hair, now with strands of silver, and fox-like features. She had pulled, cajoled, and sometimes yanked him into this profession he had not taken to naturally. She wasn't clinically obsessive-compulsive like some of his clients but she was quite capable of holding her own with them. He and Pat were almost a perfect complement to each other, a strength of his was a weakness for her and vice versa. She had aged, as did everyone he knew, but he appreciated her engagement with the aging process. She was doing pretty damn well against this indefatigable foe.

"Pat. What's up?"

"Are you in the mood to meet with Peter Goodkind? Huge urgency. Wants to come over here now."

"Did he say what it's about?"

"What's new? His wife, the work, et cetera, et cetera," she said acidly.

Peter Goodkind was a client virtually from the beginning of ACJ, almost 25 years ago. At that time, he had issues relating to employee theft at a few of his home construction sites, minor cases successfully resolved by ACJ. There was very little to suggest that Peter would grow his business into a major success story in eastern Iowa and western Illinois. Through strategic partnering with two other investigation agencies ACJ had maintained control of the security side of Goodkind's business. While shedding accounts, Bertrand had suggested to Goodkind that he look elsewhere for his security needs. It did not go over well. Bertrand relented for

5

the time being. That said, Peter Goodkind was a difficult man, mercurial, capable of going from pleasant to irate in a millisecond. His politics were so far to the right that he could vie for the banned list on Facebook and Twitter. As the country became more divided McAbee noted that, at first with curiosity and then with increasing alarm, Peter had gone into overdrive. His comments became tinged with hatred and severe verbal violence. Pleasantries were now rare, regularly replaced by diatribes heavily leavened with anger, spite, and intolerance. Within these occurrences McAbee adopted the role of counselor, venting Peter's emotions and engaging in summaries that he echoed back into Peter's belligerence. Sometimes this would lead Goodkind to edit what was even to him over the top.

It was hard for Bertrand to determine the exact point where he knew that Peter was dealing with more than radical politics. He concluded that over the last four months Peter was dealing with the possible onset of dementia, that their relationship was entering into a quagmire, and that at the end of it all only bad things would happen.

Goodkind's business operation was up the street, a block from McAbee's offices. It was 11:30 a.m. He had a luncheon engagement at 12:15 in a nearby downtown restaurant. "If he can come over right now I'll see him. But 12:10 is the finish point," he told Pat.

She came back to his office in less than a minute. "He's on his way."

Goodkind made it to ACJ in seven minutes. It was 11:39 exactly as he saw McAbee conversing with his snippy secretary Pat Trump, she seated, he leaning over her desk and pointing to some piece of paper. McAbee straightened out as Peter launched himself toward McAbee loudly saying, "Ready to go!" and advancing toward the open door to Bertrand's office. It was important to him to get McAbee's attention as he had unnecessarily imposed a deadline onto their meeting. McAbee followed as Peter went to the small side table that McAbee regularly used for their sessions. They both sat.

McAbee said, "Peter, you seem agitated. What's up?"

Peter paused for a moment before moving toward what he knew would be construed as a rant. McAbee's eyes were fixed on him. A dead stare. He felt that this man could deconstruct and reconstruct him with his oddly changing blue and gray eyes. Over the years he had learned not to underestimate him even as this PI seemed to foster such a perception, skillfully disarming the universe.

"Big problem. Big problem. My wife, Joanna. This isn't the first time with her. She's blabbing about me and my supposed bad temper. I'm high-spirited I'll give you that. I'm wired and always have been. Why do you think I'm so successful for God's sake? I want you to put a full court press on her. She will hurt my business, real bad." For effect he shot his right index finger out toward McAbee who continued to look at him with far too much calm. He noted this trait appearing more and more in their relationship over the last few months. The more excited he was the more the calmness from McAbee. It was as if McAbee didn't care. Enthusiasm was expected dammit.

"Peter. Slow down for a minute please. A few questions. Joanna? Blabbing? Connect this for me."

"Hah. I noticed it about a year ago. She's been

7

withdrawing from me. At first I backed off. Not one of my virtues. Probably too much patience as I came to realize that she saw me as a sleeping volcano. She withdrew more. So I figured that she wanted the old Peter. Maybe I went overboard with her. She kept pulling back from me no matter what I did. I'm in the TV room she goes into the kitchen. I go into the kitchen she heads into the TV room. I drive home sometimes in midday and she's not around. I ask what was her day like and she says she was home all day. She lies to me. This is not Joanna. I think affair. That's not her either. I put Eddie on it."

"Eddie? Your brother?"

"Yes. Trust him with my life. Start tracking her I say to him. His best buddy is a retired cop. They trade off. Here's the deal."

McAbee was upset with what he was hearing. Peter, a large man, unkempt white hair and oversized glasses, was kicking this into a bad place, advancing his suspicions about a tricky situation into a war of sorts as his belligerence and anger intensified. "Before you tell me more Peter allow me a question," he asked with purposeful serenity, "why would Joanna be pulling away from you?"

"Well that is the goddamn question Bertrand isn't it? Are you listening to me?" Index finger jabbing the air a foot from McAbee's face.

McAbee's thoughts went to Joanna, a good woman. Patient and gentle. He was worried about her. He had never seen Peter to be physically dangerous but he was starting to reconsider. Negative energy saturated the office. "Very well Peter. Tell me what you want from me."

"She had a good friend, Melanie. Melanie was a screwball. Spacey as hell. Other worldly. Never could understand that relationship but they got along. Melanie was a vegan, into all sorts of queer diets. She once told me that she took 50 different pills every day. All sorts of crazy crap. Way beyond Whole Foods stuff. You name it she took it, inhaled it too – aromatherapy, the works. Into hypnosis too. Searching for past lives that she lived. Screwball! Well what do you know? She died. Brain cancer. Dead two weeks after it was diagnosed. Wouldn't go to the hospital. Probably double-downed on spinach. Goddamn weirdo!"

"Joanna buy into any of this?"

"No, not really. Except for one thing. Melanie kept screeching about some witch with magical powers. We had Melanie over for dinner once. She brought her own, didn't trust cooking from anyone else. She starts telling me and Joanna about the witch. She says that *I* should see the witch. Do me good. Can you believe this? Some wacky Russian called Lady Alexandra. So Melanie died about nine months ago. Water under the bridge. Not missed by me, for sure. So here is the deal Bertrand. Guess who is sneaking down there to this Russian hag? Joanna! My wife!"

"Perhaps it's good for her," Bertrand said casually.

Peter slammed his hand down on the table and stared menacingly, "I continue with the narrative. I slipped a small listening device into her purse a week ago. We have the two of them on tape. Joanna and the Russian, this Alexandra. Long and short, Joanna is petrified of me. Thinks that I'm going crazy. The Russian, a spooky bitch if there ever was one, soothes her. Counsels separation. Predicts bad things for me! And for Joanna! All this is endangering my business.

This is where you come in. I want a full court press by your firm. ACJ and my company have put down years of business together. I want to know about this Russian. She has taken over the soul of my wife! You owe me this McAbee. She is endangering my business. What if this Russian is a blackmailer? The cop friend of my brother put out some feelers about her. A mystery."

"Hold on for a minute Peter. This is a domestic situation. A marriage. I don't want to get into your marriage."

"She's a co-owner goddamit! She's on all my papers." He looked at his watch. He said, "It's 12:08. Okay, I'll leave. You gotta do this for me. I'm leaving, I'm leaving." He threw up his hands, rose from his chair and sped out of the office not waiting for Bertrand's response.

After a minute Bertrand once again walked over to his window and took in the Mississippi River. He shook his head back and forth before he put on his winter wear and headed out toward Pat who looked at him in anticipation. Into his silence she said, "Normal? Or a new file?"

He gazed at her before saying "Maybe it's neither."

"That's not the way it looks from here and by the way you're running late."

He nodded as he headed toward the elevator and the wintry weather of Davenport. He already knew that as long as Peter Goodkind's company was a client he felt obligated to do some spadework on this matter.

CHAPTER TWO

Barry Fisk was his usual surly self as he entered McAbee's office. Before he could offer a greeting Fisk said, "I have information but I have discovered a bit of a mystery, that the most interesting in my inquiry."

McAbee had been thinking off and on about Barry for most of the morning. He wasn't sure why. His image kept appearing in his head. Almost from the inception of ACJ, Barry had found his way into the agency. A doctorate in history from Yale, a terribly failed teaching position at Western Illinois University in nearby Macomb, Illinois, and then a chance encounter with Bertrand who was working one of his first and surely one of his most daunting cases. He used Barry as an independent contractor to assist with the case. By good fortune, McAbee found a research genius. Over and over again as the years passed Fisk proved himself to be indispensable. McAbee had purchased a large reservoir of tools for him to improve his research skills and with those he awoke the hacker in Barry. Ethically, he flinched at Barry's illegalities and yet he used the information that was garnered. McAbee knew his own hypocrisy.

On top of it all Barry was mean-spirited and exceptionally

negative. His personal battles with Pat Trump were highly charged, ultra troublesome, and had almost led Pat to resign her position with ACJ. Such a move on her part would have probably caused him to close down the agency altogether. In other words, he was a huge management problem.

As he looked out at him as they sat across from each other, he observed once again that Barry had aged poorly. His combative face was run through with deep furrows, his eyes were red-lined and the pouches under his eyelids were puffed into a dark gray. And to add insult to injury his five foot or so frame manifested an ever enlarging hump on his upper back along with a terribly skewed set of shoulders grotesquely aslant with each other.

"Before we get to that, how are you Barry?"

"I'm fine. Why?" He shot back sharply, defensively.

"Just wondering. You look a little frayed."

"I'm fine Bertrand, especially so since your whiz girl out there isn't around."

"Oh, Pat. Yeah. She's off today. So what do you have?"

"Joanna Goodkind first. Manic-depressive. Lots of meds. Need to know?"

"No. What else?"

"Cops have been to her house twice. Both times called down. Husband related. Nothing physical. Yelling, screaming at her in the report but when pressed by the cops she backed off. He's wildly successful as you already told me. He's also wildly radical. Even the most wild of the Trumpers back away from him. I guess I look at them as your typical husband-wife team after 25 years of a rotten marriage." Barry pointed to a red folder and said, "Details in here. But you pretty much already told me what you knew about her. Most of what I have is confirmation of that. Questions about this?"

"No. Not at this point. It's the Russian that I'm interested in."

"Yes. Some highly unusual items about her. Plus mega blanks. There's lots of hiding and concealment around her. My research is still incomplete. But I'll tell you what I have. Records have been tampered with. Interesting gaps. Always suspicious. Currently she goes by the professional name of Lady Alexandra. She owns her house, an almost mansion along the cliffs overlooking the Mississippi. All of this is detailed in the blue folder. The house is registered under the name Alexandra Speranskya. Age 53, age could be more, could be less. Some kind of trick occurred at her birth. I don't think Speranskya is her real name but at birth this is how she is registered. Could be her grandmother's name, could be given to her out of thin air. I'll keep looking. The fact is that when she leaves that hospital in the lower east side of Manhattan, that's her name. Hospital shuttered in the early 80s. Records missing. Largely served Russian immigrants. No need to tell you how adept the Russians are in treachery especially if they can get their hands on original documents. But something is going on about her origins. Maybe some illegal immigration. She moves to upper Manhattan in a section called Inwood, not far from the Bronx. She attends Public School 52, graduates from George Washington High School and then is admitted to NYU from which she graduates in 1988 with a degree in finance. She was a straight A student. Could easily have gotten in anywhere if she wanted to. Now the problems start. She disappears for almost eight years. Off the grid totally. No phones, no presence anywhere. Then, suddenly, she's back in the known world. She's employed by Procter & Gamble. A short stint in Cincinnati in 1996, then onto St. Petersburg, Russia, late 1996 to 2001, then to Minsk in Belarus, with occasional trips to Ukraine and the Baltic States, until she resigns from P&G in 2003. She is a translator in these countries. She leaves P&G in good standing. In 2004 she shows up here. Stays in Davenport at the old Clayton Inn for a month and then buys her place outright. $310,000. Cash on the barrel-head. She incorporates in 2005 as Lady Alexandra and registers her business in the State of Iowa as Psychic Readings. Yelp and other online sites are unambivalent. She has a devoted number of followers. Most tell of her ability to read the future and treasure her counsel. There are no pictures of her on any of these sites. That's interesting. However, I managed to get one from P&G personnel records from 2003. So, more mystery surrounding her. She runs a successful business, client-oriented and yet she hides or at least that's my interpretation. Clearly, she's not a stage performer. Doesn't do birthdays, Bar Mitzvahs and so on. Bertrand, there is considerable concealment going on with her but so what? This doesn't mean that she's evil or anything close. Just secretive. Same could be said of me."

Bertrand smiled and said, "That's true with one big differential."

"What's that?"

"Your client orientation is quite unalike. Yelp would not help your cause."

Barry shrugged dismissively.

"Peter Goodkind is worried about her influence on his wife Joanna. He feels that Lady Alexandra might be dangerous. That she has a control over Joanna. The gaps in her vita are curious. Those grammar and high school records? Parental names?" Bertrand asked.

"Haamer. Father not listed. Mother is named Liisa Haamer. No indication that she was a widow. Haamer is an Estonian name."

"Why the Speranskya name then?"

"Can't determine. Maybe the father."

"What do you know about Liisa Haamer?"

"She was born in 1940. Estonian. Immigrated to the U.S. in 1956. A large percentage of the population in northeastern Estonia is Russian. She came from that region. Alexandra's name Speranskya is a very Russian name."

"So Alexandra is born to a single mother?"

"Maybe. As I say lots of fudging around Alexandra. I have more on Alexandra's mother, Liisa. She dies in 1995, cancer. Alexandra sole heir. Negligible estate. Her death ties the issue of parentage off except for the father and the name Speranskya."

"Barry I'm like you. I don't like the complications. Missing parts. You'll stay on this, of course. But as of now there is no indication that Alexandra has any marks against her as being a crook."

"No. The contrary. Some of the posts swear to her ability to conjure the future, see into the past and penetrate the present. Most amazing. Right now the answer for Peter Goodkind is that neither he nor his wife is in danger."

"I see. Anything else of note?" as Bertrand noticed Barry's legs moving back and forth, a sure sign that he was holding another card in his deck.

"Well, one more oddity about her from her admirers.

She has been called a healer by some of them, not just psychological but physical. Scary stuff if you're into that kind of weirdness. Cancers, tumors, blood diseases, viruses, eating disorders, etc. You'll see in this blue folder." Barry slid the red folder over the blue one. He tapped on it. My bill is in that folder. I guess I'll have to wait until *she* gets back."

"Yes Barry, that's true. Pat will get it out to you ASAP. Thanks for the research."

Barry left without another word. Bertrand removed the picture of Alexandra absconded form the P&G site. He studied the woman's photo. She had quite a look about her.

CHAPTER THREE

Augusta Satin had once been a detective with the Rock Island, Illinois, Police Department. She resigned upon marrying a physician, had two daughters in quick succession, and then her husband abandoned her, moving to Wisconsin to set up a practice there with his cute physician's assistant. He had no intention to pay alimony or child support. A cad of the first order.

A friend had recommended the ACJ Agency run by a former classics professor named Bertrand McAbee. The decision to hire him had changed her life. Not only did his agency secure a hefty set of contributions from her wayward former husband but she had met a man she loved, the troubled stoic who was miscast as a PI. McAbee himself. Long ago she had stopped analyzing their relationship. It wasn't a physical thing but it was profound. Yes, he was remote at times especially when involved with one of his complicated cases. Not an easy person.

After his agency had secured alimony and child support for her – the method as to how this was done was never disclosed to her, and when she asked she was told by McAbee

Joseph A. McCaffrey

that it was off limits. She suspected that a heavy hand was used. But the less she knew the better, he had said obliquely.

Slowly but surely she was hired on a spec basis for certain jobs. Eventually she was pretty much a regular with ACJ as her relationship with McAbee deepened.

She quickly discovered that the ACJ Agency had its problems. Barry Fisk, the computer whiz, was impossible. His interpersonal skills were of graveyard level, his relationship with Pat Trump especially strained with acrimony. She thought the world of Pat Trump. And then there was the formidable Jack Scholz, ex-Marine, Special Forces, who knew? An over the top sociopath with a cruel streak mined in the tunnels of hell. And yet they all became part of the McAbee outfit; he was trying to control these four galloping horses. There were other players in the agency, all of them by way of being contractors, but the core was Augusta, Barry Fisk, Jack Scholz, and Pat Trump.

Bertrand and she had met for lunch and while at it he had made a request of her. The Goodkind account. Wife Joanna was having problems. She had been reliant on a psychic. Would Augusta be kind enough to schedule an appointment with this Lady Alexandra and get a sense of her? She asked herself, not for the first time, when wouldn't she be kind enough to do just about anything he asked of her?

She drove up icy Gaines Street, turned left at the top of its rise on Eighth Street and went west to the address. After she identified herself at the gate, it opened and she passed through. She went toward the door of the impressive house, caught the incredible view of the Mississippi River and then rang the bell. The door was opened by a 60ish woman who wore a black dress covered by a clean white half apron.

The maid had a round, kindly face. She said, "Miss Satin?"

"Yes. I'm here for an appointment with Lady Alexandra. 1:30."

"Of course. This way please. I'll take your coat if you wish. My name is Maria."

"Thank you," Augusta removed her coat and handed it to her.

She was brought into a small room with a beautiful Persian carpet. She was shown a seat at an ornate round table that sat close to the middle of the room, an empty seat across from her.

The maid said, "Lady Alexandra will be here shortly. I can make coffee or tea and of course I can get water or a soft drink."

"No. I'm fine, thanks."

Maria left, closing the door behind her.

Augusta wondered about listening and/or monitoring devices. She was especially alert to cameras. Because there was a fair chance there was a device she was careful about being too observant while being observant. The carpet was stunning by any account and she began there by leaving her chair and crouching down close to it, examining the design and color while taking in the bottom half of the room as well as a subtle glance under the table. She saw nothing as she stood while doing a brief scan of the upper half of the room, pretending to have a knee event that forced her into an awkward turn. When she sat she knew that it would be a step too far for her to inspect the floor lamp. If there was

19

monitoring, any inspection of that lamp would be a dead giveaway to an observer that she had an agenda beyond the consultation.

She sat in stillness but on high alert.

Alexandra had watched Augusta Satin cross from her car to her house noting the long pause as she looked out over the Mississippi River Valley.

Augusta Satin was about six feet with a body that appeared trim and athletic. Her African heritage was exhibited with pride by her care of a well-attended medium afro. The gold rings in her ears were large, her black framed glasses contrasted nicely with her light brown complexion. She walked with an air of confidence. High curb appeal her realtor client would say.

Her appointment was made through Maria who was now showing her into the house. Maria had indicated that Augusta needed counsel urgently on a delicate matter. She had heard three women talking about Alexandra's skills in the shower area of the YWCA. Maria reported that Satin thought that it was a message from God. That she was fated to overhear the three. Alexandra was very attuned to such occurrences and totally understood Augusta's reasoning. Helping her was another matter still. She channeled people when God allowed it. She knew that nothing was certain in the realms that she inhabited.

She gave Augusta five minutes from her coming into the house until she would enter the sacred room. Alexandra had learned about every creak and every noise in the house that led to the Persian room as she called it. It was named after the early 19th century carpet from Iran that fitted almost perfectly into the room. It had been scavenged in a closure process in 1995. She had had it valued just before moving to the Quad Cities from Cincinnati. She was told $75,000 at a minimum. Its coloration, sophistication, age, and striking beauty was obvious to any observer. Very few clients failed to mention and re-mention its effect on them.

It was her custom to come upon a client as though she was catching a butterfly in midflight. To sense them before their defenses became a moat. She hoped that silent as a cat movements went unheard or unfelt. Few clients sensed her, felt her presence. They had varied levels of recognizing this gift. She wondered about the African as she gently turned the knob of the closed door that led into the Persian room. She shook her bracelets just slightly as she came upon her, noticing that her body had already stiffened slightly. Augusta Satin had some pieces of the gift.

She sat across from her. Satin had an angular face, pronounced features, strong jawline, enlarged lips, straight nose and beautiful hazel eyes. Her hair had some ribs of white. Alexandra put her at a similar age to herself. All told she was a stunning woman. "Augusta, I am Lady Alexandra."

"Pleased to meet you. Thanks for seeing me on such short notice."

Alexandra raised her hand, palm outward. "Please close your eyes and give me your favored hand. Do not speak again, please."

Augusta complied readily to the request. It was now a matter of capturing her complexities. The feel. Sometimes Lady Alexandra received no return, defenses too high. But this hand released energy. There were messages to be deciphered. Alexandra also closed her eyes and listened

with her senses. She listened for the body first. It took
several minutes until she was satisfied. Messages clear. As
she then turned her attention to Augusta's mind she felt
uncomfortable. It was as if she found her way into some force
field, contradictions. Deceits? She stayed in there as long as
she could and then separated her hand. "Please continue to
keep your eyes closed." She looked very closely at Augusta
now, a bit confused. She was not fully as she had presented
herself to Maria. Certainly part of what she received from
the African was suspiciousness. "You may open your eyes
now. A minute please?" She arose and opened the door and
went across to the kitchen where she found Maria. "Maria,
prepare two cups of tea. Small cut, black and loose. Bring
it to us when I ring." She went back to Augusta who had
lost some of her, was it confidence? Enthusiasm? Of course
since she had some of the gift, she would. Surely she felt
what had happened. A draining of sorts. She asked, "Are
you okay Augusta?"

"Yes. A bit woozy I think. I feel that something happened
between us. Odd."

"I am having Maria prepare some tea for us. It will be
here shortly. You are correct. An exchange was made. I was
able to listen into you. You have what I call a gift. You can
be read and you probably have the ability to read, perhaps
you know this?"

"I'm not quite sure what you mean."

She felt that Augusta was being disingenuous, furthering
her read that deceits resided in this woman. "Allow me to say
a few things to you. Then we can have some tea. You are not
physically well. There is a problem. Are you aware of this?"

Augusta hesitated before saying, "Well yes. I guess

so. I have an area around my right elbow and upper arm. Psoriasis. Other than an annoying itch, dry, flaking skin and visual distastefulness I am well. I am having it treated," she said with a slight defensiveness.

"May I see it?"

Augusta gave her a look of confusion before rolling up the right sleeve of her woolen turtle neck sweater, exposing her arm.

"May I touch?" Alexandra asked.

"Okay," she said after a hesitation.

Alexandra reached across and placed her hand at the midpoint of the skin eruption. She closed her eyes and summoned her energy to flow through her fingers into the affected region of Augusta's arm. "Thank you Augusta."

She rolled down her sleeve. There was an obvious apprehension in her, her self-assurance shaken by Alexandra's forwardness.

"There is more Augusta. One or both of your breasts. I am concerned. Please see a doctor as soon as possible."

"Oh. Yes. I am due for a checkup in a few months. Very dutiful about that. But that's not…"

"Augusta. Listen to me. Do it without delay. Not months from now," she spoke firmly at this puzzlement of a woman. Alexandra was convinced that she had read cancer in Augusta and as she concentrated she sensed the origin of it.

Augusta blinked hard three times before saying, "It has been a family curse. I will do what you say."

Augusta was taken aback by this strange woman. From the minute her hand had been held she felt that her ploys were neutralized and that now she was on the defense. That somehow this woman with a Russian accent had snared her. She wasn't frightened so much as she felt naked, exposed. There was no reason to fear her but there was every reason to create barriers against the intrusions.

She looked into Alexandra's eyes, a deep brown iris, almost black, set against her black pupil, the surrounding sclera, enlarged it seemed. She felt as though she was being pulled into her. She looked away having observed a long elegant face, narrow with irregular points, her chin, her nose, her ears. Her hair was black and full down to her mid-back. A loosely fitted silk blouse of dark blue covered her chest and arms. Augusta reflected about watching a chess match with the two players only feet from each other. She was outmatched by this woman. It was a rare feeling in her as she tried to regain some footing.

"But you did not come about physical matters," Alexandra said softly. "Tell me about what bothers you. This pressing matter."

Augusta had memorized her presentation. "I am in love with a man who is much older than I. He loves me but oddly so. Our relationship rests on respect and our history. I have met another man. I have yearnings for him. Matters are coming to a head. I feel paralyzed by indecision. It is said that you see things that others don't. That's why I'm here."

Lady Alexandra's gaze bore into her. Seconds went by before she spoke. "Your hand again please." She took it into hers and silence fell between them. "Augusta Satin. First off, you are a good woman. I read that clearly. Whoever this interloper is, this man you're yearning for, he is of no importance to you. His very existence as a factor in your life is fanciful, passing. You have given him an existence where none is merited. You may leave this older man but not for this reason. *That* man is complex and his influence on you is deep. You know this and your chronological age is telling you that there is a time coming. That is an issue with you. A passage across that sea may be coming upon you."

Augusta sat in amazement. Alexandra had seen through the yearning for another man move and yet she caught an issue that Augusta was concerned with, the age differential between her and McAbee.

"However interesting your presenting matter is for you I sense that this is not why you are here with me Augusta Satin," she touched a button to the side of the table.

"But…"

"No Augusta, don't. It's not becoming of you. Allow me to continue please. What I do here is not trickery. With some clients I do nothing, I can do nothing. I hold a hand and I read nothing. For whatever reason I am blocked. I accept that. I say to the person that this is the case. They go. Perhaps they say bad things about me, that I'm a fool, a fraud. The profession I am in allows for these criticisms. I accept my limitations. Some readings that I do are limited. It goes back to my own impediments but more frequently what I am allowed by the other. But there are some that lead me beyond a read to almost a channel. It is as if I am given access to a soul. These are people who have the very gifts that I have but they frequently are unable to access them or they fear them because of what may be seen or foreseen. You, Augusta, are very open but you are tangled. What I am saying to you is that I do not deceive. I do not lie."

Augusta simply nodded as her hand was released. Within seconds there was a soft knock on the door.

"Yes Maria. We are ready," Alexandra said softly.

Maria came in and placed a tray on the table. On it were two steaming cups of tea, a pitcher of milk and a small tin of sugar. On each saucer there was a spoon. Two paper napkins were on the tray.

"This tea is very special. I hope that you enjoy it. It is my final custom to do a reading of the leaves. Please keep the tiniest amount of liquid in the cup, Augusta," Alexandra said.

Augusta pinched her right thigh, a gesture by her to awaken herself. To make some return in this one-sided affair. "Your accent? Russian. Are you from there?"

Alexandra smiled. "No. I was born in America. My mother, though, was Russian. We were earnest Russians. Only that was spoken in the home. My English pronunciation will always have that mark. As perhaps you know I only came to this area in 2004. I was born in New York City. There are a surprising number of Russians in that city."

Augusta caught very clearly in her words 'as perhaps you know'. She felt as though she had been outed by some mythic force beyond her comprehension. "I am finished with my tea." She faced her cup outward to her. Alexandra nodded as she took it from Augusta's hand.

"Now let's see if there are messages in the leaves." She brought the cup to a 45 degree angle and began to turn it slowly. The loose leaves stuck to surfaces along the inside of the cup. Some of the leaves were in clusters, others alone. Her eyes narrowed in concentration. After a minute she looked closely at Augusta. "Augusta, the leaves don't lie but our interpretations are sometimes wanting. But in this case? I think it is clear enough. You have come as a herald. An agent of warning." She removed a pencil from somewhere as she pointed to a vertical, slightly diagonal line of leafs. At the top end there was a horizontal line. "You see the angel, you see the trumpet?"

"Well yes, I suppose," Augusta said, not quite convinced of her interpretation but now fully appreciative of this strange Russian's insights.

"But there is more in the cup Augusta. Do you see this single vertical rib topped by a single tiny leaf? Do you care to interpret?"

Augusta saw it as an easy interpretation. "I guess it's a candlestick?"

"Good. But I disagree. It has to be seen in concert with the angel and the trumpet. I see it as a stick of dynamite. You are a harbinger of danger Augusta. Whether you know this or not, it is the situation I believe. Now to mine."

Augusta watched as Alexandra swirled the leaves in her cup. She observed her stare hard at the cup, a slight flinch in her eyes.

"Nothing. I will swirl once more."

The motions were repeated. Augusta peered at her closely, disregarding the cup that turned in Alexandra's hands. She felt an alarm snake across the table even as the psychic remained still. Too still.

"Well, nothing that is of concern for us. I must prepare for another client now, my friend. Please take care of yourself physically, of course. But also watch around you. You have caused concern in me. I will add you to my list of clients. Come again if you wish."

Alexandra watched Augusta walk towards her car. For whatever reason the African was clearly transmitting dangers. Twice she had swirled the leaves in her own cup. Twice, almost a never event, an angry standing bear manifested itself. Something Russian was on the horizon.

CHAPTER FOUR

Alexandra Speranskya was distracted by her judgment about being ineffective with the two clients who came by after the African left. A whirlwind of thoughts destabilized her. She had no doubts after the second swirl of her own tea leaves disclosed the same message. The bear, Russia, was on the prowl, a message of danger in the air. The conduit for the bear was the tall visitor who unknowingly had a gift. But Augusta was duplicitous, not about the bear but about the reason she presented for her visit. Somehow there was a connection but it was currently beyond her discernment.

She was alone now in the house. Her watch read 4:50 p.m. The gray skies were rapidly darkening and a predicted front yielded winds with an erratic and vexing howl.

There were two biographical pathways that could lead Russia back into her life. Neither one seemed likely but it had to be one of those, one remembered easily, the other vigorously repressed.

She poured herself a large glass of orange juice along with a generous pour of Stolichnaya vodka, at the end adding two ice cubes. Her fireplace, properly logged by Maria, was lit and then she sat. She asked Alexa to play some Bach. Then and only then was she prepared to travel the two ways alert to any possible change that may have occurred recently.

She closed her eyes and thought back through her life in a series of framed episodes that she saw as telling. She had the ability to isolate these frames, convinced that they were quite accurate. She began on path one.

In 1986 she was befriended by a classmate at NYU. She was also a Russian. Her name was Olga. They would meet for coffee when their classes overlapped. She enjoyed Olga partially because she could observe her efforts at being obscure. It confirmed her knowledge of Russian émigrés, their personal combat with resisting America, doubling down by being secretive and untrusting. She had been brought up with a similar outlook. What she misread, now as she looked back, was that Olga was scouting her, vetting a proper word. Two years later, a few months before her graduation, Olga asked her about her future plans. She told Olga that she had a preliminary offer from Procter & Gamble but was apprehensive about moving to Cincinnati. She would have to decide soon, however. Olga asked if she would be willing to meet with a friend who was involved in a local family-run business. Alexandra consented.

Next, she brought up that frame, the replication of a pivotal meeting. He was about 30 years old, a long, narrow face, a black beard hanging three inches down from his chin. He had a dark complexion. His eyes were what made him stand out. They were light blue. They reminded her of the sled dogs she saw on television. After introductions and some small talk, Olga left. His name was Timofey.

"Olga tells me that your speak Russian? Both parents Russian?" He asked in a very low voice, almost growly.

"Yes."

"Olga tells me that you are discreet and very bright."

"I'm not stupid," she replied with a bit of sauciness. She didn't particularly like his approach to her. That would change over time but not at this point.

Unsmiling he said, "I am associated with some businesses that operate out of Brighton Beach. There is a Russian enclave there. Are you familiar with it?"

"Yes, Olga has told me about the area. She lives there. But I have never been in person."

"I have need of a trustworthy and smart woman as my businesses are growing."

"Smart woman? Why not smart man?"

"I don't trust men around money," he answered abruptly inviting no further discussion.

"So am I being interviewed for a job?"

"Of course. I would not be here otherwise," no smiles from this intent man.

"Exactly what is the nature of your businesses?" she asked warily. She knew about the rumors of Russian *businesses* out of Brighton Beach. The Russian mafia.

"We operate in areas where the corrupt American police departments cannot operate."

"I don't understand?" she asked with false innocence.

"As I look at you Alexandra Speranskya I think that you understand all too well. Olga is a good judge of character. She has already taken you through a number of steps. Your discretion is of Russian quality," he smiled slightly showing a number of extremely white teeth.

"Why me?"

"You are Russian, you speak Russian. You are bright.

You majored in finance. You are *not* from Brighton Beach, this is most important to me. That you have no connection to the place. Otherwise you would have conflicts. It is impossible to be brought up there and not have questionable entanglements. That leads to double crosses, betrayals and so on. Do you understand?"

"*That* part of what you are saying, yes. But these businesses?"

"They are not legal except for my cover, a tobacco store, cigarettes, cigars, pipes, and so on. It barely makes a profit. Sometimes not. It's irrelevant to my success."

"So, just what is your success?"

"It could be said that I trade in vice. Gambling, prostitution, drugs, protection. Most essentially it is a cash only enterprise. I do not believe in paying taxes. What true Russian does?" Again with the half smile. "I feel that I am only here in this rotten country by default. I am a Russian through and through. I have no regard for this country. It is a stopover for me."

"This job. Exactly what is it?"

"You would be the inside captain. You would never be allowed to be on any action other than the books and the coordination of activities. I will personally train you to the job."

"You are inviting me into a life of crime."

"Crime? What is that? I am a supplier of services."

"I find you a bit tense when you said that I would not be expected to be in action. Am I right?"

He regarded her carefully, and then he retreated into himself for some seconds. In a very low voice he said, "I will tell you. You are a replacement. Irena was occasionally used for collections. It was a mistake. She was hurt."

"Hurt?"

"Beaten up so badly that she had to quit. She went to Sofia in Bulgaria. She is being cared for."

"You need to explain this."

"In my business there are enemies. She was seen too often and then she was singled out. A warning to me."

"How badly was she injured?"

"She is in a wheelchair. Her legs were broken. She has had seizures. There is enough money for fulltime care in Sofia for the remainder of her life. But in answer to your question you would never do collections. You would be purely inside. Out of danger."

"I have an offer from Procter & Gamble."

"Ah, Olga mentioned. New York is bad enough. Ohio? The Midwest?" he waved his hand dismissively. He took from the inside of his coat an index card that he held in his hand, writing facedown. "You have two months before graduation. I am impressed with you. Here is my offer. Think about it. Olga will be our mutual contact. I am leaving now." Again, the brief smile. He was gone.

Alexandra took the card and read its details. It was double what Procter & Gamble had offered.

Another meeting with Timofey, six weeks or so later. More frames.

"I have conditions Timofey. They are not negotiable. I received a scholarship offer from NYU. They want me to pursue a doctorate. Olga told you?"

"Yes. Let me hear," a very serious frown on his face.

"I do not want to be physically present in Brighton Beach."

After a few seconds he nodded. "I'm listening still," he said.

"I do not want to be a payroll entity. Cash only. I wish to be a cipher. I want deniability. Your business is high risk. I worry about the FBI."

"As do I Alexandra. I always worry. I can set your duties into a business front that I have acquired in the lower eastside of Manhattan. I always pay in cash. Health policies you will have to purchase by yourself as you want to be walled off from the operations. I understand all of this. What else?"

"My mother has begun to decline. I will need understanding from you relative to her possible care."

"Within reason, of course," he said quickly.

"I want you to detail the specifics of the job. No misunderstandings."

He adjusted his sitting position at the small restaurant on 23rd Street and Sixth Avenue in Manhattan. Leaning in his said, "Before I do so I have requirements also. Some of these precede what I am going to say."

"Yes?"

"After I detail my business to you, you may decline to be part of my organization. That is fine. It is your judgment. I want you to vow to me that what is said to you will never pass from your lips to others, regardless of your decision." He stopped and looked at her expectantly.

"But of course. I don't want to be on any Brighton Beach hate lists, particularly yours. You have my assurance."

"If you take the job I will need a one month termination notice from you if you need out. If your performance is inadequate I will give you one month severance. Note there is nothing in writing. You would exist but not exist. I am careful about notes and physical evidence. As you say, deniability. Are you ready to hear specifics?"

"Please."

He removed a small card from his breast pocket. He placed it down on the table. His writing was miniscule. She could see that his words were in Russian. There were 15 rows of writing. For over one hour he covered the bases of his business. She was stunned at the breadth of an organization that was oiled by cryptic words and obscure gestures known only to those who needed to know. He concluded, "Everyone in the organization speaks and is Russian or close by. They have all sworn loyalty. But as I said we are under constant siege from our enemies. They are abundant."

At that very moment in this particular vignette Alexandra Speranskya made a life-altering decision. She reached across the narrow table hand extended. They shook as she said, "Yes, I will accept your offer."

CHAPTER FIVE

Alexandra continued her foray into other frames dealing with her employment experiences with Timofey. Another Stoli and oj was fixed as she recollected her extraordinary experiences with Timofey's empire. The man was a genius – insightful, a memory from the heavens and with the energy of a battalion of Marines. And all through their years together, 1988 – 1996, eight or nine years depending on how you count, there was never once from him, nor from her, the slightest hint of sexual attraction. Yet as a team she felt that she would never again experience the efficiency of their business relation. Up until the very end he was true to her terms of employment.

She did the books, transferred funds into Zurich banks, delegated orders through to his agents and within a year he was calling her his chief operating officer. An apt title. Central to her psychological well-being, besides the physical, was her anonymity. No one, other than Timofey and Olga, knew who she was. This was essential given what had befallen Irena. Payments for *her* were made out of the Bank of Zurich into a facility in Sofia, Bulgaria.

Her estimation was that little was unknown to her about

Timofey's businesses, perhaps, as she now looked back, *nothing* was unknown. The trust seemed absolute even as she became aware that Olga was his mistress. And Olga? There was no tension between them, Olga instinctively knowing that Alexandra and Timofey had no interest in each other.

All that said, the job was not easy. Some of the businesses that she had to manage were sordid and caused revulsion in her. Sexual enslavement constituted 10% of his business. Beatings, drug addiction, violence, and occasional deaths surrounded it. Anticipating a protest from her, Timofey argued that he was plowing over the same ground as the Latinos, the Italians, the Jews, other Russians, and assorted enemies that were always waiting in the wings should he relent. Left unsaid was the answering equation – better us than them.

The drug business was the most profitable and likewise the most dangerous. Four operatives for Timofey were murdered over the years as she noticed that his features became more and more haunted as time passed. On occasion, especially before the end, she observed his hands shake, eyes blinking too rapidly. He was jittery. Yet his memory and attention to detail never faltered.

Frame after frame flittered through her mind before she stopped and isolated on her mother for a few moments. Her Estonian mother, the kind and resilient Liisa, came under attack from ovarian cancer. Timofey funded her expensive treatments at Sloan Kettering. Alexandra's days of absence were covered by the resourceful and generous Olga. And through it all Timofey fully supported her at every turn of the six month trek toward her mother's death in 1995, that year full of tumultuous changes as it turned out. She blocked out any invasion of her mother's frames into her consciousness, her pain still pulsing in her.

The inevitable and intended frame rushed toward her. Her mother's death just a month gone. Her recall of their meeting was as fresh as it was if it occurred yesterday.

His disguise as a Hasidic Jew was well done. Convincing. He probably took the subway from Sheepshead or Brighton Beach. Brilliant Timofey, multifaceted in his genius. After her training, with disguises on his part, he limited his one-on-one connections with her as she set up in the lower east side of Manhattan. Their meetings were relatively rare, as it turned out. He was forever concerned about her safety and anonymity. Valentine's Day – 1996.

Timofey, not as a Hasim. His neon blue eyes with blood highways coursing through them, coming unannounced.

"My dear Alexandra. The end has come. Olga was car bombed this morning. Blown to bits." His head falling down into his misery.

She waited on him not knowing what to say.

"I am closing shop. All the emergency plans that we discussed those years back are now in play. I am leaving for Paris tonight. I do not intend to ever come back to this foul country."

Alexandra now collecting herself. "Oh Timofey. I loved Olga as I know you did. I don't know what to say. Why Olga?"

"The why is obvious to me. The Italians and the cops. I knew we were coming to the edge. I need you to close up everything. No traces. Just shut down and disappear. I have enough money in Zurich to live many lifetimes as you know. You have been superb Alexandra. I am giving you this suitcase. In it is roughly a half million dollars in cash. It is for you. Do whatever you have to do today and walk away from here this evening. Yes, there will be loose ends but it is not our problem. My people always knew that the whole enterprise could blow up in an instant. It has. You will never hear from me again, with an exception."

Alexandra gave singular effort to remain in control of herself as Timofey went on.

"I am going to give you a phone number. Please never call it except under the most extraordinary of conditions. Just leave a message. If I am alive I will respond to you in some manner. If it rings it is alive and you can assume I am as well. If answered, say 'Brooklyn – I'm here'. If it is a dead number than so am I." He looked at her anxiously.

She knew that he wanted to leave. She said, "Timofey, I am at a loss. How do I thank you for everything?" She started to tear up.

He stood. "Alexandra! You are the strongest person I have ever met. Stay that way." He ran his hand across her hair.

He left abruptly and the frame disappeared. And now? Twenty-five years later she recalled the memorized phone number.

And then there was that one last frame that she had held into herself. It was the tea leaves two weeks before Olga's murder. At the time she could not make out the meaning of the message. She had drawn it on paper, however. She went upstairs to her bedroom and removed an 8 ½ by 11 inch sheet of paper. It was as obvious now as it should have been then. Many tea leaves clustered at the bottom of the cup forming the image of a car. Unmistakable and then on top of it a heavily populated arc of tea leaves randomly dispersed. Clearly the explosion of Olga's car. She sat on her bed and cried. A rarity for her. She looked through her window, south, and saw through a cloudy night the lights atop the Centennial Bridge that stood between Davenport, Iowa, and Rock Island, Illinois. The long rows of lights atop the bridge had an aura around them caused by the frozen air of the night.

CHAPTER SIX

She returned to her sitting room on the first floor. Another drink. It was time to examine the other road. She hated going into the many frames that served as the definers of her experience on this road.

Alexandra was born in 1967 to a single mother named Liisa Hammer, herself born in 1940. Liisa was Estonian formally, but Russian in language and outlook. At an early age, 1955 was Alexandra's best guess, Liisa came to America. When asked for specifics Liisa was uncooperative and refused to disclose details to Alexandra who eventually stopped asking. Russian was the required language at home all through her life with Liisa. She was brought up in upper Manhattan on a small street in Inwood, Dongan Place. Those details constituted the easy frames.

Liisa made her living as a skilled seamstress. But there were men from the neighborhood. Alexandra knew what that was about. Conditions were not easy for them. Rougher frames but manageable.

But she knew that she would now have to conjure up the disturbing frames involving her overbearing, vile, and abusive father.

Somehow, someway, her mother became entangled with a man who was outsized, a fearful presence. She would come to know him as Alexei Raspin although she was cautioned over and over again to never mention the name outside of the small, one bedroom apartment on Dongan Place. She never did, not out of obedience to the caution but rather in deference to the shame she was told to feel.

His appearances in the apartment were rare enough, perhaps two or three times a year. It was as if he was checking out a rental property. By the age of five Alexandra had been schooled by her mother in the essentials of their relationship to this man. He was her father. Liisa looked on her daughter as being her greatest achievement in her life. No regrets there. But this man? Many regrets.

A frame: Liisa and Alexei facing one another in the small kitchen across the pitted oil-cloth red and white cover over a small wobbly kitchen table.

"I need money for her. It is hard on me," Liisa said in exasperation. Alexandra in the bedroom listening intently at the door, peeking out furtively.

"You get what you get you filthy bitch. How much do you make as a whore? *You* should be giving me money. And you think I'll leave here without seeing my daughter. Backward fucking Estonian bitch."

And now the resounding slap that Alexandra felt as though it had been delivered on her own face. The yelp from her mother and two more loud slaps, thunder claps to her young imagination.

And then his low, growl of voice demanding that she, Alexandra, be brought out for his inspection. A scream from her mother and a firm 'no' immediately followed by the noise of a chair falling to the badly chipped linoleum floor. Another scream followed by scuffling heading toward the bedroom door, Alexandra retreating away from the door, petrified. The door swung open her mother pushed forward, bent in pain, her arm twisted behind her back, tears escaping as a torrent from her fear-filled eyes. Her mother hurled onto the bed and the demand from this long-faced monster for Alexandra to come to him.

Shaking, Alexandra complies. He grips her by her shoulders, his breath sour borscht and alcohol. "You are my daughter. You are a Rasputin! You are a noble child. When I come here I demand that you come to me and present yourself as such. Do you understand? You are no longer a useless baby."

"Yes," Alexandra shaking, tears welling in her eyes.

"Leave this room now. Go to the kitchen. I have business with your mother." He steers her through the door which is quickly slammed shut. The consequential curses and moans from him, the sobs and muted screams from her mother. Alexandra frozen in shock and fear.

Time spent? She doesn't know. He comes out to the kitchen, Alexandra on the floor, sitting, braced against the oven door. He checks his fly zipper. He tugs it up from its half-closed position. "Girl," he growls, "I am your father. Your mother must accept this. You also. I will be back again. Next time we will not have this happen again. Now! Go tend to your mother."

He heads to the door, turning toward her he says, "What are you waiting for child. Now!" He makes a threatening nod, removes a wallet from his pocket and tosses a ten-dollar bill onto the floor before leaving. Alexandra rushes to the bedroom. Her mother is sitting on the edge of the bed, bent over, barely audible sobs. Alexandra comes to her and reaches for her hand as she sits next to her mother whose left eye is badly swollen. Blood running down her legs. Frame done.

Alexandra gets up hastily from her couch. The first of too many memories for her. Her mind is now back on the African as she searches for connections.

She receives a call from a long time client. Another woman dealing with the bitter Quad City winter and an abusive stepson she inherited in a now broken marriage. She soothes her, relieved by this lesser chore before heading back to the frames.

By the age of seven Alexandra is passed into a special program at P.S. 52. She is labeled 'precocious'. Her mother is overjoyed with the news. So little brings her joy. Alexandra presses about her father. Why is he called Raspin when he leans into her and shouts that he is a Rasputin? Her mother slowly surrenders information about this man and his infamous father Grigori Rasputin. She recounts that she fell in love with him instantly during a very vulnerable period of her life in 1966. As quickly as she became ensorcelled by him, enough to conceive Alexandra, she became hateful of him. He was a man who owned women by having sex with them. From then on he determined that they were his possessions, to be used at will. Pushback by her mother was met with physical punishment. Not disclosed in this recital, because as yet unknown, was his belief that his possessiveness extended to Alexandra, who was subjected to sexual abuse at the age of 13 by this same monster who traded mother for daughter.

Alexandra wept as she relived those frames involving four episodes of rape by her father. After the last incident she became aware for the first time of her power, her gift, that her mother informed her had been transmitted to her by her vicious father. A dangerous gift, possessed by only a few. Alexandra had called for her father's death. All those frames coming at her with accelerating force, each delivered with a psychological kick as she relived these experiences. She put into slow motion the death episode. He had finished with her as he stood before her quivering body. He reached down and slapped her across the face, 'Welcome me daughter or it will not get better for you.' He turned to leave, a huge presence at the doorway. It was then that she focused her mind to call down his death and as she did so an unknown energy blazed through her. She knew then, more so now, that she had connected to a force beyond her. Alexei Rasputin was discovered minutes later by a screaming neighbor – he had fallen down a flight of stairs close to her apartment. His neck broken, the ugly sneer still on his face as Alexandra viewed him from the top of the stairwell. His eyes were open, a stunned look in them. Alexandra knew. She had successfully murdered him. Any remorse was beyond consideration.

But as she traversed these unsettling frames to their violent end she speculated that perhaps some reconnection in these frames was somehow coming to be.

Her last thoughts before sleep were centered on Augusta Satin, now convinced that she was a messenger of things to come.

CHAPTER SEVEN

McAbee had concluded from Augusta's report that Lady Alexandra was a serious woman engaged in the shady business of fortune telling. Yes, she had gotten the best of Augusta, not a mean feat, but Augusta was not exactly conversant with the wizardry in this arcane art. Augusta had been spooked good and hard. And Joanna Goodkind was most likely in a state of permanent spookness. But if being so had positive effects so be it. Peter Goodkind was another story altogether. Bertrand thought about how to approach the imminent meeting with him, a supposed "setting things straight."

At his request, Barry Fisk had performed a strip down on Peter. The primary focus was the past year to present. The request turned out information about Peter that caused McAbee to now see him in need of hospitalization. Far right politics like far left politics always had its share of menacing figures bent on altering the course of the world. They seemed unable to understand the color of gray, a color that held its few truths like one would hold a newborn baby. That color scrutinized the world with a careful skepticism. As he dwelled on this, he could picture *himself* there while finding it logically impossible to see Peter in such a setting. Peter had many truths that provided no room for dissent. He went to the right and built an armed fortress of ideas. But Fisk had detected a clear drift into militaristic and threatening language. In one post he argued for a citizen ownership of military-grade weapons such as bazookas, landmines, and artillery pieces using the same argument coined in the phrase 'People kill people, not guns!' His many arguments would lead off of a simple premise and that would trigger a universalization of such, such as his right to self-defense leading to open gun carrying, etc.

His journey into white nationalism, anti-semitism and a particularly fierce hatred of the Me Too and Black Lives Matter movements alarmed McAbee. Peter Goodkind had gone over the edge. For Peter the way to deal with such movements was through mass arrests and penal colonies in Northern Montana.

Bertrand was surprised when Pat came into his office, closing the door. She looked nervous, her hands fisting and straightening. "Bertrand, Peter is waiting out there. I told him you were on the phone. He has Joanna with him. Also his brother. Joanna is wearing sunglasses but I got a side glance when I left to come in here. Her left eye is almost closed. Cheek purple. Should I call Scholz? The police?"

Bertrand thought about it before responding, "Call Jack Scholz. Brief him and tell him to come if he can and bring some muscle too. I'll come out in a minute."

Jack Scholz was the toughest guy McAbee ever encountered. Still to this day, he wasn't sure which service entity he was associated with. When he conjectured Marines something said or alluded to would pause the thought. He did know, from previous cases with associates of Jack, that he had performed a number of missions that were top secret, off the books and murderous, for the United States. Jack was also amoral and unscrupulous. Competency, though, he had in spades. When McAbee was in trouble or was up against vile opponents Scholz was his default. Augusta Satin cringed at his usage, Barry Fisk detested him and Pat stayed as far from him as humanly possible. However, at the end of it all, Jack Scholz was necessary in the world that McAbee had entered.

Bertrand steeled himself as he entered the anteroom. It was as Pat said, as he saw Peter and his brother each take one of Joanna's arms and stand, ready to follow Bertrand's beckoning arm toward his larger meeting room as he deemed his office too problematic for the coming session. The sizable rectangular table had eight seats, one at either end and three to each side. Peter's brother, Eddie, was at least 10 years younger than he and seemed to be in good shape even as he probably weighed over 250 pounds. He had played for the University of Iowa Hawkeyes football team, a lineman. Joanna was making effort to shrink, to conceal herself as Bertrand sat at the head of the table. Eddie went to Bertrand's right and then guided Joanna next to him and away from Bertrand, his hulk essentially serving as a shield. McAbee was not meant to get a good look at her. He thought of moving and sitting across from her but decided it was an unnecessary gambit at this time.

Once seated Bertrand led, "Joanna, Peter, and Eddie, the family Goodkind. Peter, I yield the floor," he said in as friendly a manner as he could summon. He noted that Peter was quite subdued for the moment. But he couldn't help but feel that a tsunami was forming somewhere in the froth.

Peter began, "I brought Joanna along, Eddie as well, for what I feel is a necessary meeting. As you all know, Joanna too, for the record, I have had some recurring concerns about my wife's behavior. She's a liar for one as well as a traitor to me and my company. She has entrusted herself to a charlatan Russian who now sits in a position to do serious damage to my reputation and that of my company."

All the while, Bertrand angling in his chair to get a better view of Joanna who seemed to shrivel further into herself.

Peter continued his oration, which was now beginning to pick up momentum. "Shortly we will be proceeding over to our corporate attorney to reestablish my company in new language that will allow for greater legal safety. Furthermore, I am requiring your agency, Bertrand, to maintain a check on my wife by means of an ankle bracelet and whatever else you deem necessary to keep her under close surveillance while she is being treated by a trusted psychologist that my company has used in the past for troubled employees. Joanna has agreed to all these conditions as she perceives herself as an addict of sorts under the control of this venomous Russian."

In the meantime, Eddie appeared to have spread his mass in such a way as to totally obscure McAbee's sightlines of Joanna. A pause was too long for Bertrand to maintain a silence. Finally, he said, "Excuse me a minute if you will. I'll be back shortly." He got up quickly and left the room. Pat was at her desk and looked relieved at the sight of Bertrand who said, "Anything? I just have a minute."

"Yes. Jack will be here soon. He's picking up someone."

"Let me know when he's here. Just send me a text."

"Are you okay?" she asked.

"Frankly, I don't know what to say, Pat."

He walked back to the meeting room and as he opened the door he caught the end of a snarly command uttered by Eddie, "and keep your fucking mouth shut." Eddie turned and glared in a way that suggested that Bertrand was a voyeur of sorts.

Bertrand went back to the head of the table, picked up his pad, and walked over to Peter Goodkind's side of the table, across from Eddie as he sat beside Peter directly facing Joanna. He and Eddie exchanged stares while Peter pulled his chair away from Bertrand so as to face him at a fuller angle. Bertrand glanced quickly at him and saw that Peter's face had reddened. Both brothers were now put off as Bertrand finally took a full look at the beleaguered Joanna. She was a mess. He remembered her as a scrupulously careful person about her presentation. Makeup, hair, clothes, accessories, the whole of what Aristotle would classify under his treatment of predicaments as *equipment*, and proper only to humankind. He said, "I want to speak to Joanna, preferably, alone."

Peter, now at yell intensity, said, "No way! She is not of your concern."

"Actually Peter, she is."

Eddie, on edge, said to Peter, "I told you. He is not reliable. Fire the sonofabitch Peter."

"Joanna, speak to me. You're safe here," Bertrand pleaded.

Eddie now in full throttle hollered at McAbee and

Joanna at the same time, his head swinging back and forth, "No, you won't say a word to this clown! Peter, we have to go. I told you this was not a good idea."

Bertrand, trying to buy time, said to Peter who was beginning to move his chair outward, thus following the lead of his rising brother, "Peter, how can I follow your directive without securing Joanna's full knowledge and consent?"

Peter stayed put and roared across the table, "Joanna! Tell Bertrand that you consent."

Bertrand's phone buzzed. He quickly read the text, [Jack and companion here].

Joanna proceeded to remove her sunglasses. Eddie grabbed for them but she tossed them across the table. She had two black eyes, maybe a broken nose, and a grossly colored cheek. McAbee arose and now in his own shout to Peter, "What the hell are you two thinking?"

Eddie was up and now grabbing at Joanna as Peter shrieked, "Get the bitch out of here!"

Bertrand went to the doorway and yelled for Jack who was there in an instant with, to the joy of Bertrand, Buster Spriggs. Buster was retired from the Marines as a Master Gunnery Sergeant. A ghetto kid who did some professional boxing before joining the Marines, Bertrand knew him as one of Jack's most trusted men. He said to Jack, "Block the door." By this time, Eddie was nearing the doorway with Joanna's right arm bent upwards behind her back. She was in a daze. He figured that she was drugged.

"You heard the man," Jack said very softly. "You're not going anywhere."

Eddie released Joanna, shoving her against the wall and

moved toward Jack and Buster. He attempted a head butt on Jack but caught an elbow to his eye instead. Buster then stepped in and in quick succession, brought Eddie to his knees wheezing in pain from three quick thudding blows to his stomach.

In the meantime, Peter was reaching inside his coat. He was armed. Bertrand grabbed his right arm impeding his grab for his gun. He yelled, "This one has a gun. Help!" There was just enough time to disrupt him as the three of them brought Peter down and disarmed him. Jack then went back to the gasping Eddie and searched him. He wasn't armed.

Joanna collapsed to the floor in full sob and despair. Pat Trump entered the room and went to her.

Later, as Bertrand recounted the events to Augusta, he concluded his commentary in the following way, "Augusta, before they came I thought through all of the possible outcomes of the session. By far, this exceeded even my most dire expectations."

CHAPTER EIGHT

Augusta tensed when she heard his recitation of events surrounding the Goodkind family. That there was actually a gun present in such a volatile meeting?

"On top of it all I lost another client. Curious situation. ACJ has been doing security for that company for years. Ultimately it was a matter of protecting the company from its owner. The cops wouldn't arrest him or his brother Eddie. Peter has a permit to carry a weapon. His enemies have multiplied because he leans in to taunt them. Joanna would not press charges," Bertrand was explaining calmly.

But Augusta knew that Bertrand's equilibrium had been weakened. In the past he could manage the upsets better than now. His call to Jack Scholz was inspired even as she considered Jack trigger-happy and dangerous. "Is Joanna safe?"

"Yes. I think so. She's at a house of a friend of mine. A retired prof, Mary, who was up to the task of taking her in. Right now Peter has no way to track her. She is using another phone that we had in the office. The problem is she wants to see Alexandra. If she does she runs the risk of being seen as Peter will probably have the place surveilled. I can't save her from herself," he said shaking his head.

"Can I do anything?"

"Maybe. Let's see. Perhaps you could talk with her after Sy has a go with her. He'll advise her of her rights and also get in place a restriction to any contact by Peter or his brother. According to Peter, Joanna owns 50% of the corporation. I don't know if that's true but I'm pretty sure she's quite leveraged."

"It's very difficult to demonstrate dementia. He'll just argue that he's a free thinker or whatever. This can only get ugly. I think she is in real danger," Augusta said.

"I get that. I've spoken with Jack Scholz. If I can't get all the parts in order, we might have to go in Jack's direction. But Sy warned me that I might have some serious legal exposure. To be careful. I see his point but I won't let it prevail. I agree that her life is in danger."

"Does she have family?" Augusta queried.

"A sister who she's in schism with. She lives in Durango, Colorado. A dead end. I have Barry hunting around in the cloud for any possible data. So far nothing. Technically, we're not in this anymore. Joanna is not and never has been a personal client of ACJ. Peter was but no longer is. It's a non-case case. I do feel obligated to see her through this up to a point. She's cooperative but she was pretty upset when I told her to stay put. I have very little control over the matter in many ways. But I do have a question for you."

Augusta had listened to Bertrand mull over the details confronting him. She sensed his circling around her as he probed the corners of the matter.

He went on, "When you came back from your meeting

with the Russian, Alexandra, you were impressed. Tell me again why?"

An interesting question she thought. She had been trying to get to the bottom of why. What had happened within a week left her awestruck. She had hesitated to say anything to him because she felt Bertrand's skepticism all along during her recitation of events around her visit to the psychic. He could be very resistant to the type of person or occupation represented by Alexandra. "Okay Bertrand, you ask and I will tell you some things. The woman was simply overpowering. Her manner of operating, her insights and her, to find a word, control. Yes, you were right. I was unprepared for this kind of person. I never met anyone quite like her. You wonder about Joanna? I don't know Joanna Goodkind, but from what you have said she simply would be no match for Alexandra."

"But you said that she told you that you have gifts?"

"Yes. She said that I must get in touch with them. That part I'm not sure of but I do take what she said with respect."

"I hope that Lady Alexandra is not in danger. Peter Goodkind was furious with her, feeling that the Russian was capturing Joanna in some web of sorts."

"I don't see her in that light. But she did sense *my* duplicity. But there's more here Bertrand. Perhaps you'll understand my take on her with this." She was wearing a red wool turtleneck sweater. "You remember that I have had some serious issues with psoriasis."

He nodded.

"Have had it for years. Never goes away but it abates and then roars back sometime. Very unpleasant, annoying. Itches too much. Well, it had come back a few weeks ago at full strength. I didn't tell you this at the time when I reported back to you after my meeting with Alexandra. What she did made me uncomfortable. She asked for permission to touch my affected arm. I allowed her to. I pretty much forgot the experience. You know if it's not itching I typically don't notice the psoriasis much. I feel it in the shower, of course. But," she hunted out Bertrand's eyes, "Bertrand, it's gone! Totally gone!"

The skeptic in Bertrand winced. She knew that it would be quite a reach for him to attribute a power to someone like Alexandra. Finally, he said, "That's an extraordinary story Augusta. I'm happy for you. But I'll have to say that cause and effect are not demonstrable."

Augusta nodded before going on, "Something else for you to ponder. My family, mother's side, has had a history of breast cancer. I've mentioned that to you. When I visited her she held my hands for some time. A few minutes felt like an hour. She immediately brought up the issue of breast cancer, insisted that I get an exam immediately. I didn't sense anything wrong and I was waiting for my regular exam months down the road. Well, after I left Alexandra I took her advice. I went to the doctor right away. They've done tests. I am waiting for a decision on a biopsy. Dr. Durant said to me that she was glad that I upped my appointment. So, Bertrand, you see how I'm overwhelmed by this woman. And remember, she had my number about why I went to her, chastising me for being a phony."

McAbee had listened to Augusta closely. He didn't, intellectually, think that such skills couldn't reside in a human being, their validity must be tested against a series of logical gauntlets. He knew that it was unlikely that he'd ever buy into such powers. But Augusta was persuasive and she also was pretty hard-headed about matters of 'forces' or 'special agencies' in people. "What would you think about going back to her? Telling her why you had gone there in the first place, tell her what has transpired in Joanna's life and see how she reacts."

Augusta consented, "Okay. I will. I have to admit that I'm looking forward to it."

Bertrand went on, "You know Augusta how cases that look simple sometimes blow up on us, become seemingly unmanageable and stress ACJ almost beyond its capacities. What's interesting about this matter is this – it's not a case. Technically, we have no business in the matter. This is what old, wily Sy was trying to tell me. Do I listen to my attorney or do I hang around?"

CHAPTER NINE

Augusta had some hesitancies about visiting Alexandra. She had been outed by her, her flimsy presentation stripped away by Alexandra who drove into her with a true psychic's scalpel. To be uncovered while performing a mission for ACJ was one thing. But to be rewarded with a healing of her psoriasis and a prophetic warning about breast cancer made her feel truly ashamed. In cases where she had been outed there were no rewards, far from it, screaming and threats more likely. But Alexandra rewarded her seeing some kind of value in Augusta that seemed to intrigue her. Furthermore, she had invited her back.

This time, however, she and McAbee agreed. Come clean and from that position try to determine if or how ACJ could help in getting Joanna Goodkind into a different orbit.

So Augusta walked toward the doorway of Lady Alexandra's house at 4:00 p.m. while being buffeted by gale-like winds of a steady 30 miles per hour with occasional gusts up to 40 with a temperature of five degrees. She gazed quickly at a Mississippi River spewing wild waves in seeming anger at the low, dark gray sky.

As before, she was shown into the room with the extraordinary carpet whose beauty called for the attention that she gave it, absorbed by its meticulous weave. For the entire day she had felt her senses quickened. Was that because of this coming meeting? It wasn't long before she sensed Alexandra, a second later the gentle tingle of her bracelet confirmed her presence.

Augusta, psychologically prepared this time, peered closely at her as she sat. She cautioned herself immediately as she thought that Alexandra had aged a bit. Her eyes, particularly, had lost some of their intensity. There was a touch of redness along the lower outside whiteness of each eye. None of this squared with her memory of this remarkable woman.

She said, "I'm pleased that you came back, Augusta. You've been in my thoughts with frequency. Your hands, please."

Augusta complied, this time with alacrity as she observed the long fingers and nails that went well beyond how Augusta pared her own nails. "Eyes closed, please," this request leaving Augusta feeling that she had been caught snooping, which, of course, she was. Then she felt it again, it was as if she was being transported, a part of her lifted away. Her supposedly built-up defenses and preparedness for this meeting wanting, a gate left open in her fortress as Alexandra came through unimpeded, Augusta defenseless.

Alexandra spoke, "I am trying to get at your center Augusta. There's clutter. Not as much as last time. I sense extraordinary strength in you. Quite remarkable. You open but then make strong efforts to shut down, to shut me out.

Stay open with me Augusta. I think it's important for both of us."

Augusta knew that she was right even as she persisted in what was becoming a futile struggle; she could not win against this woman. Her hands were released. She opened her eyes. She was met with a gentle smile.

"You came back, Augusta. And not because you like my Persian carpet?"

Augusta returned the smile as she felt a peacefulness come over her. "I have come back for an assortment of reasons. First, my gratitude to you for my health. I am attending to my breast issues. They were pleased at the OB-GYN center for my observing the changes that had occurred. There was no reason to tell them otherwise. They wouldn't have believed me. But we both know. And then there is the psoriasis issue. Allow me." She stood, rolled up the sleeve to her loosely fitting woolen sweater. Her arm was totally free of the skin disease. She rolled down the sleeve as she sat. "That touch of yours is amazing. A full cure after all these years. I am overwhelmed by your gift. I am not a believer in the transcendent. But something is going on and it's coming through you."

Alexandra remained silent as she nodded her head almost imperceptibly. She was curious as to how the African would handle her dissembling to her at the last meeting.

Augusta looked downward and away from Alexandra's gaze. After a few seconds she looked upward to her eyes and began, "Alexandra, I have come back here to clear away the deceits that I brought into our last meeting. You were correct when you confronted me. And, yes, I did bring up an issue that disturbs me but it was insincerely presented, a smokescreen to cover my real intent." She stopped and asked for some water. It was brought. She drank half of the 10 ounce glass of water before starting. "I am a private investigator. I work for a firm here in Davenport. It is called ACJ. Bertrand McAbee, the man who runs this agency, was asked to investigate you. To expose you for a client of his."

Alexandra held up her right hand, palm out, toward Augusta. "Before you go further, I have become aware of this agency, ACJ, in my work. Also this man McAbee. Not an entirely pleasant set of associations. But not all bad, I will say. This client of ACJ you would be reluctant to name, obviously. So, I will do it for you. Peter Goodkind." She stopped abruptly, awaiting Augusta's reaction.

Augusta simply nodded. "I came here in full doubt about your business. This doubt was also shared by my boss, Bertrand McAbee. He even more so. The charge was that you were a shakedown artist. A fraud. That you were abusing trust."

Alexandra, again, held up her hand. She appreciated Augusta's protection of her client but it was no longer acceptable to her that this game of shadows persist throughout the meeting. "Augusta please. I implore you to be totally candid with me. You are speaking of a client of mine, Joanna Goodkind. I know of Peter's hatred toward me. Your agency, ACJ, surely has a one-sided version of these matters as presented by Peter Goodkind. Joanna has been brutalized by this man who is suffering from either insanity or dementia or both. So, let me lay out the terms of this session. You, originally, were sent here on a simple mission, to uncover some unsavory information about me via a complaint by Peter Goodkind. Fair enough. Why not? Now please proceed," she said softly so as to avoid any confrontation but also to lay down her cards in hope of complete reciprocity from Augusta whom she felt was not quite removed from her defenses. There was a long silence.

At last, the Augusta responded, "There is no benefit to my cloaking the purpose of my mission. We, I mean ACJ and myself, of course, fear for Joanna Goodkind. There was a confrontation in Bertrand's office with Peter Goodkind and his brother Eddie. They fear your influence over her. Joanna had been beaten up. She is presently hiding in a location that Bertrand feels is safe. Unfortunately, she would not press charges against her husband. Bertrand is trying to secure a restraining order against Peter and his brother. But there is an issue for ACJ. Peter cancelled the long-term contract between ACJ and the Goodkind Company. But Bertrand doesn't represent Joanna. So to put it in his words, 'we have a non-case case.' Additionally, he has been warned by his attorney that ACJ may have legal exposure. A no-man's territory. He left it to me as to how much I should reveal to you in hopes for your help with Joanna. I have been totally open with you."

"Do you have a safe way to bring her here?"

"Bertrand feels your house is being watched. Apparently, Joanna Goodkind owns 50% of Peter's business, which is very successful. Peter is scared besides being dangerous. Joanna desperately wants to see you. We are afraid that she will just come on her own. We, obviously, can't control her. Bertand concurs with your opinion about Peter Goodkind. He is not right in the head. Would you be open to come to the ACJ offices, meeting Joanna there?"

Augusta felt a change in the atmosphere in the room.

When asked later by Bertrand, she responded that she couldn't put a proper answer to it except that when in the presence of Alexandra she thought that all of her senses were alive, that she saw things with a clarity that she rarely, if ever, felt before. Alexandra had pulled back, not physically, but with her psyche. Alexandra's eyes were downcast, unresponsive to Augusta's presence. Augusta pressed, "Not a good idea?" For a brief moment she felt the dynamics of their relationship shift. This bothered her. Something was amiss.

Finally Alexandra said, now looking intensely at Augusta, "Your question, my leaving here, raises an entirely different set of issues not related to you, yet related to you."

"I'm confused."

"My friend Augusta. When I told you that the tea leaves were a portent, I was serious. You were, and I still think, a sentinel. An early warning system. Although you came here about the Goodkinds you were also a piece in an elaborate puzzle."

"I don't see your point."

"You couldn't without some facts. But perhaps you understand that you have been gifted some powers that let you see or manifest things beyond the obvious?"

"Well… I'm not sure. I have experienced a change since we met. It's hard for me to place it."

"Those were powers that you have but your awareness of them was absent. I am a good judge of this. But back to my story as to why you were proven to be a sentinel. When I read my tea leaves I was shocked at what I saw. I did it again, the swirl, the same message. It was a consequence to your alert as the sentinel."

"I still don't understand, Alexandra."

"I am so concerned about that series of events that I have not left this house since then. I am agitated, fearful. I will not leave to see Joanna in answer to your request."

Augusta was caught off-guard from these disclosures, not sure of how to process what this complex woman was telling her. She decided to remain silent. It was Alexandra's recital.

After a lenthy delay, Alexandra went on. "I see no reason to relate my full story to you. After all, you are here about Joanna Goodkind. I will say some things to you. I am Estonian on my mother's side, a Russian Estonian. My father was Russian, a complicated man – largely absent and when present very abusive to both my mother and myself. His background was controversial to say the least. It was through him that I discovered my powers, my gifts some would say. I believe, also, that my powers were passed onto me through him. He is long dead, my mother also. Through a progression of life experiences I finally came to this area. For peace of mind, I established a business as a psychic. I have a modest clientele. I never advertise. But I am a psychic Augusta. I am a healer. I have gifts." She stopped to reflect on how much she told Augusta; there were secrets in her life that would die with her. She questioned herself as to why she even disclosed this much to her.

Augusta reached across the table, startling Alexandra. She took her hand and said, "Alexandra I feel that I have caused a problem for you by my presence last time. Not only because I was disingenuous but I brought out some image in the tea leaves."

"Yes Augusta, you did. But you may have saved me

with the warning you gave. Here is my conclusion. It is based on two consecutive readings of a bear. That bear is Russia. I have no conflicting reads. When I get that clarity I do not wander around trying to talk myself away from my interpretation."

Augusta let go of her hand. Did she feel a slight tremor from her? "But why would that distress you? Have you ever been there?"

"Yes, while a translator at Procter & Gamble. But in and out. No contacts really. It has to lead back to my father whose very existence was problematic. Or it may be related to a job I had before P&G, but I doubt this. My father had his history through his parentage. But why now? Why me? I don't know. All I know is that there is a distant rumble and you were the sentinel. There is much more to you than you realize."

"Are you scared?"

"I am apprehensive, a first cousin to fear. As to Joanna I will be happy to meet her but only here. I'm most sorry."

Augusta was turning over all of this information, wondering how Bertrand would construe the different threads from this meeting. She said, "Well, then, we will make it work somehow. But as to your anxieties, I have no answer. I am dumbfounded to be honest."

"Maybe you are more than a sentinel, maybe you are a guard." She rang and asked for tea, as before. She wanted another reading with Augusta.

CHAPTER TEN

As in an almost exact replica from her last appearance, Maria brought the tea on a tray, along with sugar and milk, two teaspoons and two napkins. She was gone in a flash.

Augusta said, "When I tell Bertrand about your use of tea leaves he becomes quite suspicious."

"I don't see you as different from him. True?"

"Well... yes with reservations. You have caused me to rethink what occurs here. I have experienced some very odd things. Some kinds of energy. And then there are my physical events. But the tea leaves? I'm not as doubting as Bertrand but I honestly feel they are a reach."

"I see," she sipped at the hot tea. "All the way back to the Egyptians, the Sumerians, and probably long before then there has always been a belief in a shaman, an agent who could traverse two worlds, the physical one that we live in day by day. The one that we experience now as we sit here, sip tea, and speak to each other. We all have that awareness, attest to it easily, unthinkingly. Some are given to distort that reality, people on drugs, mentally disabled. But most see this world, its materiality, its presence, for what it is. So even your counterpart, this Bertrand McAbee, would not quarrel over this. We all agree," she said with a smile. "But now the separation starts between us. So, I will tell you of my experience. I have no doubt at all that there is another reality beyond our senses. It is there and present but not for all. In my profession I see it all the time. People are obdurate, skeptical, closed off or, as I think in your case Augusta, unable to find the key in their soul that allows them into that world. The passage is quite unnerving, scary. But once in this other world there can be no going back to the simple way of the day-in day-out material reality. I have a gift, I *know*, not just believe, but *know*, that I can traverse this other world. I do not live in that other world but I can travel in it. It far supersedes this physical reality, which is really a weak copy of this greater world. The other world can manage our physical world, can affect it, can change things. Alter this reality in ways that I am unable to fathom, sometimes. Yes, I have gifts but I feel that I only understand a miniscule bit of what is there. You are looking at me, Augusta, as though I am speaking nonsense. I think that your boss has done some damage to you with his skepticism. He, perhaps, has inhibited you." She stopped and sipped more tea.

Augusta was troubled. She was in awe of Alexandra but she was in awe of Bertrand McAbee. Those two worlds were so apart, irreconcilable. "I'm listening closely to you, Alexandra. You are saying things with which I am unfamiliar. Please go on."

"Messages are sent, actions are taken, by that world. Without the gift these are never accounted for, understood. People speculate about chance, good luck. Good luck because they cannot get their hands around there being another world. I am a medium with gifts, limited yes, but I have them. I try to stay restrained. Careful not to overreach, to misuse. I feel that I have a Ferrari within me but I stay in first gear. When I became aware of what I had, I swung into a high gear once and actually changed the course of someone's life, irrevocably. I became stunned and frightened about what I had." She stopped and looked across the room at the light near the window.

Augusta asked, "I think I see what you are saying. Through a glass darkly as St. Paul would say and my Lutheran theology professors at Augustana College would discourse about."

"Well, at least you sense a glass in front of you and you can see darkened images. The ancient Egyptians were acutely aware of this other world. They devoted most of their civilization to trying to understand that world. They had a priesthood devoted to traversing this world. They called some of their priests psychopomps. Their job was to successfully transport souls from one world to the other. A fictional invention? I don't think so. The Greeks had similar, the Persian Zoroastrians, Hindus, and so on. So, your McAbee would label them as superstitious?"

"I'm not sure of that. He rarely dismisses things out of hand. He identifies as a skeptic. So he's not quick to dismiss but he's also not quick to accept. But a psychopomp? I don't know about that. And tea leaves?"

"Ah yes. Tea leaves. It is not they that is the issue in themselves. It is my ability to be a channel from the unseen world through the leaves to us. I have this strength. Sometimes I know what the leaves are saying, it is evident. But sometimes I fail to understand. I am an imperfect instrument. So let us begin. I see your cup has only a slight amount of liquid in it. Would you be kind enough to rotate it as I did before?"

Augusta took her cup and tilted it about 45 degrees. The leaves spread across the inside curvature of the cup. They fell into place, almost as preordained, varying shapes as they fell onto each other, beside each other, left, right, up, down, diagonal. Unlike the last time, she paid close attention to the shapes and looked for a possible theme. If she had a gift such as Alexandra suggested, why could she not also capture the messages in tea leaves? After seconds of intense reflection she shrugged her shoulders, shook her head and said to Alexandra, "I can't capture anything in this cup. Do you wish to see?"

"If I may, yes." She held her palm out for Augusta to hand over the cup in its tilted position. Alexandra studied the leaves and after a short time said, "This is a positive message. There is a sense of two people," she used a pencil and pointed it at two columns shaped, she said, like two people, she then pointed to a single horizontal line that reached between the two people. She said, "You see a sign of cooperation, of friendship. To me it is clear. We must stay close, help each other. That is our strength when facing Peter Goodkind."

Augusta asked her to return the cup. She studied it for at least a minute. Finally, she said, "I see your point, I mean I see how you got to this conclusion. But because we like each other could it not merely be a projection on your part of what you wish for? Believe me, I'm not trying to be a bitch about this but I am sharing my doubts."

"No. Not at all. I went through the same questions

that you're raising. It's easy to self-deceive. There was a philosopher back in the third century of this era. His name was Plotinus. I have studied him over the years. Very difficult to fathom but then suddenly I came to understand. A bit anyway, as he was far deeper of mind than I. He refused to write anything down, deep distrust of the written word. But he had a student named Porphery. He was an avid note-taker as he listened to Plotinus. Was most likely present at his death in 270. Suddenly, there are scam artists walking around Rome and Alexandria giving false interpretations of this great mystical philosopher Plotinus. Because of that Prophery publishes his notes, the book comes down to us as *The Enneads*. Plotinus is forever credited for this book as it should be, even though it was penned by Porphery. I don't mean to rattle on. Forgive me if I bore you. But in defense of Plotinus' experiences with the other world he would say, in my judgment, don't knock or deny something that you never experienced. There is no good response to that retort. I know what I know. To that point Augusta, Peter Goodkind will not stop his efforts. He has a field of targets, not just Joanna and myself but your boss, and I'm unsure, possibly you. Caution is the key for all of us. Tell McAbee to make Joanna a client, then protect her."

She took the forewarning without comment but with trepidation as Alexandra was more and more taking a hold on her. At last, Augusta said into a long silence, "You have not yet read your own tea leaves. Do I get to hear that?" she asked as lightly as she could.

"The last time you were here, you may have noticed, I swirled them twice in a hope that I was mistaken about the message. Self-delusion. In both swirls there was a bear. I saw the bear in conjunction with your reading as the sentinel."

"The bear? Soon to come out of hibernation. The Spring?" Augusta asked.

Alexandra shook her head. "I wish that was the case. I am Russian. My father had roots back in Russia. The bear represents Russia, the Russian bear. You were the sentinel foretelling the coming of the bear, Russia. My concern is quite high. Little good comes from the things of that country and in my case none. So, yes it is time for my leaves." She raised her cup and swirled the leaves in the thin envelope of water until they came to rest on the sides of her cup.

CHAPTER ELEVEN

"Ah. As I thought. Augusta, it is your time to become a leaf reader." Alexandra handed the cup across to her, careful to maintain the angle of the cup

Augusta took it and peered into it. She saw it immediately, surprised at herself. There was a clear image of a standing bear, arms outstretched. "I see it clearly Alexandra. A standing bear, arms outstretched. Am I right?"

"You are. Exactly as I see it. It is of great concern to me. It frightens me. I have never experienced so much clarity, so often, in the leaves. Something is amiss."

"But you said that you were only in Russia for Procter & Gamble. Your father, long dead, your mother, an Estonian. Have you had other direct business with Russians? In your past?"

"Yes. But that is settled long ago. I worked for a Russian in New York. Some businesses. But those days are long gone. There were Russians, actually much of the old Soviet Union, living in America was represented. Local businesses in the New York area. I was once an irrelevancy, not known and I am sure, at least until now, that I was forgotten. But perhaps it is otherwise. All that I can do is wait for further signs. Frequently, matters clear up and my concerns overblown."

"I hope so. But just in case there is trouble and you need help call me and I can try to get the ACJ Agency into the matter."

"Yes. Then I could meet your Doubting Thomas, McAbee," Alexandra said lightly.

"We will speak with Joanna. Perhaps we can devise a way to her get her here unnoticed. I am glad that I removed the obstacles to our relationship and that we have a common goal in helping Joanna Goodkind."

After Augusta was shown out, Alexandra went back into the Persian room and sat. She gazed at the carpet as she weighed matters.

As Augusta was driving back to downtown Davenport she called Bertrand's cell. He answered on the first ring. "Augusta, I'm concerned. How are you?"

"Okay Bertrand. Are you still downtown?"

"Yeah. I'm in my office."

"I need a drink. You gonna buy me one mistah?"

"Sure. As long as you don't drink two and send me into the poor house."

"I'll see if I can order a half a drink. How about The Snapper? I'm driving and will be down there and seated in ten minutes. If you don't hurry I just might allow myself to be treated to a free drink by an admirer and who knows what happens from there."

"Okay, okay. I'll be there in eight minutes. I get the message."

The Snapper was an old-time bar that was two minutes from the ACJ offices. It was in an alley and upon entering it he had to descend a ten-step stairway. The place was quite dark. Bertrand said to himself that the bar was sponsored by the lousy winter. Darkness into near darkness. He arrived before Augusta. What he hadn't told her was that he stayed in his office precisely to meet with her and hear what Lady Alexandra had offered as a solution to the Joanna Goodkind dilemma. He found a table in a far corner.

Even in darkness he sensed the arrival of Augusta. He knew her presence by instinct. He arose from the small table in the many cornered place and went toward her, advantaged by being accustomed to the dark. He came along her side and took her hand whispering, "Can I buy you a drink babe?"

"Bertrand, dammit, you scared me," she laughed.

"I'm way over by the pillar. You know where it is. What can I get you?"

"A double shot of Jack Daniels. No ice and a glass of water, if you can afford it."

"It'll be a tough month for me but I can make it."

When he came out with her order he also brought an alcohol-free Heineken for himself. He said, "I'm drinking heavily tonight."

"Yeah, I see. I'll call an Uber for you," she said sarcastically.

"You were gone a long time. Did you get right in to see her?"

"Yes and yes. Alexandra is one complicated woman. I've never met anyone quite like her. Bottom line, she won't leave her place. Joanna will have to go there if she insists on seeing her. Ever since I met with her, she has not ventured out of her house. She's scared Bertrand."

"Of Peter Goodkind? For Joanna? For herself?"

"As to Peter, she's in full agreement with you. Dementia, psychosis, whatever. She's quite worried about Joanna. I told her of the assaults on Joanna and your having placed her in a safe house. But that she's not a client of ACJ."

"Is she scared for herself or for Joanna?" he persisted against the unanswered question.

"More for herself and that's not due to Joanna. That's an entirely different matter. I'll explain later."

"I reached out to Joanna. She has signed on as a client. Needless to say, Sy is furious with me. He says that I am highly likely to be sued. But I did it anyway. We'll have to figure out how to get her over to Alexandra undetected. Peter called me this morning, he piled on about five minutes of abuse before I hung up on him. He's not the same man anymore. But Lady Alexandra, you said there was another issue?"

Augusta was worried about wading into tea leaves and psychopomps with Bertrand who sounded a bit testy as he sat in this darkened bar and drank his alcohol-free Heinekens. "Well Bertrand, I'll tell you providing you don't give me the 'you're crazy' look."

He laughed. "Of course, I won't. Why would I do that to my best friend."

"What if your supposed best friend is taking a dive into the other worldly?" she asked lightly with a glimmer of a smile.

"Out with it Augusta. Let's hear this."

"Okay. You asked for it and yes it does go to tea leaves but something else. Surely you've heard of psychopomps?"

"Yes," he said neutrally.

"She feels that she has gifts bestowed on her through her father. Long dead by the way."

"Gifts?"

"Healing, predicting, and maybe more than that."

"More than what?"

"Affecting the course of events. But I didn't push her on this. I'm not sure what she meant. I have to be careful about prying. After all, I'm the client, not her. By the way, the bartender shorted you on this drink. There's no way that was a double Jack."

"Got it. I'll try again." He got up and headed for the bar. He was back in a short while. "This one looks larger. I really hit the word 'double' this time." He handed her the drink, observing to himself that Augusta was not a drinker of note. "So she perceives herself as an intermediary between this world and another, an unseen one but obvious to her?" he asked.

"Yes, that's the size of it."

"And? Your analysis?"

"There you have me. I went over there today psychologically armed to resist her. To get her to stay focused on Joanna Goodkind. And I succeeded up to a point. She concluded, by the way, that Joanna should become a client of ACJ. So you were at one with her on that. But when it came to her seeing Joanna in your offices or elsewhere she was quite direct in refusing to do so. It had to be at her place. It was from there that things went odd. She picked up my skepticism pretty quickly and surmised that I had been *ruined* by you. *She* didn't use the word, ruined. I cannot get by, Bertrand, the healing of my psoriasis and her call about possible breast cancer. She has something in her, a power or as she calls it a gift or strength. That's when she started to speak about the other world, the not material world. She also scolded me for not getting in touch with my gifts that she feels I have. And when I'm with her, I do sense a current of energy that I've never sensed before in myself. So, I asked her why she won't leave her house since the last time I visited. It came down to her reading of the tea leaves and the occurrence of a bear."

"Come again on this Augusta. A bear?"

"Exactly what I thought at first. She identifies herself as a Russian. She read her cup twice when I was there before but she didn't disclose what she saw in the leaves. She said that in both cases she saw a bear and through her gifts she was positive that a threat was coming, Russian-related. It has caused her to stay home."

"She was in Russia with P&G, but why would the Russians bother with her?"

"There is something in her background that tracks back to there. She's scared."

"Did you offer our help?"

"Oh yes. I told her that I would speak with you if she wished. She never said either way. But now here's the bombshell Bertrand. We read my leaves today; they call for cooperation between me and her. After she points out what the configuration says I see her point. Then she swirls her cup. She hands it to me. My God, I see a standing bear arms outstretched. Can you believe? She now seems doubly scared. She said that she worked for a Russian many years ago but saw no reason for that to be in play now. Her father was Russian, the other possibility. She thinks that her gifts came from him. But he's long dead. So, in either case she is befuddled. And yet she's scared. And at the end of it all I think she actually has the powers or gifts that she asserts. Am I crazy to you?"

He sat back by awhile and thought. Finally, he said, "Augusta, you're the least crazy person I ever met. I take you very seriously. As you know I'm very skeptical about gifts and powers. But I don't rule out the possibility. Let's focus on Joanna who is absolute on her need to see her. Another believer, by the way, in your court. As to the Russian phenomenon, I just don't know how to handle it. There is a bizarre quality to the matter. Someday, I'd like to meet Alexandra. We'll see. How about some Italian food at Mario's? I'm buying and I'll drive."

"Perfect!"

CHAPTER TWELVE

Joanna Goodkind remained in the safe house for two days. The bruise on her left cheekbone now an ugly purple/black, both of her eyes half-circled with black rings. Her left eye was crisscrossed with numerous red lines. The professor friend of McAbee, Mary, was kind and vigilant. But on this third day Joanna was determined to break her barely made promise to McAbee. She had to see Alexandra, deciding against McAbee's plan.

She slipped out of the house and drove west across town from Bettendorf to Davenport. She knew that her heavily applied makeup was in a losing battle with her facial injuries. Her large, dark sunglasses prevailed more satisfactorily in covering her compromised eyes.

As usual she drove up to the gate and pressed the intercom button. She told Maria that she was there. The gate opened, she parked her car and came to the front door. Maria was waiting. Joanna could see that she was shocked at her appearance but after a few seconds of controlling her distress urged Joanna to enter the house. Not saying a word she hugged Joanna, took her coat and showed her to the usual room, leaving, she said, "Lady Alexandra will be with you shortly."

Joanna sat, immediately feeling a sense of comfort along with a flow of tears. She closed her eyes, folded her arms and placed her head downward into her arms; her tears were uncontrollable.

The light touch on her forearm took her away from her mental confusion caused by thoughts racing through her head with bewildering speed. Sitting erect she saw a box of Kleenex. She removed her sunglasses and heard a groan deep from Alexandra's chest.

"I'm so sorry to come to you in this state," she said between gasps.

Alexandra replied, "We have all the time you need. Breathe deeply. Collect yourself. Coffee, tea?"

"Coffee, black," feeling her tears ebbing, her breathing coming under control.

Alexandra left the room and was back in a moment. "Maria will bring coffee for the two of us. Are you ready to engage with me, Joanna?"

"Please. Yes."

"Close your eyes, extend your two hands toward me." She did as told. Alexandra felt the tension and apprehension in the touch, soon followed by the draining of Joanna's emotions. There was much more than just sadness. There was terror. Joanna had been subjected to severe abuse by her husband. She held her hands for at least five minutes. There was no possibility of all the torment leaving her. Some would be permanently etched into her. She removed her hands. "Joanna, speak with me about what has happened. Do not edit. Do not follow a prepared narrative. Just speak as things come to you. Stop when you need to. Pay no attention to time." There was a knock at the door. She went and retrieved the tray from Maria. Coffee was poured from the carafe. Alexandra chose to say nothing further as she observed Joanna sip some coffee from the mug. She was now in a much better zone to proceed.

"You said it would go this way. It did. I am sure that Peter has gone over the edge. My relationship with you makes him so fearful. You the truth-teller, he the mad man. He wanted me to sign over my share of the company. I said no, not until I spoke with you. He went into a fury and beat me until I surrendered. He forced me to take some pills. I don't know what they were but they threw me into a haze. He called his brother Eddie. They decided to take me to ACJ. McAbee. The security agency for his business. He intended McAbee to place an ankle bracelet on me for control. When he thought I was totally comatose, I heard him arguing with Eddie who had bad feelings about McAbee. When we got to ACJ, to his credit, McAbee challenged the pair of them in his office. Hazy as I was that challenge gave me the courage to say no. McAbee saw what was done to me. They tried to leave ACJ with me. It was so hard for me to even move. Then two of McAbee's men came and they essentially chased Peter and Eddie from the ACJ offices. McAbee spirited me off to a former colleague of his and I have stayed with her for a few days. Hidden. When you said I could come I left for here. I'm sure that McAbee will be very unhappy."

"Why would that be?"

"He was afraid that you'd be under surveillance. That they would try to seize me, make me sign papers, and then maybe commit me. He was very apprehensive."

"*Were* you followed?"

"No. There was no way for them to know that I was hidden away in Bettendorf."

"How about around here?" Alexandra asked.

"I'm sorry I didn't notice. I am out of my wits."

"Of course, I understand. Do you happen to know a woman by the name of Augusta Satin?"

"I know of her. She works for ACJ. Peter would speak about her. He said that she was a former cop. Why do you ask?"

"I'm not sure yet. But there is a confluence of events."

"Peter, when he was without symptoms, would joke. He thought that they were an item. McAbee and her. That they hid what was pretty obvious to him. I don't know the truth but there was a time when Peter was very observant."

"I ask because Augusta came here at the behest of your husband who asked McAbee to determine how much of a fraud I was. As we both know, Peter is very worried about me. Worried that I am a danger to his firm. That I am insincere, manipulating you for my own gain. I…"

There was a commotion outside the door. Alexandra arose and quickly opened the door. Joanna stood and peered out into the small hallway and saw Maria, arm bent behind her back and the massive hand of Eddie Goodkind over her mouth. He screamed at Alexandra, "You Russian cow! Hand over Joanna, now!" He then released Maria and shoved her against a wall. He removed from his coat a gun and pointed it at Alexandra.

Joanna pleaded, "Okay, okay. I'll come. Just put the gun away!"

Alexandra threw her arm across the doorway, blocking

Joanna's path. She said to Joanna, "No! Stay where you are." She then turned her attention to Eddie. She said, "Leave now and nothing will come of this; persist and you will not leave here alive."

Eddie looked at her curiously. He yelled, "Like hell..." Was it fear that Joanna then saw in his eyes? A glimpse at something beyond him? Whatever it was, to her subsequent shock, Eddie's hand shook rapidly, he tried to steady his right wrist with his left hand but to no avail. He dropped the gun. He looked down on the floor, but his body seemed frozen. He then dropped to his knees trying to reach for the fallen gun. He fell face forward.

Maria went to him. She touched his neck checking for a pulse. There was none. Eddie Goodkind was dead.

CHAPTER THIRTEEN

Joanna Goodkind was back at her refuge. It was close to 5:00 p.m., darkness full. Augusta Satin sat across from her. A long day. Alexandra had called the police immediately after Eddie had fallen dead. She tended to Maria while keeping a close eye on Joanna. There would be no fabrication she said. Eddie's death was natural. Joanna's beaten-up face would be explained just as it had happened. Her consultation with Alexandra was natural, occurring often enough. Maria the innocent victim. The fallen gun a demonstration of the tension Eddie was physically unable to bear.

Because of the weapon, Joanna's appearance and Maria's crying and physical complaints the police were super cautious, unwilling to leave things as they appeared. This meant a team of four officers, a lab technician, a photographer and individual and group questioning that went on for hours. Alexandra called Augusta at 1:00 p.m. briefing her. By 4:00 p.m. the cops were willing to call it a day. Eddie's body would be subject to an autopsy. Peter Goodkind went into a frenzy, so much so that he was hospitalized. The one question that was unanswered was how Eddie had breached the compound. His SUV was found a block away. Clearly, he was scouting for Joanna's appearance. But his penetration of the grounds would be investigated.

And now at 5:00 p.m. Augusta sat, said little, and tried to reassure Joanna. Both Alexandra and Bertrand separately thought it was a good idea. Bertrand insisted that Augusta go armed fearful of Peter Goodkind finding some way to his professor-friend's house.

"I'm here Joanna if you'd like to talk about things. Bertrand has made me aware of what went down in his offices. I guess that Eddie had a heart condition." She stopped. There was enough for Joanna to comment to if she wished. The silence between them was unnerving for Augusta. For Joanna, with tightly knitted eyebrows and puzzled expression, the anxiety was pronounced. Finally, Joanna spoke in a low and halting voice, "I went to see Alexandra. I needed to. She has been my source of sanity. I always felt secure and safe at her house. So relaxed. We were just getting into things when there was so much noise outside the room we were in. When I saw Eddie I freaked out. Maria was pushed around like a sack of potatoes by him. Then I saw he had a gun. Oh my God! I made to go with him. I didn't want Alexandra and Maria to be harmed. Alexandra put her arm out and kept me behind her. She has the arms of strong man. I couldn't get beyond. Then she squared off to Eddie who looked ready to fire the gun at her. She told him to leave. Nothing would be said. But he wouldn't leave. Then he started to shake. He dropped to the floor, gun out of his hands, he fell forward. He was dead. The rest of the day is a blur. Alexandra insisted that we not make up anything. To tell the truth. We did."

"Cops treat all of you fairly?"

"Yes. One of them was a woman. She saw my face. She knew. The others, all men, fell in behind her. By this evening they'll see that only Eddie's prints are on the gun. Not ours."

"Tell me more about Eddie."

"Ex-football player. Harsh, tough, macho. Not crazy like Peter. But vicious, arrogant. As Peter has been deteriorating Eddie started to play a more prominent role in the businesses. He also had no love for Alexandra. I am…was, as scared of him as I was Peter."

Augusta sensed an incomplete story. Nothing was false but not all that was true was being said. She wondered how the police team saw things. The death of Eddie was convenient. Unless the autopsy turned up foul play, not much more could be said. Yet she felt she had a 500 piece puzzle but there was a missing piece right in the middle of the puzzle. In the past when she had these insights or hunches she would usually repress them. Perhaps too quickly. Alexandra, on the other hand, perceived her as gifted. She no longer doubted Alexandra's abilities maybe it was time for her to no longer doubt her own. "Alexandra was very brave to face down a man with a gun aimed at her. And shield you. You've both been through a lot. And for you, it seems that things don't stop Joanna. By the way, did Alexandra say anything to Eddie other than to leave the house and put the gun down?"

Augusta noticed Joanna look away, perhaps surprised by the question. A hesitation. "One thing. She did as you said. Put the gun away, leave the house, and nothing further will occur. Then she said… well it's not clear what she meant."

"What's that Joanna? What you say to me will be kept private."

There was a long delay. Finally Joanna said, "She warned him that if he charged ahead he would not leave the premises alive. I remember saying to myself what does that mean? Within seconds, Eddie's face showed confusion; he seemed fearful. Like a hex had been placed on him. He shuddered, his gun hand started to tremble. He dropped the gun, then he crumbled to the floor. He was dead. I know that she's a powerful woman but I can't comprehend what I saw. What it suggests."

Augusta listened in astonishment. Joanna said that she needed sleep and it came to her almost immediately as she laid back on the couch.

Augusta called Bertrand and reported some details to him. He would arrange for one of Jack's men to cover the house for the night. Augusta didn't mention the warning that Alexandra had issued to Eddie. She needed to process it. Tomorrow would be sufficient.

PART TWO

RUSSIA: QUESTIONING

CHAPTER FOURTEEN

"So you ask my dearest friend Vladimir, are traits inheritable? For example, can adherence to the principles of the revolution be passed along the path of genetics? Can a person develop a trait through personal discipline and then somehow have that become part of their DNA and thus become eligible to be passed down to the generations to come?"

"More or less Adam. That is an issue for me."

"A debate took place at the beginning of the socialist revolution. Precisely on this issue. For some, possible. For others, impossible. No one argued against eye color, baldness and so on. Physical traits are very much in the genetic codes. The facts are overwhelming. But your question created a chasm. Some pure communists were inclined to affirm a passing of psychological traits. Theory-wise it made possible the creation of a new society. A true communism became theoretically achievable. There could be a society where all are created equal and a corresponding extinction of selfishness and individualism, those traits sewn into capitalism. Our optimistic political theory demanding the crushing of original sin, a sour and negative theory perpetrated by theists. Instead of Jesus Christ, some of our intellectuals went for genetics."

"If you'd stop gulping down my vodka in liters, respond to me very directly, please, my friend and corrupt philosopher."

"Well, I know you enough to understand what you want me to say. If you promise not to exile me to Siberia, I will answer," he said jokingly. He did not fear President Putin. They had grown up together in St. Petersburg, lifelong friends.

"Yes, you drunken son-of-a-bitch, I *will* send you to Siberia if I don't get a straight answer from you," Putin said as he shook his head in mocked exasperation. The Russian President knew that there were only two men with whom he could feel totally relaxed and uninhibited. Both were companions from childhood. Besides the philosopher, Adam, sitting across from him, there was his right-hand man who operated out of the Kremlin, the infamous Dimitri whose self was made of steel, the exception a heart of unwavering devotion to Vladimir Putin. If Putin was angry then so was Dimitri. If Putin was sad, and so on. Adam, on the other hand, was allowed the spear of truth.

"I will give you my opinion, comrade. It is not, I fear, what you want to hear. DNA cannot be changed. What you get is what you are. If my atheistic father went to Mount Athos, lived with those depraved maniacs and became a spiritual guru and assimilated all of the traits the monks strove for, none of them could be passed on to me through genetics. Yes, if I was around him all the time I might also become a spiritual guru but it would not be due to genetics. Just cultural conditioning, period. In other words, you are a mean fucker not because of your DNA but because of the people you hung around with, the customs that you were exposed to. There is another angle to this question, the fucking Chinese. They are trying to change people by shaming, surveillance, and retraining camps. They may eventually work their way into editing the genetic code. But none of this goes to your question directly. Whatever the case, don't forget it is only because of me that you are half-human," the philosopher laughed loudly before a sputtering cough caught up with him.

"Your radical materialism is unable to explain some things. I have felt a mysterious hand operating in my life. Like you, I was brought up as a materialist. I understand perfectly well what you are saying. But I think that the materialist philosophy is too glib, simplistic. A whore who will sleep with any occurrence in order to conquer it."

"Vladimir, I believe that you are going through what the religionists call the dark night of the soul. Something has a hold on you. In your words, it it's religion-based then you are in the arms of the greatest of all whores in the universe," Adam said crossly.

"Perhaps you are right, Adam."

An hour or so later Adam left the Kremlin in the limo ordered by Putin. By that time Adam could barely walk; he was assisted by two guards. Vladimir Putin shook his head. Adam had become an alcoholic, a Russian trait that he had long abhorred.

Sober, he went into his own private chambers. He sat in his lounger. Yes, drunken Adam, the most brilliant man he had ever met, had one thing right. Putin was having a dark night of the soul, the provocations for such were easily identifiable.

It all began when he was introduced those many years ago, at age 16, to an old man who was said to be a prophet. He had predicted, quite precisely, Putin's ascendancy to power. Occasionally, he would have a fleeting memory of that chance meeting. But now, with the recent occurrence followed by his meeting with Wilosky, he felt it necessary to force his way to a coherent understanding of related but seemingly unrelated phenomena.

In what was becoming a night-time ritual, he opened his wall-safe and withdrew the single sheet of paper that he had stashed in it.

The hand-crafted page, very thick and stiff, had the Romanov crest etched in a dark maroon on a pale blue page.

Putin handled this very page with reverence, as perhaps a priest would handle a chalice. He read the message four times, slowly, and then placed it back into his wall safe. He retired to his bedroom convinced that forces beyond him were unmoored.

That very page had been passed to Dimitri by the Director of Archival Records. Following a State order, the entire archival records of the Soviet Union were being examined, reclassified and placed into an electronic database. Deniken, the Archival Director, had estimated it was a 10 year job. Previous efforts to do this had ground to a halt because of budgetary considerations, politics, and typically the inertia of the Russian State. But this Deniken was new to the job and was known to be a high achievement man. At the urging of his advisory board, Deniken chose 1905 as a starting point. In that year a huge revolt against the

Czarist Romanov government was violently suppressed by the Czar Nicholas II regime. Many historians argued that it was that event that slow-burned to the fuse that would bring about the 1916 Russian Revolution and the violent end of the Romanov dynasty that had lasted for almost 300 years.

The archiving was tedious work. The massive number of records were acting as a centrifugal force as they now occupied three massive warehouses. First, Deniken decided to proceed chronologically year to year, day to day. If the manuscript was created in April of 1905 then it would be placed in that year by specific date, the standard way. But there was pushback to that approach. Shouldn't that year be based on themes, e.g., foreign policy toward Japan, toward Germany? Should the thread follow particular events through to their ends? Some even argued that the year by year approach be scuttled entirely in favor of particular events that ran through many years. He put together a committee to offer recommendations. After two months of internecine war, he realized that his death would come long before any completion of the project. To the surprise of many the completion of three years, 1905, 1906, and 1907 (calendar-based) was achieved. He was praised for having put order into chaos. But then the critics, agents of order they claimed, attacked him for creating chaos. Welcome to Russia, he thought as his now estranged wife placed three novels by bureaucracy-hating Franz Kafka on his bedside table. In addition, on top of the Kafka tomes, she placed a Russian translation of a German book entitled *How to Kill Relationships*. It was a disgusting book which, in the very giving, began the self-fulfilling prophecy.

At last Deniken was called into a meeting with the

current cast of powerful figures for an accounting. Praise for his accomplishments was sparse. It was evident that he was going to redirected from his approach. When he was asked how long it would take for him to reach the pivotal year of 1916 he said, disingenuously, three years. Even the simplest of mathematicians in that ignorant group instantly realized that the 10 year program was more likely a 25 year slog. It was then that a mysterious man who sat off to the side of the great table caught his attention. He was noticeable because he was not noticeable. The meeting had been trudging forward for two hours. He was ready to resign or be forced to manage a gold mine somewhere in the outer reaches of Siberia. Suddenly that unnoticed man said, very gently, "Please." Every motion and voice in the room went still, frozen. God had appeared. "Continue on Comrade Director Deniken. But today, start with 1916. If you complete it in six months, come back here. You will be assigned an additional 40 professionals with cataloging and library experience. This meeting is done."

Archivist Deniken had a reasonably good relationship with one of those in attendance. In the hallway he asked who that unnoticed man was. He saw a brief stare of fear in the man's eyes.

"His name is Dimitri. When he speaks, Putin speaks. You do not need to know anything else. Just do what he says." His walking away steps would have found him a place on a track team.

Two months later a woman by the name Anna Osokin requested a private meeting with Deniken, an unusual request but she had indicated that it was a grave matter.

She had a folder in a hand that shook. A woman of

about 50 years, she was pudgy and socially awkward. His inquiry, previous to meeting with her, indicated that she was a faithful party member and librarian from Volgograd. Anna was gone in five minutes and he was in possession of the folder that she had brought with her.

The high grade sheet of handmade paper was signed at its bottom with the name of the head archivist in the year of 1921. It was counter-signed again in 1937 by still another head archivist. In 1964 it had a hand-stamp of the Archival Department along with a scribbled signature and small handwritten note, 'As seen. File away. Top secret.'

All that was not without precedent. His eyes then wandered onto the contents of the page as he was trying to fathom why this woman from Volgograd was almost apoplectic. It was handmade paper, a light blue with a majestic maroon crest. When he read the contents, its author and the year of creation, he felt a shiver along his spine. A meeting was arranged with the aforesaid, Dimitri.

Dimitri looked at him indifferently as Deniken handed the folder to him. With a slight motion of his index finger, Dimitri had the Archivist Director Deniken follow him into a small room. He pointed his finger downwards and Deniken sat. He was about to say something but was silenced by a quick stab of Dimitri's finger.

He watched Dimitri open the folder. Even the expressionless eyes of Dimitri appeared to be spooked. He looked up several times as if to make sure that Deniken was there. "It is good that you brought this to me. Inform that woman from Volgograd that she will be rewarded. Make sure that neither of you are to ever mention this matter to anyone. Punishment would be beyond imagination. Thank you, comrade."

Two weeks later Deniken read in *Pravda* about the unfortunate death of a librarian from Volgograd named Anna Osokin. He felt terror in his heart. Her death was an apparent suicide, the newspaper declared.

CHAPTER FIFTEEN

The Orthodox priest, Father Damien, was jarred alert by his desk phone. It rarely rang. When it did his psyche roared to a full alert. He picked up, "Father Damien here," he said cautiously.

The gravelly man's voice commanded flatly, "You're needed here within the hour. There is urgency."

"I understand," simultaneous disconnecting, now, on both ends of the phones.

He robed quickly, left his quarters and was on his way for the five minute walk to the residence of Vladimir Mikhailovich Gundyayev – AKA Patriarch of Moscow and all Russia – Kirill. He conjectured about the urgency of the call, estimating that high risk was in the air. This was beyond the crowded schedule that he regularly coordinated for the Patriarch.

Father Damien was 43 years of age. He had been vetted carefully by Orthodox officials from the time of his interest in serving God. A Georgian from the Russian occupied territory of North Ossetia in Georgia he was a Georgian in heart but a Russian in tongue. He was a stellar student with a notable religious bent. His childhood fascination with the exotic rituals of the Orthodox Church never ceased. He engaged in theological studies in Tiblisi, Georgia, but soon he moved to Moscow at the urging of the Georgian Patriarch who saw him as a useful piece in his complicated relationship with the then Russian Patriarch. When Kirill assumed the patriarchy of the Russian Orthodox Church in 2009 Father Damien was assigned into a coterie of officials around the new Patriarch. By 2015 he was appointed as First Secretary to Patriarch Kirill. His right hand man, in effect.

With a flow of the right hand and a small tip of the hat, he was escorted by an armed guard and then shown into a seven doored circular atrium. He went straight ahead and knocked on the door to the Patriarch's study. It was opened immediately, another guard in use.

Patriarch Kirill was seated at his desk. Brusquely, he flicked all ten of his fingers quickly inwards as he then motioned with a slight upward nod for the guard to wait outside.

Damien looked at the exhausted face of Kirill. Except for the thinnest straws of black the Patriarch's white beard squared off about eight inches from his jaw line. His eyes had a mordant cunning that Damien had come to estimate as inward and plotting. He had rarely seen him smiling, ah yes, there was the virtual rictus when Pope Francis met with him a few years back, Kirill's hatred for the Roman Pontiff hard to disguise.

Kirill pointed his index finger downwards. As Damien sat at that command the Patriarch's finger now slid across his lips and then quickly pointed upwards. The message was clear, repeated often as it was now. Be cautious, cameras and listening devices were typically omnipresent. Father Damien nodded almost imperceptibly towards Kirill.

Kirill said, forced jollity, "President Putin desires our presence at the Kremlin immediately. He has sent a limo. It will be here within minutes. Let us walk in the garden. I have another matter. I need fresh air."

The priest perceived that he himself was trusted at a level of 75%, a level that was off the charts for a man such as Kirill. Accordingly, grains of salt were always added to what he was told. However, the salt never *ruined* the broth.

Father Damien, on the other hand, saw Patriarch Kirill as a snake inserted into the garden of the Orthodox Church. His career trajectory was too closely matched to the rise of the Putin gang. Furthermore, nothing of significance ever happened in the Kremlin or the Patriarchy without one or both of them in the know. Kirill was careful to never disclose the nature of his ascent into such an elevated position and Damien went along with what he saw as dishonest and a travesty to *his own* beliefs, which were faith-based and fervent.

As they walked to the snow-filled garden Kirill, inches from Damien's right ear, whispered, "Petrov found four additional devices in my study. I am being watched again and listened to more so than ever. I have no idea what this meeting with Vladimir is about. He wanted you present. There was tension in the communication. Your presence will also be of great help to me. My relationship with Putin is currently very strained."

"Yes, of course, I will observe and help as much as possible." He did not believe Kirill about a strained relationship as he saw the Kirill/Putin association as that between two pitbulls cooperating with each other about their food supply while keeping a close eye on each other for suspicious moves. In this case the 'food' was the furtherance of the Russian State – a return to a lost greatness such as when Josef Stalin controlled the affairs of the nation. Putin's cynical and vile manipulation of the Russian Orthodox Church through the likes of Patriarch Kirill screamed to the heavens and hopefully would one day be righted under the ascent of a man such as he, Father Damien.

Nothing further was said as they headed back into the residence and its vestibule, awaiting the arrival of the limousine. Silence fell between the two; they both knew the wisdom of that.

CHAPTER SIXTEEN

Putin sat at his huge desk. His eyes were faced downwards, apparently perusing some documents of State. Kirill and he were shown seats facing this great man. Damien construed Putin to be a vile fraud, worse even more so than Patriarch Kirill seated beside him. The reading important documents ruse went on for at least a minute, he and Kirill the subject of this silent reminder of their place in the Putin-world.

Finally, his eyes came up and faced outward. The unmistakeable impression left by him – oh, I had no idea you were here. Putin's steely blue eyes fastened onto Kirill's until he got back from Kirill what he was looking for, surely some sign of submission. His stab of a look at Damien was almost dismissive, yet it had more scrutiny to it than ever before. Something new there as Putin had maintained a consistency of indifference toward him throughout all of the past meetings that he was allowed to attend. Other meetings between Kirill and Putin that he was not allowed to attend? God knows. Well, then again, maybe God would not desire to hear what these two thieves spoke of.

Putin spoke in low tones with crisp, impersonal intonation. "Patriarch Kirill, I want your advice, your cooperation and your discretion." No hellos, no introductions.

Was the coolness meant for Damien? To throw him off some speculation? Who knew? This was Putin the master of nefarious techniques.

Kirill responded in his usual gruff intonation but with proper subservience glued to his words, "It will be my honor."

"Rasputin," Putin said, with his eyes narrowed, boring into Kirill.

Damien shot a quick sideways glance at Kirill whose suspicious eyes, for just a millisecond, showed confusion. Kirill cleared his voice, "Ah, yes Mr. President. Your wish on this?"

Another long pause in this subtle duel. But Kirill's response toward the name *Rasputin* was deft.

"Your estimation?" Putin remarked through zippered lips.

"Mr. President, he is 100 years plus. *Dead.* His legacy and his life confused many. To some he was a saint; to others a devil, a perverted man. Controversy surrounds him."

"I did not have you here my dear Patriarch to listen to your observations of others. I am asking for *your* opinion."

Damien had never heard Kirill pronounce on Rasputin. He assumed a negative from his derogatory comments about the so-called *True Religion*. It was a form of Christianity practiced primarily in the far out reaches of Russia and replete with odd and condemned practices by Kirill's Russian Orthodox Church. Probably, Rasputin who came from that ilk, would be scornfully denounced.

Kirill, put on the spot by Putin, cleared his voice twice, thus giving him precious time to avoid a hasty and perhaps dangerous response to Putin the Great. "I believe that he was beset with highly skewed forms of good and bad. Some saw the goodness, such as the Tsarina Alexandra or Alix as she was known, but for everyone like her there were numerous others who felt his evil ways." He then stopped abruptly.

Damien had seen this quality in Kirill and he admired it. Kirill was like a jeweler who once he cut the stone properly knew enough about what he had achieved to not go further.

Putin leaned forward and placed his jaw into the palm of his hand. "Yes. A good answer. He made a lot of enemies, especially in the upper ranks of the Romanov Court. A lethal place. He went from a spiritual status to a political one. Like driving a freshly gassed automobile into a ring of fire, it seems. Caused him to be murdered. So tell me Patriarch Kirill, the powers that he supposedly possessed? A psychic. A healer. A prophet? Do these exist in anyone?"

Damien enjoyed watching these two likely atheists fencing with each other over theology and spirituality. A pretend game played in front of a true believer, not played for him but in spite of him.

"I think that if you *believe* all things are possible. Belief enables." Again, the abrupt stop.

While holding his jaw, Putin's chair bobbed back and forth as he gazed at Kirill. "Some type of healing occurred," Putin said pensively. "Tsarina Alexandra was no fool even as she doted on her hemophiliac son. She was convinced that Rasputin healed him. But there is something from our cavernous archives that has been brought to me. A Rasputin note from 1915, a year before his murder. I will not share it with you at this point. I keep it in my private safe. A note of prophecy. Like the Tsarina, I am not a fool. Furthermore,

I don't dote. My vision is quite clear. Date to date, point to point, he predicted *my* coming to power. He was not the only one." The bobbing stopped and his lips sealed up. It was Patriarch Kirill's turn.

"Prophecies, like horoscopes, are held in doubt. Words can be parsed in so many ways and if they are used to confuse many interpretations are possible," he stopped, line in the sand as it were.

Putin straightened his posture, collecting himself, "I reiterate the rescued note from the files is quite clear and specific," he said with a touch of ire at the patriarch's possible rebuke.

Damien steeled himself to hear about the true purpose of this session. The sparing had reached its endpoint as Putin was focusing a laser on Kirill who perhaps was not seeing what was coming at him. Kirill probably more atheistic than Putin might be disgusted with Putin's mention of psychics. Then again, he cautioned himself about underestimating Kirill.

"Ah, I see. As the note is that precise in its meaning and context and given that it is in the handwriting of Rasputin there is cause for an inquiry?"

Putin appeared to be mollified as he looked at Kirill as one might look at a beloved child who had occasional bouts of stupidity. "Yes. Precisely. *But* neither my hand nor yours can be associated with such a controversial inquiry. Mockery would ensue. *But* I will engage indirectly through our various services. There is a scientist named Wilosky whose work deals with genetics and indirectly with these powers of healing and prophecy. It interests me. A scientific explanation is always preferred to a theological one in the

Russia of our days. However, for the Orthodox Church to direct its gaze at the theological would hardly be surprising. *But* you personally must keep a distance. As you know the hardcore Bolsheviks have no love for you and the Church you lead. As you well know, the Orthodox Church is ascendant again because of policies created by me. Furthermore, there has been a push by a few Orthodox zealots to pronounce Rasputin a saint. A good cover for an inquiry."

Kirill said, "I understand."

The mob boss was laying down the law now and his capo, Patriarch Kirill, was kneeling ass-up. Damien wasn't quite sure what exactly was expected by Putin but from past experiences he knew that there would be no confusion on anyone's part by the time they left this dictator's fortress.

"So, your companion Father Damien," his eyes now swung over to Damien, "so quiet, so unassuming. My file on him indicates a man of religion. A man who can sit comfortably with healing and prophecy as being entirely possible. For a Georgian, he is a bit too quiet for my taste. But he manifests discipline. He has heard us and understands the issues. He is to make inquiries. Surely there are notations, reports that were not seized and destroyed by the Bolsheviks 100 years ago. Fraud or Saint is the question." His eyes now back on Kirill. "If and when evidence points to some divine gift I will share Rasputin's note with both of you. But you, Patriarch of Moscow and all Russia, you must stay clear of this and of course my name must never be associated with your charge." With that, President Vladimir Vladimirovich Putin nodded once and went back to reading his reports.

On the way to the limo Kirill whispered into Damien's ear. "We will walk in my garden. Don't leave."

Kirill was uneasy about this entire episode that had just passed. He believed that there were too many moving parts and he detested the manner in which Putin had inserted himself into his formal relationship with Damien. Putin actually had the nerve to mandate a mission for his subordinate. And his take on Father Damien? Competency beyond compare. But trust? No. Pure and simple he trusted no one, especially believers and Georgians to make it worse.

In the garden, now in virtual darkness, he said to Damien, "Be very careful with this assignment. Anything you turn up must be reported to Putin through me. Never communicate with him except through me. I want complete and full reports from you at all times. Understood?"

"Of course I will try to do as you say Patriarch Kirill. As always. As you know I did not seek this out."

"Yes. That is one thing I do know for sure. And I think I know something else. President Putin really wants to believe in Rasputin's powers. There is much more to this than meets the eye. You may go now Father Damien."

CHAPTER SEVENTEEN

Father Damien sought the counsel of Father Matthew. Matthew was considered the most learned historian in the Orthodox Church. He was located in the Novodevichy Convent, an historic center for the Church that was returned by the Putin government to the Orthodox Church in 2010. The Bolsheviks had seized it ages ago and it was used for diverse purposes by the Russian State. Parts of the vast complex had important artifacts, some buildings housed museums. Matthew was stationed there as a sign of the growing Orthodox swagger as the Church and Putin were engaged in their *pas de deux*.

Father Matthew welcomed Damien, serving tea and biscuits for the occasion. They chatted about the convent, about church attendance, and various Orthodox patriarchs. It was quite general and certainly not provocative. However, Damien noticed, Matthew's face was tightening especially around his pressed lips. This was not a social call as they both knew. Before he could state the agenda Matthew said, "So, Father Damien, you are not here to make friends. What is the purpose of your visit? When people come from the Patriarch's office there is a specific purpose involved. Please."

Matthew, 50ish, had a short beard on an otherwise cleanly shaven face. He was thin, small of stature and his movements concise, orderly, and purposeful. "Of course Father. Patriarch Kirill has allowed me to examine the life of Gregori Rasputin. There is a possible inquiry into sainthood. I have read a significant amount of literature about him and his times, including having a good run at the show trials performed by the Bolsheviks after their overthrow of the Czarist regime."

Matthew appeared to relax. Perhaps he had perceived Damien as a messenger of bad news. Historical matters, on the other hand, were his forte. Whatever the truth, his face had lightened up. "Damn the Communists. For every manuscript kept by us they destroyed hundreds. The Church was the archenemy of the atheists. The Bolshevik atheists were as bad as the Mongols or the Teutonic Knights, the bastards. What exactly do you want from me?"

"Father Matthew, my mission is quite secretive. It is important that it never become public. If it happens that it does we will be forced to put a false face to it. In that spirit, I need access to any hidden papers in the possession of the Church that have been held onto only by the few. Also, I wish to speak with anyone who could be considered a reliable source. I realize that anyone with direct personal knowledge of Rasputin is dead but there should be, at least a few, who were conversant with figures who had firsthand contact with him. This is so important to our Church, Father Matthew."

After his recital of his needs a dead silence came between the two men. Finally Matthew spoke, "Father, I do not wish to provoke you. You are a Georgian, yes. I know you work with Patriarch Kirill, yes. But what you are asking demands a direct order from Kirill himself. I, too, have been sworn to secrets. Your requests fly straight into that mountain."

"I understand Father Matthew. In fact, I am pleased with your requirement as it speaks to your professionalism." He then opened his satchel and removed from it an official document signed by Patriarch Kirill and with the crimson waxen shield of the Moscow Patriarchy beneath the signature. He handed it to Father Matthew. The message was short and to the point. All cooperation must be given to Father Damien, there was no specific reference to Rasputin.

It was to be used in all instances where hesitation was shown to his request for assistance. It would be the first of several times he would use it. He was struck by Matthew's study of the letter including, as a final piece of scrutiny, his holding it to a light bulb in search for the watermark that he knew was in the fabric of the parchment paper. Matthew held the letter on the tips of his fingers and lightly shook it up and down, as if weighing it. He gave it back to Damien and then excused himself.

About five minutes later he returned. He said, "You must excuse me for my due diligence Father. This is a very serious request. The Church is layered in knowledge pertaining to sources and access to certain papers. I am at the very top layer. Quite a privilege. I have authority to study any and all Orthodox materials. There are only four of us with such permissions. A mistake by me, at this level, would be unforgivable. In the old days, my nose, ears, and lips would be carved off. I'd be blinded and sent to some freezing monastery deep in Siberia. And some were, actually. I just spoke with Patriarch Kirill, personally. You might guess that we four have a password code. It is two layered, that gets us through to him immediately. What you presented to me is accurate and true. In effect, for this specific mission, four of us becomes five. Let us talk."

Father Damien determined, then, that there might be some extraordinary knowledge around Rasputin, well beyond what was known by the many. In multiple ways, the Russian Orthodox Church was the reverse side of the coin to the Russian government. There were secrets and there were secrets.

Father Matthew detailed an approach to Damien. He indicated that he had spent two full months on the Rasputin files some five years previous due to the centenary of Rasputin's assassination in 1916. He felt that what was available about Rasputin was probably as complete as what the Orthodox Church had in its possession. The materials were centralized in two areas of Orthodoxy. All of the different patriarchies, regardless of changing political boundaries, and differences in affiliations, had vowed to maintain without question access to the four approved scholar-priests, now five.

Accordingly, he insisted, gently but forcefully, that Damien venture to these two locations, St. Sergius – north of Moscow, and the Lavra complex in Kiev, Ukraine.

Damien agreed to do so but then persisted for names of individuals who had contact with secondary sources. Father Matthew left the visitor room. When he came back, he gave a list of two names. Perhaps another would be available soon.

Damien then pressed him. "In your studies of Rasputin, did you investigate his supposed ability to heal and to prophecy?" In the posing of the question, he observed that

Matthew winced and looked away quickly as if to evade his gaze.

Recovering quickly, Matthew said, "I do not want you to be influenced by me. But I will say this. There is no way to refute that he had such powers. All that you can do in the matter is demonstrate that such things happened and then determine *if* it was anything other than a divine gift. You must decide. If you complete your inquiry, I might be happy to chat with you, Father Damien."

Damien thought that Matthew's use of the word *if* was odd.

CHAPTER EIGHTEEN

Damien drove north out of Moscow. The trip took about one and a half hours. His visit was known to the authorities at the Sergei Holy Trinity Monastery. He had been there often enough since being assigned to Kirill who had offices on the grounds as well as in the Danilov Monastery in Moscow that had become over time the official residence of Kirill.

The complex had many buildings and was considered by many to be the spiritual center of the Russian Orthodox Church. Church foundations started to be erected in the 14th century by the esteemed St. Sergius, a man of singular religiosity. Since then it became a sprawling complex. In 1993 it was inscribed onto the World Heritage list. Walled, Damien saw it as a place meant to keep people in but also to keep people out. Its famed frescoes dated back to the 17th century. If its walls could talk, its story would be never-ending.

He parked in one of the reserved spots for the Patriarchy near the entrance. Before he got out of his Lada he saw an elder – a *starets* – monk complete with the black regalia for orthodoxy leaning on a large walking stick. He brought the fingers of his right hand together and waved them toward himself as he turned and walked slowly to the gated monastic entrance, and then through a large archway leading into the complex. Damien followed him and was eventually brought to a small two story white painted brick building whose plainness on the outside was in stark contrast to the well-lit main floor on whose walls were hung some magnificent and aged icons. He followed the monk into a large room. There was a lounge chair set beside a window that took in sectors of the complex and a long rectangular table with six leather chairs. The monk sat and pointed across the table for Damien to sit.

Over the years, Damien had seen representations of St. Sergius, the long face and beard, the saintly eyes and expression. He was struck by how the elder in front of him matched up so well to the art. He sat as directed, estimating the monk to be somewhere in his 80s or even 90s.

"My name is Zacharias. I have been ordered out of my skete by our esteemed Hegemon. I have not been in company, other than some religious services, for years. I understand that you have resurrected the name of Grigori Rasputin." The monk's eyes never wavered as he stared at Damien who noticed a thin white film over Zacharias's eyes. He was partially blind. His voice was melodic, low pitched and had the slightest creak in it. Anyone hearing it would hear the voice of an aged man. Just as Damien was about to reply, the monk held up his hand, "It is because I knew a priest, Father Isaac, who had personal dealings with Rasputin that I have been asked to be here. I will tell you what I know." He paused and then asked Damien to go across the hallway and get him some water. He did so as he found a young monk positioned near the entryway to the building. Damien had not seen him when he had entered. His request was accommodated.

When he arrived back with the water Zacharias was asleep. Damien sat and said nothing. Zacharias opened his eyes about 10 minutes later, blinked and could see enough to find the water and sip it. "Excuse me. This is what I recollect. The priest I knew was my mentor in those days. The Church was heavily persecuted by the Bolsheviks. I will admit that I was an agent of that regime and was no more than an undercover operative for the Communist Party. The intent was for me to sow distrust. I was 18 when I was assigned here by the NKVD as an agent. I was told that I would be here for only a few years. It was 1948. Stalin had softened his suppression of the Church late in the war, 1943, 1944. But make no mistake, the security service kept an eagle's eye on the Church. I was told to zero in on Father Isaac who had connections back to the regime of the Romanovs. He wasn't trusted for that reason, also because he was seriously religious. A believer. The very worst kind of character for the atheists. So I was assigned to Father Isaac by some traitors in this community. Of course, he saw right through me. He knew what I was. But he saw something in me. He engaged in a fight for my soul and he did it through Rasputin. And you ask how so?" He gave a slight smile. Damien determined that this was going to be a monologue. He remained quiet. Zacharias went on after another sip of water, "Much later in our relation, by then he had won the battle for my soul, he told me that I was the good Rasputin." He made a slight pound on the table, a gesture of humor in his reminisce. "Rasputin came to St. Petersburg in 1904. Father Isaac was a confessor in the Nicholas II court. He knew much about the intrigue and betrayals in that weakening Romanov regime. Rasputin was a Khlysty. Yes, he was Orthodox and identified as such but in his core he was a Khlysty. I was told that you were studying Rasputin. That I was to fill you in because I was a novice to Father Isaac. Surely you've become aware of the Khlysty perversion, a maniacal interpretation of God's providence. Rasputin was a wanderer, a *strannik*, in that cult that he tried to merge with our holy Orthodox Church. In Father Isaac's view he was a heretic to the Church much as I was a Communist heretic to the Church. He said that he tried to work on and with Rasputin to no avail. But he would not let *me* get away with my dishonesty that easy. As you can see Father Isaac was quite successful." He gave the slightest of smiles as he sipped more water. Damien had yet to say a word, noting that Zacharias seemed to be fighting exhaustion and roaming slightly in his presentation.

"Father Isaac observed Rasputin insert his way into the complicated sinews of the court. He heard the rumors that Rasputin had a checkered past. That he came out of a section of Siberia rampant with paganism, superstition, and Khlystic practices. Rasputin didn't just show up in 1904, he had support from some religious authorities, letters, referrals. Father Isaac would say that a new person coming into that court would be subjected to a host of distrustful figures who feared new people. At the time there was an obsessive interest in the Russian peasantry and mysticism, seen as the embodiment of the Russian soul. From that interest there was fascination and zeal for another world within reach of the gifted few." Another sip of water, closed eyes and a lengthy pause.

Damien held onto his silence. Zacharias might see any questioning as interrogation. God knows what Zacharias's retreat into a skete – a monastery of one – with its extraordinary silence, asceticism and self-imposed loneliness had done to this man's psyche.

"So Rasputin came into an environment that was welcoming to what he brought, the peasant, the mystic. He befriended people with great influence. Father Isaac would speak of his blue eyes that could, if one was fertile for such, penetrate into the soul. There were two Montenegrans, sisters, daughters of the Montenegran King, Nicholas Njeges, named Militsa and Anastasia. Both of them married into Russian Court figures of importance. Rasputin connected with this pair of sisters. Very close. They would serve a conduit for him directly into the Romanovs themselves as they were particularly close to Alix, Nicholas' wife – the tsarina herself. The pair of them were called the black women. They had pitch black hair and were born in Montenegro, famed for the black practices of sorcery, bewitchment, and the occult. When Father Isaac watched these women's influence increase he became concerned for the future of Russia. In 1905 there was the peasant revolt against the regime. It was put down by terror and violence. But such is never forgotten. Russia also lost a war with Japan in 1905. Many external forces pressing on the regime but Father Isaac feared the black women and their types more. The one, Militsa, was steeped in mysticism, speaking with the dead and a variety of other occult practices. At first, she and Rasputin seemed to be made for each other as long as he understood his place, he was a vassal to her. Any penetration into the Czar's family would only come through her and be controlled by her. The two of them especially powerful individuals. Well, Rasputin won that battle of wills. The rest you know." He closed his eyes for some seconds. "Czar Nicholas and Alix had five daughters. Then, finally, a son. But the son was cursed – a hemophiliac. The slightest cut, a bleed that never ends. The boy's life in constant danger. He is having an episode, Rasputin now known comes to the rescue and the boy stops bleeding. A miracle worker! Tsarina Alexandra absolutely convinced that she has encountered a man of God, a healer. Even the Czar himself is convinced. Rasputin has broken through. He is God's gift to the Romanov family. More and more he is a visitor to the family. His fame rises. But who and what is this man? He is brought in secretly to the living quarters. Spends intimate time with the family. His presence a salve to be used if and when the boy bleeds." He napped for a minute.

"But all this is noticed and now Rasputin will have to deal with more than just his new found enemies, the black women. Other enemies come at him with full force. Father Isaac observes all this. He knows how vicious the court is. He is also aware that the Tsarina is susceptible to the supernatural, to the intervention of God into human affairs through the occult. She is a German by birth and has the German affliction, if I may say so, a fixation on process and implementation. Her love of her boy has no bounds. Rasputin comes into that gulf of love and sickness, his arms outstretched so as to connect these divides, this holy man, the elder. Father Isaac hears of Rasputin's charm and power over the royal family. Father Isaac is not one to hastily deny Rasputin to be a healer. Healing is certainly within the scope of Orthodox practices and is a gift given to the chosen by God. He then hears that Rasputin has made prophecies that have come true. He is seen by some as a man of God. A peasant monk who has harnessed the powers given him by God. Prophecy, also, is a gift of God."

Another long pause, a brief nap, seconds.

"But Rasputin's enemies come out after him and his reputation with a vengeance. Women are attracted to him. Insinuations are made about his being a Khlyst. Their practices are examined. Group nakedness, wild dancing, sexual abandonment, and drinking. How can it be a religious practice? This is not part of our tradition. It is sin. So Father Isaac listens carefully in the confessional and interviews several prominent Khlysts. There is this theory in that movement that to secure a union with God we must purge ourselves of all passions by bringing them to exhaustion. In other words, have so much sex that the very thought of it is repulsive, to dance so wildly that the idea of dancing is vile and so on. Then in that state of exhaustion we are ready to meet God with no interference of our lower appetites. Their vile qualities have been washed from their being not by self-control and discipline but by running them into exhaustion. In addition, they practice flagellation, another facet, beating each other in a frenzy while engaging in wild dancing." He took another sip of water.

Damien observed that Zacharias's eyes were inward and half closed as if he was communing with the long dead Father Isaac. He, again, refrained from saying anything, fearful to break the flow as it now came to him that Zacharias had almost memorized his delivery. Silence fell in the room. Zacharias asleep, again.

Sudden wakefulness, he proceeds. "More and more

rumors crowd the court environment. Rasputin's hold on the Royal Family becomes widely known in St. Petersburg. Newspapers taunt the family. Rasputin is made out to be a fraud. He is savaged over his beard, his hair. His eyes are said to be maniacal. If one falls under their gaze capture of your soul takes place. The push against Rasputin is full of frenzy yet Father Isaac remains open to the possibility that Rasputin is truly holy and is merely the subject of court intrigue. He weighed it all in his careful way. He tried to engage with Rasputin but he was brushed aside by him in a way that said he was too unimportant. Father Isaac notices Rasputin's growing pride and arrogance and its odd interplay with his saintly monk appearance. He concludes from gossip and the confessional that the more Rasputin is attacked the more Tsarina Alix supports him, perceiving the attacks as the work of evil. It is, it seems, inescapable that when the boy bleeds only Rasputin can recover him. War starts in 1914. Rasputin pleads for Russia to avoid war. Predicts only bad can come from it. But to no avail. Apparently, he also predicts that the Romanov family is in danger. Along with other predictions his reputation grows as being a psychic."

Another long pause.

"The rumors of his heavy drinking and womanizing further erode his reputation. If he is khlyst this would not be contradictory. He has a large retinue of female followers. He is said to be a hypnotist. And then in 1916 he is murdered by a clique of haters. These things you must already know." He stopped again, sipped some water and looked closely at Damien. "So I believe you are interested in Father Isaac's conclusions about Rasputin?"

Finally, Damien was allowed to speak. "Exactly. I see that you have great regard for Father Isaac. You are evidently a man of discernment. Yes, please."

Zacharias stroked his beard, pitched his eyes downward and said, "A man or woman can be given any power that God chooses to give. Some given gifts are left unopened. There can be many reasons for that but chiefly it pertains to faith or the lack thereof. Father Isaac believed that Rasputin was given the gift of healing and probably prophecy. That when he came to St. Petersburg in 1904 he possessed these powers. Rasputin knew that he held those powers and that many could sense them in him. These powers are magnetic and draw people to their possessor. But these gifts carry an extraordinary responsibility with them, for example, a healer is by definition also a curser if passions mingle. So also for the psychic who instead of using that power in the expression of prudence uses it for odious purpose. Rasputin was a peasant, poorly educated, barely literate, who came from the darkness of obscurity into the brilliance of fame and recognition. As he rose high in that environment he was overwhelmed by the praise, the allure of recognition. But he was also detested and feared. Ultimately, it broke him and he resorted back to his origins, Khlystism. But Father Isaac believed that once God bestowed a gift it would be as a non-removable mark, permanent. So, my good Reverend, I have been told of your quest. I have thought back to the many discussions I had with Father Isaac about Rasputin. Undoubtedly, Father Isaac believed that Rasputin had the gifts. But in the end the gifts probably led to his destruction."

"These gifts that you speak of Elder. Are they truly of

God or merely effects of magic and wizardry?" Damien asked in a sharpened voice.

"Hah. I think that you would have sympathized with the haters in the court. You see there is one pillar that I will always attach myself to – Father Isaac. He is the fulcrum. He I knew. He was brilliant and dispassionate. I must always return to his judgment. I am now prepared to take you to the records that we have that escaped the Cheka, the NKVD and KGB."

Three hours later Damien was leaving the grounds of St. Sergius. The records that they had were inconclusive. Many were resentful and highly judgmental of Rasputin but there were a stubborn few who supported him. Three notes were written and signed by Rasputin himself. They were scrawled, there were misspellings and the overall impression was that Rasputin was essentially unschooled, which was not to gainsay his probable brilliance.

CHAPTER NINETEEN

Damien flew into Boryspil Airport in Kiev, Ukraine, via Aeroflot. He was disappointed that a third lead at Mt. Athos had suffered a severe stroke, was uncommunicative and was not expected to live more than a week. So, he was down to this one last source who resided in the famed monastic complex the Kiev Pecharsk Lavra or simply Monastery of the Kiev Caves (Lavra). It had its great history dating back almost a millennium. Like much of Russia, Ukraine suffered its indignities, invasions by Tatars, Mongols, Lithuanians, Poles, Nazis, etc. The Lavra is the residence of the Metropolitan of the Ukrainian Orthodox Church. So, Damien knew that he had to tread carefully given the schism between the Russian Orthodox Church and the Ukrainian Orthodox Church, the two countries in a contentious relationship given Russia's invasion of the Crimea and its support of Russian military enclaves in Eastern Ukraine. But because of the pact of the four historians he was told that he'd be welcome and so it was that he was picked up at Boryspil and driven into Kiev proper and into the sprawling Lavra complex.

There were still caves at the complex. Some monks chose

to live in that style of rigor and solitude. This is where he was told that Simeon lived. He was the son of the chief guard of the Winter Palace in St. Petersburg. His father, thus, was in direct and frequent contact with Rasputin.

"Elder Simeon is 91 years of age. He is sickly and steadfastly refused to meet with you on two grounds. One, that he's exhausted, that he has finally reached God and that such would be a distraction to his prayer-life. Two, you are seen by him as part of the Russian patriarchy and he wants nothing to do with you. But we convinced him otherwise," a young unhooded monk told Damien in reasonably friendly tones. "He resides in a cave and goes about his religious rites in a studied manner. As a warning to you he is not known as an effusive man. Affectionate neither. He considers most life on the planet to be a waste, a distraction. I fear that he perceives your mission as such. So, yes, he will cooperate but understand who is your respondent. Controlling how he acts by us is impossible and being overly zealous on your part would be inadvisable," saying the last few sentences in a sort of sinister manner. "We will awake him shortly and see if he is disposed to come. Fair enough? Please wait here."

"Of course," Damien said to the already disappearing monk as he once again questioned why he was doing this. What was really behind Putin's interest in Rasputin?

Fifteen minutes later the young monk came back with a grizzled looking specimen from another age. Monk Simeon smelled badly. He was a small man, perhaps five feet plus an inch or two. His beard was full and seemed tangled in numerous spots. His flat features accentuated his small stature. His brown eyes were shrunken by two thick and overgrown eyebrows. He was a very unhappy looking man. The young monk inquired of Damien, "Should I stay?"

"Please stay close but for now I'd like to interview the elder alone." He left abruptly, perhaps pleased to be out of the way.

"Elder Simeon, my name is Father Damien. The very idea of disrupting you from your holy life is very trying for me. So, I will be brief."

"You are not a Russian. You are a Georgian. Odd." He said in very clipped tones.

"Very true."

"How are you not in Georgia? God knows that they need God as much as the damned Russians!"

Smiling, he said, "All that is true. I was sent to Russia from Tbilisi. By the Patriarch there to better relations."

"Ah. What do you want from me precisely?"

"Rasputin. I know his history well. From Siberia to the Court to his murder. What is being held to question is this: was he given gifts by God? Specifically, healing and prophecy. Your thoughtful opinion Father?"

Simeon faced downwards for a few seconds. Then his gaze was directed at Damien. "I will tell you what my father said about him. He was convinced that Rasputin had celestial powers. When Rasputin came to the Court he was in possession of these gifts. He actually healed my father who suffered from severe headaches. One touch of Rasputin's hands – they were gone. He also told my father to retire and head to the West. The end was coming. This in 1914. My father didn't listen then but he did escape a while later. He was lured back to Russia by some empty promises in the early forties. They promised him a military command, filthy communists. They put him on the front lines, he was in his late sixties. He was dead in a month. To the end he would actually pray to Rasputin. He called him a saint. His enemies overwhelmed Rasputin. It was too much for any man."

"What about the alcohol and the women?" Damien asked the monk who had sat back in his chair.

Leaning forward again with a baleful look he said, "How can a seemingly sensible Georgian such as yourself ask such a foolish question? The communists in 1917, the foul and corrupt Court through the teens, they were all bent on one common goal the crucifixion of this saint." He started to get up from his seat, "There is nothing else to say about this. Tell your Russian Patriarch to wake up and start proceedings into raising this man of God into sainthood. Enough for me. You are a waste of my time!"

Damien was on the plane back to Moscow that night, after having reviewed some sparse material about Rasputin. At the end of his two hour study of documents in a library room he concluded that his knowledge had not advanced.

CHAPTER TWENTY

Father Damien's Aeroflot arrived back in Moscow's Sheremetyevo Airport at 10:05 p.m. When he cleared the airport's controls and entered the immense terminal, he was approached by two men, unmistakably FSB or some associated organization of Russian goons. They had all the necessary embellishments and physiques. Leather coats, shaved heads, huge bodily dimensions attached to six feet and over frames. Both appeared to be in their thirties. They approached the Georgian from either side. Goon one said quietly, but with no compromise in his voice, "Father Damien." Both snapped open their wallets at the same time, one second, then closed. "We are here to collect you and take you directly to the Kremlin. Follow us," he ordered.

Damien was surprised but not surprised. This was Russia. Would it be the same in his native Georgia? Now? Its move to the West now at full gallop. Yes, he concluded, but with a softer tone to it. But a state apparatus was not all that different all around the globe. Just a matter of style.

He observed that it was an important trip to the Kremlin as he was escorted to the nearly empty airport curbside, watched over by a Moscow cop who stood within

20 feet of a black Mercedes. The powerful car sped through the lightly travelled roadway from Sheremetyevo into the gated Kremlin guardposts. With a barely observed set of security protocols, they must have been expected, they reached a small parking area. He was led into a building, into an elevator and brought to the top level. He was not sure where he was but he knew that he was close to the heart of the monster, the atheistic side of Russia regardless of the new script that Putin was following. He ended up in a posh waiting room, luxuriously decorated with wall carpets from various localities, some from former states no longer under the umbrella of Russia, the former Soviet Union. Others were from areas in the largest country in the world, Russia itself. A secretary came out to him and offered tea or coffee. He chose coffee. The two goons sat across the room from him in full glare. They were not offered coffee. When it was brought to him in a handsome ceramic mug emblazoned with the Red Star, it sat on a silver tray that had a server for cream and a sugar vessel with a small spoon. Two cotton napkins were also presented. So, he was being treated with respect and kindliness for the moment. How long that would last was guesswork. He then noticed that every piece in the serving tray had the red star attached to them. He poured a small drizzle of cream into the mug and two spoonfuls of sugar. Normally, he didn't drink his coffee with these additives but he used them as a way of showing spite to the two goons, including a small 'ah' after his first sip. He chided himself for his pettiness but he did feel a shot of pleasure too.

After about ten minutes, a thin, short man came out from behind a door. To Damien he appeared to be a man trying to escape notice. A cipher. He reminded him of the Bellini portrait of Mehmed II with his hooked nose and skirting downward glance. He was not an attention seeker and yet there was a clear *gravitas* to him. He noticed that the two goons had stood to attention.

"Father Damien, my name is Dimitri. Thank you so much for accommodating us for this visit. If you wish more coffee, just say the words. Please be kind enough to come with me." He placed an arm on the rising priest and said to the goons, "One of you stay to return Father Damien to his residence. Whoever is the other can go home," he said, now with a sharpness in his words. He turned back to Damien and said, "Please follow me."

They entered a large room. The walls were crowded with pictures, original oils it seemed mostly from Russian history. On a shorter end of the rectangular room it appeared that all of the pictures centered around the Napoleonic war, a few pictures detailing the burning of Moscow by the French. He was escorted into a circular arrangement of antique leather chairs. "Please sit Father. I'll be back in a moment." Dimitri left through a narrow doorway, difficult to spot.

Minutes later, Dimitri came back with a heavy-set man who looked the worse from alcohol. He was introduced as Adam. He seemed familiar but he could not place him. Adam went to a corner in the room and opened a cabinet. A bright light came on. In a gruff but friendly voice he yelled out, "Anybody want a drink?" Neither Dimitri nor Father Damien responded. There was a sound of clinking ice cubes.

Precisely at that point, President Vladimir Putin entered the room. Alexandrov felt his stomach constrict. He understood he was sitting among the giants, two of whom he did not know personally. Putin waved his right hand down, they all sat, the heavy man just making it back from the bar in time.

Putin spoke, "Father Damien, welcome back from your trip to Kiev. My two oldest friends. Adam," he waved toward the man with the drink, "and Dimitri. I wish to hear about your trip and your conclusions. By the way, Patriarch Kirill was notified. He will not be here," he said dismissively.

All three men looked at him expectantly. Father Damien wondered if any of the three men he faced had a sense of humor. Deciding that it was worth a try he said, "I don't think the word saint and the word Rasputin belong together." He smiled. Putin glared hard at him, Dimitri was somber, and Adam, God bless him, laughed loudly. Enough for being a comedian. "I only found two knowledgeable sources of sound mind, one in Kiev, the Lavra, and one at St. Sergius. I listened closely to both. There was one other but he was incapacitated due to old age and a stroke, beyond my reach. The documents held by each complex were interesting but did not shed any significant light on the question at hand. So, you must understand my limited exposure to worthwhile sources in *my* sphere – religion."

Adam said, "Okay, okay. We understand the epistemological restraints. Who were these two esteemed sources and what did they say?" He said lightly.

Damien realized by his mid-sentence that the drinker was not to be underestimated. Dimitri and Putin said nothing.

"Both are very aged men. They are both ascetical in habit and quite devoted to Orthodoxy. The Sergius monk was more outgoing while the Lavra monk was withdrawn and I'd say harsh. Both of them were straightforward. Although I could cut a slight distinction in what they said, at the end of it all, they both felt that Rasputin was gifted by God. A *bona fide* healer and psychic. The one based his thinking on a man whom he admired and respected, a mentor who weighed things carefully. The other based it on his father's copious personal experiences with Rasputin."

Putin spoke, "These sources? Your judgment on the two?"

"Sincere. They are both men of integrity. Whether they are accurate is another matter. The St. Sergius monk the more trustworthy."

Adam charged in, "I don't understand what you just said? We don't need a skeptic, Father, hesitant about making a judgment concerning accuracy."

Adam wasn't hostile but he was the kind of man who probably liked to contest others in unstructured dialogue. He conjectured that he probably taught at one of the universities in Moscow. "I understand. I am a man of religion. I believe in the supernatural. I believe that God works through us no matter how imperfect we are. All of Orthodoxy is in accord with this view. Rasputin was highly imperfect and eventually was overwhelmed by fame and court antagonists. However, even with all that in account I do believe that he did in fact have the gift of healing. As to being a psychic, I am less sure. But there is something else for consideration. I believe that he could project himself into others and create conditions that he could control, not through hypnotism, which he did study but I think only to use it as an accelerant. There was a rugged genius in the man. I didn't mean to offend when I said saint and Rasputin does not correlate."

Putin interjected, "I am surprised with your analysis.

You are saying your conclusion is that he was supernaturally gifted."

Adam, a new drink in hand, said, "And did he have these gifts regardless of your theological musings? I am not a believer Father Damien. So, if these gifts as you call them, are actually present, do they merely come from our DNA? Much like high intelligence or blue eyes?"

"To me that is logically impossible. Only the theological and faith can explain what is obviously divine in origin."

"Father, do you ever experience the presence of someone? Yet there is no noise or indication that they are there?" Adam queried.

"Of course," Damien replied.

"Am I to assume a supernatural gift?"

"We are speaking about the similarity of an ant to a polar bear."

Adam roared with laughter and then said, "You are a worthy opponent. Are you sure that you're an orthodox priest?"

Putin said, pointedly, to Adam, "Thank you Adam. Enough for now. Father, if you have other thoughts on this matter, please contact Dimitri. He will give you his card. I may have you back. Patriarch Kirill should only be told one thing – that the two monks you spoke with had *nothing* to offer. Thank you."

He was escorted from the room by Dimitri. Damien noted that he had said nothing in the meeting, his face stiff and unreadable. He gave him his card.

"Father, call me at any time. Make sure that you comply with what the President said." He signaled to the waiting goon who acted toward him with much more courtesy than at Sheremytevo.

CHAPTER TWENTY-ONE

It was close to midnight after Father Damien left. Putin looked at Adam and Dimitri. He asked, "Impressions?"

As usual, Adam was first to speak, a slur to his voice. By previous standards, however, he was reasonably sober. "So, the priest believes. What's new? He interviews a few decrepit monks who actually believe that all the misery they inflict on themselves will lead to eternal life. If heaven doesn't give them anything better than their pathetic lives on this earth, what's the use? Eternal life in a fucking cave. Hah!" He peered closely at Putin before continuing, "Vladimir, I know you've had some unusual occurrences and you need an explanation but I would recommend that you avoid these Orthodox cretins. The Romanovs left the door open for Rasputin. I know a historian at the university. A wise man. He puts the fall of the Romanovs to four factors. Rasputin was one of them. A sign of very bad judgment. They let him stick his big nose in the tent and soon enough he's pissing all over the place. Gifts my ass! Rasputin was a conjuror, a magician. Like Jesus himself. A phony!"

Putin held his hand up. Adam stopped. "All these years Adam. You've never changed. I feel as though I am listening to you from forty years ago. There is one problem with your opinion. It doesn't explain what has happened. The monk who was just in here offered a perfectly rational explanation if you could get beyond your atheism. But even still, the central question remains, are there people who can heal? Prophecy? Perhaps even alter events from their mind? There are plenty of examples as you know. Also, there are only a few who could claim all of these powers. Do you even allow for such?"

"I allow for the illusion, not the reality." Adam excused himself, needful of a bathroom.

"Dimitri?" Putin looked toward him, tired of Adam whose skepticism was as hard as a rock.

"You have never shown Adam the communication from Anna Osokin that was passed on to me from Archivist Deniken. Perhaps it is time?" Dimitri asked.

"I don't know. He's drinking so much. I'm worried about his health and, of course, his discretion."

"I understand. He is becoming a menace to himself. But he's loyal all said and done."

Adam reentered the room and immediately went to the bar. Putin and Dimitri exchanged knowing glances. Adam came and sat.

Dimitri said, "I was impressed with Father Damien. He did due diligence with regard to the question. I do believe that Rasputin had some extraordinary power residing in him. Whether supernatural or natural, it was there. The question you have raised maintains. Can this power be passed on genetically? The Wilosky investigation shows evidence of a son fathered by Rasputin who escaped Russia and went on to America. If he was true to his bloodlines he more than likely was sexually driven, like his father,

Rasputin. Now the question is this, did he sire children and are any of these alive? If so, are they also gifted and how could those gifts be harnessed by Russia. A worthy question to investigate. To hear it Adam's way there is no question. The matter is closed, any evidence to the contrary rejected."

Putin sat for about a minute and then asked, "Adam, how sober are you?"

"I'm fine. Been a lot worse, rarely better," Adam said in a way that implied he sensed a change in the atmosphere.

"Adam, I'm going to show you something. I have kept it from you. Only a few know about it. I wanted you to read it with an open mind. It involves what we've just been talking about. But if your mind is shut tight or you are too drunk, this is not a good time, my friend." Adam had the unique ability to change horses, drunk to sober, or at least a semblance thereof. Putin sensed that Adam was back to being a close friend rather than a scolding lecturer. "Allow me a minute," Putin said as he headed out of the room.

In Putin's absence, Adam said to Dimitri, "I went too far, didn't I?"

"A bit. But to do otherwise would have come across poorly. Pay heed to what he shows you, Adam."

Now back, Putin sat and removed from a leather folder a single sheet of parchment, light blue with maroon engraving, as far as Adam could see. Putin said to him, "Handle this with great care," as he gave the stiff page to him.

Adam saw that the maroon markings involved the crest of Czar Nicholas II. The paper was handmade and cut to imperfect ridges. The writing was not that of a learned person. He looked to the bottom of the page and saw the unmistakable signature of Grigori Rasputin, barely legible but consistent with the writing above it. He read it three times, each with greater care. He put his drink aside, on the third reading his intent was to memorize, harder now due to age, but still within his range. A slight smear of sweat broke across his upper lip, his forehead soaked in drops of water. Finally, he looked at Putin and Dimitri. "I am astonished. This has been vetted for authenticity?"

"It has," Dimitri responded sharply.

Putin interjected, "Read it aloud Adam. Perhaps a reading from a skeptic will have me understand it in a different light."

Dimitri noticed that the letter was shaking slightly in Adam's hand.

Adam started to read.

> For the Future:
>
> I see clearly the end, the beginning, the end, the beginning, the end, the beginning, the end, the beginning, the end, the beginning, the end and I see no more. The Romanov family will be terminated by a revolutionary who will be replaced by a Georgian – ruthless, replaced by middling scums to be replaced by a radical who will subvert the entire enterprise, I see a drunkard without an anchor to be replaced by a stern but capable leader from an intelligence service. From there I can no longer see beyond the early twenty-first century. That's for another.
>
> Grigori Rasputin, 1916

Adam stood and gave the page back to Putin, almost with priestly reverence. Dimitri had never seen Adam so confused, maybe hobbled, with his belief system so strenuously challenged. Adam sat and said to Putin, "I am aghast Vladimir. I have never experienced such a revelation. The specifics on the page are beyond a magician. It is a map from 1916 to the present. It is the work of a psychic. I am at a loss. But now I understand your quest. I best go now. I have opened my mouth too much tonight."

Putin hugged the departing and chastened Adam. When he came back he said to Dimitri, "We should plan our approach tomorrow. To see Adam, our skeptic, succumb to this is both heartening and frightening. I think we are on the back of a tiger. Would it be possible to find a descendant of Rasputin who could continue a look into the future? Knowledge of this is still secure?"

"That is a matter of huge importance Vladimir. Only archivist Deniken knows of it. Anna Osokin in dead. There are four of us who know."

They hugged. Dimitri left and Vladimir Putin placed the paper into his safe. He knew that sleep would not come easy.

PART THREE

RUSSIA: PLANNING

CHAPTER TWENTY-TWO

Lena Dzik drove across the Paton Bridge. She looked down and across at the Dneiper River, not happy about her assignment given to her by some faraway Dr. Petrov Wilosky in St. Petersburg. She had been ordered away from her duties as a FSB intelligence officer in the Russian Embassy in Kiev. They didn't give her a choice, no say at all. An officer with over 31 years of service to Mother Russia and still treated like last week's garbage by the chauvinist bastards who ran the station. And again who the hell was this Wilosky? And why her?

Lena was a lifelong resident of Kiev. Her parents had immigrated to Ukraine in 1920 in the service of Red Bolshevik Russia. Her grandfather had been a celebrated hero in implementing the great terror famine of 1932 and 1933. Millions were killed due to Stalin's purposeful policies of repression and genocide in Ukraine, a satellite country to Russia. Lena's father, on the other hand, also a bureaucrat serving Moscow, never rose in importance when compared to his father. Lena Dzik was a product of this history. She considered herself a Ukrainian Russian, *Russian* accented and underlined. Ukraine had been part of the Russian

Empire. Had been so for centuries even though there was always the fringe element that sought independence from Bear-Russia. She graduated from Taras Schevchenko University in 1987. Her degree was in economics. She spoke four languages fluently, English among them. Upon graduation she was fastidiously recruited by the KGB, her sympathies toward the USSR known by her academic advisor, award winning professor and a newly discovered quality in him a KGB procurer. And so she went fully into the celebrated KGB (later to be called the FSB). With bitterness she watched Gorbachev be finessed by Ronald Reagan of the imperialistic United States as the Soviet Socialistic Republics were peeled away from the Bear's claws. But Ukraine? How could that be? Kiev? Next to Moscow and Leningrad (now disgracefully called St. Petersburg once again), Kiev completed the Russian trinity of capital cities. And the temerity of the Ukrainians – a separation from Russia in 1991. Maybe on paper but not in her heart. She reasoned that she would only die in peace when the breach was snapped back to its oneness.

She was ecstatic when Putin clawed back the Crimea from Ukraine in 2014 and then went on to undermine Ukraine's sovereignty over its Eastern industrial expanse. And in all of this a concerted effort to destabilize the corrupt Ukrainian separatists – her part in all of those efforts significant and current.

But privately, only disclosed to one close friend, the only one she really had, she was distressed by Putin's courtship of the shady and absurd Russian Orthodox Church. She was more inclined to treat those idolaters as Lenin and Stalin did, all but drowning the litter of robed frauds.

Putin's perverse regenerating of Orthodoxy was politically useful to him. Russia's agrarian soul, the 'real' Russia, bit hard into this apple and that gave Putin his cult not only in Russia but also in many of the regions where Orthodoxy still breathed its foul breath.

She observed the benefits of this filthy contract between Putin and the Orthodox Church as the majority of churches in Ukraine were under the control of the Moscow Patriarch Kirill who was clearly a Putin puppet. Accordingly the Russian controlled church in Ukraine readily complied in efforts to undermine the Ukrainian government limping along to align with the European Union and its puppet master the United Fucking States of Fascist America. To make matters worse the Orthodox Patriarch of Constantinople (Istanbul) freed the Ukrainians from ties to the Moscow Patriarch. In effect, the Ukrainian Orthodox Church could have its own Patriarch. A staggering mess, further stressing the strain between Kiev and Moscow.

She had never seen an Arctic ghetto but the two words came at her as she looked east, now nearly at the end of her trip. There were five twelve story tenement buildings on each side of a narrow strip of land, two one-way streets pointing in opposite direction to each other on either side of the land. This arrangement separated each row of the horrid gray complexes. She parked her car and looked around carefully. No one was visible on the snow packed street nor on the island of ice, snow, several steel benches and a few miserable trees that constituted the land strip between the five of the one and the five of the other tenement buildings that stood across from each other.

As she looked up at the apartments she observed broken

143

blinds, haphazard shades and a variety of badly worn, drab curtains. Amidst the darkening sky, the architectural pollution of the environment and her depressing assignment she proceeded to Building 3, Floor 10, Apartment 12. Only a fool would expect the elevator to work. Lena Dzik was not a fool. The elevator didn't work.

Vlad, a true believer in the inseparable bond between Ukraine and Russia, opened the door. He had been alerted by Dzik about her coming to visit his grandmother. Dzik snapped her ID at him and said brusquely, "Your grandmother and I need privacy. Have you prepared her for me? Alert?"

"More or less. She's in her 90s," he shrugged. "She's in the bedroom. In her chair. You can have all the time you want with her. I'm going to visit a friend next floor down. My phone is on." He didn't like the looks of this wizened bitch Lena Dzik. She had short, cropped black and white hair, dark brown suspicious eyes, and a narrow face. She projected an intelligence out of his league. But there was that binding that they shared, Russia over Ukraine.

She moved by him and went into the cramped apartment as if she owned the damn place. Arrogant bitch. He left for downstairs.

Her bedroom was tiny. A single bed pushed up against the wall, a narrow rocking chair, a floor lamp and a small bureau. The woman in the rocking chair sat stiffly, a blanket laying over her lap, a nightgown encased her to within a foot of her slippered feet, black woolen socks covering the remaining flesh.

"Your grandson told you about me? I am Investigator Dzik," Lena said with no hint of kindness.

The woman stared at her through glazed over eyes. She said nothing.

"Is your hearing good?"

The old woman's head went backwards just slightly. She again said nothing.

"I am involved in some important work. You must cooperate with me. Did your grandson speak with you?" Lena now wondering if she was on a fool's mission. Was the old lady dealing with dementia? But as she looked closely at her she dismissed the thought. The fixed look from this old goat was really one of defiance. Tough, old people were always hard to crack. So now in a falsely softened tone she said, "Your grandson, Vlad, yes? He spoke with you about my visit? The motherland needs your help about matters of the past. Your name is Marta? Yes?"

Marta sniffed the officiousness of this murderous pig. She was KGB or whatever they now called that filthy blood-soaked agency. She had heard stories of reform, a new openness, a more humanitarian sensibility. Another layer of duplicity to the KGB's arsenal of treachery. Whatever they wanted to know would only be used in some heinous undertaking. "I am Marta, yes," she said stiffly, knowing that she had to reply.

The spy removed a folder from her beaten-up briefcase. There was a sheath of papers held together by a large clip. "Allow me to review your vita. Tell me if there are mistakes. You were born in Leningrad in 1926. You answer to Marta Verlovsky. Your parents were insignificant toadies in the

Romanov's court. These unimportant roles were to their good fortune when the revolution came. They survived the culling of thousands and thousands by the Bolsheviks. After the overthrow of Czar Nicholas your father worked barges, your mother a floating maid at State-run guesthouses. You were the youngest of three children, the other two were brothers, both lost fighting Nazis in 1942. Your father died in 1939, heart, and your mother disappeared. Assumption – one of the many starved during the Nazi encirclement of Leningrad. Records scant as you can imagine. Is any of this incorrect?"

Lives of her family reduced to a few flippant comments, a bit of derisiveness in her inflections. The communist cunt.

"I await your response Marta. I wish to get back to the city center before the traffic rush. But I will stay here if I must. If necessary, I will have you removed and brought to our embassy and then on to Moscow. This would not be pleasant for you. You may think that you're a Ukrainian but you're not. You are a Russian. Please act as such. Patriotism is expected."

"What you said is correct," she said slowly. "What you said about my mother, not so."

"Of course. Your family is not the issue. You are. You were never a member of the Communist Party. Your father was under constant watch because of his employment in the Romanov Court. He was a suspected sympathizer. But he was shrewd enough to keep a low profile, including an abiding silence about his predilections. But we have three sources who claim that he was adamantly anti-Bolshevik. There was much mayhem in the 1930s. Stalin was aggressive, the economy was weakened, and the Germans were on the rise. With all that, you disappeared in 1937. One notation, edited eventually, has you as missing and presumed dead. There were a number of murders in Leningrad, a compulsive serial killer acting out. Yet you sit here now, alive. You are required to give me an accounting but before you do so understand that I have a large amount of material about you. Do not lie to me."

Marta observed her as she went through her recital. There was that omnipresent stink about all of them. The true believers! Their Communism raging through their veins. Her father's hatred for them coursing through her veins also from an early age, now habitual, as hard as diamond. Lenin versus Czar Nicholas II. "I do not know what you want me to say."

The expected reprimand came as if an order. "Start with your time as a child. What were you inculcated with by your Romanov ass-kissing parents?"

"I remember nothing of that period except for hunger, cold, and misery. My parents struggled to keep us alive. There was no time for doctrines."

"You remember not to remember Marta. You are quite lucid for your age. It is too late to perform an old age ploy. Although I think your memory is only good for a few minutes. It is assumed, quite correctly by me, that you were bombarded with Czarist fictions by your retrograde parents. Admission or not, it is taken for granted. 1937? Smarten up now Marta."

Marta wondered how much they knew. How much was in those clipped pages? What exactly was the sow after? She answered, "In 1937 I was sent by my parents to Finland.

As a servant-girl. One less mouth to feed, one less child to worry over."

"Servant-girl?"

"I did as I was told. I was a girl. Obedient. I was to serve Alexei. Together we traveled with Laura across the border to Helsinki."

"Then what happens? Be precise with me."

"I only have faint memories. You are pushing me beyond my abilities. I have flawed recollections."

Lena Dzik had quickly abandoned her feigned and erratic humanity with this crafty old woman. She was as sharp as a pin and as cagey as a fox. But Dzik, contrary to what she claimed, had barely enough in the papers supplied to her to snare this czarist in front of her should she resort to lies.

"Tell me about this woman Laura. It is the first mention I have of her. She is not in the file."

"She was there and gone."

"This Laura? More!"

"Only a week or so with us. Always in motion and then gone. She helped those escaping the Reds. Much admired," she said truculently.

"So then Alexei and you? Did he rape you or seduce you or both?" Dzik watched her flinch. It was a guess. She hit Marta with her most penetrating of looks, signaling to her that the files had much information.

In a low and guttural voice Marta shot back, "He did neither. Your file is laden with lies."

"Laden with rumors I concede. Lies? Not really. So you are a 12 year old virgin in Helsinki. Untouched by human hands," she said mockingly, trying to poke at the hostility in Marta.

Marta returned the stare, not biting on Dzik's hook.

"Well? Go on," Dzik said impatiently.

"We are on a freighter. It stops in Bergen, Norway. We spend several days there."

"Where exactly in Bergen?"

"Please with your stupid questions. How am I to remember?"

"Was it a hovel like this apartment?" Dzik asked sharply.

"No. We were always well-cared for. But could I tell you where exactly we stayed? Of course not."

"Proceed," she ordered.

"We end our journey in Canada. Some port, I don't know. Some days later we end up in New York City, smuggled in. A truck."

"And you reside in the United States until 1947. We know this. But you come back to Eastern Europe – Kiev. Your mother, now reappeared, has had a bad turn of luck. It is not clear in the file but she ended up in Ukraine, an intricate part of the Russian Empire. You become a charwoman at St. Andrew's Basilica. You support your mother. You marry, 1954. You are 28 years old, he is 45. This husband of yours is a known traitor but, as we both know, so are you. He is arrested in 1958. Sent to Siberia. Dead in 1961. Useless piece of trash!" Dzik paused her vicious recital. No reaction showed on Marta's stoic face. Tough old crow. "Do you wish to contradict anything that I have said?"

Marta stared through her, hatred evident as Dzik sat in silence for a minute.

"You have a daughter, born in 1961. Presumably by

this traitor fool of a husband. But who knows given your moral compass? She lives, she marries, she dies. She has a son. But unlike you he is a patriot. Vlad, your grandson, a true Russian. He cares for you even though you should have died ages ago rather than sucking up monies from this rogue country that can't buy a bottle to piss in."

Marta reached into the pause. "If you have no more questions leave me alone, KGB scum."

Dzik was surprised by the strength of this woman whose life she had just eviscerated. She continued her assault, "I could go on for some time about your miserable life but you are not the reason why I am really here. In the old, old days you would have been shipped off to Siberia and left to die. When you came back to Europe in 1947 you came because of your mother and her health. An allowance given to you by some sentimental bureaucrat. Perhaps you gave him sexual favors?" Her goading now as a horse in full gallop. "But your baseless life is not relevant. Although I do hope that you carry my comments into your awaiting grave. You know why I am here Marta. And if I do not get truth from you, you will end your days in Moscow. Ukraine will no longer have to support you, your grandson will inherit the apartment and you will be given over to some expert torturers in Moscow who take great joy working on czarist trash such as you. I need to know everything about Alexei, your master. We have much information about him so lies by you will be quickly determined. Do you understand Marta?"

Marta's belligerent stare maintained.

"Answer me! Goddamn you old lady or I will have you removed this instant!"

After a few seconds Marta responded, "I understand but you must understand. I know little. I was incidental. A servant. He was a man of character. I did not know this when I was assigned to be his servant." Marta said carefully.

"It was not that simple in those days to escape Russia, to make Finland, to make Norway, to make Canada, to make America. This woman Laura? She was a busy bee and suddenly she disappears. How so?"

"Who am I to say? My participation in the trip was not of my doing. I was told and I went. I was to be Alexei's servant. No matters of importance were ever discussed with me. I did as I was told. But understand something, Bolshevik! This Laura was one of many who helped him. You filthy communists had many enemies in those times. But names and particulars? What do you expect from me?"

"You were with him into your adulthood. You claim he never touched you? I can't tell now about how you looked then. But you were probably passable for this lecherous fool." With joy she saw the old lady finally react.

With extraordinary passion Marta said, "Alexei was no fool. He was a great man. You! Bolshevik bitch! How dare you!" Tears slowly came into her eyes, then dripping down across her wrinkled cheeks.

Dzik knew that this was the time to strike, seize this moment of passion and wind the old lady into admissions and determine what secrets she possessed. "Go on!"

"Lower east side. That's all I know. An apartment."

"Your sick mother? How did you find out?"

"Alexei told me. In Russia it is said everything is a secret but everything is known. My mother's illness was reported to me by him. How he heard I don't know. I was told by him to go to Ukraine. Four weeks later I was with my mother, here in Kiev."

"When did you last see him?"

"At a pier. There in Manhattan. I never saw him again. He blessed me and told me that I would be gifted with good health."

Dzik blew air out from her compressed lips before saying, "I suppose he had a medical degree also?"

"No. He didn't need to, Bolshevik unbeliever. He was a healer. Occasionally someone would come to him to experience the gifts from God that he had. You could never understand," she said with great strength.

Dzik realized that Marta was still star-struck by Alexei. That she probably never got over her time with him. "So, you come here. Not an easy world to reenter. His underground contacts had to make this happen. Who were they?"

"All gone. Swept up by Bolsheviks and all of your campaigns of brutality and horror. Now here I am at death's door facing a Bolshevik trying to track down a dead man. I have nothing further to say. Bring me to Moscow. I am not afraid."

Dzik's bluff had been called, she knew. Wilosky had ordered total secrecy around this inquiry. Taking her to Moscow was out of the question. She had pieced together some new data. She could come back, of course. She placed her notes back into her briefcase, arose and said, "Marta, you are a curious woman. In awe of a ghost. I will be back."

She called Vlad. "Your grandmother is very difficult. She yearns for the czars. If and when I come back I expect more from your efforts at getting her to cooperate." Vlad didn't respond, he was a surly man even though he was given high marks by the FSB for his pro-Russian views.

As she drove back to Kiev Center she thought again of Wilosky. Somehow he was on the hunt for the man called Alexei who had disappeared into America back in the late 1930s. The only connection that Wilosky had was old Marta who knew more than she was saying. If necessary Marta could be brought to the Russian embassy in Kiev. Dzik would not be averse to torturing the old viper there. It wouldn't be the first time. It would be Wilosky's call, of course, this man who had the power to issue orders to the FSB in Kiev.

CHAPTER TWENTY-THREE

Lena Dzik, back in Kiev Center, called three men, looking for the right man. No one man gave her the answer, but all of them contributed. The right man's name was Victor, no last name, please, the last of the three said. Just say that I recommended him. He will oblige. "Anything relating to Bolshevism up to 1939 he knows. Incredible scholar, memory of a million elephants. After 1939, probably forget it," he said.

So Lena called Victor, a Moscow telephone exchange. Victor was talkative. Probably because not many gave a damn anymore about 1939 and back. Finally, after unnecessary babbling through an aged voice, too friendly and off point, she felt that she could pose the question. "So Victor, a longshot. In the late 30s, but probably this was ongoing long before, the Czarists were still escaping from our motherland…"

He interrupted. "Yes, that is so but the doors were getting bolted more and more. Stalin was at his most malevolent. But yes, escapes were possible. There are numerous instances. God help the poor bastard of a guard who was on duty during a successful one. I am familiar with some of these instances."

"I am speaking of 1937."

"A great time to get out, but unnervingly difficult."

"I'm interested in middle men. Facilitators."

"Yes. There were some infamous ones, almost all eventually discovered and shot."

"Leningrad to Helsinki."

"One of the most used routes out. Because of that it became terribly dangerous. Stalin's counter-steps multiplied. Escapes drove him mad. It wasn't just czarists by the way, most of *them* were gone one way or another. Plenty of Bolsheviks wanted out seeing how the revolution had become a farce. Jews also coming to understand that anti-Semitism was metastasizing. So there was plenty of demand for facilitators, sherpas really, leading the way out."

Dzik felt a stab of impatience. He was a prattler. But at least he wasn't a piece of silent granite like many of the old-timers who had seen or read too much. "I have a first name only. Helsinki presence. Dealing with a czarist."

"Yes?"

"Laura."

There was a prolonged pause. Finally he said, was his statement given with some kind of reverence? "There was only one Laura that I know of who assisted czarists but not just czarists. Incredible woman. I will tell you what I know from my memory. She herself was from a Romanov circle. Nobility. Most of her family was tried and executed in 1919. Some ended up in Siberia at the work camps. Death by prolongation. A lucky few got out, Finland and Latvia, maybe Estonia. In 1919 she was only a few years old. At the time you speak of, 1937, she would have been about 21 years old. Laura Kevenskya. I believe that she knew every expatriate in the Baltic States and Scandinavia. Inspirational. Brought a new hope into the demoralized. She was on the assassination list of the Communist Party. She was protected, of course, by anti-communists. Helsinki was a dangerous city at that time. Spies lurking in every corner. Everyone looking over their shoulders. Informants, betrayers, and so on. She was extraordinarily well-connected because of her heritage and trusted even at her young age."

"What became of her?" Dzik was quite sure that assassins from the Communist Party would finally get to her.

"She went underground by 1939. She made a lot of money on the way. Escapees paid handsomely. Apparently she went up near the Arctic in Norway. Her aliveness was established later on by the KGB in 1956. She was killed around 1957. Don't know the particulars. You can take a good guess," he said sourly.

Dzik admired this man's memory. "Family?"

"Yes. She married a Norwegian, one child. A daughter. But I don't know anything about that child."

"This Laura. If I may, Victor. You seem to have an abundance of respect for her?" Dzik asked trying to be as coy as possible.

He replied, "You are correct. My great uncle, a Jew, was brought out by her. I don't forget. I always kept track of her. Her child?"

"Yes?"

"There are no winds meant to hurt her I hope?"

"No. Of course not. Just a standard inquiry by a minor department. I don't think anything is to come of it. Just completing a report is all. Thank you Victor," she disconnected, comfortable with her lie.

She immediately called an old colleague in Oslo who worked out of the Russian embassy. She gave her the name Kevenskya and asked her to run a check in Norway for this child of Laura.

By the time she arrived at Kiev Center the next day she was called by her Oslo contact. There was a hit. Laura's daughter Irina Kevenskya had been married, now a widow, living in Oslo. Last name of Jorgenson. But she changed her name back to Kevenskya.

CHAPTER TWENTY-FOUR

When Lena Dzik arrived at her office two days later she found a sealed envelope on top of her desk. She slit it open and removed from it a single sheet of paper. On the page was a letterhead with which she was unfamiliar. It read as Bureau of Exceptions, Saint Petersburg, Russia. A tiny Russian flag adjoined the lettering. Her first instinct was to question the authenticity of such an entity. But her experience with Russian bureaucracy caused her to put that suspicion away.

She read:

> You, Lena Dzik, are expected at 3:00 p.m., January 3, in St. Petersburg. Kominsky Tower, Room 303. This order has been personally approved by President Vladimir Putin's office. There is no acceptable excuse for failure to appear. Bureau of Exceptions. Wilosky

She looked at her watch. It was 11:00 a.m. She had five days.

Dzik entered the Kominsky Tower at 2:55 p.m. The two stuffed suitcases that had been hurriedly packed were in the trunk of her Lada. This concerned her as crime in St. Petersburg was up substantially in the past year. She showed her ID to the parking attendant and with as a threatening look as she could establish asked for alert eyes. She gave him a 100-ruble note.

The elevator brought her to the fourth floor, room 303. The lettering on the opaque windowed door merely read 303 Private. She knocked but heard no response. She turned the handle and walked into a nearly empty room where there were two plastic seats along a wall. A door to the right apparently led into another room. Lena was unsure about what to do but she finally knocked at that door.

It was opened by a small man whose white hair was disheveled. He had long sideburns, bushy eyebrows and a crunched up face, his chin, mouth, nose, and eyes entirely too proximate to each other. She figured him to be in his mid-60s. The word 'peppery' came into her mind for this man.

"You're Dzik from Kiev."

"Yes."

"I'm Dr. Petrov Wilosky. Come in."

Dzik followed the quick-stepping man into the room which was banked with some impressive computer hardware and at least five active screens. It was ill-lit as it depended on light emanating only from the screens.

"My desk is in the corner. Come over here." He stooped to remove a few folders from the seat that he expected her to sit on. Wilosky then went to his chair and sat down, almost disappearing behind an array of printouts and folders on top of his desk. He pushed them to the sides of the desk and peered over toward her.

"So, you make it here on time. A good sign. I know much about you. You have only heard of me, on the other hand, incidentally. Very few know of me or of my work. Allow me to share a few things with you. I am a scientist. I have a doctorate from the Leningrad Institute. My work has been in genetics. I have published widely in that field. I have spent several years in the USA in advanced research in the field, Stanford and Harvard most recently. I am well-known to a few but I am otherwise obscure and I intend to remain so." He gazed closely at Dzik, then he went on as if entered in a 100 meter dash. "Four years ago I came upon a scientific article, well-done for a change, from India. It intrigued me. I set about doing my own study of the matter. It took me two years but I slowly came to a conclusion that there was something of extraordinary value in a field where disdain toward their findings is the rule. Some months ago I was summoned for an interview with Vladimir Putin. We spent two hours together. We discussed my work. He knew of me, enough so to understand that I am not a crank. He became intrigued. In fact, the very issues that I raised with him had been of great interest to him at varying times in his career. He told me that the KGB, for instance, had also shown a keen interest about the matter but the agency could never move beyond that into any scientific validations. Some discreet inquiries from Putin's office affirmed that the questions that I am raising had pretty much been dropped over the last three decades."

She observed that as Wilosky spoke his zeal increased. This scientist was excited as evidenced by his rushed words.

"So, you wonder?" he asked as if just noticing Dzik.

"I do since I've been sent here to presumably work with you," she said in mild exasperation.

Wilosky picked up on it. He stared at her, "If I am correct in my findings you are being given the opportunity of a lifetime."

"And if you are wrong about the supposed opportunity?" Dzik rejoindered.

"Then you go back to Kiev," he said flatly.

"And you?"

"I retire. This will be my last major piece of work, I assure you."

Dzik decided to press him at this point. "Since you seem to know so much about me you most assuredly know that I am not a scientist."

Wilosky looked impatiently at Dzik. He then said, "I wanted a professional doer. Honest, experienced and *not* from St. Petersburg. A digger. You were assigned to me by Putin's assistant, Dimitri. You know of such a man? When I ask for something it is given to me promptly. Hail to Vladimir Putin! Hail to this Dimitri! After you questioned Marta, I thought that it would be weeks before you would arrive. Do you see now why my work is perceived to be of utmost importance?"

Dzik was impressed but she also felt apprehension. Being unnoticed by Putin was in the long haul better than being noticed by him. She knew the name Dimitri. He was the right hand of God to Putin himself.

"You have heard, what Russian hasn't, of our illustrious history with psychics, healers, and prophets?" the scientist queried.

"Of course," she replied warily.

"Those types were common in the Russian Empire during the time of the Romanovs, that entire 300 year span. With the Bolsheviks taking control of the country, 1916, 17, 18, such pretensions were discouraged, in fact it was unsafe to proclaim oneself as a prophet or worse still a healer or a psychic. They were branded as counter-revolutionaries, pimps for God in an atheistic state. Siberia or bullets to the head or both the preferred way to deal with them."

Dzik's attitude toward prophets, healers, and psychics was neutral but if they became annoying she would not hesitate to support their being sent to Siberia. Let them heal wolves or preach to bears, the crazy bastards. However, she had to admit she never met personally with any of these types. Raving drunks, yes, but not these, for whom she had a proclivity to associate with drunkards. She nodded and said, "I understand. Your point is unclear to me, however."

Wilosky peered at her, his eyeballs slightly misaligned with each other. "There is so much to say. It is not a straight road. But I will tell you this: healers, prophets, and psychics will be our focus."

"Now I see your point. Are they becoming an issue here in St. Petersburg?"

"*No*," Wilosky replied just short of a scream. "The more the merrier." He chuckled.

The chuckle reminded Dzik of coal sliding down the chute at her childhood furnace's coal bin, in preparation for the Ukrainian winter, an erratic rumble. There was something about scientist Wilosky that she didn't like, but worse people than he were easily remembered. Maybe that was it; Wilosky was coy, condescension mixed with it. She didn't respond. Wilosky would have to clarify.

Instead, Wilosky changed course. "I know that it had to be a tiring trip for you. More tomorrow on the matter. You are, at State expense, to stay at the Hotel Red Star. One week. By then you are expected to find a studio apartment close to here. Your pay will be enhanced to cover this. I understand that you have no immediate family. That's good."

Dzik did not care for this turn of direction. Her family or lack of was not this man's business. It was bothersome that Wilosky had been briefed, thoroughly probably. Then she thought of Putin and backed off commenting.

"One other thing. This mission that we will be on has the status of top secret. You are warned not to speak about our work with anyone. All communications with others must be circumspect. Any violation by you will be met with severe punishment, your career and potential pension forever terminated. I want to hear you say I agree."

Dzik tagged him with another observation, officious bastard, before saying "I agree."

"This is good. You may leave now. I expect you here tomorrow morning at 8:00 a.m. More will be disclosed to you."

CHAPTER TWENTY-FIVE

The office building was centrally located, not far from the headquarters where Putin officed when in the city. Wilosky, much to his credit, had secured an expensive espresso machine. Lena was shown it by him at the office adjoining his own as soon as she arrived the next day. *In toto* there were four separate rooms. The non-descript outer office, Wilosky's (the largest), a room with shelves of books, two fax machines, an elaborate copier, and assorted other standard office equipment. She noted that all of it looked new unlike some of the junk used by the embassy in Kiev. And then, of course, this elaborate De Longhi expresso machine. She could feel Wilosky's eyes on her. Dzik said, "Is it permitted for me to use this machine Dr. Wilosky?"

"But of course. Your boss was contacted and asked about your personal habits. One thing stood out that I could fix. Your love affair with coffee. Thus the machine. And from what I can see enough coffee to last until the end of the century. We are highly privileged in these offices. The Putin regime has given me extraordinary authority. I ask around about machines such as these. I am told this is a good one.

I requisition it, it is here the next day. But remember Lena, great rewards are tied to great results. Let us go next door."

Lena was shown into the fourth office. There were several file cabinets, a grandiose mahogany desk, an executive chair and a placard with her name on it. By the window was a smaller desk and chair. Wilosky pointed to it and said, "A secretary is on order. But the vetting process is painstaking. We will have one shortly. Phones and two computers will be installed later today. Questions?"

"No. Most extraordinary. I am impressed."

"For this week and part of next you have one job only. On the book shelves next door, on the left of the entry is an entire set of books devoted to one topic, one man. I want you to read as much as you can. I want you to live in his soul and his mind. For the moment he is your case as it were. A murder victim." Wilosky paused, clearly expecting a response from Dzik.

She said, "And this? This man?"

"Gregori Rasputin. And in case you are wondering much of what we will be doing will be centered on this man. Much studied. Many contradictions. You are to become an expert."

Dzik knew of Rasputin. Who didn't? Well, she was given her marching orders. She'd have plenty of coffee, a nice office and for a week or so, maybe a stress-free existence.

CHAPTER TWENTY-SIX

Four days later when Dzik sat she saw a file on her desk. There was a note attached to a stack of separately clipped pages. Files among files. The written note read:

> Lena,
>
> Sooner than expected, I must leave. From here on in I will be deeply engaged with some very involved research. My trip to Moscow includes another meeting with President Putin. In this folder are a series of notes that detail where I am in my investigation into matters that you will now actively engage in as I get more involved in pure research. Do as you see fit. Keep up on Rasputin and be free to do what is necessary. Only contact out of necessity.
>
> Wilosky

Dzik read a two page piece referred to as Memorandum to Self (July):

I must admit to a spasm of fear as I was led into Vladimir Putin's office in the Kremlin. He is a muscular presence, as if anchored into the ground. He is quick to smile but even quicker to scowl. His blue eyes are forever weighing, scanning, and calculating. I felt, not true of course, that the slightest error on my part would provoke his calling guards to send me on the way to Siberia. He informed me that he was alerted to my research by Dr. Asinov, a friend of mine. I repeated my hypothesis to him that genetic makeup goes well beyond inherited physical traits. I pressed my point to include complex psychological processes. I brought to his attention the study from India that appeared to demonstrate that the healing skill was a feature involved with such processes. I mentioned a purported saying by the ancient Greek philosopher and physician Empedocles that are three kinds of people who enjoy gifted madness: healers, prophets, and poets. Putin interjected that he agreed about poets. He did not refer to the other two mentioned by the Greek. Essentially, I told him that I was studying in these areas, especially the features of healing and prophecy. He informed me that the KGB had speculated about inheritance matters but that little came of it. He, on the other hand, had great

> interest in the subject. He asked me to draw up an action plan and have it submitted to him within two weeks. Note, this was a two hour meeting that sometimes got to be very detailed. Great secrecy was demanded by him.

Dzik wondered again how she was chosen to be part of this secret mission.

Next in the file was a short one page undated memorandum. It gave her the answer as to how she was chosen to investigate the old shrew in Kiev, Marta.

> I described the kind of person I wanted from our security agencies to a Dimitri. I quickly learned of his importance. He assigned to me a woman. Said to have an outstanding record! A pusher but with a reputation for being unyielding. Perhaps she is fit for the job. Dimitri had been aware of her for years. She was on a short list for a weighty assignment.

She wondered if she was meant to see this memorandum. It was almost positively the Dimitri of Putin's inner circle, thus her assignment was both perilous and exciting. Dzik got up and went into the adjoining office for another espresso.

Next in the folder was a fifteen page summary of correspondence between Wilosky, an Italian scientist from Padua and an Israeli from Tel Aviv. Dzik realized the discussion was beyond her ability as the three men made comments that were built on a complex knowledge base.

The subject dealt with Proteomics. She ascertained that this involved the application of science to the study of protein gathered by genes. The Israeli focused on there being several billion proteins in a single human cell. New laboratory instrumentation and incredible data-mining tools made the study of these proteins the foundation of Proteomics, e.g., newer mass spectrometers could be used to study thousands of proteins in a single referent. Copenhagen was the site for a conference in the summer of 2019 that had as its focus "Ancient Proteins." Apparently Wilosky and the other two had met there. The correspondence summaries appeared to show a friendship had already blossomed between them. The Italian mentioned his work on some medieval texts from Monte Cassino, the foundation monastery of the Roman Catholic Order of St. Benedict in Italy, the Benedictines. He was permitted to remove an ink sample, just barely the size of a pinhead, from a manuscript. His protein analysis enabled him to determine that the Benedictine scribe had a venereal disease. When he reported his finding, the Head Librarian at Monte Cassino became upset and demanded an end to the Italian's work. Unnecessary scandal! However, the biochemical analysis of the proteins removed by a pinprick from a single letter from one word on a page caught Wilosky's attention. The Italian stressed that the best of the tiny samples came from pages where handling was evident. He further stated that the scribe was the most probable suspect but that other hands had perhaps touched the manuscript from where the sample was taken. Sarcastically, he suggested an abbot. The proteins, in short, were the equivalent of a biological and chemical annotated autobiography. This new science was packed with possibilities for uncovering the secrets of the past. The Israeli spoke of Proteomics as archeology on steroids. Wilosky contracted with the pair who had become good friends and collaborators. Wilosky said he had a one page letter in his possession and from it he could take a tiny sampling, and yes, he knew that the techniques could lead to the destruction of the sample itself. Wilosky submitted the sample to them and the results of their investigation were returned to him. The memorandum ended at that point.

Dzik quickly scanned the other materials. There was no further report about this research in the entire file; she thought that curious.

The next clipped set of pages dealt with a series of memoranda directly from the Archival Department. She read the documents closely. Lena sensed a high amount of tension, speculating that there was probably resentment toward Wilosky. His guardian angels, Putin or Dimitri, were probably somehow endorsing him as a VIP with virtually unlimited powers relative to documents held by that department, or so it appeared to Dzik seasoned as she was with Russian bureaucracy.

The bureaucrat's first response to Wilosky (there was no record of Wilosky's entreaty) read as follows:

> Comrade Dr. Wilosky,
>   Please accept my delay in responding to your most unusual request. Because of the sensitivity of your inquiry it was necessary for me to validate your standing. I fully understand, now, the importance that has been given to your inquiries. I

assume that more questions will arise as we move forward. Grigori Rasputin was, and still is, a complicated man. Allow me to begin to respond to your inquiries. Rasputin was quite promiscuous. Extensive investigations were done by several major commissions after Bolshevik rule had been asserted. He was constantly enveloped in the context of those hearings even when he was not the principal subject under investigation. An inescapable presence. His murder (assassination) in 1916 was and is still quarreled over by many. You report that you have a significant interest in him. So what I say above cannot be a surprise to you. But allow me to get to your specific inquiry. Rasputin was married. He sired five children in that marriage in his province of residence, Tobol, in Siberia. Specifically his village was Pokrovshoe. As per our conversation you have no interest about these children. I will not, therefore, detail their sad fates.

Dzik shook her head as this crafty bureaucrat was covering his ass when dealing with Wilosky. He was complying with his orders while being coy. She continued to read the report.

We have three instances of reported illegitimate children. All three of these

171

> children were from Czarist women who in each instance were sent to Siberia where they were unable to adjust to the rigor of that environment. Their children met the same fate. Accordingly there are no further materials available about Rasputin's progeny.
>
> Sostov

Dzik was a bit shocked at the tone of this bureaucrat's message given that Putin was in the circuitry. She noted that Wilosky responded vigorously with a written reply.

> I find your response to my inquiry to be dismissive. I am upset and demand a formal response from the director supporting your work. I made it very clear that there is both urgency and delicacy about full research into my request.
>
> Wilosky

Good for you, thought Dzik. She appreciated how Wilosky countered in this cat and mouse game with some obscure official who probably bristled at being under the paw of a scientist. The next piece demonstrated that nerves had been hit. The tone of things had changed.

> Your concerns have been brought to my attention, Dr. Wilosky. It is of great importance to us that you are satisfied with our responses. I have removed your inquiry away from this official, about to retire, and

into the hands of my very best investigator. But do please realize that your question about progeny does involve speculation and intense focus. I am asking for your indulgence and time for my investigation to delve into this matter.

Igor Deniken

Yes, thought Dzik, the bastards were now on alert. Old Vladimir Putin himself could send a missile up their collective asses. Wilosky was gracious in victory.

Thank you for your promise of a thorough response to my complaint. I await the results of your inquiry with the gravity that my question demands.
Wilosky

Two weeks later the following was received by Wilosky. Lena Dzik was caught off guard by what was discovered.

Dr. Wilosky,

As I mentioned, your Rasputin request about progeny carries with it speculation. As I understand you have had a professional interest in this extraordinary man. If I may say so, many Russians are intrigued with him. His presence in Russian history is complicated and staggering at the same time. My most competent investigator, Stefan, was charged with reviewing the exact questions that you raised. You were dutifully informed about the three children traced back to him. We confirm that the three women and their children perished in Siberia, either en route or while there. But according to the notes from your original request your probe went deeper. The files and cartons at our closely guarded and sprawling centers are a challenge. As you can imagine secrets are, after all these years, still secrets. The amount of data is simply overwhelming. To further complicate matters the rise of Josef Stalin created unusually difficult conditions relative to what preceded his rule. Put simply, there was suspicion around historical inquiries. His reasoning, apparently, was why would there be any curiosity about Czarism? Researchers, therefore, were intimidated and materials were seen to be dangerous by their very presence. Historical evidence was not destroyed, fortunately, but it was conveniently placed aside, perhaps stashed is a better word. With the Gorbachev-inspired collapse of 1989 there was a period when scholars were allowed entry into some of our historical records. That was very controversial and as you know much of that permissiveness has been curtailed. Some materials about Grigori Rasputin were released especially those concerned about his dealings with Czar Nicholas II

and his German wife Czarina Alexandra
(Alix). The peculiar relationship Rasputin
had with Alix has been scoured over to
say the least. But your inquiry seeks to go
beyond what is generally known, and to
this cause my investigator, if I may say, has
tunneled into records and cartons that, in
some cases, have not seen the light of day
for years.

After another espresso, she went back to reading the
report sent to Wilosky by the Archival Department.

A most unusual discovery was made in
the caverns. I will say this. I am shocked
as well as proud. Pride due to the efficacy
of my best investigator, Stefan, and shock
as to what he discovered. Allow me to
state this as clearly as the matter allows.
A carton of materials was mislabeled. It is
my judgment that this was purposive. The
materials were never meant to be found. The
carton was labeled as follows. 'Irrelevant
nonsense, time better spent elsewhere.' As
you will see a serious intellectual crime was
committed by someone who probably had
Czarist sympathies. But regardless of these
musings on my part here is what was found.
Among Rasputin's many sexual conquests
was a nun named Veronika. She gave birth
to a son in 1917. His name was Alexei. This

Veronika disappeared into the hinterland of our great country. Veronika, as a nun, had cursory contact with the Czarist court. This would explain a Rasputin liaison with her as he was a court regular. The Czarists, of course, went underground as you can imagine, with the rise of Lenin. Even today, there is a notable segment of the population with Czarist sympathies. It must be assumed that Veronika and her son were protected by these interests. This same Veronika died in 1937. She had been dead for about two weeks according to the local police. Some notes were discovered in her tiny and frigid apartment. These notes were passed to a local KGB officer. It is believed that this officer committed the filing crime that has been turned up by Stefan. Because the materials had been registered by the local police he could not destroy what was found. Deceptions like that were punished severely. In the carton are two items of great interest. There is an unsigned note to Veronika to prepare her son, Alexei, for movement to Helsinki. He was to be under the guidance of an agent familiar with escape routes out of Russia. The handwriting is of such quality that it must be assumed that the writer was highly educated. A servant-girl by the name of Marta Verlovsky was chosen to be a companion to Alexei according to this note. The second piece is a handwritten note to Veronika. It is a short note. Considerable age, back to 1916 perhaps. It reads, "God is with all of his angels. As an angel, celebrate your gift. R"

My handwriting expert studied this note. He said he believes that the writing is from the hand of Gregori Rasputin. A photograph of Rasputin was found in her apartment in front of which was a small burnt-out candle. All of these items were found in this mislabeled carton. It is highly likely that this Alexei was the son of Rasputin whose days were numbered at the time of his writing this note to her in probably 1916. I await your instructions Dr. Wilosky.

Yours,
Igor Deniken

Dzik was impressed as she turned to the last page in this exchange. There was a copy of a note sent by Wilosky to this Igor Deniken.

Thank you for your perseverance. I am most impressed. It is imperative that I be given the original note sent to this Veronika.

Wilosky

Dzik came onto still another two pages. They read as follows, a note to self.

> The name Marta Verlovsky was supplied to Putin's aide, Dimitri. In short order she was determined to be alive and living in Kiev. I asked the already recommended agent Lena Dzik to interview her. She was not happy with my giving her an order to do a thorough investigation of this Marta Verlovsky. Dzik comes across as a difficult woman. Dzik's background check before meeting with this Marta revealed verification of Marta's stay in America. Her personal interview of this very old woman brings up interesting details. I feel that we are finally getting a strong connective thread. Lena Dzik is quite good at what she does but she is seen by me as a resentful agent. The target of this investigation is, at least in part, the man called Alexei. Dzik also determined that the escape guide was named Laura Kevenskya. Laura Kevenskya was murdered in 1957. She has a daughter living in Oslo.
>
> Wilosky

Dzik was surprised to find such a judgmental note about her in those two pages. Wilosky was correct, of course, she was resentful. Well, he was probably playing head games with her.

Dzik read through three other files. She found them to be irrelevant, files opened and then closed for good reason. Lena Dzik grasped that this assignment *was* actually a career-making chance. She wondered how she had come to the attention of Dimitri the right hand man of none other than Putin himself. Perhaps her fidelity to communism was seen as an asset in Moscow as opposed to the deriding of her beliefs in the Russian Embassy in Kiev. Her perception of Wilosky was changing. He was a subtle and astute character who led her into a submission. Someday in the future, maybe, she could reverse the relationship.

CHAPTER TWENTY-SEVEN

Wilosky was led into the Kremlin and up to the offices of President Vladimir Putin. In the anteroom he was wanded thoroughly, hand searched meticulously and all items, belt included, placed into a discreetly situated plastic bin. God help the sorry bastard caught trying to smuggle in some kind of threatening object. Putin's personal aide, a thin, muscular man of about 40 years asked him to sit. "The President will be with you momentarily." Ten minutes later he was led into another room. A well-dressed, smart-looking woman, 30ish in age, smiled as he was handed off to her by the aide. She said, "President Putin will be with you shortly. May I get you something to drink?" Wilosky politely refused as he sat in the seat indicated by her proffered hand. Five minutes later he was sitting across from Putin separated by a huge desk. His immediate perception was that the President was edgy, impatient.

"I won't have much time today. The tiresome Americans are acting like asses again. Have you ever played chess with an impulsive teenager? It takes them four moves to my one to achieve the same end. They think that they can throw money around and neutralize the world. Imbeciles! Dangerous! But tell me what you have ascertained."

"Mr. President, thank you for making the time." Putin bowed his head an inch, accepting the courtesy. "All of Rasputin's known children are dead. As far as is knowable, there are no progeny – the bad news. But there is a development. This may be the good news. It appears that he impregnated a hanger-on, a nun, at the Romanov Court shortly before he was murdered. Of course, there are probably other women but we have no record. As you well know, the monk was a libertine. However, following this long dead nun's materials, she seems to be the mother of a son by him, named Alexei. The same Alexei was spirited out of Russia and ended up in America."

"Yes, yes of course. What is the phrase? Only in America. So that you know, I have already been alerted to this by my chief advisor, Dimitri. But go on."

"We are making every effort to secure knowledge of this same Alexei. I thank you for the continued assistance that you are supplying to me."

"It is surely impossible for this child to be alive, of course."

"Yes. That is true. Age-wise there is no hope to find him alive. We are seeking any progeny of *his*. It is complicated by the secrecy around our pursuit. Who we allow to know. But progress has been made. But we need some help in New York City, if it comes to that."

"Sit back for a minute Dr. Wilosky. Allow me to recount an episode in my life. When I was a teenager, 16, I was introduced by a party member, a recruiter really, to an old man. The elder was said to be a prophet. I held him in scorn, me a know-it-all teenager. I felt that prophecy was inconsistent with the communism that was taking hold over me. The recruiter, afterwards, told me that this supposed prophet was 91. This elder took my hand and held it for what seemed an hour then he released it. He pointed to the party member, waving him over. He gestured toward me, I'm sure that I was glaring at him, thinking old fool. I will never forget what he said, 'When the current system collapses this young man will become leader.' Then he dismissed us. Just as we were at the exit he shouted, 'Grow up youngster, stop the nonsense.' It took me a while to dismiss my prejudices against prophecy but as I advanced my career I was and am open to prophecy. Thus my interest in your work."

"That old man?" Wilosky asked.

"He died a week later. But prophets *are* out there," Putin said slapping the top of his desk, as he continued, "A colleague of mine, KGB, stationed in England, became fascinated with an English group. They were attesting to premonitional behavior. He was impressed. Some people in that group reported extraordinary premonitional abilities. When he disclosed his interest in that group to his KGB superiors in London he was shut down, harshly. There was, and still is, a strong resistance to this kind of phenomenon here in atheistic communist Russia. This is why I want you to be careful. I don't want my enemies to be aroused, to see me as crazy. Their minds are closed. We must keep them in their cages as it were."

"Of course Mr. President. But you must know that when I ask for something it is given to me with alacrity. But I have never tried to compromise you, I assure you."

"I don't worry about that. Also strings are regularly

pulled all over this country by diverse actors. There is a specific string devoted to you Dr. Wilosky. My involvement is quite cloaked even as you are treated as essential by my regime." Putin gazed at the clock that sat on his desk. "I have wandered. I only have a bit of time. Tell me of anymore scientific findings."

Fifteen minutes later Wilosky was being led out of the office by Putin. As with other times he was awed by the personal power and energy field that emanated from the President. He observed in the anteroom three men who looked at Wilosky with annoyance, as though he had wasted their time as they waited. Wilosky rated the three as dangerous looking. As all three arose to greet Putin he observed that they immediately morphed into subservience as Putin came up to them. It was indeed good to have a protector from on high.

CHAPTER TWENTY-EIGHT

Irina Kevenskya carried her shopping bag back to her apartment, northeast of Vigeland Park. She lived in the Majorstuen district of Oslo. Her mother, Laura, had moved both of them from near the Arctic into this neighborhood which at the time was shabby and rundown. Laura had told the five year old Irina that it was best for both of them to stay low. Reason? Laura had a bad history with Russia, so much so that there was reason to be alert to danger. When pressed by Irina she was merely told that smuggling people out of Russia was dangerous, that she had done it, and that Irina had a strong Russian bloodline going back to the Romanov regime. Irina's father, a Norwegian, had drowned in a sledding accident shortly after her birth.

When her mother was murdered in 1957, she was caught off guard by the treasure left to her by her frugal parent. Still a girl, now cared for by an aunt, she would never be in want as she pursued a successful career in photography. Now, herself elderly, she lived in semi-retirement, accepting a few jobs here and there. She was weighing an offer from an Oslo travel agency to go to South Florida for a week to take tantalizing photos to be used in a campaign to lure

Norwegians, tired of winter, to succumb to the enticement of sun and heat next year.

Only recently, after decades of neglect, had she begun the perusal of the contents of one of two large suitcases that had been kept by her mother whose instructions were, 'If something bad happens to me – read sometime if you wish, you may find them interesting. Ultimately, you probably should destroy them. Whatever you wish my dear daughter.'

She had pretty much finished the larger suitcase's contents. There were a number of short stories written by her mother, an unfinished novel, and a few short descriptions of escape routes from Russia. Yes, her mother Laura, had been a risk-taker dealing with a horrible period in the history of Russia. But her mother could not escape the murderous apparatus of the Kremlin. She understood why her mother always seemed to be on alert, constantly looking around. And the knife left to her by her mother that Irina carried in her bag? Irina cherished it, understanding its historical context. She had yet to explore the second suitcase.

The day that changed her life of complacency came with suddenness.

She had volunteered to instruct an adult class about the use of photography on iPhones at the local Lutheran church. She was accustomed to the dark gray sky at 4:00 p.m. as she entered her apartment. About to close the door behind her she was shoved hard falling to the floor. Startled, she looked up and behind her. She saw a man and a woman. The man was quick to put his hand over her mouth as he pulled her upright and forced her forward into the apartment.

She breathed in his rotten-smelling breath as he said in harsh Russian, "I will remove my hand from your mouth if you nod your head that you will not yell. If you do I will hurt you."

She nodded through a long and desperate sigh as he released his hand from her mouth. He then pulled her half upright into her small study. He sat her forcibly into a recliner. He placed his index finger vertically across his lips and stepped away from her.

Facing her now was an austere-looking woman in her 50s. She crouched slightly and came within two feet of Irina's face. "My name is Lena. I will leave you in peace if you cooperate with me. If you don't, you will suffer. Do you understand? Boris, tie her hands behind her."

She had no option. Her life was at stake. Her hands now braced against her back. It was a question of whether or not she could get out alive from these two menacing characters. She breathed deeply in an effort to control herself. "What is it that you want from me?" She observed Boris going on a prowl in her small and studiously neat apartment.

"Your mother. It's about her. Not you. You are irrelevant, I think. But that also will be determined before we leave you, alive, maimed, or dead," the Russian woman declared in a staccato voice that seemed well-trained in projecting threats. She spoke through curled and tightly zippered lips.

Irina heard the first noises of chaos from her bedroom. Drawers, it seemed, being hurled against walls. She had kept her apartment with meticulous care, not a spot anywhere, not the content of any drawer in her house without purpose and the precise placement of each and every item. She closed her eyes and shook her head. The violent slap across her left cheek caused her to gasp and mouth, "Uh, uh," as tears welled in her eyes. "What is it that you want from *me*? My mother is dead, decades."

"What do you have from your traitorous mother? A saboteur against the Russian State. But this you know, your innocence about her has been long spent."

Irina had to make a choice. There was little other than a few objects from her mother – a necklace and matching bracelet, a picture of her as a young girl with her mother and father, a small enamel cat, and the knife. She said nothing about the suitcases that were stored in her allocated storage unit in the apartment building basement.

"I have nothing. A picture. She left me nothing."

"The picture," the Russian snarled.

"In my living room, please stop from destroying my apartment," she pleaded while hoping that her lie would stand them down. The name of this vile woman, Lena, she recalled. "Lena, please."

Dzik called Boris who was continuing the bedroom wreckage. He came. She said to him, "Watch her." He stood over her, broad shouldered with a mustache that smothered his upper lip. Stalinesque. Dzik came back with the framed picture. She asked Irina, "This is it?"

"Yes," tears in eyes.

Dzik opened a small bag, the type a doctor would use on rounds in the old days. She removed from it a small hammer. Then she laid the frame on the floor and smashed it. She didn't have to do that, of course, it was for effect. She removed the small picture and placed it in her purse. She said to Irina, "What else?"

"Nothing. That picture is all I have."

"You're wasting my time. Lying bitch." Another resounding slap.

Irina, wimpering, said, "Please leave now. No police will be called. Just leave."

"Hah! Police! You are in no position to negotiate. I have all the cards and we have all night." Dzik nodded at Boris, as she cupped her hand and made a gesture toward her mouth. Boris acknowledged, plodded back into the bedroom and brought back a pair of panties that he had probably flung across the room from a bureau drawer. He grabbed Irina's head back and as she opened her mouth to scream he pushed the panties into her mouth, half of the pair hanging out and down across her chin.

For a fleeting moment Dzik thought back to Marta, regretting her unusual show of leniency toward the old fox. She reached into her bag and brought out a powerful battery operated hair remover. The type used by Russian military on new recruits. She had observed that everything about Irina was balanced and neat. Her carefully arranged whitened hair. "Do you know what this is Irina Kevenskya?" The terror in Irina's eyes duly noted.

Irina shook her head pretending ignorance.

Dzik smiled slightly to her lie. Irina knew. She signaled to Boris who now grabbed Irina's neck and held it tightly. Within a minute the head of this sobbing woman was shaved down to stubs. Dzik gave her a few minutes to contemplate the enormity of her transgression and the subsequent misery that was in her future. She slapped Irina's face, gently this time. "Now! Daughter of a traitor come out to me about what you have from your mother before I begin on your fingernails, toenails, tits, oh that's just for a start. I will give you a few minutes to contemplate. If I have Boris take your underwear from your mouth and you promise not to yell I will also allow that. All this unpleasantness is unnecessary you know. Nod your ridiculous bald head if you will behave."

Dzik had participated in, and led other, routines of torture. Secretly, she had become an adept handicapper about when and how the tortured would break. The materials that had been collected about Irina Kevanskya demonstrated conclusively that she was very unlike her mother Laura, by all accounts a courageous bitch even when captured by a KGB hit team and tortured without mercy before being shot in the head and dumped in the Akerselva River in Oslo. She conjectured that Irina would break by the third yanked fingernail on her right hand. If she did in fact have materials they would be yielded at that point. If Irina had lasted through all of her right-hand nails, Dzik was prepared to relent.

Just as she was fastening the pliers onto and around the middle finger, Irina gave out. There were two suitcases in the basement storage area. Boris was sent. He returned with both.

She asked him, "Seen?"

He responded, "A stupid old man passed by me. Eyes down. Concentrating on the steps. Never looked at me."

Dzik said, "He's a Norwegian. A stupid people. Reached their zenith as Vikings a thousand years ago. What would you expect? Watch her, I want to review the apartment as old Irina is a bit of a liar."

She came back in 15 minutes, now crouching in front of Irina. "I see that you have a nice bundle of money in your accounts. I assume it was given to you by your traitorous mother who pillaged escapees in return for her betrayal of mother Russia. We will leave shortly. You will be tied up to your bedpost, mouth gagged. If you persist you will be able to free yourself by tomorrow morning. By then we will be long gone from your pathetic country. I have permission to kill you but I won't. I urge you to keep this affair to yourself. Collect your life again and go on. *But* if somehow what has happened here comes back to hurt Russia you will learn to see just how gentle I was. If I had the time I would read to you what happened to your mother. You had five percent of what she went through Irina. Never forget that." She turned to Boris and ordered him to bind Irina.

CHAPTER TWENTY-NINE

Lena Dzik brought the two stolen suitcases into her office in St. Petersburg, noting that there was still no secretary. Both pieces of luggage were aged, beaten up. Two large belts around each, securing them fast. One of the suitcases had been opened given the different shaded areas caused by the belts. The other seemed to have never been.

She chose the one that had been once opened while trying to guess at why Irina seemingly never perused the second case. The belt would not yield to her attempts. Besides a handgun, she always carried a knife. A sharp knife. She cut through both leather straps with ease. The standard cheap lock she picked with a paper clip and then spread the two sides apart. She counted four full writing tablets, six distinct typed manuscripts, and fourteen books. Fortunately, Laura had neat handwriting and wrote in Russian. Dzik read the first few pages of two of the writing tablets. Laura Kevenskya was a fiction writer. The two she scanned told of life in the Arctic area of northern Norway. They were simple stories detailing her run-in with a pack of wolves, the other her coming up to a herd of elk. They reminded Dzik of the Russian writer Turgenev. Laura was an accomplished writer.

The typed manuscripts were novellas, one in particular an elongation of the tablet piece. The fourteen books were collected stories by Tolstoy, Dostoevsky, Pushkin, Turgenev, and other writers with whom she was unfamiliar.

The effort to capture information about Laura was not in balance with the result. She would see to it that the entire contents of the suitcase were destroyed after closer scrutiny.

She suspected more of the same as she repeated the opening process with the second suitcase, this more recalcitrant and ungiving of its contents than the other. Dzik was not inclined to smile when her efforts paid off. She knew that the assault on Laura's daughter, Irina, was a longshot and was likely to yield little or nothing. At the end of it all there was the cold comfort of retaliating against traitorous Laura's daughter, Irina. There was always that. A price should be paid in the grand scheme of things. So, even if nothing was gained about the activities of Laura there was an evening of the scales. But smile she did. This suitcase was replete with information specific to Laura's betrayal of her country.

There were numerous maps, some printed, others hand-drawn. The escape routes drawn in meticulous detail, along with abbreviations of names and currency exchanges. Routes went in many directions, to the south, the Caucasus, to forests of the north. The schemes and planning were extraordinary. Laura Kevenskya was an accomplished and brilliant spy far smarter than the fragmented NKVD apparatus around Josef Stalin. She got the best of them.

She found routes into Turkey through Georgia and Armenia, some through Georgia and Azerbaijan into the Caspian Sea through to Iran. Others into the Black Sea and out to Romania or Bulgaria and some routes into Greece. She sat in awe of Laura who would have been an extraordinary asset for the Motherland, Russia. But deep in her soul she had to admit that a talent such as Laura could easily have been extinguished by the vile, chauvinistic bastards in the Kremlin.

There were no names spelled out. Her multiple contacts throughout all of the regions that she used only had initials. She remembered reading the KGB reports detailing her execution and the extreme torture that she was put through. The seething comments of the KGB torture specialist who was unable to break her as they killed her with a thousand cuts only to destroy what remained of her with a bullet to the head.

She pored over records, noting that vast sums of money passed through her hands in some instances. A Jew paid in gold bars and diamonds for an escape to New York through Greece. A Russian Orthodox priest paid with two icons from the 11th century, escaping to Bulgaria and eventually bound for Paris. To this point she had found 47 engineered escapes.

The day was slipping away from her as she made her seventh espresso. Outside her window she saw blackness punctuated with heavy snow. She was down to the bottom of the suitcase when another slightest of smiles crossed her lips. She came upon a faded white envelope inscribed as follows: A and Marta V. A small map was handmade, detailing the escape route from Moscow. An ambulance was employed for part of the long trip, Laura as nurse to a bandaged A and Marta as a bereaved daughter. That got them to St. Petersburg with a man lettered in as Q.

The border from St. Petersburg to the Finnish border was approximately 400 kilometers. Her notes showed that she used five contacts and some hefty sums to pull off the escape into Finland and eventually Helsinki. Further on her notes made mention of Bergen, Norway, and the Port of St. John's in Newfoundland.

There was a small inscription that read NY with a small cross next to it. At the very bottom of the note she read: *In memory of the Czar*. Dzik interpreted that to mean there was no charge to get them out. There was now a confirmation of Marta's strained confession of the trip.

She noticed the elusive use of just the letter A. Surely Marta's master, Alexei. By the time she fully explored the suitcase there were a total of 52 escapes before Laura called it quits to her very dangerous profession.

Dzik was unsure about what to do with the second suitcase and it contents. To turn it in to the FSB would be to invite inquiries about how she secured the materials and had interest in them. That night she decided to keep only those materials pertinent to her investigation. The rest she would burn. It was time to rid herself of Laura Kevenskya and her pathetic daughter Irina.

CHAPTER THIRTY

Dimitri sat in President Putin's office, 5:00 p.m. precisely. Vladimir was exchanging comments with President Assad of Syria. He could tell from Putin's clipped comments and some of his facial expressions that he was not happy with the Syrian. Privately, Dimitri had had reservations about Russia's involvement in the affairs of that troubled country. But, as always, he said nothing especially so when it came to foreign affairs. He knew his value came to performing tasks given to him by Vladimir and maintaining vigilance for anything adverse that could come at him.

Like Adam, he had his doubts about Rasputin and his supposed gifts. He was an agnostic leaning into atheism but there was always that minute doubt that kept him from it. From his speculations he thought Vladimir Putin to be of the same mindset. Everything changed when Deniken passed forward the found document with Rasputin's predictions. It was such a monumental revelation as it foresaw Putin's tenure in office. That along with Putin's teenage experience with the aged psychic was enough for him to go into overdrive.

In anticipation of this meeting he had called Lena

Dzik in St. Petersburg at 1:30 a.m. She would be met at Passazhirskya Terminal in Moscow. Seats on the train had been arranged for already. The four hour trip would be by bullet train (Sapsan) leaving St. Petersburg at 9:00 a.m. and arriving in Moscow at 1:02 p.m. She would be met at the station by agents. To his mild surprise she asked only one question, "One day?" He told her to bring a suitcase to which she said, "yes." Conversation ended.

What Lena didn't know is that he had been watching her progress as a KGB agent from the outset of her career. She was fluent in German, French, and English. Although she was classified as a Ukrainian she was unmistakably a Russian patriot, her family having had deep Russian roots. She had been inserted into some Ukranian separatist cells to such an extent that her work delayed by years the eventual severe break by Ukraine from Mother Russia. Never once had she been outed even as her cover was exposed. She had foreseen the possibility and finessed the Ukrainian scum into believing her to be friend of their causes. He knew that she wasn't liked in the male-dominated FSB in Kiev. In fact, he felt that efforts had been made to undermine her career. Yet he observed her closely and had arm-twisted an agent to report back about her. He recalled the last few sentences of his report, not meant in praise but seen by Dimitri as just that. 'Lena Dzik is seen to be a mean-spirited bitch who will do anything to advance the interests of the Russian State. She has the personality of a viper. I cannot support any advancement in her career. She is quite secretive and for a Ukrainian, extremely honest.'

There were many other particulars in her file. He would ask about those as he peered at her on the screen that received the footage from the hidden camera in his waiting room. She was quite observant. He speculated on whether she was adroit enough to pick up on the hidden camera. Or maybe she just didn't give a damn, assuming that everything was being taped in the current high tech environment. She had a tight mouth, a short, severe haircut and projected a strong appearance. Not someone to play games with. She had to realize, of course, that she was now in the 'A' league. Noticed. He did not question for a minute that she knew who he was. He messaged his secretary, "Send her in. Ask her if she wants anything to drink."

So, Wilosky was correct, she thought. This was *the* Dimitri, right-hand to God himself. The agenda, still seen only dimly, had extraordinary implications. Dimitri was compact, rail-thin, perhaps around 5'8". He was bald on top, the side hair clipped short. There was a military precision around his movements. There was a reptile quality in the man accentuated by a thin face and hyper-alert brown eyes. He came out, quick movements, from behind his desk, the top of which was bare except for a large Apple computer that sat to the side of the desk. She noticed that he had touched the keyboard and the lit screen went dark.

He showed her a cushioned seat on the far side of the room. He sat across from her. He had a curious way of self-effacement, a humility of the powerful. He sat and gazed at her. Then he said, "Lena Dzik, pleased to meet you. You know who I am?"

"Yes."

"If you feel the need to use a last name for me it is not necessary. I rarely use it, mostly for official documents. I don't have to tell you that your very presence here signifies that serious issues are involved. I report directly and daily to President Putin. When I speak you can assume that he is speaking to you. Question?"

"No sir. I understand that. Your relationship with the President is well-known in the service, especially."

"Your involvement with Dr. Wilosky connects you to a mission of great importance. Right to the top of this Kremlin. I read your report about Marta Verlovsky. Probably the best you could get from a very old woman. But she gave a confirmation of yet another detail."

"I could bring her into the Russian embassy in Kiev. Torture would probably not help in this instance. But...if you wish..."

"No. I don't second guess good ground people. I think that you squeezed out of her all that was possible. Your daring approach in Oslo with Irina Kevenskya was superb. Many questions answered. Have you become conversant with Rasputin? Enough time?"

"Yes and no," she responded.

"Please?"

"By yes, I mean I was allowed time to get engaged with the man to an extent that I know pieces of him very well. On the other hand, there are dimensions that are unknowable. He is a complicated human being."

"And?"

"I am a Communist of the old school. I do not believe in worlds other than this or in unscientific conclusions. His pretense at being a healer or some sort of prophet is absurd. The Tsarina Alexandra was a foolish German whose love of her son blinded her. She was ready-made to be gulled.

Rasputin, dishonest to the core, insinuated himself into the Court."

"Wilosky left documents for you to read. You are familiar with them?"

"Yes."

"Your orthodox communism is well-known, actually. Your interests and your professors when you were a student in Kiev certainly aligned with what I perceive in you. Your analysis of Rasputin is consistent with classical Bolshevism. As you know the President has made efforts to return Russia to its religious past. He sees the religion of our fathers to be part of Russian DNA. That the Bolsheviks went too far. That Lenin and Stalin misread the soul of Russia."

"I have never articulated a position on his rapprochement with Orthodoxy," she said defensively, fearing that she had already flown too close to the sun with her waxen wings.

"You don't have to Lena. Your whole life has been one of consistency. I do appreciate your honesty, another feature of your personality. You should know that I have had a close eye on you ever since you came over to us upon your graduation. You had been assigned a rating rarely given. Your work as a double agent with the Ukrainian radicals became necessary reading for me when it was passed forward. I could tell even then that there was hostility toward you. It was sexist. They feared you in the Kiev Embassy. You were just too damn good."

"I had no idea that any of my work would be forwarded to you."

"As I gained in influence I insisted that it become a protocol. They are obedient now even though resentful. Your efforts in the Crimea after our seizure of it from Ukraine was outstanding. Also your work in Eastern Ukraine with Russian sympathizers is unmatched. So, to make a long story short, I have watched you gain excellence as a true Communist fully dedicated to Mother Russia. If I may, your moment has come. It happens to some people, the right time, the right place. When I saw the inevitability of this particular matter, its taking on a life of its own, the Kiev connection, my awareness of your excellence, your stalwart love of Russia, you became the chosen. And so it is that you are here."

Dzik was both honored and frightened. She was on Mt. Olympus! She could feel the pull of power in her stomach. In one of the few times in her life she felt gratified, respected. But this mission? Was she overmatched? Had she already said too much? Exposing her bias? "I am quite honored Dimitri."

"At the completion of this affair, assuming that all things are done properly and that you live up to my expectations, you will be given a choice, either to assume the ambassadorship at the Kiev embassy or to come here to Moscow and work directly under my command. But… enough of that. Just a few more things. Your command of English?"

"Excellent. I have always been good with languages. If necessary, within a week of total exposure it would come back to me perfectly."

"You were in New York City, United Nations, for a week in the mid-1990s. Impressions?"

"Hamsters are interesting. Run, run, run. That's the West to me. New York is the epicenter. They look like they're getting something done. Constant motion. A total waste. It is all based on selfishness. It will do them in eventually."

"That view Lena is consistent with what I know of you. My question, though, pertains more to your ability to fit in and move around that country if such was necessary. Can you act like a hamster but not be a hamster?" She saw the faintest sign of a smile on his stern face.

"Ah. Yes. I see. I believe that I can do anything if the purposes of what I am doing are clear."

"Be assured they will be." He looked at his watch. "We have one more meeting Lena, five minutes from now."

CHAPTER THIRTY-ONE

Augusta arranged a meeting with McAbee at his office at 10:00 the next day. She arrived fifteen minutes early hoping to have a conversation with Pat Trump who was smiling at her.

"You will need an hour to unravel all those clothes, Augusta."

"More than that," as she removed a woolen hat, scarf, gloves, winter coat and loose sweater. "It's brutal out there. I had to park two blocks away. The winds are up to no good. How are you Pat?" She went about translating all of her gear onto a seven armed post that was already handling winter gear.

"I'm okay. I was dropped at the door by Ed who in his retirement needs tasks. He actually likes to pick me up and drop me off. A win-win for us. And you?"

"Yeah, doing well. Nasty stuff dealing with this winter. I guess we've had worse but I can't remember. Are you going to get to Florida this year?" Augusta asked now seated to the right of Pat's desk.

"Still not sure. Can I get you some coffee? Hot cocoa?"

"Did you say hot cocoa?"

Pat laughed as she went behind her desk toward a tray that sat on a window shelf. On it were a number of carafes, bowls, and assorted necessities that allowed for wish fulfillment. Over her shoulder she asked, "Some cookies?"

"No, no. Thanks. Weight."

"Oh sure. Miss America denying herself a cookie." She brought Augusta a steaming cup of cocoa.

"You're not having any?"

"I have my own vices," she said with pressed lips and expanded cheeks.

Pat was a smoker. She was a rail thin smoker. Augusta and Bertrand had discussed the matter often, concerned about the effect it was having on her. Augusta let any comment go. What was the use? She asked Pat, as this was the reason for her early arrival, "How is Bertrand doing? He's dropping clients with a fervor that I didn't think he'd pull off."

"I think that some of them were prepared. Others have resisted, in some cases, with anger. It's like they're saying who the hell are you to check out? Interesting. And new clients? Forget it. I know you're onto the Goodkind matter. I never saw him to be so happy as when Peter Goodkind fired him," she smiled.

"I'm afraid that while we no longer represent Goodkind that the related matters are quite complicated. Bertrand would say that it was a tar baby. Touch it and you'll never get free."

"Have you changed your mind about taking over? There still are plenty of files. Jack Scholz and Barry Fisk need the work!" She pounded her fist on her desk, a mock gesture.

"Well, I was considering it but you just talked me out of it," Augusta said lightly.

At that, McAbee came out of his office. He wore a blue, high-necked woolen sweater, black corduroys and he had on his usual sneakers. He was still pretty trim. His high cheekbones, blue-gray eyes forever shifting in color it seemed, a short haircut to the sides of his otherwise balding head. He was about 5'10" and surely weighed in at about 165 points with a margin of error about five pounds. In his late 70s, he looked younger. His movements had slowed, however. Rather than the continuous action of a movie, watching him made it seem that she was looking at photographs, the easy momentum no longer there. His smile was captivating. Augusta told him often enough that he needed to display that more often.

"So why do I tremble when I see the two of you talking together? Plotting perhaps? Gossiping?" he asked while nodding his head up and down, a smile on his lips.

After a few more minutes of easy banter between the three of them Augusta and Bertrand went to his office.

Pat always wondered about them. The chemistry between them was intense. It was obvious that they loved each other, their awkward efforts at concealment, laughable. Perhaps they fooled others but not Pat. Did they sleep together? That was the question she couldn't answer.

They hugged each other for quite a while, both acutely aware that they were dealing with a tiger in the form of a case.

McAbee had been already informed about the death of Eddie Goodkind, the travails of Joanna, and the hospitalization of Peter. But he was about to hear something that would alarm him as it had alarmed her when she questioned Joanna last night. Bertrand's skepticism was about to take a broadside hit.

Hugging ended they sat and gazed at each other. Augusta broke the ice. "Joanna first. I visited her this morning. She's frazzled. Her doctor prescribed Xanax. She took three 50 milligrams while I was there. It helped her. She went to bed to nap. Your prof guardian, Mary, has a friendship with a retired nurse who came over. They'll try to keep her relaxed. She really needs to see Lady Alexandra again. What do you think?"

"She's an adult. We can't do anything to stop her even if we wanted to. You know I'm leery of Lady Alexandra but then one of the brightest and most insightful people I know, *you*, thinks highly of her. All's the more not to get in Joanna's way. But she shouldn't drive if she's pumping in all that Xanax."

"Mary would drive her. She knows. She has her car keys."

He nodded his approval but added, "There may be value to your driving her. Another chance to see Alexandra. Think about it."

"There's something else. Brace yourself, Bertrand. If true, it's scary."

Augusta went on to give a very detailed description, as accurate as she could put it together, of the events around the break-in, the threats and ultimately the death of Eddie Goodkind. She noticed that Bertrand's attention was quite apparent as he stared fixedly up and above to his left, always a clear sign of close and calculated listening. When she finished there was a lengthy silence.

At last, he said, "I think that I hear your concerns correctly. You have an admiration for Alexandra. You attribute to her the ability or gift of healing. Your psoriasis and breast issues a testimony to such. What has happened is quite extraordinary. I'm not inclined to agree completely with you but I do not dismiss it as impossible. Healing, as a gift, is not out of the question for me but I'd like you to define it very carefully. But you've gone further into the matter of her gifts and this is where the trail gets darker. You know that I always lead with skepticism. That's just me. I'm not in any way trying to deny you or diminish your observations." He looked at her carefully, reinforcing his statement. "You have been overwhelmed, I think that is a good word, by her gift of discernment so much so that it can incorporate the word psychic. That's quite a jump the one to the other. But, in effect, that's the business that she's in and it's a business that I'm leery of – no big surprise there. I know that you were also skeptical before you met her. There's a long history of deception around psychic practices. But I don't discount the possibility. I believe there are people who see way beyond what others see. For such people I understand the word usage – gift. So, each one – healer and psychic – in themselves is quite a rare possibility but when you tie them together there is something well beyond just an extraordinary woman. But now I become a harder skeptic because of the implications in what you have observed. Really? Eddie's death?"

"Yes Bertrand. You have me fair and square but where you're an even harder and more demanding skeptic about her I am becoming a middle hard believer. And then this most difficult wall," she said thoughtfully.

He went on, "In baseball they talk about 'Five Tool' players. Excellent at every dimension of the game. Flawless as far as the restraints of the game go. Your assertion about the death of Eddie Goodkind, if true, brings this woman into a totally different dimension. Let's just say that all three gifts reside in her. A healer, a psychic, and now a bewitcher. She would pretty much run the gamut for gifts that are beyond the reach of any human known before we pass into theology and Jesus Christ. She lives in obscurity. She has a faithful clientele but before our involvement I had never heard of her. My conclusion is that she is hiding otherwise she could not escape the notice of the world."

"Everything you say has merit Bertrand. I went over, very carefully, Joanna's memory of things. She had no doubt about what she saw and heard."

"But Alexandra lives in fear of something, it seems? This lends credence to her purposeful obscurity. She knows what she has and is not afraid to share a bit with her healing and psychic abilities but she might be afraid to display the bewitching quality. Telekinesis involves moving physical objects, e.g., bending a spoon. But you're going well beyond. This gets into sorcery and witchcraft, very dangerous realms, especially for a person of goodness as you present her. But let's postulate that she has all three of these gifts. A person like that is potentially very dangerous, good intentions aside. If, as you speculate, she hurled a curse at Eddie and he did in fact die from it do you really want to spend any more time with her? She would have the power to murder within her psyche. Yes, Eddie was threatening with a gun in hand. Yes, her reaction can be construed as self-defense, but that *kind* of self-defense could have no limits. Her goodness and strength of character has held it in check. Let's say as we don't know her history. But how many people with extraordinary abilities have misused them and have had the very great abilities capture their souls and lead them into perfidy?"

Augusta listened to McAbee's discourse about the issue. His analyses were causing her to become alarmed. Everything he was saying had a probability. "I'm not sure of how to proceed Bertrand. However, there is evidence that Alexandra is fully imbued with the ways we've been discussing."

"Let's keep thinking about this. Our client is Joanna Goodkind. We can be pretty sure that Lady Alexandra has tremendous empathy and concern for her. A good influence. That's the compelling question – the safety of our client. In a way, Lady Alexandra is a distraction from our purpose. A distraction to watch but she is not the first object of our business."

CHAPTER THIRTY-TWO

Lena Dzik was on edge as she was led into Vladimir Putin's office by Dimitri. She said to herself that what was happening was well above her pay grade. But then she caught herself at this negative self-talk. Probably, if fortune had played a different hand of cards, she would be sitting in the President's chair. Finally, she reached into her courageous heart and realized that she was as capable as the two men she now faced, one directly in front of her, Putin, the other to her right. She could feel the weight of Putin's observation of her, his eyes penetrating across and through her if such was possible.

Putin spoke first. "Lena Dzik! You commendations are most excellent. Your negatives are from the right people to have negative evaluations as they were from known sloths and rabid foxes. Dimitri," he bowed ever so slightly to his left toward Dimitri, "has been very observant of you for years. You are an agent held in reserve for special missions. Your time has come. The secrecy around what you are being tasked is absolute. Whatever ultimately comes of your work should die with you, Dimitri, and myself. Is that clear?"

"Of course, Comrade President," she said in a slightly strained voice.

Putin nodded and then went on with a low-toned gravity. "It has come to our attention that the Russian Orthodox Church and specifically Patriarch Kirill have raised Rasputin from the grave, as it were, and are pondering sainthood for this man. We understand that he authorized advanced background checks, interviews of principals, analysis of documents over to a priest of high influence and mind, a Father Damien, part of Kirill's coterie of officials, to probe the matter. While I have tried to create a warmer relationship with the Orthodox Church, a political necessity if we are to ever recover the Soviet Union of old, I am aware of the dangers of that institution. Thus, close surveillance of the Church is ever utilized. Is it true that you have had misgivings about my tilt to the Orthodox Church?" His piercing look now aimed directly at her eyes.

She was stunned. How did Putin know of her anger and dismay about his tilt to the Orthodox Church? Only one friend was told. Would he disclose this? No way. Yet he must have and accordingly, under what circumstances? They must have trolled through her entire life. Amazing. And yet she realized that she was part of this entire system of intrusion, investigation, distrust, and so on. After all, she had done such to others on countless occasions. Why the surprise? She answered, "It is true Comrade President. I think of the Church as a reactionary institution. Many of its adherents still worship Czar Nicholas II, that Bolshevism was evil. Those tigers do not change their stripes. But I do see it as a political gesture and I am pleased that the frauds are under surveillance by you. My admiration for you has no limits.

Your remediations for the damage caused by Gorbachev and Yeltsin are beyond mere praise."

"Good. Good. I take you at your word. However, be careful who you talk with. There can never be a misstep in what you are being tasked with. Understood?"

"Most assuredly."

Putin liked her. She was as advertised by Dimitri who had put a no holds barred on backgrounding her. He especially liked her frank response about her concealed antagonism about his approach to Patriarch Kirill. If she had denied what her seemingly only friend had disclosed she would have been outposted to far Siberia. "So Dimitri, it is time for you to outline our charge to Lena." Putin sat back in his chair prepared to listen.

Dimitri moved his chair closer and at a more favorable angle to face Lena. A few index cards were removed from the inside of his jacket. "Lena," he spoke softly, "I will give you the overall approach of your mission. Precise particulars – locations, names, and so on are in a folder in my office. In general terms, here are your mission particulars. In New York City, especially certain areas there, Russian exiles are many and they tend to congregate together. In those concentrations we have inserted agents. No surprise there for an agent of your caliber."

Lena nodded.

He continued, "Among the exiles, there are many stripes of persuasion. Some are devoted Communists, Stalinists, Yeltsinites, and so on. Of concern for us is a small Russian Orthodox Church in a place called Brighton Beach. A large number of Russian emigres in that area. At any rate, this Church, Saint Nicholas, has its roots back into Czarist times.

The adherents there despise Bolsheviks, the revolution, the murder of the Romanov family, you can imagine. There is an obsessive fervor to them. It is a congregation of about 300. But their zealotry and proactive stances make them equivalent to 3,000. There is also a considerable amount of wealth in the congregation. We have watched this group very closely, needless to say. We have tried to penetrate but so far we are unsuccessful. We have an agent who attends services but there is a tight clique within the whole. We cannot tap into this closely-knit circle. They are of the old days and they do not circulate, as a rule, in the cyber age. We considered trying to place you in the group but it probably would take a decade or more or ever to get into it. Besides the adoration of the Romanovs, its regime and practices, they have been avid in their conviction that Rasputin is a saint, that he must be recognized as such by the Russian Patriarchy. Their research about Rasputin is estimated as formidable. Of course, it is not in the interest of the Russian State for any of this absurdity to gain traction. But as you have heard from Comrade President the Orthodox Church here in Moscow is exploring sainthood possibility for this maniacal fraud. So to the point. We are virtually positive that Rasputin himself fathered a son by some nun, a hang-around creature in the Romanov Court. I understand that you know of this from Dr. Wilosky?"

"Yes. I do," she replied with a hint of wonderment.

"You have had other confirmations such as in Oslo that make us quite assured that this Alexei, who was accompanied by Marta, is the bastard son of Rasputin. There is an almost zero chance that he could be still alive. However, we need authentication about him in New York City, and if not there, where? As I am sure you are discerning you will be going to New York City to undertake an investigation. We are especially interested in any progeny from this man, Alexei. I have been in touch with a reliable agent of ours named Ivan Brodsky. He is with our mission at the United Nations. He is an attorney, very devoted to our country. He has been briefed about some of the issues that we are concerned with. You can trust him but I warn you that his views on a number of matters might be seen by you as aberrant. You have my assurance that he is indelibly loyal, nonetheless. Questions?"

"No. I understand."

"The cover for the matter is the supposed theft of three paintings from the Hermitage in St. Petersburg. It is essential that you be very careful not to ever speak about your true mission with anyone, specifically to locate progeny from Rasputin's bastard son Alexei. Ivan Brodsky knows some particulars but not all. Other than him, no one knows of your quest. That inquiry is part one of your mission. But there is another angle, another approach. Let me explain. It demands a high degree of deceit. You will be given a forged letter, to be shown, but *never* to be surrendered. It will falsely be from Patriarch Kirill to initiate a secret investigation from his offices concerning Rasputin and a bid for sainthood. The letter will state that any inquiry about the letter's legitimacy will be denied by the Church for political reasons. The forgery is without parallel. It includes the name of Father Damien whose work has already been leaked by us to the head priest at St. Nicholas. If he sends you on your way, fine. Don't overplay your hand. I think, however, that he will bite and perhaps you will gain an access to what might be known about Alexei. Then again, they may know nothing but this I doubt. Does all of this make sense to you?"

"Of course."

Putin interjected, "Remember one thing Agent Lena, this is all about ascertaining any information about any progeny from this Alexei. If you discover such that will become the third rung on this ladder." Putin then waved his hand forward. Dimitri and she were being dismissed.

One door down the corridor she entered Dimitri's office. He handed her a folder. Later, in her hotel she found detailed instructions among a new credit card, hotel accommodations, airplane tickets, and five hundred $100 bills to be used as needed to secure cooperation. There was a phone. The note said it was totally secure for text messages and was keyed such that the messages could only be sent to Dimitri. If any special requests need to be made they were to be done on this phone only. By the way, it would be best for Ivan to handle the money as his familiarity with the United States was one of his notable assets. After all, money drove Americans. She was to leave Moscow for New York City in two days. She would have diplomatic status.

CHAPTER THIRTY-THREE

Later in the day Augusta drove over to Joanna's safe house, driving along the Great River Road. She crossed the virtually hidden border from Davenport into Bettendorf. The Mississippi River was in a fury, unsettled, almost confused, she thought, under assault from the winds and cold. She accepted Bertrand's suggestion that her driving Joanna to Lady Alexandra's place was a good idea, hoping that Joanna was still in place and not already there. When she was allowed entry to the residence she found Joanna sitting in the living room, arms on a table, head buried, sobbing. Bertrand's professor friend, Mary Bridges, was trying to console her.

Mary, an elderly gaunt woman with a kindly face, turned back to Augusta and said, "Joanna really wants to go to Davenport to visit her friend, Alexandra. I have many reservations about that. She's not quite herself."

"May I speak with her alone, Mary?"

"Ah, of course," she said leaving the room.

Augusta sat next to Joanna and placed her arm around her. Joanna looked up and through her tears smiled, ever so slightly. She said, "I'm a mess Augusta. Mary won't drive me.

I've unsettled her, I'm sure. I won't touch the Xanax again until tonight. I'm not as bad as I seem. Would you be good enough to drive me to her?"

Twenty minutes later the pair of them drove through Alexandra's gate and parked. Augusta noted the presence of another vehicle in the visitor's parking area. She hoped their unannounced visit would not be problematic. Maria allowed their entry and brought them into the kitchen. She said, "She is with a client. Last of the day. I'll speak with her when the client leaves." Augusta thought her to be frazzled, nervous around them. Well, no wonder, after the episode with Eddie Goodkind. They were served coffee and they sat alone, Maria disappearing. From the moment she consented to drive Joanna to their sitting at the table no words had passed between them. There was little doubt in her mind that Joanna was traumatized, talking would probably be counterproductive. Augusta was pleased with her own self-control in the matter.

"So, here are two of my favorite women," the voice came to them before their awareness of her presence. "I'm happy you came. It was a light day for me, three cancellations. The weather." She placed her hand on Joanna's head. Almost instantly Augusta could actually see Joanna's entire persona uncoil, her face relaxing, her body letting go of the stiffness caused by her tension. Augusta, too, began to feel a lessening of the stress of the day. *Amazing* was the thought that flew through her mind.

"I'd like to see each of you, alone."

Augusta nodded appreciatively while Joanna stood up and thanked Alexandra profusely.

"Augusta, if you'd be kind enough to stay here in this

area. Maria is around somewhere. Just pull that cord over there." She pointed to a sash. "It was one feature of this place that I treasured when I bought the house. So old-fashioned," she said smilingly.

Maria did, in fact, return shortly. No cord pulled. Within 20 minutes Augusta observed Maria preparing the tea, then delivering it into the Persian room. Would McAbee consider all of this part of a scam? As she went through this trail of logic she wondered, as she frequently had, did Bertrand believe anything? Was truth for him not truth but degrees of probability? He referred to himself as a monk sometimes, sometimes a stoic, sometimes a handicapper coupled with the comment, 'there's not a sure thing except death.' She loved him but he was a tough customer, a difficult man, intellectually hard-bitten.

They came out soon from the Persian room. Joanna looked as though she had just been to a spa. She went from being slightly elderly to a middle-aged, conditioned athlete. Lady Alexandra, on the other hand, looked preoccupied. Her eyes knit tightly, strained. "Augusta, I need about five minutes. Just go in when you please. I'll be there shortly. Joanna will be fine right here." She left through another door leading away from the kitchen and back deeper into the house.

"Joanna, you look so much better," Augusta remarked.

"Oh I am. Thanks for driving me over here Augusta. Means so much."

When Augusta entered the Persian room she immediately went to the standing lamp near the curtained window across from the table and seats. She explored it, acting the part of an appraiser just on the off-chance that there was a hidden camera or listening device in the Persian room. She was satisfied that there were no bugs in the lamp, knowing that certainty was not possible without a tear down of the lamp. She then sat. The door to the room was opened with a considerable amount of noise. Unusual. Alexandra entered the room and sat across from her. She waited for the request to extend her hand. There was none. Alexandra sat and looked into Augusta's eyes, a scrutiny marked by worry, apprehension, and concern.

Finally, she said with an air of resignation, "I am unable to communicate with you as usual. My mind is unsettled. Some of that involves issues that I'm engaged with, some of it concerns you Augusta."

"I hope that I have not distressed you," Augusta said plaintively.

"No, no. Not directly anyhow. Allow me to talk without interruption." She waited, Augusta nodded slightly in assent. "First, thank you for driving Joanna. She has been beset with terrible encounters. Hopefully we managed to cage some of them. Your help and that of your friend, McAbee, has been generous and beneficial. Now that she is a client of the agency I hope assistance for her continues in a suitable fashion. A worry that she raised with me concerns the events around Eddie Goodkind. First, let me say that I have her permission to raise this issue with you. I try never to divulge information about any session I participate in. Eddie Goodkind climbed the wall, he then hurt Maria when he kicked in the door and snapped the chain and sent Maria for a tumble. He then twisted her arm forcing her toward this room. It was close to these events that Joanna and I came out into the hallway. He was holding a gun, threatening, and demanding that Joanna come with him. Some minor details Joanna did not know. I do because of my conversation with Maria. What she could report on the matter, however, squares with what I have just said. *But* this is where there is concern on her part. She worried that she should not have repeated to you what I said to Eddie. It is true that I told him to leave and the matter would end. If he did not he would not leave the house alive. In a time span of seconds, as he was intent on staying, Eddie Goodkind was dead. Joanna feels that I was betrayed by her as the disclosure to you puts me in a bind, a murderer perhaps. I would appreciate knowing how you processed this information?"

Augusta was preparing herself for this question, aware that it was a natural progression to Alexandra's recital. But as she thought about an answer she could not help but feel that she was being drawn into a complex web. "To be honest with you I was and am perplexed. Firsthand, I know of your gift as a healer. My psoriasis and my breast issues. I have felt the power of your presence, your discernment, and your, to put words to it, psychic abilities. You have overwhelmed me. And so as not to deceive *you* I want you to know that I have discussed these issues with Bertrand McAbee. Joanna's recount of the Eddie Goodkind warning and then his death totally unsettled me. It hints of gifts beyond anything I have encountered or ever heard of except in a movie or television show. I have no doubt that you are a most extraordinary woman. That said, I am still grappling with the Eddie Goodkind issue. But under no circumstances do I see you as a murderer."

"Murders of the innocent. Inexcusable and vile. There

are murders or killings of dangerous and violent people, those who do not heed restraint toward others, justifiable to defend against. Eddie was in this category. You understand that I can detect physical problems in others. Can I say to you that I detected a physical problem in Eddie and I knew that he was in danger if he continued on his course of action?"

"It is possible but unlikely Lady Alexandra. The question for me is this – are you so gifted as to be able to hurt someone? From your mind to the physical world? Bertrand put it to bewitchment, or, he used the word sorcery."

Alexandra, anger in her eyes, snapped back, "No. Sorcery is the invocation of evil spirits, vile entities. I do not do this. Tell your McAbee he is wrong to suggest that," she slapped her right hand on the table, accenting her indignation. "What was done was done Augusta. You should never be fearful or concerned about my mission in life to help others where I can."

Augusta sensed the dodge in what she was saying. She offered an explanation consistent with what Augusta knew of her but it was offered as a way to assuage Augusta's worries. But as Alexandra went on she was implying what she did had self-defense in play. "I'm sure of that Lady Alexandra. After all you are fairly invisible here in Davenport. Bertrand suggested that you might be in hiding precisely because of your gifts or powers. But it's quite obvious that's untrue," she said placing herself midway between McAbee and Alexandra. 'Let the games begin' she told herself.

"I will go on. I mentioned Russia to you. The tea leaves, inescapable. Something is brewing out in the mists. Of that I am sure. It may be beyond my abilities to withstand what is coming. McAbee? He seems to have some considerable insight even as his assertion of sorcery is terribly wrong. But where he is correct I admit. I am in hiding in a way that I do not wish to be obvious, to stand out. I desire obscurity. Why? It's not important to detail that to you. It is interesting that he perceived that. Does he have gifts?"

"Occasionally I think so. He sometimes drifts into a trance of sorts. Very momentarily. Not sure. But if you pressed him about his insight into your desire for obscurity he'd simply say it was a matter of logic."

Alexandra laughed but it wasn't merry. It had disdain attached to it. "Your agency, ACJ. I might be interested in securing your services. Is there some way I can meet your friend and colleague? As I have said I have heard of him in my practice. Not all good. He has some twisted corners."

"I'll run it by him. He finds you intriguing, I'll tell you that."

"As do I him."

CHAPTER THIRTY-FOUR

"I will be seeing off Lena Dzik this morning. A review of things. Anything you wish for me to include in her orders, Vladimir?"

"A few things to make more explicit. If the trail runs cold for her then we let it be. A failure is not on her unless she acts stupidly. She was impressive. But I think that there's an element of fanaticism in her. We would never want her in any politically sensitive position."

"I hope that she can handle, if it comes to be, our deception about Rasputin's sainthood inquiry being supported by Kirill."

"Ah. She's a FSB agent. They are brought up on a web of deceits and lies. She would or should think that she was being insulated by us from a danger. No agent should assume that there is absolute transparency. Lies are either direct falsehoods or deceit cloaked in the withholding of vital pieces of information. Dimitri, you're going soft on me, are you?" he said smilingly.

"Of course not. We are very protective of our own people but ultimately they are dispensable for the greater good of the State. That's another part of any training given to her. Anything else?"

"Yes. This mission is very important to me. Tell her that she is to use whatever force she must. Permission to use *deadly* force, no. But as we both know we will disown her if it comes to her being compromised."

"Yes."

"And her familiarity with America and its ways? Her linguistic skills?" Putin asked.

"An accent, of course. But she is a skilled linguist. Her familiarity with America is so-so. That's why we have the U.N. contact. He's blind to the true, true intent behind this endeavor but not to his obligation to assist her in every way possible."

"Well, then, Dimitri we throw the dice."

Dzik was driven to Sheremetyevo International Airport (SVO) for her flight to JFK, New York. Her diplomatic status made the airport procedures simple. She was seated in first class, much to her delight even as a tinge of guilt passed through her. Was this consistent with communist theory? A cab was taken from JFK to the already booked hotel, the Grand Hyatt, a stone's throw away from the United Nations' complex on the east side of Manhattan. Her first contact was to be Ivan Brodsky from the Russian delegation to the United Nations. He was highly regarded by Dimitri. She was in her room by 2:00 p.m. After a shower and a nap of 45 minutes she called the number for Ivan. He answered immediately. "You are here?"

"Yes." Both of them assumed that listening devices were

omnipresent. There would be no appreciable length to their discourse over their phones. "I'm ready if you are."

"There's a bar there on the mezzanine. I can be there in one hour. I'll find you. Have your winter wear with you."

"Yes," she replied.

Augusta had dropped off a much more relaxed Joanna. Mary met them at the door to her house. It took much longer to get back to Bettendorf because Augusta was concerned about a tail. Was Peter Goodkind, hospital and all, still alert enough to order such or did his brother's death force him to back off? She didn't observe anything of note.

The office doors were locked but Bertrand sat near the entryway after she had called to make sure he was there. She was let in immediately and they proceeded to his office. They hugged, a ritual of necessity for both of them, then sat. She noticed one of his Loeb books open by his recliner. It was green-covered, she couldn't make out the author. She knew he was knowledgeable of both Latin and Greek although he had complained that Greek was becoming a hazard for him. He attributed it to age and not spending enough time with the books.

Lightly, she said, "I see you're reading those old Greeks again. Old, dead white men, I hear my youngest daughter proclaim."

"How about your other daughter, Anastasia?"

"No. No way. She's too sophisticated to utter that kind of crap. Pretty racist thing to say such when you're trying to undo racism."

"I don't care for phrases leading political parades.

They're like train engines hooked up with and pulling 100 cars of dynamite."

"So? What are you reading?"

"Actually, I'm looking through the famous Greek physician Galen. What does he say about healing? Still looking. Lots of volumes by him. Smart man but very limited because of the times he lived in and his being too associated with some of Aristotle's ideas. But Galen can still pack a punch."

Augusta thought to herself that she had better turn to the case or else she might be subjected to a blow-by-blow description of the relationship of Galen to Aristotle. "So Bertrand, I have some news for you." He immediately left his ruminative state and looked at her with curiosity. "I brought Joanna to Lady Alexandra today. Whatever Alexandra does in these sessions, works. Joanna is much better, relaxed. But for how long? I don't know. She's back at Mary's place. No tail that I could see. Mary is a nice woman. But I detect some steel in her. Right?"

"Oh yeah. Mary can be a hardball player. They fooled with her at St. Anselm. Really played games with her from what I could make out. She made an exquisite explosion of fury. They ran for the hills even as they continued to sharpen their nails for a different kind of assassination. When they attacked her again, they lost again but this time she had a fierce Chicago lawyer. The college settled out of court. I don't know how much Mary received from the bastards but let's put it this way, she's not going to be in want. So, yes, Mary is tough. Did she show you her shotgun?"

"What?" Augusta said in surprise.

"That's another part of Mary. Joanna is in good hands," he said nodding his head.

"So, after Lady Alexandra saw Joanna I was asked to stay and meet with her. Of course, I did. Here is the nub of what she said. She realizes that she is capable of healing. She has no doubt, nor do I. She is comfortable with being a psychic, within limits. She will not concede readily to being able to cause harm to others, as in the case of Eddie Goodkind. She dodged me. The dodge was apparent. I believe that she thinks that she has this power but would not own up to it. I mentioned your word sorcery to her. She became very angry and dismissive of you for saying such. But she is quite worried about an impending danger. She might consider becoming a client of ACJ. She wants to meet you. She has heard good and bad of you. She did confirm that she craves privacy, hiddenness by hiding. She was struck by that insight that you had."

"What's your recommendation Augusta?"

"Nothing to lose Bertrand. Could help Joanna. Who knows? Maybe Lady Alexandra could cure you of your skepticism," she said in a cheeky way.

PART FOUR

RUSSIA: ON THE GROUND

CHAPTER THIRTY-FIVE

Ivan Brodsky came up to her from behind. He said, in Russian, "If you go outside the front door, go right about 100 meters, on your right is a small tavern. It's called Together. I will go now, come in five minutes. I will be in the back, left, at a booth, facing towards you. See you then."

She waited for a few seconds, turned around, and didn't see anyone except for a couple three seats away. 'Good' she thought. He's careful.

Brodsky had been given some detailed information about Dzik and her mission. Her picture showed a harsh-faced woman somewhere in her fifties or early sixties. He had heard the phrase on American television and found its mark in her picture, 'resting bitch face'. He figured she'd be worse-looking with an 'active bitch face'. She was profiled as a serious idealist, unscrupulous in her duties as a FSB agent. When on a mission she was obsessive. She had the support of Putin as well as Dimitri himself who had informed him. This last assertion was meant to alert him to be extremely cooperative with her. Other observations about her character indicated that she was a dangerous crow. He knew the score. He would be absolutely careful around her.

She came into the tavern, blowing into her ungloved hands, the heat of the place snatching the cold from her lungs. When she came deeper into the darkened areas he held up his hand, ever so slightly. He observed that her outerwear was inadequate for the winter that New York City was in the clench of.

She sat. He said, "I'm Ivan. I am prepared to assist you in every way I can. Welcome to frigid New York City," he smiled, she didn't.

"This bar? Safe?" she said in low-pitched voice.

'No,' he thought to himself. 'Of course I would bring her to an unsafe place with mega listening devices all through.' Instinctively, he didn't like her. She had as much lightness of being as a toilet bowl of vomit. "Oh yes. Very," he said cheerily into her face of cement.

"How much do you know about my mission?"

Lying, he said, "Enough. I understand that we're to discern what we can about a probable thief. A political escapee from Russia in 1937. Progeny of his who might know of some art thefts from the Hermitage. Demographically, he's long dead but there might be some still living who knew him or about him. The problem is that there is no current information about any progeny of his. His name was Alexei, his mother was named Verlovsky, long, long dead."

"Then you know plenty. You need not know much more," Dzik said, asserting her control over him, "but I will give you a few other particulars. We know he lived in this disgusting city from 1937 on. He was accompanied out of Russia by a young teenager, still alive, named Marta. I interviewed her in Kiev. Quite uncooperative. But what can you expect from escapees? She made one comment that

I found interesting, I think that old witch was enamored of him. She said that he was a healer. That people came to him for such. That is our best lead. He has a parentage that involves the Khylisty movements."

"Ah. Interesting. The great healers who healed by unhealing," he said, again lightly. Did this FSB cow have any sense of humor? *No*, most assuredly, he deduced from her passing from a resting bitch face to a dead bitch face.

"What assets do you have available for this investigation?" she asked in an acid tone.

"I have five people I can utilize. I have been told to avoid any embassy contacts. Is this still true?"

"Yes," just as she said this a young woman server dressed in a black blouse and slacks came to the table.

She asked, "What would you like?"

Brodsky ordered a Modelo, Dzik a glass of water. The waitress looked at her for a few seconds in dismay. She left with a shrug of her shoulders.

"Russian immigrants," Brodsky said, "were particularly drawn to the lower Eastside of Manhattan in those days. Allow me to pass this information along, including his being with a young teenage girl named Marta. We will start to comb the area tomorrow. There are still some there from the old days. But later arrivals and many from the lower Eastside began to drift away from there to Coney Island, the Rockaways, Brighton Beach to name a few. Lot of Russians in New York City area. Surprising."

"I have noticed that you have not taken any notes. Is your memory that good?"

To himself he thought, 'No, my memory is horrid. I have dementia. I can't remember my name or who this horror is who sits across from me.' He said, "Very good. Ask and I will repeat precisely," he said, now not as lightly as before.

His Modelo came. Dzik's glass of water was put down sharply by the waitress who placed the bill on the table. She fled the scene. Probably had a good look at Dzik.

"I will be in my room, 919. Here is my cell number. Encrypted." She said it to him with planned speediness. "I have other business for tomorrow, perhaps a few days. Call me each night at 7:00 p.m. exactly for reports. Emergencies, though, at any time. I cannot emphasize enough the importance of this mission, comrade."

"Understood. We will begin inquiries tomorrow morning. My people will be all over the lower Eastside."

"One more point. Of necessity, I need for you to repeat every detail of importance, including my phone number, now, please?"

There was a part of him that suspected this ploy from her. Fortunately, he had an extraordinary memory. He was pleased with himself as he gave her a two minute recital of what had transpired, including an accurate recital of her encrypted phone number. Having done, she arose immediately and left. At the front door of the tavern she put on her light trench coat. He wished a freezing on the FSB hag.

CHAPTER THIRTY-SIX

McAbee called Lady Alexandra for an appointment. The phone was answered by mild-voiced Maria. He said that he was a friend of Augusta Satin. Maria's response surprised him, "Yes, she was awaiting your call." A time was reserved for later that afternoon. McAbee again read through the vetting report done by Barry Fisk. He was most intrigued by the blank years between her graduation from New York University and her employment with Procter & Gamble. Basically an eight-year void. And then there was Barry's concern about her birth records, suspecting some finagling with the documents. An enigmatic woman with a mystique coursing through her.

Alexandra observed McAbee's Camry pass through the gate, it was 3:00 p.m. She had cleared her calendar for the remainder of the day, convinced that he was somehow a part of the emerging drama around her. He parked and came out of his car very carefully, watchful for wintertime hazards such as black ice. He was observant, quickly eyeing all in front of him. He stopped for several seconds to observe the Mississippi River and then he proceeded to the doorway. Maria would take it from there, showing him into the Persian room. She weighed what she knew of him. There were, to the best of her memory, five clients who had dealt with ACJ. Three of them were hardly supportive. They had been in messy divorces. Each in their own way had felt the wrath of ACJ as it delved into finances, affairs, drugs and other behaviors that could compromise them in either alimony and/or child custody disputes. Two of them were in wonderment and subsequent anger about how some information was acquired. The complaints and fury always led back to the supposedly unscrupulous McAbee. In all three cases, however, she had learned that the wronged women themselves sought the work of investigators. It was obvious to Alexandra that ACJ was just better at the nefarious business.

The other two women were quite positive about McAbee. He had brought resolution to one of them who had her identity stolen. Her ACJ benefactor, the client said, was a strange little man called Barry with a bad gait and poor communication skills. He worked for ACJ. The other was in nothing short of adulation about how McAbee and his firm had handled a dangerous stalker. Somehow he disappeared from her life. How? She didn't know and she didn't care. A strange man named Jack showed up, spoke with her, and then he was never seen again by her. He identified himself as an ACJ investigator sent by McAbee. This client had met McAbee once. She adored him because of what he managed to do. But she ended her recital of the events with the comment that McAbee was a good listener but very hard to read. But he knew how to get things done.

The door to the Persian room was closed. She came up to it stealthily, typical for a first meeting. Noiselessly she opened the door. Simultaneous to that she saw him rising and turning towards her. Surprised at this she said to him, "Kindly sit Dr. McAbee." He did without complaint, not offering his hand to shake. "Please indulge me, sir, close your eyes and give me your hands." He did so. She guessed that he had been coached by Augusta. She had very few men as clients and to a man they never gave ready compliance in offering their hands and closing their eyes.

She held his hands, lots of strength in them for his age. But they included resistance to her. He was creating a wall as she was creating a ladder to surmount it, but as the ladder was extended the wall did also. She decided that it was futile to go on. She released his hands and told him to open his eyes. His graying/blue eyes would hardly allow for any view into this man's soul. He was an arch non-believer to her gifts, she wondered if it was merely skepticism or did he pass over into cynicism. Or at the end of it all was he in denial?

She said, "Your resistance to me is quite strong. Did you gird yourself or is it your normal state?"

"Girded actually. Nice to meet you, by the way. You can call me Bertrand."

She had been given the terms of the coming joust by this man. He was closed up tight but he made one mistake, his fore-knowledge of her presence at the door. She had perfected the art over the years. There was no discernible noise. She was sure. Yet he sensed her, his wall build-up included a sensor for her hiddenness behind the door. So he was a man who had gifts but was not about to display them even as he had unwittingly done so. But on second thought it may have been a purposeful announcement to her. There was a shrewdness to him. A chess player. His statement also manifested a desire to establish some kind of control.

"And I am referred to as Lady Alexandra. But you can call me Alexandra. You have been spoken well of by Augusta. She has schooled you a bit for this meeting. However, I don't see you as needful of schooling. I have had encounters with you through my clients. Not all favorable."

"As I have had of you. Not all favorable."

"May I ask you a question?" He nodded. "Why have we begun in such a… contested manner Bertrand? Are we at war?"

"War? Hardly. But to be totally honest with you, you are an enigma. Augusta Satin is an extraordinary investigator. A woman of high sagacity. A healthy skeptic. She is struck by you, feeling that you possess some amazing powers. A healer, a psychic, and perhaps, a… bewitcher. Three professions floating into somewhat metaphysical tiers, each more into the beyond when tiered upwards. How could I not be impressed when she recounted her experiences?"

Alexandra waited. Did he have more to say? Apparently not. He had a good command of silences. She noted that. "She has been exposed to a very large share of things given our short times together. She has seen what she has seen and has heard about what she has heard. I have made no representations to her beyond explaining what she has seen or heard. You have heard what you have heard but you don't accept me or the world that I inhabit. Do I have it correct?"

After a considerable pause he said, "Yes. That's how I assess things. Augusta, though, tells me of tea leaves and an overarching fear of Russia, the bear of your leaves. To me, that's a stretch beyond logic. I'm not trying to pick an argument with you but surely you see my point."

"Of course. You are not the first to dismiss me as a crank or a charlatan. Because the profession is riddled with insincerity and treachery you then use a broad brush to paint me into these categories. But Bertrand you are wrong. The barriers that you have put up before you ever came here tell me of a man bound up, knotted, by logic. Your type of logic blocks any inquiry into things possible. Fortunately, Augusta is not so hard-bitten as you. There is a chasm between us. You are not prepared to give me any opportunity to explain myself. Your behavior borders on boorishness. Do you see?" This said with a scorching stare at McAbee. "Furthermore, I am not asking for your approbation. You are stuck in the deep mud of your own doing. This meeting is, I thought, about your providing protection for me. But you must take me seriously. If you think me to be a crank then your instructions to your people will be given with your tongue in your cheek. You would provide a disservice rather than a service." She finished, her eyes flashing heat.

McAbee was chastened. She was correct, he came armed to the hilt. "Okay. You're right. I did you a dishonor. I can't experience the things you do or have done..."

She interjected, "Oh no, not so easy Bertrand McAbee. You have gifts. And you know it but you locked them in a safe before you came here. Can you open yourself a bit, anyway?"

He ruminated, concerned that such a departure from logic, could lead him into being a mark. Another Augusta? But that dismissive thought about his best friend caused him to alter directions. Alexandra was scoring points on him by her own use of logic. "Okay. I will try to suspend my skepticism. But that doesn't mean that I can't ask questions of you. I really need to comprehend this fear of Russia that you have. It can't be just based on tea leaves. There has to be more than that. I have questions."

"Yes?"

"I want you to answer me in a field of trust. There must be antecedents precipitating this fear. Nothing that you say will go beyond this privacy between us. Not even to Augusta should you require that. No notes will be kept, no transcriptions, no anything that could possibly be construed as violating what I have just said. You ask me to trust you, I ask the same."

"I will need to consult the leaves. Alone or with you present. After all, I don't want you to have seizures," she said with the slightest of smiles.

He laughed. "No. I think I can handle it. If *I* have to drink the tea also, please just give the slightest bit. I am not a tea drinker."

She looked at him and nodded. Then she said, "No. I understand. Your mother was, though, I can sense."

McAbee felt the first dart penetrate his mind, his Irish mother a tea devotee. He said nothing but felt a jab. Was this a cheap parlor trick?

Ten minutes later, in three mild sips he was down to the required leaf sediment that would allow for the swirl. This carefully dictated by Lady Alexandra who, herself, drank from a full cup.

"So now Bertrand, tilt your cup to where you can allow for the leaves to cluster on the side of the cup." He did as asked. "Tell me what you see," she said softly.

He looked carefully over the scattered leaves, pasted as it were, to primarily one side of the cup. The most obvious vision entailed a fairly large block of leaves that almost made it to representing a rectangle. He told her this. She asked for the cup and looked.

"Ah. This is the very wall you presented when you appeared here. This exercise, however, is mostly to the future. It bespeaks security. Things are safe with you. You see Bertrand? You have passed the first test. Now I'll do mine."

She swirled the leaves in her cup. He watched her long and steady fingers do something that had to be long practiced. She studied her cup and then said, "A bird. Upward flight. A profound statement about the matter. I will trust you to the extent that my Russian soul allows. Ask your questions."

For some reason, not quite sure but it concerned the element of trust, he did not ask to see her cup. "You are Russian. Do you speak it?"

"Da."

"Your mother was Estonian. But a Russian by orientation?"

"I see. You have unearthed things about me already. That would take some skill. This from that short man my client referred to? This Barry?"

"Yeah. He's quite good. You're not as hidden as you think."

"Yes and no Bertrand. Continue your verifications."

"She was a single mother in a time when there was a lot of social condemnation for such. Your birth records are scrambled."

"So, you know everything, explain," she said with a mild consternation.

"The name Speranskya was given to you. Not your mother's name, Haamer. If that's important to this I need to know why there was a switch. The inference is that it was your father's name?"

"My God! No! So your small man is not all he's put out to be. Hah! My mother had a great love for her mother's mother. Her grandmother. That's the name given to me. And to further the concealment it is the maiden name for her grandmother. A tribute."

"So, why the subterfuge?"

"It really wasn't, as far as I could ascertain. My mother was a Russian Estonian in New York City. Trust is hard for Russians given our history. Add to that an uncertain land. But you need to know more. My father."

The pause in her recital caused him to stare at her face. Was there a tear in her eyes? An anomaly in such a hard woman. He said slowly and gently, "Your father."

"My mother, Liisa Haamer, found out that he was a cad of a man. Dangerous and vicious, midway through her pregnancy. She was determined to create a chasm between him and me. She turned out to be prescient. A vile man. An abuser. He died outside of our apartment in upper Manhattan. But only after he had, drunk as usual, sexually accosted my mother, but also me when I was not even bodily ready for him." She breathed heavily. She had never shared this story with anyone, there was relief but also apprehension about McAbee. Was he a good man? She recalled Augusta and the leaves and came to terms with what she had said.

"This man. Russian too?"

"Yes," assiduously guarding from McAbee the name Raspin that the predator had clarified for her as being short for Rasputin, he the son of one of the greatest figures of the 20th century, he would proclaim. McAbee didn't need to know this. She had already allowed him to get under her guard.

"Your school records? You were precocious."

"My mother saw achievement at school as the portal for success in this country. I was also innately bright. I was noted as such by my teachers. You have my school records?"

"Your mother? How did she manage? Those had to be tough times for both of you."

"She was a very expert seamstress. She took in jobs." She would not disclose her mother's occasional sexual encounters when need required such. McAbee was nosy.

"So you went to NYU. A marvelous record there. My man, Barry, says that you could have gotten in anywhere, graduate school. Business?" He stopped short.

"I did get into business. Almost eight years."

"That cannot be deduced from your records. You basically disappeared. Were you in Russia?"

"No. Russia? Please! But Russian, yes. I was involved in a business that was off the books. A manager. For Russians in New York this was not uncommon. A fear of governments and a detestation of taxes. No more needs to be said except that besides illegality there was the overlay of violence. This enterprise was shut down in a single day and the owner fled to Europe. I have not heard from him since. While I was at NYU I had been offered a job from Procter & Gamble. A translator in Eastern Europe, especially where Russian was used. When the business ended I reached out to them and

I was immediately employed. My mother had died in the meantime."

"So you went to Russia?"

"Oh yes. Also to Lithuania, Belarus, Latvia, Ukraine, and others to where Russian was used."

"Is that the cause of your concern about Russia? Something from that experience?"

"No. Nor do I think it relates to my previous off-the-books job," she answered very firmly. "Of that I am not totally positive," she added.

"Okay. So you leave Procter & Gamble and come out to Davenport. On the face of it there doesn't appear to be a context. The choice doesn't follow the arc of your life if I might say."

"Now you once again have placed your logic against inspiration, my gifts, and my desire to become obscure."

"I don't understand."

"And knowing you, you may never. On the other hand, you may know all too well. I will explain but it involves tea leaves and a cruise. There was a service operator on the Mississippi River. When I left P&G, I felt that I needed a vacation. I contracted for a barge trip from south of Minneapolis to Vicksburg, Mississippi. Obviously we passed through many cities and towns along the way. Most were small towns but there were others that had significant size. There were four that struck me. I researched them when I got off the barge in Vicksburg. It came down to two. The Quad Cites and St. Louis. The tea leaves and my coming to this area for several weeks decided me. So I bought this marvelous place."

"You used the word *obscure*. I would choose the word

hiding. Why hide? I don't understand that and yet I think it is related to your apprehension about Russia," he said in a speculative manner.

"Good. But your logic has blind spots. You see Bertrand I already knew, for years, about my gifts. I could heal by touch or simply observation. Not all the time as such frequently requires at least a tacit consent from the other. But I could and did. I also saw things that others didn't or couldn't. It was noticed by some. I realized that this could put me on public platforms. Attention. I did not want that. I did not want my life to be exposed. So I went in this direction. Lady Alexandra. I make a satisfactory living, I have investments, but also live pretty obscurely. I decline public notice."

"Still not sure about these choices. And Russia? Fear? There has to be more to this."

"Of course there is. But I will be sparse with what I tell you, for in knowing you yourself might come to danger. To use your word, poorly selected but I'll allow – I *can bewitch*. Eddie Goodkind was not the first. My father was!"

McAbee was taken aback by this disclosure. Was Alexandra mad? If she was, it was difficult to discern it. Carefully he said, "Go on."

"You must see my concerns. I could be pictured to be a dangerous person. If any of this came out, my life would be a catastrophe. For some I could be seen as someone to weaponize. I can't have this Bertrand."

"I understand your concerns if not your powers. But, again, where does your concern with Russia fit into any of this?" He persisted sensing that Alexandra had pulled back away from him, just slightly, her back stiffening a bit.

"The answers to your question are my powers that you

are unwilling to admit to. But one way or another I'm quite sure that the bear, Russia, is stalking. I'm not quite sure why. But it is."

"Why would they give a damn about you? It has been years since your foray into that business with P&G and Russia?"

"I had other business with a different Russian," she said mysteriously.

"I feel that you do not want to open up about this with me."

"Yes. You are correct, Bertrand, not at this time anyway. It is a secret that I think is unknowable. Your communications guru, the man who doesn't communicate well, would never be able to discern this secret. Let us end this part of the discussion. It has to stay within me at this time."

"One more question?" She nodded. "If I was told a name would I see your point?"

"Very good. The answer is most assuredly."

"I'll let it rest there. I fully appreciate the confidences that you shared with me."

"The answer to your next question is yes."

Bertrand was surprised. He hadn't asked the question that was on his mind. "Excuse me?"

"You may share with Augusta what I have said. That man, Jack, also. After all, I wish to become a client of your firm."

Bertrand laughed. "Well, you are beginning to get under my defenses. My walls as you say. But you do it by sapping not climbing."

"Your walls are too high Bertrand. But maybe someday you will let me through."

"I will talk this over with Augusta and yes, as you anticipated some of this with Jack Scholz. If I am correct he will want to come out here by necessity."

"Thank you sir."

Alexandra watched McAbee walk toward his car. The scarf that he had placed around his neck had not been tucked properly into his overcoat. One piece flopped around, at least two feet outward into the wind. He stopped again to look at the great river. There was a quality that they shared. Was it muddy and dark or wild and turbulent? Maybe both?

CHAPTER THIRTY-SEVEN

The bearded priest, Father Leonid of Saint Nicholas Church in Brighton Beach, came out to the visitor parlor, his pallid and suspicious face catching Lena with a stare perfected in some horrid monastic setting. She had to be careful with this maggot priest. She led into her prepared opening at full gallop. "I have a letter for your consideration. I am prepared to show it to you but you must consent to give it back to me after you have read it. Total deniability is essential given the nature of the matter."

"On the phone you said that you represent the Patriarch Kirill. Accordingly, I cancel a meeting to accommodate you. Now you present some restraint on me. I don't understand what it is that you are about. Just hand me your letter. I will read it and I will give it back. Then I will consider my options," he said sternly.

She thought of the pleasure that it would bring to her to place an electric prod on this robed bastard's genitals as she handed him the forged letter from Patriarch Kirill. She reminded herself that this was a very chancy ploy.

He took it from her, just short of a grab, and then reached inside his robes for a pair of reading glasses, placing them on the tip of his overly large nose. He seemed to have read it ten times before he looked up at her. He then went to a desk in the parlor and withdrew a powerful-looking magnifying glass. He studied the letter, the paper, the ink and whatever else his slinky mind conjured up. Finally, he said to her, "This is so out of the norm that I must wonder about this. And you? What is your story?"

She held her hand out for the return of the letter. He shook his head back and forth, violating the terms of the agreement between them. Apparently he thought he was in a power position and could do so. "Our conversation ends if the letter is not given back to me immediately."

"I will determine that," he said defiantly.

"Let me make something very clear to you. I am a special agent to the Patriarch. He has demanded that I pursue Grigori Rasputin's sainthood credentials. An extraordinary amount of work has already been given over to this effort in Russia. Father Damien had led that effort. In his research he found mention, I don't know the details, of progeny here in the United States. This could prove to be problematic if true. Your church has been on the vanguard for Rasputin's sainthood. Patriarch Kirill does not want to be compromised in any way. He feels that Father Damien has gone as far as he can. Thus, I am here. We are on the same side, Father. But I demand the letter back into my possession immediately."

"And if I walk out of here with it?"

"You won't," she said tersely.

"Excuse me?" He got up. Dzik had been assessing him from the start of the meeting. Not a young man, he moved slowly but with the clear intent to leave the parlor with the letter in hand. In one fluid move she grabbed his robe's flap at the arm, leveraged his weight and sent him to the floor. He held the letter even more tightly in his hand as he growled out a curse at her. With a well-practiced judo chop on his wrist he surrendered the letter. She stood over him. "Now we either cooperate or I leave, if I leave I report the incident to the Patriarch Kirill personally as I will be back in Moscow shortly. Dishonesty from a priest of God is abhorrent," she said in full disingenuousness.

Slowly, he got up using the arm of a chair for aid. He then sat. Nothing was broken but he was astonished at how adroit she was. It wasn't out of the question that she was employed by Kirill. She probably was so but he couldn't be positive. He said, "Just what is it that you want from me?"

"As I said Father, I want to know if you have any information about progeny here in America that flows back to Grigori Rasputin. It's not complicated."

Close to the same time Ivan Brodsky's team spread out across the lower east end of Manhattan. The age group that they were most interested in was the elderly. Each member of the team was provided with adequate cash to facilitate cooperation. Helena called him at 2:30 p.m. She requested his immediate presence. She's pretty sure that she has a hit, she reports jubilantly. He can't believe his luck, if true. Anything to rid himself of the FSB cow. He quickly taxied down to Third Street and Second Avenue. He stood in front of a well-worn seven story hotel that had been given over to the mission of assisted care. He entered the facility and found Helena sitting at the side of a grungy lobby. On a stained old couch with Helena was an old woman. Eighties? But he noted that she and Helena were having the best of times together. Marvelous Helena who could coax secrets from graveyard tombs. Helena rose and greeted him, always deferential, the best trait any woman ever could possess. He was cheerily introduced by her to April Wenger who happily matched up perfectly with Helena. They were both extroverts, cheerful in disposition and ready to help.

"So Mrs. Wenger, excuse me, April, I should say," Helena began, "You knew of a man called Alexei?"

"Ah yes," Wenger came into the conversation with a loud and high-pitched voice. Ivan felt as though a saw was cutting across his throat. "I think that I know this man that Helena had been talking about. A long time ago. Late 1960s, early 70s. I was in my early 20s, when I met him. I was a hippie to end all hippies," she proclaimed with a loud laugh, "I was quite a thing to behold. My father had fallen quite ill. We only lived five blocks from here. He had a virus of some sort. Really sick. Lost weight, seemed like a pound a day. We were poor. No health insurance or anything like that. I was afraid for him. My mother had taken off for California with some asshole long before he got sick. I was doing all sorts of drugs, you must know." Ivan listened to her and hoped that April Wenger was not taking him and Helena for a prolonged ride to nowhere. "So there were a lot of neighborhood creatures around this section of the city, still are. There was some innocence about me as I asked around about my father's illness. A grocery man, ran a small grocery store on the corner, long gone now office building in its stead, told me of a man called Alexei. He had secret powers, yes, that is what he called them – secret powers. This shopkeeper was Russian. He had a thick accent but he meant well I think. But you can never tell with Russians."

Thank God he and Helena spoke with only barely noticeable accents. "So I ask him how do I find this man and how much does he charge? He'd find him for me. Come back the next day, same time. Sure enough he's there. Oh my God was he a fright to see."

Ivan cut in. "April this is very important. There is a large estate that has come open and his name is on it somehow. If you can help us determine that this is the man we're looking for, I know he's dead of course, I can give you a reward."

"That's mighty tempting. My whiskey supply is thinning out."

"So you said he was a fright to see? How so?" Ivan asked.

"Well, he had a beard down to his chest. Had a wild look in his eyes and boy did he take me in. A leer that could take in a whorehouse of 50 girls. My cutoffs were up to my ass and I had a nice large rack. He was pretty much salivating. I saw him nod to the grocery man. Like *thank you*." She laughed again.

"So did he visit your father?"

"Yup. Visited me too on the kitchen floor. Payment you know. Might have gotten the clap from him but not sure, I was no nun in those days."

"Your father? What happened?"

"Well this Alexei starts some kind of strange chant. Gibberish. May have been Russian. Who knows? Then he commands me to get some cooking oil, salt, and a spoon. He does some kind of service. What do I know? After it my father naps and we cut the deal."

"Cut the deal?"

"I thought I just told you. I'm on the kitchen floor being

mauled by the son-of-a-bitch. Well, at least he didn't cost me anything."

Ivan was surprised that April Wenger was still alive given her lifestyle and attitudes. "Did you ever see him again?"

"Oh yes. One of those denizens who hung around here. But I found out that he had a reputation for being a healer. My father, by the way, he got better soon after Alexei worked on him. But, two years later he had a fatal heart attack. I headed off for Frisco and stayed out there till I came back in 1985. No. I never saw the guy again if that's what your question is."

"The grocery man. Did you know anything about him? Kids, wife?"

"He had a son. I think he took over, or was supposed to. Don't know anything about a wife. The son's name is Maksim. Strange one then and stranger still now."

"Now?"

"Yeah. He lives here. Up on the sixth floor. Maksim Yetashandshaky or some screwed-up Russian name that never ends. By the way, Helena, how come you stopped talking?"

"Oh," she laughed, "Ivan is the boss and he's the very best at what he does." Helena turned toward Ivan and gave him a big wink and smile. Ivan said to himself, 'That one is pretty damned talented, she'll probably become my boss one of these days.' True to his word he gave two $100 bills to April Wenger. Now to find Maksim, but first to call Dzik. She might want in on this. He reached her right away. She listened to his very abbreviated story.

She said, "Don't move from there. I'm in a cab coming back to the Hyatt. I want to be in on this. Address?"

He gave it and he, Helena, and April sat in the lobby awaiting the Bolshevik.

CHAPTER THIRTY-EIGHT

Father Damien was in his apartment. Night had fallen in Moscow along with a fresh snowfall of six inches. He was rereading some Turgenov stories of the Russian hinterland. A text blipped on his phone. It was from Father Leonid, the controversial head priest of St. Nicholas in Brighton Beach, New York. Damien had dealt with him on several occasions. Patriarch Kirill thought him to be a pest but someone to keep an eye on. The text read, [Can you call me on a safe line? Urgent!] Damien's eyebrows flew up as he shook his head. He muttered, 'Safe line? Are you mad?' That still, he would call and hopefully Father Leonid would realize that everything said would have to be cryptic.

Father Leonid responded to the call, "Yes. Thanks for calling back. Are you safe?"

That was coded, the 'safe' being an inquiry about the security of his phone. Damien replied, "How can I be safe when we have a half of meter of snow on the ground!" he said lightly hoping that Leonid would understand.

He did. "About our request for a consideration for Rasputin's sainthood. A parishioner of great importance and wealth requests a status report. I understand that you have shown an interest of late."

Damien was upset. How did Leonid find out about his inquiries? Only a select circle knew that Putin had put him to an investigation. However, his queries at St. Sergius and the Lavra in Kiev were probably leaked to him. Carefully, he responded, "Well Father Leonid there was some interest in exploring this matter. So, it was entrusted to me to look into the question. I did and it is now shelved for the moment. There is no active investigation going on at present."

"So if I told you that a woman who works for Patriarch Kirill came to me a bit ago with some official letter furthering the probe into Rasputin's life, especially a questionable part of his life, what am I to believe? She would not allow me to keep the request letter and if I asked Kirill he would deny that any probe was on, she says. She had the odor of KGB all over her."

Damien knew that indiscretions had already occurred in the conversation. He did not think that Kirill would support any further investigation of Rasputin without it going through his office. Furthermore, no woman worked for Kirill who did investigations that would entail engaging with the likes of an arch-conservative priest such as Leonid. And if ever there was such an investigation, this very conversation proved that it was false. The Russian Orthodox Church a mighty bastion against women inserting their noses into Church affairs? "I am not aware of any such person. Her name?"

"Lena Destoya. A Ukrainian, accent off just so slightly, at least that's who she said she was."

"I know of no such person." Now with full duplicity he

said, "She may be an American spy playing some kind of game with you. I would be careful with her but maybe you should play along and see what comes of it." American my ass, he thought. This is FSB all the way. Probably right up to Putin. Kirill would never be behind what Father Leonid was exposed to.

"Thank you." Leonid ended the call.

Damien went to his recliner, a glass of vodka in hand, and sat. He was trying to fathom what was going on. What was Putin's motivation if, in fact, he was behind the subterfuge? What was the hidden agenda? Why would he be left out in the cold?

CHAPTER THIRTY-NINE

Adam was the first to arrive. He was sent for, and as usual, not asked about his plans. What could he do? Putin had good alcohol too. He wondered, as he poured himself a large glass of vodka on ice, if he was going to have to endure another session on genetics, character, and special attributes. Maybe not. He knew, from the quick and judgmental glances from his old friend, Vladimir Putin, that he was concerned with his drinking. Putin only knew half of it. Adam had made a conscious decision two years ago to advance his death through alcohol. The world became too dark for him. What better way than to be perennially half-drunk every hour of the day except for his spotty and bedraggled sleep patterns. So, he sat awaiting the coming meeting.

Doors open and in come Vladimir and Dimitri. He, and these two, friends from early childhood, now ending up at the top of the heap. They breathed the air of power, lived off of it, protected it as if it were gold bullion. And yet at the end of it, futility. Vladimir had become a gangster and the regime a mafia. Russia stood for nothing but pretended to represent something. Putin's Russia could cause more disruption than any other country in the world, assassinations, cyber warfare, tyrant supporters, sport cheaters, whatever would cause the Kremlin to be recognized and feared for what it was – a nasty child with an ingrained inferiority complex among the great nations of the world.

But Dimitri and Vladimir, they were his very best friends. He would never desert them, warts and all. He arose from the couch unsteadily greeting the pair with a raised glass.

Putin said to him, "Easy on the vodka, Adam. I need your brains for this session. There is a match for your brilliance. Maybe he's even smarter than you. I don't think he drinks!" he said not warmly. Dimitri laughed, always intent on protecting the friendships from fraying. Putin hit a button on the side of his desk, he said, "Show in Dr. Wilosky."

Wilosky was surprised. He knew Putin, of course, and Dimitri, the great provider for all things needed. But who was the other? Wild-looking but with calculating and intelligent eyes.

Putin came forward; there were introductions. Adam was the name given for the third man. All four of the men sat on a squared setting, each with their own couch. "So, you have news for us Dr. Wilosky," Putin said.

"I do. First off. The scientific evidence for traits other than physical being passed through DNA is firmer than ever. How deep this goes is the question. The research from India has been confirmed."

"Give me an example," Adam asked abrasively.

"Let me propose, learning languages."

"Nyet. That can be explained by brain passages. Areas

of the brain that have been activated. That's physical. You must understand I am a materialist. There is nothing else."

"I beg to differ. Another example. Healing has been demonstrated in Indian research."

"What the hell is healing? Nothing but psychosomatic interactions. How to explain the placebo effect found in almost all drug efficacy tests? People get *cured* by suggestions that a drug is efficacious even though they have just swallowed a sugar pill and whatever crap they put into the placebo pill. We don't need to get into metaphysics to explain a brain function. Hocus pocus. Vladimir, this is pseudo-science," he took a huge gulp almost emptying his glass, ice tingling faintly.

Wilosky shot back at him, "No one is suggesting metaphysics. Not necessarily, but some might argue otherwise. The fact remains that placebos can heal people. Instead of pills why not hands? Suggestion the key."

"Go on," Adam said with a slight concession to the scientist. He was placated that metaphysical explanations were not necessarily being advocated by Wilosky.

"Harder to explain, of course, are psychic abilities. These phenomena are totally validated. Many examples."

"Lucky guesses?" Adam responded.

"Specificity is the cornerstone of my argument. If I merely say that an airplane will crash this year there is an absolute truth to this occurring, anywhere from a small one seater to a passenger jet. It's meaningless, akin to saying that someone will die today. However, if I say that X will die in a motor accident, tomorrow, outside of Moscow at 2:00 a.m.? That's quite a different thing. Harder to explain when it occurs. Do you remember that Michael fellow in

St. Petersburg? He was able to recreate crime scenes, find bodies. The police there used him regularly. Then he died, the skills died with him. Regardless of metaphysics, the ability is there. The Indian research has multiple examples of the trait being passed on to children. We have anecdotal evidence but because of people like you, sir, scientists are afraid of studying the phenomena. Reprisals!"

"While you're at it I suppose you're going to suggest some form of telekinesis. Magic!"

"There are data for this power."

"Telesuggestions. The evil eye. Curses. Tricks that can be played on weak minds. Superstition."

"You are a philosopher with a pre-set mind. Mystery is alien to you. It will always be. We can waste time here arguing all day. There was a period that I passed through that found me on your side of the argument. Now I feel it's immature, binding, blind."

"Ah." Adam went to the sideboard and filled his glass. No ice this time.

"Other things Mr. President," Wilosky went on, "We have numerous proteins available relative to Rasputin. Your allowance for the removal of a dot from the note found in that dead woman's dwelling? Absolute certainty it was from Rasputin himself. I have studied his life very carefully. I have no doubt that he sired that child by her. I have only the tiniest of doubt that Rasputin had some very special powers and I feel that it was very likely these could have been passed onto his son. An answer to your specific request, President Putin."

Adam snorted, "Bah!"

Putin arose, "Dr. Wilosky, thank you." He turned to Adam, "Adam, you are free to go right now."

When only Putin and Dimitri remained, Dimitri was asked, "Thoughts?"

"A difficult session. I appreciate Wilosky. He's a hard scientist. Adam is a philosopher. The odd thing is that they agree on much until it involves a jump into genetics," Dimitri said.

"I am more than convinced that this can be settled if we can find progeny from this son of Rasputin."

"I have more on this."

"Oh?" Putin said.

"Our play with this priest Leonid in New York? It has been foiled."

"How?" Putin said gruffly.

"After Lena made her request the priest tried to abscond with the letter. She had to wrestle it away from him. She got it back but she put a bit of a hurt on him, physically and psychologically. Those robed morons are not used to women using judo. He had been alerted to Father Damien's inquiries about Rasputin and sainthood. Leonid contacted Damien about Lena. Phone. We have it in entirety. Father Damien told Leonid to steer clear of any cooperation with her. I called her and told her to step away from that approach. She was outed, I fear."

"Damn Damien! We will ruin him at the proper time. What about the other angle?"

"Last I heard there is some promise there. I'll keep you informed."

CHAPTER FORTY

Lady Alexandra went back to the Persian room. She needed alone time. She had just endured the likes of a man she had never encountered before. He had been sent by Bertrand McAbee. An investigator for ACJ. If McAbee had been a wall, this one, Jack Scholz, was a far-off planet. Never to be reached in the next few centuries, she conjectured. She wondered what McAbee had told him about her. His questioning about threats was demanding and obtrusive. When she said it was based on unusual vibes from her various skill sets he gave her looks as arched as a gothic cathedral. But he never challenged her. He listened carefully and then told her that she had multiple vulnerabilities. If she had time, he could seal up the house and grounds to cover 95% of her weaknesses, pointing out that in this business 100% was a pipe dream. The more she listened to him the more she felt that she was listening into the American National Security Agency or the Central Intelligence Agency. Even with her gifts this man would be a dangerous enemy.

"So, Mr. Jack, there is one room that is off-limits to you. Please follow me." She brought him into the Persian room. "This is my place of business. My operating room as

I could put it. No intrusions. No devices. No entry. Do you understand? Do you accept this?"

He was taking in the room with great care. He said, "Behind the lamp, then the curtain there is a window to the outside. That's a high vulnerability. Can I at least work on the outside of it?"

"No. It must be left as it is right now. To ease your mind it is locked from the inside. But, no, no work there."

"Fine, 90% coverage," he said acidly.

"Yes, 90%. I'll take that," she said.

Arrangements were made. He said that two others would be on the grounds. It would take a day, maybe two, starting today, soon. There would be cameras all over the property, almost impossible to spot, latest in spyware.

She felt that she had taken a bath in a tub of ice cubes. She hoped that when he was finished she would never see him again.

CHAPTER FORTY-ONE

Some traffic delays later, Lena Dzik arrived at the assisted care building. The driver told her that she was one nasty bitch after she refused to tip him. She just shrugged thinking that he got hurt more than she did in the exchange, she familiar with insults, he apparently unfamiliar with being stiffed. Pakistani scum.

She walked through the doors of the facility and quickly saw Ivan, a woman of about 25, cute and fashionable, Helena she would learn. Then an old lady with large earrings, a blonde mop of hair, a face full of rouge and powder, and with enough lines on her face and neck to fill a geometry textbook. She hoped against hope that this old shrew wasn't the source of the supposed breakthrough that Brodsky had hinted at.

Ivan, too cheery and loose, got up. He welcomed Lena, introduced Helena and then April Wenger, a spent item. Did Ivan pass any money to this creature?

Dzik noticed that Wenger recoiled a few inches when she sat across from her, wondering what the old woman had against her.

Ivan seeing all this silent brew of tension spoke about

what April Wenger had said to him and Helena who herself sat in silence.

Dzik said, "So, you are a fountain of wisdom April?"

"And who the hell are you?" Wenger shot back instantly disliking the foreigner with the noticeable accent.

"I'm Lena. Don't get angry at me. I'm just here as a friend."

"Is that right? Friends like you, scowl and all, I don't need."

"Ah. Excuse me for a moment," as she squeezed out a five percent smile and simultaneously bent her index finger back and forth toward Ivan. A private session.

They removed themselves to about 20 feet from Helena and April Wenger. Harshly Dzik whispered, "What does this old goat have for us?"

He told her and also included some history about April and Maksim who lived upstairs in the building. That was the key to what April had reported, he concluded.

"Did you give her any money for that?"

"I did. $200." He saw her wince. He also saw in her eyes frustration, as she briefly bit down on the lower left side of her lip. He calculated that she was unable to leave well enough alone as she went back toward April Wenger.

"So, you have been given money and this is all you have? You gulled my friend here and took his money? What else do you know?"

Ivan thought that Dzik, the ultimate Russian bureaucrat and FSB tyrant, was going to meet her match with this American hippie from another era. He winked at Helena who raised her eyebrows slightly. She was onto this coming drama.

"Listen to me Lena or hyena whatever the fuck your name is, you can go straight to hell! The more I listen to you the more I hear Stalin or one of the goofs who succeeded him. So stay out of my space! This is my home, my building. Keep it up and I'll call the cops you belligerent bull-faced ass."

Dzik froze, her eyes bulging. In the real Russia, April Wenger would have been brought down to some prison and they would have beaten her to within an inch of her life. She looked over at Ivan who seemed to have a slight smile on his lips. She'd have a go at him in the future if she had a chance. "Go buy yourself some cheap wine or dope you old used-up wretch," Lena said now moving out toward the information desk after she told Ivan to leave Helena in the lobby.

Ivan requested the room for Maksim while using the mashed up last name roughed up by April. It was close enough, 603. The man at the desk had a whimsical look on his face. They entered the elevator that trembled as it crawled upwards. Dzik said nothing but he could feel dark mold coursing over the divide between him and her. They went to the door of 603. Dzik knocked. A booming voice shouted, "Yeah! Come in."

Dzik gasped involuntarily. The apartment was a disaster. Maksim was a hoarder. Dzik remembered sitting in the embassy in Kiev a few years ago. The ambassador, drunk as usual, had on a television show from the USA that he wanted everyone to see. It was about hoarding. Some obese woman from somewhere in the American South was being spoken with by her friends who had come to tell her that she was out of control. They called it an intervention. The camera flitted around the house. Everyone in the Embassy was laughing hysterically at the stupid American and then, by logical extension, stupid Americans. At first, Dzik smiled a bit, she not given to laughter. Then she was revolted. This was a show about zoos, captured denizens being gawked at by self-righteous others. In reality, such a woman should be publicly whipped, brought to a barracks, chained to a wall, hosed down daily and given one piece of bread a day. Hoarding would stop and she'd lose weight in addition.

And this Maksim? Well, he was huge. His place was without a visible empty piece of floor. Papers, magazines, old boxes, rags, food cartons. An odor from hell. And there he sat behind a desk filled with junk up to two feet high except for about a foot of open space where Maksim could peer out at Lena and Ivan.

"Who are you? What do you want? And no, I'm not cleaning up. If that's your agenda get out now," his voice near a scream. He then reached into his desk drawer, a squeal from wood harshly scraping wood. Watching Maksim's shoulder Ivan noticed that he pulled something out, the suggestion of a weapon.

Dzik whispered into Ivan's ear, "You try first." Ivan figured that Dzik was not used to dealing with American exceptionalism at its most exceptional, probably knowing that she might get both of them shot because of her pissy arrogance.

Ivan said, still less than two feet into the apartment disaster zone, "We've come for information. Your memory of the past."

"Money," Maksim held out his hand from between the stash of papers on either side of his desk.

"May I come forward?"

"Yes. Only you. Not her. Evil eye there."

266

Ivan almost fell twice as he ventured across the ocean of garbage. He held out a hundred dollar bill. Maksim grabbed it and put it below the desk, out of sight.

"Ask your question."

"I just spoke with April Wenger. She said you'd remember. Allow me to explain." He recounted April's story about her father and the healer named Alexei. There was a long silence.

"My father was a good friend of his," his voice softening considerably. "They would go down to the bathhouses on Sundays. Massage. Then they get laid by some Irish girls. Sunday nights they'd get drunk. Two would-be kings."

Ivan said, "It's Alexei that we are seeking out."

Maksim held out his huge hand. Ivan was able to get a better look at him as the sun behind Maksim was hidden by a cloud. It also helped that the window hadn't been cleaned since being put in ages ago. He was all facial hair, unkempt, food stains and particles popping up, wedged into coiled places, a Brillo pad on steroids. There was an elongated arc of beard that went from ear-to-ear. His brown eyes were hidden a bit by his cheeks that seemed to reach upwards giving his face a scrunched look. His hand then went into quick finger-grabbing, going back and forth. He wanted more money. Ivan was distracted. There was a more pervasive odor than at the doorway. It was from Maksim. He smelled like gorgonzola cheese. Cheese was one thing, Maksim was another. What Maksim was physically Lena was spiritually. What a horrible day! "More money?" he asked.

"Now you're cooking."

He placed another hundred into his lurching hands.

He wanted to look back at Dzik but didn't dare. He asked, "Alexei, they say he was a healer. Any truth to this?"

"Alexei – hah! My father who hated everyone loved that man. When Alexei died it broke his heart. Healer? A lot more than that. My father said he could literally take pneumonia or tuberculosis right out of a person. Yeah, he was a healer. Big league."

"One might ask if that was true why wasn't he working at a major hospital like Presbyterian or Sloan-Kettering? A famous healer. Makes no sense."

"Yeah, well it does. He was a very scared man. He didn't ever want to be made public. My father would say that someone, somewhere, was after him."

"You said he died. Where? How?"

Again, the motion of grabbing fingers. It would be useless to barter. He figured that by now Dzik was sharpening a pair of hedge cutters to cut poor Maxsim's balls off. He didn't look back. He withdrew another hundred dollar bill and placed it in the yearning paw.

"Alexei fell down a flight of stairs way up in Manhattan. How do I know this? It was my birthday. My father's address and phone number was in Alexei's pocket. There was a small birthday cake in the fridge for me. When they called my father with the news, he went to the kitchen table and wept. He took a cab up there. The body was at a hospital. When he was leaving I remember to this day what he said to me. 'Eat your own fucking cake!' Can you believe that? Me on my birthday. Broken neck, Alexei."

"Year?"

"1980. November third."

"You wouldn't know the address where the accident occurred, would you?"

"I throw nothing away. There are my father's papers. I have them but I'm not positive there is anything relating to Alexei's death. We can look. That will cost you $300 since I'd have to go downstairs. Not a desirable task."

Dzik screamed. "That's enough you fat fuck! You've been given too much money already."

"Get out of here both of you!" he screamed back, reaching down toward his lap or somewhere. A gun?

Ivan was calculating the matter. Dzik was a fool. Maksim was a money grabber, but not a teller of tales. He was confident that Maksim was a truthful man, as long as you kept inserting money into his greedy hands. If he had more information it could well satisfy Dzik's request. Another scream from Maksim who was reaching for a landline phone. Cops, just what was needed to make this a catastrophe. He stepped to the side of the desk in case fat-assed Maksim did have a weapon, giving him a clear shot at Dzik. He held his hand up to her and said to Maksim as he was pulling out three $100 bills. "Here's the money. Let's not get too excited." In the first sign of some emotion other than sullen anger he saw her face flush. A true communist! She had money obsessions to such an extent that she could have lost the best possible lead they would ever have. Oh sure, in Russia they could beat it out of Maksim. Forget it here though, forget it.

Maksim got up, a huge effort as he moved out from behind the desk. When he came close to the door, he pointed at Lena Dzik. "One word from her, you'll never get anything."

"Understood," Ivan said, not looking at Dzik. He hoped his career at the United Nations was still alive, her mean-spiritedness and vindictiveness reflected in her face. At least, for now, she backed off. The reek from obese Maksim was overpowering. He wanted to send Maksim and Dzik down in the elevator together, himself absent, as he hopelessly knew there was no way to pull it off.

They went to the cellar in the bumpy and turtle-speed elevator. He noticed that Dzik almost had sex with the back wall of the contraption, as far from Maksim as possible. Ivan wondered if dry cleaning would succeed in getting the stink from his clothes. Doe-eyed Helena would never see him in the same light if she came near him.

The cellar was composed of closets, each matched to a room number. Maksim said, "I have four of these. Deals. Need more." He pointed toward one of them, "But this closet is the storage area that would have things from my father. Give me room," he said as he opened the closet. Glad to give the obese bastard all the space he wanted Ivan backed away, Dzik still further. Hopefully, she had come to terms with the limitations that the situation demanded. Unexpectedly, the closet was fairly neat.

Ivan saw him remove a black leather pouch. He opened it. "This is all that I have on the matter. My father's notes, the place of death, disposal of Alexei's body and so on. There is nothing else. Five hundred dollars and you can keep it. These would be the first things I have given over since seven years ago. You have no idea how hard this is on me," holding the pouch close to his stomach.

Ivan was convinced that any delay on his part would allow for Dzik to conjure up some way to beat up miserable

Maksim and steal the pouch. He reached into his pocket and took out five $100 bills, after all this was money meant to facilitate cooperation. He handed it across to Maksim who counted out the money, an elbow being used to protect the pouch from a grab, while quickly glancing at Dzik. Ivan noted that Maksim had good instincts about people like Lena Dzik. Satisfied, he handed over the pouch, saying, "I'm staying here for a bit. We're done."

Briskly, he and Dzik walked back to the elevator. She put her hand out. Ivan gave her the pouch. They parted in the lobby. Nothing was said by either. He went over to Helena who was talking with April Wenger. April looked up at him and said, "I see you met up with Boris," now laughing hysterically, "you look pale and you don't smell like a flower."

CHAPTER FORTY-TWO

Back at the Hyatt, Dzik began to examine the contents of the pouch. There was a death certificate for an Alexei Raspin. Death from a fall, broken neck. The certificate was signed by a medical doctor, approved by the city coroner (a stamped signature) and signed by Sergei Yashansky. That was, of course, Maksim's father. The accident took place on the fourth floor of a tenement building, 30 Dongan Place, Inwood area, in upper Manhattan.

Raspin's address was listed as an upstairs apartment over the Yashansky's grocery store. The NYPD found no evidence of a crime. Interestingly, Yashansky got the police report. Bribe? They attributed it to a blackout or seizure at the top of the ten-step stairway and a subsequent fall. Death was ruled as instantaneous. The police report included neighbors in the six apartments on the fourth floor. Added notes indicated that three of the six were not at home during the incident; they were interviewed on subsequent days. Of those three, no one claimed to know him. But of the three present in their apartments at the death, one did think that he had seen the man once or twice in the past coming from apartment 4B. A young woman in 4B was questioned. She said that she had never seen the man before, stating that her mother was out. No follow-up was ever done.

A subsequent check on the deceased showed no record of the man, probably an illegal Russian alien. Since it was seen to be an accident no further action was taken on the matter. The body was released to Yashansky and Dzik figured that the corpse was cremated or buried somewhere in New York City.

Lena sat back and thought about the day and this information about Raspin and Yashansky. She removed the dedicated phone from the safe in her room and texted the following to, she presumed, Dimitri:

> [Possible breakthrough here in NYC. Need some research. A man called Sergei Yashansky – his ties to Russia? Grocery store owner, son Maksim. Also the death of a man named Alexei Raspin, close friend to Yashansky. Raspin reputed healer. Sudden death at 30 Dongan Place in Inwood, Manhattan in 1980, November 3. Need name of tenant in apartment 4B at the time.]

Within minutes there was a reply, presumably from Dimitri:

> [Cease all inquiries with priest. Stay on current probe, however. Research will be done on requests.]

Dzik was stung by the order. While she had to be physical with the robed fraud she thought that she had reached an understanding with him, that he'd comply with her investigation about Rasputin and the sainthood ploy.

Not unusual for her, she slept poorly, her mind in frequent twists and turns. She awakened at 5:45 a.m., showered, and went to the lobby for breakfast. She texted Ivan at 6:30 a.m. figuring that the *bon vivant* was still asleep, certainly not serving his country. He was told to come to the Hyatt lobby at 8:00 a.m. and from there they would taxi up to 30 Dongan Place wherever the hell that was, she shook her head.

Back in her room at 7:10 a.m. after a disgusting American breakfast she was texted the following:

> [Sergei Yashansky is from a family of czarist-sympathizers. The family arrived in the USA in 1919. Sergei was watched by the KGB up to 1985. Has son named Maksim written off as a fool. No further interest in him. Raspin is a different matter. Nothing on him. There was a suspected charlatan named Alexei operating in NYC for some time. Hearsay, as he would be one of many. As to apartment 4B occupant at 30 Dongan Place. The name was Liisa Haamer. She died in 1995. Records indicate a Russian parentage but one with Estonian heritage. Emigrated to USA, naturalized citizen. Had a daughter named Alexandra. More time needed to research as there is no marriage

recorded nor is there an Alexandra Haamer.
Records oddity. More time needed.]

Ivan arrived at the hotel at 7:40 a.m. He went into the breakfast area and poured himself a cup of coffee. He took one doughnut. He used Dzik's room number when asked by the server, some kind of remuneration for having to deal with nasty Lena. At 7:57 he left the restaurant and went toward the hotel entrance. Halfway across the extended lobby floor he saw Dzik exiting an elevator door. He stayed back and when at the main exit he said to her, "Good morning."

Turning while simultaneously looking at her watch she said, "Yes, hello. We need a taxi."

He gave a two dollar tip to the doorman after the cab was signaled for. While progressing toward Dongan Place, she questioned why he tipped the doorman. He answered, "A courtesy." Her response was a "Buhf" or some such sound. He and Dzik simply were not meant for each other.

Thirty Dongan Place was on a curious street. Ivan saw it as a half boomerang, straight and then a severe turn halfway up the street. All told there were ten apartment buildings. Turning left off of Arden Street, 30 Dongan Place was first up, left, a dark crimson building. It seemed to have once had some class to it, some upscale decorations in stone near the doorsteps but neglect had taken a toll. Latinos seemed to have taken over as the primary residents in the neighborhood. The mailboxes were inside the dark lobby, a few with holes, where locks had been removed. Above the mailboxes was a handwritten note that read 'Superintendent – Basement'. They proceeded there, guttural sounds stood for conversation between the two of them.

The basement was dark and large, with serpentine passages. In one area they found a small mountain of newspapers and magazines while in another, an ill-lit room with a few washing machines and dryers. An older woman sat on an orange plastic chair tapping her foot to the sound of a noisy washing machine while reading a magazine. Finally they found a door that was signed 'Julius Klein – Super'. Ivan touched the ringer. They heard a sharp click-click behind the door. It flew open to a "Yeah?" Behind the yeah was a once muscular man whose body had turned to flab. He had light blue eyes, a truculent manner and looked to be in his 70s. Ivan assumed that he had never joined the white exodus a few decades ago. Behind him was an alert German shepherd who didn't bark but looked ready to attack on command.

To Dzik's credit, she was starting to allow Ivan to deal with their American contacts. He figured that her failed efforts with Maksim and her abysmal conversation with April Wenger had taught her to be careful around Americans who sensed her officious and overbearing ways. New Yorkers, especially, would not bow to this approach.

After introductions, Ivan immediately handed over a $100 bill. "We need your help." He didn't look over at Dzik who was probably sizing him up for a trial in Russia.

Klein took the money. His belligerent attitude softened. "What do you want?"

"A few questions. How long have you been the superintendent here?"

"Forty-nine rotten years."

"Good. We are trying to locate someone from the past."

"Go ahead."

Ivan detected the slightest German accent in the spoken words. For a moment he perceived Klein and his dog as concentration camp material. They would have made the cut in the old days. Ivan smiled, "In 1980 a man died, having fallen down a flight of stairs. His name was Alexei Raspin. Do you recall the incident?"

"Yeah. He was a Ruskie, beard and all. Why?"

"We think that he was visiting 4B. Liisa Haamer. But the police never pursued the matter. Raspin was an illegal, there was no interest. But we are interested in Liisa and particularly her daughter. There is a will in which she is named. But the daughter seems to have gone by a different name."

"Liisa is dead, many years ago. Cancer. Nice woman. Seamstress. But she had some male visitors if you know what I mean. But you're not interested in her?"

"No. The daughter."

"Ah yes. Quite a girl, Alexandra."

"A last name?"

Klein looked at him appraisingly. Then he looked at Dzik who had backed away, slightly behind Ivan. He found that interesting. She looked sour. He looked down at Rex, his dog, just to make sure that he was alert. There was something about this pair that he didn't like, Ivan too friendly and loose in manner, but her, barely introduced, tight and dangerous-looking. "I could probably find it somewhere in the records. Come back in a few weeks and I'll see what I can find. Maybe it will come to me if I think hard enough." The bitch came out at that and was now fully viewable. Rex omitted a very low growl. To Klein that was a sure sign that she was the one to watch. Rex could smell threat and danger. He waited for Ivan to respond to his subtle demand for more money in order to hasten his memory of Alexandra Speranskya.

Ivan answered, "We'll come back. However, for another $100 can you give me her name now? Perhaps a search of your books?"

"$200," the German said flatly.

"Very well, $100 now and $100 after you give us the name."

Klein held out his hand, took the money and said, "Ah, it just came to me. Alexandra Speranskya," as his open hand extended toward Ivan.

Ivan confirmed the spelling, gave him the money and he and Dzik left 30 Dongan Place.

In the returning cab Dzik said, "Ivan, you're pretty good at what you do but your use of our country's money is reckless. For now, you can stand down."

CHAPTER FORTY-THREE

An oxymoron! Patriarch Kirill just completed his *private interview* with Vladimir Putin. The qualities of his own voice inflection, his facial tics, position of his legs and so on, now probably being analyzed by some elite group of specialists devoted to Putin and his silent but omnipresent lieutenant, Dimitri. He was not quite sure why Putin was so adamant about Father Damien. But there was the President showing a flicker of anger toward him. That was rarely seen, Putin more the icy plotter and silent assassin. But, for reasons that he could not ascertain during the four minute interview, Father Damien's career was disrupted, if not fatally derailed.

There were times when he and Putin collaborated on policies either presented by the Patriarch himself or by Putin. Sometimes he managed to divert Putin through gentle persuasion, no choice other than being gentle. Other times he was ordered and steamrolled, his opinion not sought or if sought only to be ignored and even stopped in mid-sentence by the son of God, Vladimir Putin.

He was upset. He liked Father Damien even though in the deep registers of his heart he had concerns about the Georgian. Where were his sympathies? The Georgian

Patriarchy in Tbilisi or with Kirill and the Russian Patriarchy in Moscow? Ever since the breakup of the Soviet Union Georgia had shown proclivities to edge towards the West, even the European Union. The relationship between Tbilisi and Moscow was strained, not just politically but also spiritually. Damien came from a region of Georgia that essentially had been stolen by a Russian invasion of sorts in 2008, called Ossetia. Sometimes it is said that the difference between Georgia and its Northern neighbor Russia is an arbitrary border post. After all Josef Stalin himself came from the city of Gori, smack in the middle of Georgia.

As a seminarian, Damien was sent by the Tbilisi Patriarch to Moscow for further learning. Before long Father Damien, mentally, politically, and socially adept, had risen in the ranks and was now to Kirill what Dimitri was to Putin. But defying Putin was not an option. Father Damien was being politically assassinated by Putin. The best information he got from Putin was that Damien had interfered with a State investigation of high import. God knows what would have occurred if Kirill had asked for particulars.

The meeting took place between him and Father Damien within minutes of his return to his offices. When Damien entered, Kirill made the usual single index finger to his forehead reminding his visitor that nothing was safe from listening devices, the slightest of nods from Damien returned. He felt sadness and anger simultaneously at having to dismiss this man so much in tune with his moves. Yes, the Church was a resuscitated partner in the new Russia but not a full one, more like it had a five percent interest.

"Please sit Father," Kirill intoned, "I have some news of an appointment."

The Georgian reached into his robes for a notebook. But Kirill held up his hand and shook it for him to stop. "Yes?" Damien said.

"The Church has been subjected to a great deal of pressure to advance the cause of sainthood to the many deserving such an honor. This you know from your recent exploration of Rasputin. The job you did on the matter was restrained and brilliant." He saw that Damien moved in his seat and leaned in closely toward him, probably sensing something untoward. "I have need of a new post, formally recognized and given the power to investigate all the issues and persons around such an honor." He stopped. He felt empty and disingenuous. He observed a brief smile cross Damien's lips, a bitter smile.

Damien asked with a pretended innocence, "Who would be appointed to such an honor Patriarch Kirill." He immediately made the connection to the call from Father Leonid of Brighton Beach. It had been heard by the FSB, reported to Putin who in turn commanded Kirill to get rid of him. Ruin him. So now they would both go through this painful charade.

Kirill went on, "A new set of offices has been ordered for this job. At St. Sergius. A secretary will be supplied and the job will be undertaken without delay." He arose as did his prey. "The job is yours Father Damien. My congratulations. Please give over your current affairs to Father Petrov."

Damien thanked him copiously and left.

On his way to his office he reminded himself that he was still young and that in Russia nothing was final until you were buried. In the old days of Stalin and the reprobates around him he would had been murdered. Everything is possible until it's not possible. When he came to the office door he was approached by Father Petrov, his successor. To his credit Petrov looked embarrassed. They both knew what had just happened.

CHAPTER FORTY-FOUR

When McAbee was entering the elevator for his customary ride to his office he received a text on his iPhone. It read: [Peter Goodkind here. Seems subdued.] It was from Pat. He thought about going back to his car, calling Jack Scholz, or even calling the Davenport Police. He chose to go up and face Peter. Arriving, he looked at Pat first, who held out both hands, palms down, a signal for calm. Then he looked over at Peter who did not rise, unusual.

McAbee went toward him and sat beside him. He said, "Peter, I am sorry that our relationship has ended the way it did. Also the death of Eddie, very sad." Peter only nodded. Bertrand went on, "I understand that you were in the hospital. I'm glad that you're out. Are you okay?" A gentleness of speech in every word. Observing Peter he saw a man who seemed to be in some kind of drugged state.

Peter finally said, "I want to see my wife. I know you and how you operate. She has been squirreled away. I want you to help." This all said in a halting and soft manner, very unlike him.

Bertrand was quite watchful of this new Peter. Was he holding back the emotional equivalent to lava? He mouthed to the alert and watchful Pat, 'Jack'. This conversation could go off the rails. He wondered if Peter was armed. He certainly was not all together. "Joanna is not at your house. I know that. She is scared of you Peter. What the future holds is unknown by me. I don't, can't, and won't speak for her." He was watching Peter very closely. The old Peter would have been screaming profanities and making threatening remarks, by now.

"I need to talk with her," he again said. "You owe this to me, McAbee."

"I'll relay your message to her. From there it is up to her. Not me. Not you," Bertrand responded with a measured stiffness in his voice.

"Do you represent her now?"

"It's against protocols to give client names but in this case I will. The answer is yes, and as you know, you and your business are no longer a client. So, Peter, our conversation is over. I am asking you to leave here now. Again, I'll relay your message to her." Bertrand started to get up but Peter reached across and very forcefully grabbed his forearm. The lava within him beginning to flow.

"Very important. I will hold you responsible…"

At that point Jack Scholz entered the office. His quick glance at Bertrand and Peter picked up the large hand around Bertrand's lower arm. To divert Goodkind he said to Pat, "I'll get that package but first I'd like to speak with Bertrand. He then turned toward Peter and Bertrand, saying, "Hello Bertrand, Peter."

Bertrand wiggled his arm loose and stood. "Peter is leaving now. As you might not know Jack, his company is no longer a client of ours. Among other things I am reminding him that he is no longer welcome in this office."

"Of course, a long standing rule," Jack said picking up on McAbee's strategy. He came closer to the pair. He, also, wondering whether Peter, who looked odd, was packing.

Peter walked out of the offices, the glass doorway had its frame tested by his hard pull.

"Lots of insanity in that guy's eyes," Jack said. "I was going to come in today anyway to let you know the setup for the Russian."

"Alexandra you mean?" Bertrand asked reflexively still thinking about Peter Goodkind.

"Yeah, the Russian," Jack looking at Bertrand closely. Maybe Peter Goodkind shared some of his drugs with McAbee.

Pat said, "Bertrand, I can set the buzzer system on the door. That would control for his entry."

"Yeah, sound idea. I'm worried also for you Pat."

"I have my pepper spray and the taser that Jack gave me. I'm not defenseless."

"Good," Bertrand caught himself, knowing that he was operating in a disconnected manner, still absorbed by Peter and then forward to Joanna. "Yes, Jack, let's go into my office. Let me know about the setup at Lady Alexandra's place."

Jack gave him the essence of what he and his buddies had done. The entire complex was wired, any movement in the compound and even around the perimeter of the property was under video surveillance. At nightfall an extra layer of security would capture any movements in and around the property. All windows and doors were armed and merely had to be set by the Russian with a simple command to her Alexa device. Only one window was not armed due to her insistence. In that room there was a "pretty nice" carpet. The systems would be monitored by a group of elderly but competent seniors: "who had too much time on their hands. They'd probably do it for nothing," Jack said.

When he finished his recitation, done with military precision and brevity, McAbee thanked him for coming over so quickly, remarking that Peter Goodkind was not quite together.

When Jack left Bertrand asked about Augusta. When was she coming in?

Pat responded, "Fifteen minutes."

"I'll be in my office."

Pat felt that there was still a big part of him obsessing about Peter Goodkind.

McAbee looked over at his desk and then the giant cedar bookshelves that held his Loebs. There were six different volumes open, lying face down, covers fully exposed, four greens and two reds, this in spite of Pat's cleanup campaign. He looked around at them, sitting at different places in his office. He sought solace in them, most of the time, but not all of the time. He sat, depressed and unsettled, until Augusta stood at the doorway. Her electric smile and upbeat personality shook him out of his malaise. Hugs and cheek kissing done, they both sat across from each other. Augusta has just arrived back from her visit to Champaign-Urbana, the University of Illinois and her daughter in the second year of law school. Her daughter had been through some tough times personally. Augusta was perpetually concerned about her. Her daughter's previous drug dependency issues were always offering a specter of darkness. She said, "She's doing well, I think. She's very private, I don't always know what might be going on but I have to live with what she says. I know that I have to show a balance, letting go but I can't entirely so. She has a tendency to date some dubious customers. So, two days over there was the sample size and I think she's going to make it."

As Bertrand listened he could sense the fear in her. She must have observed something in her daughter that left her uneasy. He chose his words carefully, "Both of your daughters are extraordinary, Augusta. I hope that it works out well. If I can do anything let me know."

"You know I will. But I'm not here to throw my problems on you. Tell me about the meeting with Lady Alexandra. I had three dreams about the two of you meeting together. Hazy. But I did wake up suddenly on all three occasions."

"She's quite sure that something is coming out of Russia or with Russian finger prints, that it's hostile, that it's proximate and that it's about her. She's convinced that she's a healer, a psychic, and that she can affect events with her powers, a bewitcher."

Augusta said, "I felt that was the case when Eddie died. Joanna reported it too exactly to me. There seemed to be a power transfer. A power used against Eddie."

"She filled in all of the blank spots on her résumé. I think I have everything that she's prepared to share. Plainly speaking, she's scared, she's convinced that she has all three of the gifts: healing, foretelling, and bewitching. Somehow, she is unable to fathom, Russia has entangled itself with her life. She used the word *weaponized*. Her success in life is being obscure, hidden. But things have changed. Augusta?"

"You sound like you're not a believer, Bertrand, you think her demented."

"No. Not demented. I just have a difficult time crossing over into her system of thinking. She's quite smart, brilliant. But she's in a different solar system. But I've taken her at her word. Jack has set her up with a professional monitoring system. She is now a client and we'll give her every protection possible."

"Very happy about that Bertrand. Let's hope that it passes."

He went on to brief her about the appearance of Peter Goodkind. A big worry. Peter's desire to meet with Joanna. Would Augusta feel her out about that and what conditions she would require if she consented to such a meeting?

Augusta said that she would do so and also continue to drive Joanna to Lady Alexandra when such was requested.

Augusta, he noticed, seemed to be in a hurry. She left. Bertrand picked up a red Loeb, Latin, Seneca.

PART FIVE

RUSSIA ATTACKING

CHAPTER FORTY-FIVE

Dzik was disappointed. There was no way to track back to the true origin of the name Speranskya. She googled the name Alexandra Speranskya. There was a match to it in the hinterland of the United States, Iowa, Davenport, a city sitting on the Mississippi banks, across from the state of Illinois. She had scant knowledge of the Midwest, her work in New York City.

[Need background on Alexandra Speranskya, currently in state of Iowa, city, Davenport. If to proceed will need Boris (cf. Oslo investigation) and Vasily Gorski of Cyber Unit. Both know me and have performed dutifully in past]

Dimitri received this latest communication at 7:00 p.m., Moscow time. He hesitated in responding to Dzik. She was all that he had hoped for in regard to getting things done. But he also agreed with Vladimir Putin. She had the subtlety of a rock, not ambassadorial material. Her desire to use Boris and Vasily is what delayed his response. His files showed them both heavy handed by inclination. Add that to Lena and one would have a perilous trinity. Ivan Brodsky, the brakes on mayhem. He decided to discuss the matter with Putin, the next morning. He congratulated Dzik, telling her that her requests were being considered.

When he got out of bed the next morning at 5:00 a.m. he was uneasy, the source of it Dzik and Putin. In his heart he was wary of this entire pursuit. As Vladimir Putin had aged he noticed a quality in him that 20 years ago was similar to a candle in a dark field, noticeable but negligible. The candle had burned brighter over the years. In the past year the light had passed to floodlight dimensions. The growing obsession with Rasputin was troublesome.

But clear-sighted Vladimir was in possession of materials that convinced him that Rasputin had extraordinary powers, the candle becoming a floodlight. There was no choice in the matter, his job was to do anything he was ordered to do by his boyhood friend. And he would, unswervingly. He reflected on Adam who was presently drinking himself into a graveyard. Adam was brilliant. Drunk and all he didn't miss a trick. Perhaps he saw that candlelight long ago and foresaw what would come. Adam couldn't face, sober anyway, an inevitable lurch into false mysticism.

Putin welcomed him into his office at 8:00 a.m. Coffee and croissants on a side table, a many years custom between the two of them. Dimitri had already been through his own private briefings about the economy, threats, the military, and the seeming infinity of absurdities in this world.

"This is what I see this morning, Vladimir."

He then went on to outline how he saw the matters of State. When he was finished he would then be questioned in a way that suggested falsely that Putin had not looked over the same materials he had. It was a charade; they both knew it. Vladimir's version of dialectics. The session took one hour and thirteen minutes exactly, about average.

"Do you have time for the Dzik investigation?" Dimitri asked. He would bet his last ruble that he would.

"Yes, of course," Putin said in a tone of disbelief at the very question.

"I have good news. We are very confident that we have found the son of Rasputin, going by the name of Alexei Raspin in New York City. We have the name, with 95% sureness, of a child by him. A woman by the name of Alexandra Speranskya. She lives in the Midwest of America. We are engaged in a full pursuit of what is known of her. One thing seems obvious. She is not craving notoriety. She is as hidden."

"Now what?"

"That's where I need some direction from you. Lena Dzik has performed as predicted. Competently. Her records indicate no knowledge or familiarity with the Midwest of America, a handicap but it can be worked around. She is desirous of visiting Speranskya but wants to know about prohibitions, barriers, limits around what she does. She has asked for two operatives here in Moscow. Both are not known for their civility. One physical the other cyber. Add to that our knowledge of Lena Dzik and any sense of decorum or courtesy is probably lost once any resistance is shown. We do not want an international incident with America."

"I do not want any brutishness in this unless there is no other recourse. If she is given these two operatives what restraint do you recommend?"

"We can say that she is never to resort to violence. This

would mean no Boris. Vasily works his charms via the computer. But he can be controlled."

"Can Dzik?"

"She has true red blood. She will do whatever she is ordered to."

"You are not clear in your answer. Do you trust her?"

"I do, within limits. Orders have to be very precise. I would never give her an open ticket. Another dimension, here. She was assisted by Ivan Gorsky from our U.N. mission. He's quite polished. Impeccable judgment. Very Americanized, but a patriot. He was of great help to her. She found him heretical but she respected his abilities, even though they were corrupt in her eyes. He uses money instead of fists." Dimitri smiled into Putin's smile. "I had her give over the dollars to him. He used them well."

"This Ivan? Do you vouch for him?"

"Yes. He's quite capable."

"How much does he know?"

"He knows that we are in pursuit of three lost paintings from the Hermitage Museum."

"Can we keep him at that level of deception or would he catch on?"

"I think Dzik can control for that. But he's quite sharp. Reliable to keep his mouth shut if he learns or suspects more."

"Speranskya. Do you think she'd come here to Russia?"

"My assumption is not willingly."

"Money is not an object here, Dimitri. Give this Ivan a run at her. Millions are acceptable to me as an offer. Then, if that fails, we let Dzik have a go at her. Death is not to occur.

Also, I want Dr. Wilosky to come here tomorrow morning before you give any orders on this."

"Of course," Dimitri said.

The next day Dimitri entered Putin's offices with Dr. Wilosky in hand. Wilosky had asked Dimitri about what to expect. Dimitri demurred.

Putin got right to business. "Doctor, we believe we have found the granddaughter of Rasputin. Tell me your thoughts."

Wilosky paused his tendency to give out quick opinions. He understood the importance of this moment. Finally, he said, "There is some research out there that suggests that a skip takes place in the passing of characteristics. I have a friend who does drug addiction rehabilitation. He swears that there is a generational skip in addiction, it is not the son or daughter of the addict who suffers but rather the son or daughter of them. There is a chance, therefore, for this woman to have extraordinary powers," he nodded his head in a reinforcement of his opinion.

Dimitri watched Putin closely as he considered Wilosky's words. No read was possible.

"So you are saying that she could be the equivalent of a genetic Rosetta Stone," he smiled.

"Ah. Yes. Possible only, of course." Wilosky said cautiously.

"We will be sending a team to investigate her. Perhaps, more than just an investigation," Putin said obliquely. "What could such intrusions present?"

Again, after pausing, Wilosky spoke, "If she is the inheritor of qualities – psychic, healer, and possibly,

Joseph A. McCaffrey

though I doubt, casting her thoughts into material objects and altering them – then I believe she already knows that Russia is searching for her. There has been such a flurry of action around her existence that I can't believe she would be unaware of it. Her skills as a psychic would almost have to pick it up. Otherwise I would begin to question that she is gifted."

"So, you are saying that she is probably hyper-alert to our interest in her. And this, what should I call it, sorcery? Rasputin allegedly had it. Would she be dangerous?"

"Mr. President, I have never been overly fond of going that far. But let's say, for these considerations, that she has such? Then yes, she's quite dangerous, lethal in fact."

"I daydream, of course. Anyone with those powers would be worth a mountain of gold to a country, not in hiding which she appears to be, but now under our control."

"Most assuredly," Wilosky said, nodding.

Dimitri saw Wilosky look back toward the door, probably wanting to leave as the discussion was crossing into science fiction. Someone like Wilosky, a famous and grounded scientist, was already on a shaky tree limb. Maybe Putin was teasing him. He would do that to people sometimes. Dimitri could always tell it in his eyes and mouth. To his bewilderment, though, he didn't see any sign of such.

Wilosky was dismissed. Dimitri stayed on to preview the day but before he could get to those matters, Putin said, "Authorize Dzik's requests. Make sure she gets what she wants, plus add Ivan, the U.N. man. Have that team travel by a rental van. No planes. Keep Dzik under very tight control Dimitri. Tell U.N. Ivan whatever he needs to know."

"Of course," Dimitri said firmly.

CHAPTER FORTY-SIX

Dimitri was very specific in his instructions to her. The papers given to her by newly arrived in New York Boris would self-destruct when placed in a sink of hot water. Accordingly, she read the materials carefully and repeatedly until they were memorized. It took about five minutes for the odd-feeling pages of instruction to disappear. She wondered whether the CIA was onto such a unique invention.

Boris was his usual stolid presence. He was built like a huge refrigerator and as personable as such. But he was incredibly obedient and subservient. Her kind of man. He was another ethnic Russian whose family had been sent to Bulgaria back in the 1920s to do the work of Russia. Like her, he never lost his center; he identified as a Russian.

Vasily, on the other hand, was a man of a different ilk. He was Russian *non-interruptus*. Tall, he was as thin as a blade, wispy blonde hair, sideburns to his jawline and a nose that seemed to occupy most of his face. She had worked closely with him when she was undercover trying to choke off Ukraine's bid to become a Western satellite. Extraordinary technical skills, but with one serious handicap. He was religious to a fault. He believed in the whole mess of absurd theological gibberish of the Russian Orthodox Church. To him, Putin was the second coming of Christ, returning Moscow to its centrality in the Church of many patriarchies. He had once said to her that what Rome was to Roman Catholics, Moscow was to Orthodoxy. Such pious stupidities had to be overlooked.

She also knew that he had been busted by the authorities for hacking into some Russian Departments of State, especially those dealing with the Orthodox Church. It didn't help his cause when child pornography was supposedly found on his computer. Turning him into a loyal and docile tool of the State was not difficult, the choices stark, either submit or be assigned to a gold mine in Siberia where computers and wifi were hallucinatory concepts. Did they really find pornography? She wondered.

Ivan Brodsky was another matter. He was given a separate set of instructions. These were outlined for her but she did not get everything that had been handed to him. In effect, he was allowed a budget of ten million Euros with the stipulation that Alexandra would come over to Moscow. She would be offered a downtown Moscow apartment, a dacha and an apartment overlooking the Black Sea in Shoshi. All of the above was on offer once she demonstrated her abilities to him. He was to be an intermediary in negotiations that would be directly overseen by Dimitri himself.

Her job was to allow Ivan to use a charm offensive as the first order of business. If Ivan's efforts failed Dzik would then be permitted to use more direct methods on Alexandra, everything short of killing her. Kidnapping might be entertained, permission required.

Although she was in charge, Ivan was given too much

leeway. It was obvious to her that he was a favorite of Dimitri, thus she had to be careful around a man she saw as a fixer, a whore driven by money and what it could reap. There was corrosion around his serpentine ways. He was more Byzantine or Ottoman than Bolshevik.

Additionally, they were forbidden to fly to Iowa, too many records, too much surveillance by this phony open society of America. 'Rent a large vehicle' was the order.

And so it was that the four of them set out for Iowa in a huge Cadillac Escalade ESV in February, Vasily and Boris at her command, essentially ignorant of the core mission. Ivan was hunting down a potential recipient of three stolen paintings, but she wasn't sure how much he really knew.

CHAPTER FORTY-SEVEN

Alexandra sat in darkness. The winds had let up almost to a stillness. It was as though a pact had been made between the winds and the freeze. The winds would let up, taking a rest, but inviting into the new stillness a freeze from the Arctic. At 8:00 p.m. the thermometer had read minus 13 Fahrenheit. The overly cheery weatherman on Channel 8 predicted a near record of 20 below. Just two more degrees and we could enter the record books he bellowed, not quite nudging his viewers to run out into the streets and yell for joy just in case that extra two degrees occurred.

She was trying to box her thoughts, a mental trick her mother had taught her. Create four boxes. Color them, black, blue, red, and yellow. Four possibles. If she needed more boxes, color them differently, e.g., green, pink, purple and whatever. Just always keep them alphabetized. Her mother would joke; if you need more than eight boxes you have become insane, 'Burn them all and jump off a bridge', she would say laughingly. Alexandra smiled at the memory of her mother, whose rare laughter was so genuine.

She proceeded to place each compelling issue into a box. Into the black box she placed her fears of the bear – Russia.

The blue box was packed with Joanna and Peter Goodkind matters. The third box, red, was filled with ACJ, specifically Augusta Satin and Bertrand McAbee. The fourth box, yellow, was filled with her defenses. It was the last box, afloat in her subconscious, that was not quite developed.

She delved into the black box first. Her fears were based on tea leaf readings and intuition. Russia could have two sources, either the country itself or perhaps a situation arising from her work with Timofey those many years back. Slavs had long memories. Timofey had worked among them, making his share of enemies not only with them but also tribes – Italians, Latinos, Jews, Blacks, and so on. Never ending. Had one of these groups found him, acquired her name and was now making her a target? Thus, that as a possible explanation of the bear. There was an answer to this, perhaps. The phone number he had given to her along with the code if and when he answered. She hesitated. After all these years was it wise? She listened within herself but heard nothing. She poured herself a Stoli with orange juice.

Pausing with each touch of the number she dialed the country code of Switzerland. She listened on her iPhone, buzz buzz, buzz buzz. A voice, his, immediately identifiable, "Oui?"

She gave the coded phrase, " Brooklyn, I'm here."

There was a long pause, then, "I will call you back. Moments." A disconnect.

His voice was as controlled as always. She was overjoyed to hear him even though she continued to question herself about the propriety of the call. What alarms it might set off. When she told him of her fears would he dismiss her as an alarmist or as stupid?

In short order, a call registered from an unknown number. She answered, "Brooklyn, I'm here."

"Are you well Alexandra? The call is safe. Tell me."

She began, "I am very concerned Timofey. You know I would never call otherwise. First, are you well and safe?"

"I am both," he said tersely as was his manner.

"This will take some time. Please indulge me," she stopped speaking, giving him the opportunity to reject a prolonged narrative. He said nothing. At the end of her recitation she said, "You don't know a half of me. I have gifts that were passed through to me by my father through his father. For an unbeliever they are suspect and perhaps ridiculous."

He interjected, "What gifts?"

"I can foresee into the future, not always, of course. I can heal bodily conditions, sometimes, not always. I know that I can affect the lives of others by casting spells; this latter I have only used twice on threatening people. It is a power that frightens me. Nonetheless these exist in me. Please try to understand Timofey."

There was a long pause before he asked, "Have you ever mentioned this to others? I, for one, sensed your ability to foresee. I never put a name to it but I sensed it in you. We Russians are given to such gifts as you call them. But gifts are two-edged swords. To heal and cast spells is beyond me but I would never doubt you. Who knows about this?"

"Some people here locally are aware but I keep a low profile. I am in the American Midwest. I am afraid of the ramifications if these became too public, especially the last of the gifts. Where I live is in a somewhat obscure area."

"Specifically, who would be aware of this latter gift?"

"I have hired a security agency because of my fears. Allow me. I read tea leaves. Extraordinary messages are received through them, not always of course. Because of some readings I have become convinced that Russia is on the prowl. I am fearful. It is the reason for my call, Timofey. Is this Russian threat based on our collaboration those years back?"

Again, the long hesitation. "Alexandra, if you tell me that you have not gone mad I will believe you 100 percent."

"I'm not mad Timofey. If anything I am more alert now than ever in my life."

"You are trying to eliminate possibilities. How many are you concerned about?"

"Two. Us together, and Russia itself. I can think of no other possibilities."

"Have you eliminated Russia?"

"No. You are the one who will decide that. Do you see?" Alexandra said passionately.

"Then it is Russia. Our situation was, is, and will be forever, sealed. There has been absolutely no winds on the most sensitive of feathers except now from your call. If you are correct Alexandra then you are up against the bear itself. But why? What do I need to know to make sense of such?"

"I can think only of my father and his father Timofey. There is a bloodline that attaches to me through them."

"This doesn't go back to the Czar, to the Romanovs?"

"No. Not directly," now wondering about the wisdom of disclosing her secret to him.

"Why would they care about you? Living in the Midwest, obscure by your own admission. To what end?"

"He was a prominent official in the Romanov regime."

"So what? There are plenty of those descendants hanging around the world," his voice tightening.

"Supposedly he had gifts," she said.

After another long pause he said, "Alexandra! There were all sorts of maniacs in pre-revolutionary times claiming to be clairvoyant or miracle workers. I cannot see Mother Russia or Father Putin entangling with that. Even a prime candidate for all this, Rasputin, shouldn't raise the attention of Russia or Putin himself, I think. And thankfully, you are not a descendant of the infamous Rasputin."

She shuddered. She felt that to share that heritage with him would be to endanger him. What he didn't know about this connection is what he needn't to know, the fruit of a dangerous flower. So, she withheld this crucial datum. She replied, "Timofey, I am sorry for reaching out to you. But you were a big help. I conclude that the bear is afoot for some reason. Sooner or later it will come near to me."

"I hope not for your sake. If you have to call again, do as you did."

"Before you leave, one more thing. Please."

"Sure. What is it?" he said.

Ten minutes later Timofey was gone, hopefully for the last time. She considered her options. Then from somewhere in her heart she decided that she needed to speak with Bertrand McAbee and Augusta Satin.

CHAPTER FORTY-EIGHT

Another chair had been brought into the Persian room. It was a necessary meeting for Alexandra. McAbee and Satin sat there, both faces pretty neutral, his more so, skeptical to the end. Augusta's look was more expressive but her defenses were back.

"Thank you for coming to see me. You have become my angels. I have no one else, you see. All the signs that I use are signaling that I can trust you. So I will."

McAbee said, "Whatever you say to us will be buried within us. No notes will be kept; no indications of this meeting will ever be transcribed by us. It's the best that we can do to honor your trust."

"It's all true, Alexandra. His word is sacred. It binds me too," Augusta remarked.

"Very well. Some of what I'm about to say will seem untrue or exaggerated. None of what I say is false, no deceit is involved. At the end of it all you may wish to end your relationship with me. I'll regret that but I will accept your judgment."

McAbee nodded. Augusta said, "A separation would be most extraordinary."

"I start. Some of this you know. My mother was born in Estonia, but she was Russian through and through. I was born in New York City. My father's last name was Raspin, a Russian also. There was no marriage between them. He was a vile man, an abuser psychologically and physically of both my mother and me during his rare times with us. My mother learned to hate him soon after my conception. Somehow, at my birth, my last name was changed to Speranskya. I never learned how that was done or what she had to do to effect this. She wanted to separate me from her name, Haamer, and particularly his name of Raspin. So, in a way, I became a cypher. It was very important to her; she hated him so and I think she hated herself for getting involved with him. He tried to force an abortion on her, at the time a very risky and illegal act. But she was steadfast against him. He beat her but to no avail. My mother was a wounded but good woman. A survivor."

Bertrand was busily filling in those revelations with what Barry Fisk had determined in his search about Alexandra. Some questions were now answered. Augusta listened with her heart sensing the anguish in Alexandra's recital.

"I continue. My mother was a skilled seamstress, a tailor, but in the privacy of our apartment. In hard times, she would see men. She was a very practical woman. Reliant. She would do what she had to. Unfortunately, my father would visit us but not often. Hurricanes are not often and yet their damage is long-lasting. Welcome to my father and his world. He would beat her, rape her, and then leave, half-drunk mostly. Eventually he did the same to me. So nothing unusual here, a common enough story where wife and child abuse is present. Yes?"

They both nodded in unison. Bertrand and Augusta were good listeners. Alexandra was also experiencing a lift in her psyche, relating a story that she had never revealed to anyone. "So now I start my stray off the path and into things that you might find absurd. But I must preface what I say. My father would bellow in my ear that I was a special child. His filthy beard and rotten breath an inch from my devastated self either from seeing my mother bleeding from his punches and God knows what else or fresh from a violation of me. He would say, "I am a Rasputin! Your blood is sacred!" He would, of course, add other expletives after that pronouncement. Bitch, cunt, cow, whatever came to that corrupted mind. Then he'd leave our small apartment, perhaps throwing a five or ten dollar bill on the floor near the doorway, as if he was paying at a whorehouse."

Augusta looked downward; McAbee kept his focus fixed on Alexandra who appreciated his penetrating eyes. It was as though he was not surprised by her story. He probably had a very pessimistic view of humanity. She agreed with that. "You must understand, I was a very gifted student. Well beyond my peers. My mother was quite attuned to that, cultivated it in me. But I was not aware of the other qualities that were dormant in me."

McAbee interjected, "Excuse me. When you say the name Rasputin, am I to assume that he also changed that name to Raspin?"

"He was illegal. I don't know the name he used when he came to America. He was transported into this country through an underground for Russian emigres. He had disclosed this to my mother very early on before he showed his true self to her. I have no reason to question that he was the son of Rasputin himself. The resemblance was astonishing. Even now when I see a picture of *the* Rasputin I cannot shake the visage of my father, eyes and all. To put it another way, I am sure that I am the granddaughter of *the* Rasputin, of Czarist Russia."

Finally, McAbee reacted, his eyes suddenly adrift as they bounced around the Persian room. Was this his first test of her sanity, veracity? Augusta, she noted, kept her eyes downward, perhaps more engaged with her story of abuse. McAbee was the scholar, he would be fully attuned to the implications of her disclosure about her father. Alexandra was sensing that she was quite drawn to the two of them. Their vibes. She liked them both, even as she sensed McAbee's reservations.

"Your mother? Did *she* accept him as he said he was?" McAbee asked.

"Yes. She was staggered by it. She was very aware of Rasputin's legacy. No Russian was ignorant of what my father's father was and his history with the Czar, the Romanovs. She cautioned me frequently. 'Stay clear of this disclosure. It can only lead to trouble.' And I did. Augusta, when you came to me I discerned that you had gifts but they were dormant within you. You may not have believed me but I am correct. And Dr. McAbee? You also, but you would be a reclamation. A project," she smiled wistfully. "I go on. My gifts were dormant in me with one exception. I could heal to some extent. My mother would be subject to migraines. She would close the bedroom door, pull down the shades and place a black towel over her face. Terrible to watch. But it came to be that I could place my hand over her forehead for a few minutes. Within a short span of time the migraines would simply disappear."

"How long is a short span?" McAbee asked abruptly.

As lightly as she could she jabbed at him, "Are you part of the Vatican that investigates the merits of sainthood?"

"Hah. I had that coming. I should not have asked the question so abruptly. But your recitation is fascinating to me."

"The answer is within fifteen minutes. But unfortunately I did not understand this gift for some time. What is dormant is dormant. It upsets me as I could have been more of a help to my mother. My mother, a Russian true to her heart, was also a reader of tea leaves. But as it was, when I practiced the art I surpassed her. I never told her this but I knew from some incidents. But, still, I was in a denial of sorts. I'm very logical, scientific mind-set. Like you," staring at McAbee whose eyes would not be still. "I slowly became aware of my powers although it seems that I tried to suppress them, except in the case of my mother and her migraines."

"How did you know about your tea leaf abilities? You said you were well beyond your mother."

"I knew when my father was coming, to the day. I also learned from the leaves when my mother would engage with men, her migraines too. She could never discern these things. The leaves, the way my mother used them, were as a horoscope in the newspaper. Generalities about nothing. It was a hobby for her; for me it was much weightier even though I continued to deny. I became scared, in a very real way. When the Rasputin legacy came my way and I understood the implications, I became traumatized. No good can come from such a bad father I thought. When

I heard the Greek myth of Pandora and her wedding gift from the gods, I related myself to that story. The supposed gifts were vile and constituted all of the ills of humankind. I equated my father to the gods. No gift was a real gift in truth."

"That's a pretty savvy analysis. I get your point," McAbee said reflectively.

"So, I see these gifts as a two-edged sword. Part of my DNA somehow, for good, for bad."

Alexandra stopped her recitation. She informed them that Maria was not present in the house. She would like to prepare tea for the three of them. She did so attending to Bertrand's cup with only a minimal amount. He looked pleased that she remembered.

"So I go on now to what brings this matter to the present. It is one thing to have some healing abilities and some sensibility about the future, and some understanding of people by touching them. Rare abilities probably, but nothing that could shake the world. My usage of them was under very tight control. I did not want a public pronouncement."

McAbee registered a disagreement. "You have done just the opposite it seems. The business that you are in. Word gets out. You're not invisible here in the Quad Cities."

"Is that a question or an accusation?" she said testily.

"A question," he smiled, "remember I am investigating you for sainthood."

"I am not used to being questioned or cross-examined. I should not have reacted in that way. We have much to go. No one ever gets my full understanding of things; I am a master of concealment. I am a counselor, a sherpa, a guide. I was careful that clients left me thinking nothing other than I was a wise woman."

McAbee said quickly, "When Augusta came back from her first meeting with you she was awed by your skills. Her psoriasis too."

"That is a good point," Augusta said.

"Ah Augusta, you were transparent to me. You projected powers. I have only met two others who could compare to you. You emitted so much that I could not help myself from helping you even though you presented yourself deceitfully. I felt an obligation to awaken you from your torpor. That is why I told you of cancer and touched your psoriasis. Rare would I do that. Hiddenness is my first rule but I sensed in you a kindred spirit. I knew that you'd be back, a source of light."

Neither McAbee nor Satin said anything. Alexandra was not surprised. She was coming at them with many disclosures. She didn't intend to jar them but she could feel it happening to them. "I have gotten over my fears about the qualities that I have spoken to. There are some clairvoyants who are superior to me, there are some healers who are superior to me, there are some who intuit others better than me. Very few, as far as I know, have all of these gifts, however. When I see clients they will only see one gift. Augusta was an exception. The leaves secured my trust in her. I have no regrets."

Augusta said, "I felt an enormous surge in me. It was as though we had bonded. I had no control. It is true."

"But now I come to another room. A room that is most frightening. Augusta, I know that you quizzed Joanna about the incident with Eddie Goodkind. His sudden death, my words preceding it. And Dr. McAbee, I briefly discussed the issue with you. But, in honesty, I backed away from it. I will not accept his death as being a murder. An act of self-defense, yes, but not a murder."

"Of course not. The cause of death was a massive heart attack. It had nothing to do with you except that perhaps your words psyched him out and precipitated his heart failure. But I think that is a stretch," McAbee said evenly.

"But you have only half of what I want to disclose to the both of you. I accept that there is the possibility of coincidence but I don't think so. Eddie Goodkind was not the first to die off of a focused wish that such should happen. When I faced down Eddie I was quite sure that he was a dead man if he proceeded against me. Where did I get this idea that I could state this to him and be sure of the result? It goes back to my life with my mother, and in particular, my father. Many years ago, he had finished his rapes. He left me on the kitchen floor. He had already done so with my mother. I could hear her sobs. I was in shock, once again. This was my father." She stopped and looked away.

McAbee observed an almost unearthly look of anger in her eyes that were also filled with tears. He looked at Augusta whose face had clenched in disgust.

"I saw him take out his wallet, take a bill from it and fling it to the floor. He said, 'bitches'. It awoke in me an anger that I have never felt since. My mind became so focused to one thought – his death – instant. And deep within me I felt an aura, almost a seizure, I want to say out of body. I was no longer sobbing on the floor. A power. Hard to describe. A few seconds later, Rasputin's son, my father, was dead. He had fallen down the stairs and broke his neck. But my mind replaced the word fallen with the word taken."

As she described the scene, her face had a peculiar glow. If McAbee had been superstitious he would say other-worldly. But he fought the urge even as he was in astonishment with her recitation.

"What I am saying is this. I am a dangerous woman when under severe threat. I am also saying that I have the power to cause harm. I have steered clear of its usage. I have been tempted, of course, when I am angry about something but I refuse to bring myself into that state, a frenzy, I could say. My father generated that condition in me; me unaware of what power I had. I had never gone back to that state. Then Eddie comes with a gun and I am almost immediately in that frenzy. The words I used to dissuade him came from me but not from me. It was as though I was taken over, and in a blink I knew he'd die if he persisted. What I am saying to you both, as friends and guardians, I feel that something lives within me well beyond the simple act of healing or prognostication."

Augusta said, her voice on edge, "There is no question in my mind Alexandra that there is a uniqueness about you. It would not shock me to learn that all you have said is true, a result caused by you, not by a coincidence. I am in wonderment." She looked at Bertrand who sat impassively but whose eyes wandered the room.

Finally, he said, "Cause or coincidence, that's the question. Your bodily experiences during both episodes are definitely tilting the deaths to causality. But it strains reason. Yet I can't underestimate your argument for such. But Russia. That was the issue for us. How does that fit?"

She turned to him and said in a soft voice, "You sense in me a slight case of paranoia Dr. McAbee. I understand your concern."

"I never said that," he came back quickly.

"No. You didn't *say* it. But it's all over the room sir."

McAbee was once again chastened by this incredible woman. "Well, the thought was held briefly, I will admit."

"Unlike you, I am not a Vatican saint chaser. I won't ask for a definition of *briefly*," she smiled.

Augusta noticed a slight flush in Bertrand's face.

Alexandra went on, "I know as only I can know. You either believe or you don't. Your agency has provided me with early warning systems through that man you sent…"

"Jack Scholz," McAbee interjected.

"Ah yes. A man who shows signs of having risen from the dead. To encounter him is to touch the hand of death and violence."

"He has had quite a history behind him. But as a protection against the forces you are apprehensive about you couldn't find a better ally," McAbee said with some defensiveness, surprised about how adamant he was in defense of Jack.

"Yes. Of that I am positive. I will need help, for sure. The leaves show a bear, no longer standing still, but rather one in motion. I believe the time is coming near. I do not think it wise for Joanna to come here again. Augusta would you be so kind. I believe that her husband will soon be back in the psychiatric ward. If and when things settle I will, of course, reengage with her." She looked back at McAbee. "If I am here."

"I have another question. When your father died, did

314

you leave the apartment to see? How did you become aware of his death? Noise? Screams?"

"I heard nothing. I was fixated into my anger. But I knew that something had happened or would soon happen. The clarity in my mind had a certainty to it. I was attending to my mother when I heard a commotion outside in the stairwell. I then knew. I went out."

"What did you see?"

"There were three neighbors. One had come back from outside. He roused the others. The police were called, an ambulance too. But I saw. He was gone, his neck was broken, his face half turned from his frame, arms splayed out oddly. Face full of madness, a sneer, mouth open. Why do you ask this? You are nosier than the Vatican," she said sternly. "The scene will always be in my memory and also my reaction to it."

"Which was?" McAbee inquired.

"Joy. I don't think that I was ever happier in my life."

"How about with Eddie?"

"I was upset with him. He certainly could not compare with my father. He brought me into a state of anger by his stubbornness and his imbecility holding a gun on me. I immediately got control of myself afterwards. But I was not happy as was the case with my father. I knew the police would inquire and there were witnesses, Maria and Joanna. I did not want the police to interfere with my life. Like you, the cops were unbelievers. Since Eddie was never touched by me there was no case. No knives, no weapons, no poison. It was as though he suffered a heart attack."

"I'm not an unbeliever Alexandra. I come to belief, however, hesitantly and perhaps unwillingly."

"One would not need my abilities to fathom that," she said to Bertrand with a smirk.

"I have thought hard about Russia and you. Unless you are holding back some key information, I can't get why they're coming after you. You're an unknown to them."

"I have closed off the only other possible angle. It's not that one. I eliminated it last night. It has to be in Russia. I believe it may have a connection to my grandfather. That's the best explanation. After all, we are dealing with a country that has huge resources and great curiosities. Perhaps something was found in some file about him, some physical trait that he had. A rare disease? A disorder? Some antibody, who knows? The possibilities are countless. What provokes the interest I cannot tell. I perceive their coming. The *why* escapes me."

Augusta remarked, "You have spoken about the physical. But I think it might be more obvious. Your gifts!"

"That sounds possible," Bertrand said in response.

"I have thought of that, of course. But how would they connect A to B?"

"They're Russians. They have a sophisticated intelligence service. They're conspiracy addicts. Rasputin is a legend. For all we know you might be the only heir. They may come in peace, by the way. Or, of course, they may never come," he said.

Alexandra sighed. And, if he was attuned to Augusta's whispered sigh, he would have heard that too.

Augusta said, "We came here also to discuss your security arrangements. This is a good time to review them?" she asked Alexandra, while looking baffled at Bertrand.

"Yes," she responded.

He came back to the conversation. He realized that the two women were not pleased with him. He owned that he had been pushy with Alexandra, prying. "We have placed you on a 24 hour emergency system. I believe that Jack Scholz went through this with you. With the exception of this room everything around the property is wired. We believe that any transgression onto your property will be picked up and a response to it almost instantaneous. There are two men, highly qualified in defense, who live within a half mile of this residence, one actually a stone's throw, just north of here. They are part of the reaction team. Augusta and I are, of course, always on call, one or another."

Alexandra nodded. "That's reassuring. Russians can be blunt. If their purpose is to call down harm on me they will be crude about it. I think that I'll be well protected. There are so many ways for them to come. But this particular avenue is secure. I thank you."

"If there's nothing else we will leave," McAbee was halfway up when he sat again, seeing her right hand held out.

Alexandra said, "Allow me. The leaves."

Augusta volunteered to be first. Now familiar with the process, she swirled the contents of her cup. She perceived a mound on the top of which was a rectangle of solid leaves. "Once again, I'm not sure of this. Am I a tower on the top of a mountain? Back to my sentinel interpretation that you saw before?" She smiled at Alexandra as she handed over the cup.

"You are opening to interpretation my friend," Alexandra said gently, "but it needs more time than you are giving it. You must learn to walk into it; insert yourself into the picture, gaze around. I have done so. It is not about you, Augusta. It is a stele, a tombstone on top of a burial plot. I can't read any deeper. It could be us; it could be them. But it does portend death. Now Dr. McAbee, yours?"

He gave it to her, not prepared to make an interpretation.

She removed a pencil from the inside of her garment as she stared at him for a bit. "Your leaves depict an airplane. Flight. Allow me to demonstrate this."

McAbee observed her long fingers around the pencil as she almost surgically pointed to the wings and body of a possible aircraft. He saw why she observed an airplane as he tried to make out other possibilities. He was failing to do so.

She said, "The two of you tell a story of death and flight. I will look at mine." Her eyes squinted as she studied the remnants in her cup. "Mine is not as clear as yours. In fact, I see nothing that I can interpret. Very unusual. I assume that agency is required."

Augusta asked, "Agency?"

"Yes. What I see is yet to be decided. My decision. Yours too will indicate the future. Our agency, our actions. We can only wait."

CHAPTER FORTY-NINE

The Russians arrived in the Quad Cities. At the urging of Ivan they booked in at the Holiday Inn Express in Moline, Illinois. Dzik, as she frequently did, thought that Ivan was too familiar with America. She was alarmed at the expense of each of the four having their own room. She deferred to Ivan on those kinds of matters, concerned that she would stand out in her Bolshevik ways – an oddity that might be reported to the filthy American police by the hotel staff.

Vasily continued the work that he had been assigned since his arrival at JFK, Boris in tow. He was circling around the elusive Lady Alexandra who put herself out as a psychic. Between his own efforts and with what was disclosed to him by a source in Russian intelligence, he was quite positive that this was the person they were looking for. Why the Kremlin was so interested in her was subjected to intense personal interest, not to be articulated to the others. Boris, whom he shared a flight with, was an absolute freak of nature. They spoke no more than was necessary, which meant that they were virtual strangers throughout the trip to America. He would keep his distance from him as he was obviously a henchman. It was wondrous to see such an obviously violent man kissing the ass of the Ukrainian. And she? All during the tedious and dangerous winter drive to Moline, Dzik would deride everything she saw of America. The depraved materialism, the gaudiness of their culture, and she especially found her sarcasm when they stopped at Walmart in Pennsylvania. 'Fat pigs! Slobs! Eating their way into death!' In some ways, he agreed with her but for the wrong reasons. She wanted to impose a hard Communist dictatorship to put rigor and discipline into the American character. That was not the answer, of course, and by the way, who were we to talk? Americans, on the other hand, were spiritually bankrupt. A return to God would bring about a change in character. But he said nothing to her. He had never experienced such a driven, harsh, and vicious woman. He had worked with her before, but at a distance, when she was shattering Ukrainian networks bent on freeing the country from Russia. But now, in person, he prayed for her, even as he concurred with her opinions toward Ukraine.

Ivan was another story altogether. He was likeable, knowledgeable, and urbane. Vasily wondered whether he was already an American mole in their operation. He was just too good at what he did. He threw money around like he was a capitalist. He wondered if Dzik would use Boris to kill Ivan at the right time. Dzik knew of his own religiosity and figured that he'd be on her list eventually. How she ever found out about his own religious leanings he didn't know but he calculated that the FSB was involved. The all seeing!

Regardless of everything, he would always be a true Russian patriot, the odious characters in the service of the country notwithstanding. Ditto for his faith in the Orthodox Church.

He had determined a good deal about Alexandra. He knew about her growing up in upper Manhattan, her studies at New York University, her time at Procter & Gamble. But there was a multi-year void in her life before Procter & Gamble. Nothing came from his countless stabs at it. Dzik suggested that she was a street-whore and advised that he look at arrest records. Lena Dzik, always sinking to the lowest common denominator.

He did successfully access some intelligence from Russia as she was employed as a translator in remnants of the old Soviet Union besides some time in Russia in the service of Procter & Gamble. She was seen as sharp-eyed and a possible plant by the CIA. She was fastidious in her personal habits; the intelligence services spotted no weakness in her that could be exploited. Not much there.

How she got the name Speranskya was impossible to determine. Clearly, there was an effort to conceal her parentage, reasons unknowable, but he speculated that it had something to do with her father.

Ratings on service apps of her as a psychic were extremely favorable. She took appointments on a one-on-one basis. But her website was very demanding for a client, restrictive, even prohibitive. It was as though she was doing one a favor for allowing entry to her services as a psychic. She asserted, for example, that she preferred females. That she was not interested in servicing skeptics, that she reserved the right to terminate sessions immediately and permanently. Vasily smiled at this. He liked her attitude. She was pure Russian!

When they met as a team, minus Boris, in Lena's room at the hotel they conjectured as to how best for Ivan to get beyond the restrictions on the webpage. Primarily, his gender was the problem. Vasily argued that Ivan had just one chance. His calculation was that Lady Alexandra was 'one tough Russian.' He noticed that Lena Dzik bit her lip in anger at the comment. Vasily hoped that Ivan was successful, dreading any approach that Dzik would use.

At the end, Ivan said that he would go directly to her place, identify as a Russian, and beg for a meeting. After all, he had much to offer her. He was a friend.

Lena said, "If the bitch rejects you it will fall on your back, your failure!"

The meeting ended with Ivan smiling and saying to Dzik, "And if I succeed it will probably also be my failure, Lena."

CHAPTER FIFTY

Vasily took the I-74 bridge across the Mississippi River, going from Moline, Illinois, into Bettendorf, Iowa. He exited at River Road, Route 67, and headed west into Davenport where he turned north on Gaines Street.

Ivan and Vasily chatted as they went forward. Ivan asked him, "What do you know about this matter?"

"Hah. What do I know? I know that I was on a 13 hour Aeroflot with monosyllabic Boris. I am to supply technical support to Dzik. We are trying to ferret out the location of some stolen paintings. We have a likely source of information named Alexandra Speranskya. It is Lena's job to smoke out this malevolent daughter of a bitch. That's it!" Vasily said resignedly.

"You believe that story?"

"Whatever I am told by my superiors I believe. You only get into trouble when you think otherwise."

"A wise answer from a tech wizard. By the way, I noticed your black bracelet, a cross at its end?"

Vasily hesitated in responding, distrustful of the quick-footed Ivan. "Yes. From the monks on Mount Athos. I try to be religious."

Ivan laughed as he said, "And you profess this faith around Lena Dzik, the atheistic Bolshevik from hell?"

"She tolerates me because we worked together to dismantle some Ukrainian cells rebelling against Russia. I try to be a patriot. Plus, I don't care for the *Ukrainian* Orthodox Church."

Ivan liked Vasily, thinking that he would probably be better off in the service of the Russian Orthodox Church than the likes of Lena Dzik. "So let's review this. We have a good understanding of this Alexandra's grounds. Thank you almighty Google. I will go to her gate unannounced. You will be with me. You determined that there is some gate surveillance and an entry protocol. I will try to talk my way in to see her. You will be with me as my driver. But you will attach that device, whatever the hell it is, to some part of the gate perimeter. It is so mighty that it can pick up the sound of a worm in the soil? Another wonder of our Russian technology. No jobs really created for the masses but we can spy on the masses with great skill."

When Vasily heard the irreverence in Ivan's voice, he once again wondered about Ivan's patriotism. Was he turned by the CIA? "And then you want me to sit in the car and wait for you. But you do not want me to make use of the voice interceptor until you leave her house. Yes?"

"That's correct. Do not record anything that I say to her. I am on a special leash by the authorities. Do you understand?"

"Yes, of course. I will stay in the car until you leave and then we will go back to the hotel. Very clear. I am a very obedient citizen."

They made the turn and headed west on Eighth Street.

They parked about 100 feet from the gate to Alexandra's residence. "Are you ready Vasily?"

"Yes. The attachment is quite small. You'd have to be looking for it to see it. The wall that houses the gate will work fine. All set."

CHAPTER FIFTY-ONE

"Jack, there are two characters approaching her gate," Mark, his watcher said.

"I'm getting it up now on my screen," Jack Scholz responded.

"Boy, that one guy looks like he's out of central casting. The gray Ruskie hat. He's dressed to the hilt. The one next to him looks like a stretched Igor from the *Young Frankenstein* movie," Mark said.

"I'll alert her of their presence. Keep your eyes on the Igor guy especially," Jack said.

Scholz called Alexandra. She said, "I see them; they're outside the gate. The tall one with the gray fur hat, he wants to see me. Pure Russian. He says he comes in peace, the other is his driver. He just left. I will let him in."

"I'll have one of my men there in less than five minutes. He'll be around. Just hit the panic button on your phone."

"Yes," she said.

"My name is Ivan Brodsky," he spoke into the voice mechanism. "I am a Russian lawyer attached to our mission at the United Nations. I would most appreciate it if you would allow me to speak with you. I come in peace. I have a proposal for your consideration. The man with me is my driver. He is going back to the vehicle now."

"I need a minute to consider," she said in Russian.

Ivan looked beyond her house and noticed that in the distance a bridge and the Mississippi River. The view was beautiful but the cold began to get at him. The weather was Siberian in this state called Iowa.

The box sounded, "Come in at the buzz. Only you."

As the gate was opening, he reflected that her voice was commanding. She would not roll over. He was probably on a fool's mission.

As he pushed the buzzer to her door, he once again observed the view, the raw beauty created by the winter and its effects. A maid of some sort opened the door. She said her name was Maria. She took his coat and hat and showed him into a small room with a stunning Persian carpet. It appeared to be almost exactly fitted for the room but its obvious age said otherwise. He sat and peered around the sparse room. Maria said, "Lady Alexandra will be with you shortly." At that she closed the door.

He never heard her enter the room. A rustle of jewelry alerted him, by the time he was aware she was almost seated across from him.

No doubt in his mind. This was a Russian face through and through. She was quite handsome but in a craggy way. Her face was angular and long. Her eyes held him. "Your name again, please. Also some documentation about your identity." No hellos, no handshakes. He was adversarial until he could convince her otherwise.

"My name is Ivan Brodsky," he said as he removed his

wallet from the inside of his suit coat. He showed her his United Nations' identification card.

"May I inspect it?"

He withdrew it from his wallet and handed it over to her. She studied it for at least one minute before giving it back. He muttered, "Thank you," as he placed the card back into his wallet. He then proceeded to silently curse himself. Why in God's name was he thanking her? Her presence and her accompanying skills had thrown him into disadvantage.

"Your coming here is not a surprise to me. I was expecting such. So, Ivan Brodsky, what brings you here to Iowa of all places. A social call?"

He breathed deeply. He'd have to turn back her offensive. He had once been a very accomplished chess player. He saw her through that prism. "There has been great interest in you by Russian authorities. I come in peace; I am not a menace."

"Russian authorities and coming in peace. Two concepts that some would say stand in opposition to each other. My time is limited so state your business."

"May I call you Alexandra?"

"Knowing the Russian mind and the waters you must swim in, I am sure that I have been called by other names. Yes? You may call me that," she smiled almost imperceptibly.

Ivan laughed. "Not by me. But, yes, there are others who have used colorful language to describe you; you so hard to fathom. You are quite good at concealment. I have only limited knowledge of you. If I may, I will describe what I know of the process that led to your identity," he said in as soothing manner as he could muster, now beginning to feel that he had made strides to reestablish his position."

"Yes?"

He outlined his assistance in discovering her whereabouts and identity concluding with his most forthright move. "In short, you are the granddaughter of the renowned Rasputin," He stopped and looked closely at her hoping that his disclosure would send her reeling, her steady calmness of manner broken.

No such thing. She said, "Why exactly are you here? To give me a medal? To defame me? To charge me with a crime? Please state your purpose, Ivan Brodsky."

There was a knock at the door. Maria came forward. "Your next guest is here. He is from Jack. He is in the kitchen."

Alexandra thanked her. Maria closed the door. "I repeat, your purpose?"

So much for that brilliant move. His tactic was blunted and he was back on the defense, better to get as close to honesty and candor as he could or else he'd be tossed out. Then Lena Dzik and crazy Boris would have at her, no more chess but straight out warfare. "The authorities in Russia, I mean at the very top of the pyramid, are exploring the passing down of characteristics that are uncommon among people. I tell you the truth when I say that I only have a limited knowledge of what lies behind this inquiry. Your grandfather was, of course, a controversial presence in Russian history. To some he had powers that can only be seen as other-worldly." He stopped his recitation, awaiting some kind of response. She said nothing. Frustrated, he went on. "You mentioned that you were not surprised by my coming here. I don't understand why you said that. May I ask?" He thought of his conversations with Arabs and Jews at the United Nations. Neither would be keen to sit across from this woman.

"It became apparent to me from my readings. The bear was out and about."

"The bear?"

"Russia. What is not to understand sir?"

"For one thing, when you say readings. I can't see what is meant. Now I get what you mean by the bear. You are not exactly forthcoming to me Alexandra," now he was immediately concerned that he had overstepped as he noticed that she had turned up her focus on him, a lazer beam.

Finally she said, "Ivan Brodsky, I have a business. I have rarely in my years here allowed entry to my house someone who out of nowhere comes to my gate. You are a curiosity to me, your wearing your Russianness so obviously. You fulfilled a prophecy by coming here. But so far your arrival, while prophetic, is as dust in a windstorm. Either get to your point or leave now."

She had taken his queen, his rook, and his bishop and was now sizing up a checkmate on his king. However, the game she was playing would be useless if Dzik and Boris came here. "Alexandra, you represent yourself as a psychic. Okay. You read about a bear and you are not surprised by my arrival. I guess this to be your claim as a psychic?"

"You hear the word *read* and suppose a book, a letter?"

"Yes. Something of the sort."

"Tea leaves," she said flatly.

He froze at this mention. How could the higher authorities, read his mentor Dimitri, be in any way consorting with this granddaughter of the lunatic Rasputin?

There were enough maniacs walking the streets of Moscow. Why come to Iowa in pursuit of one? "A lost art," he said weakly.

"A science in the right hands," she rejoindered.

"There were some comments about your ability to heal. Is there truth to that?"

"There are times."

"Your grandfather was said to have the skill."

"I've heard," she stated. She tapped the table with her long right index finger.

"How about your father? We…"

"Don't bring his name up again," her eyes now charged with emotion. "Who is we?"

"I have come with another. A woman. She has a companion. If I fail in my duty they will want to see you too. The matter is a concern of the State. But I repeat, I come in peace. I come with a proposal."

"I'm listening."

"I have an offer for you to come to Russia. You would be given money, housing, attendants, and…."

"That's enough. I have been in Russia as an employee of Procter & Gamble as you know. I will not go back there especially as this offer is made off of a State concern."

"I have some specific details. Guarantees."

"Never. I desire oblivion. You have made your case and you are done. Now I have a favor to ask of you in return for my allowing you to come in here. I want to read your leaves. Is that acceptable to you?"

"Whatever you wish," he said warily.

Ten minutes later he was at the end of his cup. He knew the ritual. His great aunt practiced at leaf reading when he was a child. But between her and the witch-like woman sitting across from him there was an ocean of separation.

"I see that you know how to participate," she said as she eyed his nearly empty cup. "Do you care to swirl?"

"I'm an attorney. I am hopelessly inadequate to the task."

"Allow me then," she reached across the table and took hold of his cup. She did a quick rotation of the leaves as they fell across the tilted side of the cup. She studied the formation of the leaves. She looked across at him several times as if to match the leaves with his persona. "I was abrupt with you. There was good reason for that. Be good enough to tell me of your offer. Details."

Obviously the leaves had forced a reconsideration. He said, "A luxury apartment in Moscow, a dacha and a place in Shoshi. Also, millions in euros."

"How many millions?"

"Subject to negotiation. Let us say four."

"And in return?" she asked speculatively.

"If you are as you say, the benefits of your gifts would minimize what is being offered to you. Surely, you understand. You could not sit around watching American television, drinking vodka, and having Cossack lovers. You would work for the State." His smile was met with stoniness. So much for the disarming humor that worked frequently for him.

"I believe that there is a genuineness somewhere in your soul. As a good man, you must know that your mission is futile. Money and properties in Russia have no value to me. While gallant, you are a materialist. You have been in the wrong part of America for too long. In the leaves you are on a horse, shield and lance. But you have been felled. Defeated. Do you wish to see?"

He nodded, leaning forward to see the interior of the tilted cup. From somewhere she had a pencil that she used to describe what she saw. What she called a horse was such but its legs had collapsed. The shield and lance askew, the knight, a bowed head. He looked away and at Alexandra who was staring at him.

"Your time is done Ivan Brodsky. Thank the upper echelons for their interest. You are a good man caught in a web. Eyes open! Always!" She arose, meeting over.

When Brodsky left the house, Mark came toward her. He asked, "Everything okay?"

"Yes. He's the lamb. The tigers will be next."

"We have a tail on him and the guy with him, the driver."

"Oh yes. Of course you would," she said in a soft voice.

CHAPTER FIFTY-TWO

Alexandria sat and said to McAbee, "Thank you for coming. We have much to pursue."

"Yes. Let me tell you what we have. Ivan Brodsky is who he says he is. My IT guy, Barry Fisk, ran some checks on him. He is highly regarded at the U.N. Some files have been opened surreptitiously by Barry. If you have ethical problems with hacking, let me know now."

She smiled, "Dr. McAbee, I hack people's minds. I don't have ethical problems doing that. Files are lesser beings. I'm listening."

McAbee wondered about the accuracy of that comment even as his skepticism about her was diminishing. "He has penetrated the comment files of the U.S., Canada, Britain, and Mexico. Brodsky is seen as engaging, materialistic, Americanized, but true to Russia. Some efforts have been made by the U.S. to bring him into the fold. No go. One other interesting piece on him. The British suggest that he is quite close to an important Russian official. The official is not named as a difficult program takes over and that file is impenetrable to Barry. Bottom line, you were dealing with an important man. Not to be taken lightly."

"I could see that. Clever, smooth. But I don't think there's killer in him. But he's too nice to get too far with that rotten gang running that country."

"He's staying at the Holiday Inn Express in Moline, by the airport. He was followed by Jack Scholz's people."

"Jack! My soul shudders at the thought."

Bertrand smiled, oil and water when that experience occurred. "They rented a large Escalade. Drove from New York City. Everything is in Ivan's name. Credit cards, etc. There are four of them, all in different rooms. When Ivan came today he was accompanied by one of them. We can't determine who he is. *But* we know this. He was wearing around his right wrist a woolen bracelet with a cross at its nexus, Orthodox related. He came to your gate with Ivan. He's a tech man. A tiny listening device was placed on the inside of your gate. Very hard to see. We took it off as a result of studying the footage of them at your gate. Jack has already turned it into the CIA. He has many contacts with the U.S. government. *Quid pro quo.*"

"I suppose your Jack Scholz exults in this, more clout for future returns?"

"Most assuredly," McAbee said, "I see that you understand that game. Besides his driver, there are two others with Ivan. Of them we know nothing. A man and a woman. He is built like a tank. An enforcer? She is brusque and singularly unfriendly. Ivan fronts for them, a diplomat!"

"I understand this. Ivan warned me but in a very cloaked way. That there was more to come. Perhaps those two?"

"What exactly did Ivan want with you?"

"They want me to come to Russia. Money and houses in exchange for my services. It all has to do with my grandfather. The passing on of qualities that he had. That gang of four flushed out my father's identity and then the trace back to Rasputin himself. There are some higher-ups, *who* were never disclosed, they feel that I have inherited powers." She stopped.

McAbee said, "And?"

"And? And? There is probably some merit. I cannot explain otherwise," she said impatiently.

"The offer? Here's a leading question. What did you say?"

She raised her head high, looking down her nose at McAbee. Imperious. "Of course I said no. Do you think that I'd ever get out of there again? If I was not up to their expectations they'd have a show trial. If I satisfied them they'd keep me in a guarded dungeon. I know many things about Russia. One of them is this. If they are keen to do something they will do it. Thus I am in harm's way. In Ivan's gloved hand is a lethal fist, not his, but others."

"We will arrange for one of Jack's men to stay the night here. Also, Jack and myself will come tomorrow morning."

"Yes. That is good but all of this is not why I needed to see you. I have made some decisions. I don't want you to judge me, to counter me, to do anything other than understand and assist me. I see in you that quality. But tell me if I am correct."

"Of course I will do what you want. But in exchange I need full disclosure from you. Don't hold back. You were very perceptive of Ivan's assets. Thus, in some ways, you understand those assets and can probably use them yourself. Diplomats are diplomats. They live in ambiguities."

"A fair appraisal. I will undiplomatically explain my plan. I intend to see the two he warned of. I sense danger.

You will have a man here. I can handle danger, let me assure you. If they mean harm they will be harmed in turn. But Russians won't stop. Ultimately I can only beat them by avoidance. I called the man I worked for all those years back. A throwaway phone, no traces. He had many contacts in the underground of this country. Mostly illegal and criminal. You wanted honesty. Dr. McAbee, I am going to disappear into Canada. New identity. Foolproof escape and routes. All arranged, except for a few details. I have invested wisely. Money held in several countries and I have three bitcoins for ready cash. From the sale of this house you will take payment for your services; plus, give Maria $50,000 in cash if you would. The remaining money will go abroad. You will be notified in a way you will recognize when it happens. That is my plan. Comments?"

"No comments now Alexandra. I will help you in any way that I can."

"How about some tea?" she said, her eyes strange to McAbee.

Preparations done, McAbee drank off the small amount provided in his cup. Without request by her, he tilted the cup and watched the leaves entangle and disentangle. The process reminded him of the atomist theory advocated by the ancient Greek Democritus, atoms and void, leaves and empty spaces. He handed the cup over to Alexandra. She scrutinized it for a long time. Finally she said, "It can't be read. I can't decipher. I suppose it's best to say that it represents you."

"And yours?" he asked.

"Mine. Clear enough. What can I say? It only states

the obvious. A thin road going northwards. Do you wish to see?"

"I'll take your word for it. So lastly, when does the departure occur? Do you need help?"

"I will see you one more time. It could be a few days. It's coming."

"One other question. Why wasn't Augusta Satin invited here for this session?"

"I simply don't want her to know anything. The knowledge is dangerous. But you? I always saw you as having Teflon for skin."

CHAPTER FIFTY-THREE

Returning with Vasily, Ivan went directly to his room. He removed his dedicated phone from his briefcase that had a superbly built hidden compartment for such. He called the encrypted and highly protected number in Moscow.

His call was answered immediately. "Da?" Dimitri's voice was low, emotionless.

"I have news. I met her today. No doubt about her being Russian. She did not dispute her heritage, even the mention of the famous one." He paused reminding himself not to use any names. Dimitri, his hidden mentor, had drilled into him the necessity for complete concealment about their relationship in addition to his belief that there were few secrets in Russia.

"Go on."

"I placed every offer on the table. Rejected categorically. A return of her to us will not take place peacefully. The Ukrainian is next."

"Necessary steps. High interest still. If that fails the mission will be abandoned for now. Back to your post in New York when appropriate," Dimitri disconnected.

Ivan then headed out of his room. A meeting with Lena

Dzik about to occur. He detested her but took joy in the game he was playing with the all-powerful Dimitri and her unawareness of such. He was allowed entry to her room. He observed that one would not know that the room was ever occupied.

"So? Ivan? Your report?" she said with a dose of venom added.

"She is the real deal. She didn't deny her grandfather's connection to her life. I made the offers that I was allowed. Her response was categorical. No. It was as if she had practiced for the meeting. She remarked that she knew that Russia was in play. Tea leaves."

"What nonsense – tea leaves! Did you tell her that there was more to come. Myself and Boris?"

"Yes and no. Yes, that there would be another visitor, no as to whom specifically. I thought that I'd leave that to you and Boris."

"Vasily? Did he plant the device?"

"Yes."

"If he did it doesn't work. We have nothing from her house. Not even your conversation with her," she said angrily.

"There is no record of my conversation. He was told not to record anything until I was back in the car. Only then did he turn it on."

"Why was that?"

"Security," he answered.

She looked at him meanly. "You don't want your persuasion skills on display?"

"That's one way to look at it."

"We will go there tomorrow morning, be prepared for anything."

"I always am," he left the room.

Vasily drove the two of them. Even though he had never been in America he was acutely aware of his oddness to the culture, that he didn't fit in. However, there were peculiarities and then there was that pair behind him in the Escalade. The two of them would fit in as guards at some stalag, their grim faces staring ahead as if preparing for service on a firing squad.

He had been scolded for the failure of his listening device. He had waited to implement usage until he and Ivan had returned to the hotel. There was nothing. The device had been silenced. Only a practiced hand would know how to do that. Furthermore, the concealment had been superb. In his quick observations there were no cameras on the property. So, the failure was beyond him. It had been decided that he would go back to the gate with Lena and Boris. He'd inspect.

As he did yesterday he parked near the same spot, observing that the sun was brilliant but the temperature vile. At least the winds had stopped.

Dzik said, "If you can reinsert the device, or find it, start recording immediately. I will want a record for my superiors."

Vasily shuddered. He did not want to hear these two exert their nastiness on the poor woman, Alexandra. He remembered the only comment that Ivan had made yesterday after his meeting with her. 'That's quite a woman, tough as nails.'

All three left the Escalade and proceeded to the gate. Vasily immediately peered at the nexus between the gate and the rock wall where he had placed the device. It wasn't there. He looked down at the snow. It had not fallen. But he also noticed some footprints around the gate enclosure. Was the device recovered? He looked around with great care. He did not see any cameras. Long after this mission was complete, he still was unable to fathom how the device was discovered. Perhaps a crow had taken it? There were some in the trees. But he placed another device.

Dzik told Vasily to go back to the vehicle as she pushed a button to engage the intercom. A 'yes!' came from the speaker. "I am Lena Dzik. I am with an associate, Boris. We represent Russia. We wish to speak with Alexandra Speranskya."

Alexandra heard the edge in the voice. She had told Maria to take the day off. Mark had stayed the night and in the early morning Jack Scholz and McAbee had come to the house. They would stay the day. She had mixed feelings. Jack's aura in the house was unmistakably violent, though tempered as it was by McAbee.

The warning from Ivan, or was it merely an announcement, had set up the defenses just in case those two at the gate were malevolent. She responded to Dzik, "Come through the gate when I buzz. I have been awaiting you."

Coats and hats removed and hung, Alexandra showed the pair into the Persian room. She had added a chair from her dining room. Boris, she observed first, as he was physically menacing. He was an enforcer, plain to see. A dime a dozen through every race, ethnicity in the world. They were the five percent of every group out there, stunningly stupid but cunning, or stunningly cunning but stupid, a good candidate for Timofey's old network. He said nothing but he grunted. There would be no paragraphs coming from him.

And then she turned her attention to Lena Dzik, short black hair with abundant white streaks, late fifties, early sixties. A resting, vicious bitch face, her eyes threatening from the outset of their encounter. The pair looked at Alexandra as if she was dangerous nuclear waste.

"So, you met Ivan yesterday?" Dzik said.

That was probably her version of small talk. "Yes, I did. I believe that I was very clear with him. I have no desire to go back to Russia. If you have come here to reassert your offer it will be to no avail."

"If I told you that you were thought to be a security risk even up to President Putin, his personal intervention involved, you would maintain your recalcitrance?" Her voice steady as a hammer in an accomplished wood worker's hand.

"What is important to Vladimir Putin is your concern only. You have not told me what you do in Russia?"

"I am a government official," Dzik said, "he also."

"Yesterday I met another of you. Why do you feel that this visit is necessary when my answer was so definitive?"

"You have never run into my agency and if you had I don't think you'd be so comfortable. I have questions. Please allow?"

"My time is limited. Ask." Alexandra noticed that Boris was flexing his large, thick fingers while Dzik's eyes had narrowed, her face hardening by the second.

"The nation-state of Russia had made an offer to you. An extraordinary proposition of material goods and prestige. Hardly anyone ever receives all that has been offered. Perhaps you are a hockey star? An astronaut? A Soviet hero?

No. You read tea leaves!" She grinned meanly, intent on breaking down this fraudulent soothsayer who practiced magic. When the revolution occurred over 100 years ago they were among the first to take a bullet to the brain, or a trip to Siberia, or both. A pure atheism had no traffic with practitioners of magic like the one who sat in front of her. And then there was the genealogy. The granddaughter of the most reprehensible Czarist of them all, Rasputin. Her thoughts were interrupted.

"You should leave now, both of you. You are no longer welcome in my house."

"Don't you see? It's not you. It's your genetic material that this is all about. One way or another you will be in Russia either as an undeserving hero or a deserving traitor, held in chains would be my guess. Do you not think that we can easily remove you from this useless country? We will. You are a lone woman living in an isolated villa. Come willingly and receive your rewards, come unwillingly and receive your torments."

Alexandra stared at both of them. A war had been declared. The prophecies of the leaves had materialized in these two. And after them? There would be more, and then more. She knew all too well the hard soul of Russia. Generous, artistic, talented but so ever cruel in governance.

Boris arose quickly, fast for his size. He looked over to Dzik who gave a barely perceptible nod to him. He grabbed for Alexandra's arm. She had pulled it back as she withdrew her phone and pushed an app called panic button. She drew back to the edge of the small room as Boris stepped into her space. Lena Dzik drew a gun. The door to the Persian room opened. No Mark, no Scholz, McAbee stepped into an empty space by the door.

Dzik backed up toward the window, the lamp in front of it. The visitor held up his hands, halfway. Dzik had no intention of shooting anyone, explicitly forbidden by Dimitri and Putin. The consequences of such would have international repercussions. But she would play out her hand as drilled into her by the KGB. "And who are you? To save the poor damsel in distress? A bit old for this, yes? Her boyfriend? Does she read your tea leaves or your sweaty palms? Sit in the chair, otherwise I will shoot you. Boris, leave the bitch alone for a minute but keep your eyes on her." She turned back to the visitor who hadn't sat. "Did you hear me? Are you a fool?"

"I'll sit if it helps you realize that you are in an impossible situation. There is only one feasible way out for both of you."

"Then keep standing. I don't need your logic."

"You do," he said tersely.

Lena was puzzled by this character. He seemed to be unafraid of her, as if he had the gun and not she. "What is your name?"

"Bertrand McAbee. I'm an investigator hired by Lady Alexandra who, as you have heard, foresaw your coming."

"Lady! Lady! This undeserving crow is illegitimate, a worthless entity with supposedly some interesting DNA. Lady! Hah! We intend to take her from here. If you try to interfere Boris will handle you and/or I will shoot you dead!"

"Hear me out before you do those things," he asked as mildly and unthreateningly as he could.

"Quick," she said.

"Outside this room there are three men and one woman

345

all but one U.S. Special Forces trained. They are armed. You would never get out of this room alive. You are a Russian citizen here on a rendition exercise against an American citizen. Your name is Lena Dzik. You work in Kiev. You are FSB. That has become known. As I am speaking with you every word is being taped. Your career hangs in the balance, you must know. Your friend? We don't have him yet in identification. He's clearly a thug in your service. You are experiencing a checkmate. Your man in the Escalade is being sat with by two of my men. Keys taken. The best resolution for the three of you is to get out of this country as soon as possible. I would recommend a Chicago exit, just 170 miles from here. Thank you for hearing me out."

Her nod toward McAbee set in motion the next chain of events.

CHAPTER FIFTY-FOUR

Dzik sat in the anteroom. Nothing had changed. Well, perhaps her reception upon entering the Kremlin. Maybe it was she, her humiliation grafted into her soul by those events she would have to address with Dimitri, Adam, Dr. Wilosky, and Vladimir Putin. Her failure even more bitter as she had come close to success.

Coldness in the air, was it really cold? She shivered as she entered Putin's office. She heard the ice cubes far to her left. Adam was his name; she was never sure just what he was in all of this. He was a drunk but more than that. Wilosky was gazing downwards, Dimitri stared at her with his usual poker face. She knew that both Wilosky and Dimitri promoted and recommended her for the Alexandra Speranskya mission. And then there was Putin himself. His look straight at her made her knees weak as she sat.

Putin began, "We all have read the reports except for Adam. Relate it all to him. We will listen in," he said with a kind of controlled menace.

She looked over toward Adam who held up his glass as a kind of salute, his face the kindest among the four. She outlined the scope of the mission, the trip to New York City, and her request for Vasily and Boris. Dimitri, who had called this meeting, had demanded that the involvement of Ivan Brodsky was to be minimized so as to not affect his position at the U.N. So, she did, skirting around his involvement as much as possible. To the best of her knowledge Ivan was still in New York at the U.N. She was proud of her work in discovering the identity of Alexandra Speranskya and in particular, her whereabouts. Adam was a good listener; she kept her eyes fastened to him, as he would occasionally nod as if to encourage her. But she knew that this was the easy part. "The first attempt at persuasion was done by a man representing Russia at the U.N. This man, Ivan, was briefed that Alexandra had stolen paintings. He offered her settlement in Russia along with generous rewards for her assistances in State matters. She was adamant in refusal. He withdrew from the scene in favor of a more robust approach. The next day myself and Boris, a tough agent with whom I have worked in the past, went to her villa. We were driven there by Vasily who had unsuccessfully planted an advanced listening device near a gate to her home. He came back with me two days ago. His involvement was incidental, an IT man, by far not an agent."

Adam held up his hand to stop her. He asked, "So the soft approach by Ivan failed. I understand your FSB background. Time to remove the velvet glove as it were?"

"Yes. My understanding of the mission allowed for this."

Wilosky asked, "Most importantly was your appearance or that of this Ivan *anticipated* by Speranskya?"

"Yes, she had indicated this to Ivan. It was as if she was forewarned, messaged in advance of our approach. She let myself and Boris right in also, as if prepared."

Putin leaned forward and, was it with a snarl, asked, "Did you take any account of her defenses? That she was luring you into a trap? There *was* knowledge out there that she was a psychic."

"I do not believe in such Comrade President," she said too quickly and far too categorically, as she thought in retrospect.

She caught Adam's gaze, the slightest of nods. She dared not look back at Putin, aware of her mistake.

Putin came back at her, "You didn't answer my question. Did you ever take account of her defenses? One way or another she was anticipating you, do you not think that she would also create a line of defense?"

She wanted to hide her head in shame. That was the issue, she didn't anticipate. Her arrogance toward Alexandra and dislike of America, her disdain of Alexandra's supposed abilities, had led to the disaster that transpired.

"Go on," Dimitri spoke for the first time.

"Boris and I were allowed in by her. I repeated the offers made by Ivan. She told us to leave. To me it was either confront her or call the mission down. She seemed to be alone. Defenseless. Boris was ready and I released him to subdue her. At that moment an elderly man entered the room. He held his hands up and…"

Adam said, "Why hands up? Did you have a gun?"

"Yes. I had already pulled it to frighten Speranskya. The man, McAbee, identified himself as a private investigator, urged me to think about the forces aligned against me. He enumerated them. He must have calculated that I wouldn't shoot anyone. Too dangerous. My brief was quite clear about not doing so. He is a private investigator. My conclusion? No police involved, no FBI. But he was quite sure of himself. We were in checkmate. Then a huge misunderstanding occurred. As I listened to McAbee I nodded in understanding. Boris knew two words in English, yes and no. But he also misunderstood my nod, always used by us on missions for him to take action. He grabbed Speranskya by the hair and placed his arm across her throat, McAbee yelled out something and the room was stormed by American thugs. I surrendered my weapon trying to protect Russia from a worst case scenario. I looked over at Boris, wanting him to stop. But he had fallen to the floor, he was convulsing. Right there. I went toward him. He needed help, a heart attack, I think. One of the men who had entered the room, wiry, thin, mean-looking stopped me. He said, I will never forget, 'Let the bastard die.' I continued to move and he slapped me so hard that I fell against the wall. Although I am trained in martial arts I understood. Something about him. I dared not fight him. Boris breathed heavy for some seconds, shuddered, and then died. Alexandra Speranskya murdered him and would have done me likewise had not that investigator McAbee stepped in and removed her from the room."

Putin said, "What makes you think that she murdered Boris? And murder you if she had the chance?"

"I don't know. I've thought about it frequently. I don't like words like aura, or presence, but at that moment I was positive. She is a dangerous bitch."

Dimitri, almost inaudibly, let out a low moan.

"Vasily, I was told, had been neutralized in the van by some others of these men. He was our driver. I had no doubt about that truth. I was alone in the house. McAbee, before

Boris acted, had cautioned me to go home. Take a flight out of Chicago, not that far away. The Boris misunderstanding of my nod had cost me that move. McAbee had gone off with Alexandra. That man I spoke of, the thin man, wanted answers from me. He said that I may leave from Chicago with Vasily. Boris' body would be taken care of but first and foremost he wanted to know what this was all about. I told him to go to hell. He smiles and then punches me in the nose. I bled copiously. Then he says, 'I know your type. You give it well but you can't take it.' He takes me into another area. He has a black woman search me. Another wild creature like him. She finds the knife in my shoe sole. These are skilled people. Professionals."

"So what?" Putin said. "You are too. But they outsmarted you again and again. Tell the rest of this to Adam."

"That man, I think she said Jack or Jake. He takes out a case. Vials of liquid, some syringes. He says to me we can do this without drugs or with them. I tell him about the stolen paintings. He looks at me scornfully. He knows I'm lying. He punctures one of the vials with a syringe and jabs me in the arm. The bitch holds me and then I'm fighting within myself, I'm in and out." Dzik looked at Adam for support. He gave her a look of sadness, from his soul. A very broken man but whose compassion was meaningless. It was the others; a quick gaze took in hostility, negative judgment. "Several hours later I was slapped out of my darkness by this same vicious man. McAbee was with him now. That woman too. She was black. I thought her gentle but I was mistaken. She was almost as bad as Jack, I'll call him that – Jack."

Dimitri said, barely audible, "We have his name, Jack Scholz. McAbee has an agency, Scholz does spec work for it.

The black woman is most likely Augusta Satin. The others involved are subcontractors. At this time none of this is important. What happened next?"

"I divulged things. I know this. I have a letter from McAbee. He read a small portion of it to me. Enough for me to know that I said things not meaning to. The letter is sealed in wax. I have brought it. I was told by him to only bring it to President Putin. To hand it to him personally. I do so now." She took the letter from her inside coat. Dimitri grabbed it and inspected it by touch, smell, sight before handing it over to Putin.

Putin handled the letter briefly before placing it on his desk. He asked, "Then what happened?"

"Jack said they would dispose of Boris' body. They handed me back my phone. I was to call Ivan and tell him to fly back to New York. Several of his men would take me and Vasily to Chicago. I agreed with this. From there I flew to Toronto and from there to Moscow. I told Ivan to book us for such. He did. The vehicle was returned in Chicago and we left."

"Did you ever see Alexandra Speranskya again?"

"No."

Putin said, "So I have a letter from this McAbee. The mission has come to this? All of my concerns fall to this letter? I am severely disappointed with you Lena Dzik. Your future assignments will be arranged by Dimitri. And one other thing for all of you, but especially you Dzik, if anything leaves this room about this it will be life-ending. You can all leave now except for Dimitri."

When Dzik arrived at the exit of the building, she felt a tug at her sleeve. It was Adam. He said, "From the very beginning of this whole enterprise there was no way to succeed. But like you I never considered a defense from Speranskya. Russian arrogance bites its own tail. Goodnight Lena and good luck in your future."

CHAPTER FIFTY-FIVE

It was to be their last visit with Alexandra. McAbee figured as much as he and Augusta drove to her place. The weather had relented, the temperature was going to reach 25 degrees Fahrenheit. The Channel 8 guru was having spasms of grief, no longer able to advocate the marvelous rush of setting records. He'd have his day again when tornadoes would rip through the surrounding area adjusting to the vagaries of the spring. But that was in the distance along with the flooding of the Mississippi River, now an almost annual thing. Years ago that had been rare, not any longer.

Alexandra opened the door for them. Maria had been given time off. Jack Scholz had provided a man. He helped her pack essentials only. The Persian carpet, her table, her chairs would come with her, little of anything else. Her new Canadian identity as well as passport was secure. All three sat in her living room. She was sad-looking.

Alexandra said, "So, it has come to this. My old friend in Switzerland has been a godsend to me. I won't tell you where I am going or how I will get there. It is all arranged. The contents of my Persian room will follow. It will take weeks for that recovery. Hiddenness is the order of the day.

I thank both of you for your diligence. The two of you are most extraordinary. You know the story of the brothers Epimetheus and Prometheus. The gods offer the half-wit Epimetheus a gift, a woman named Pandora, along with a chest full of gifts. Epimetheus was a fool. He had hindsight but foresight was lost to him. His brother Prometheus had the gift of foresight. He could project into the future as well as remember the past. Trusting the gods was absurd to him. Pandora and her chest of presents he knew to be dangerous. The gods were tricksters, nasty avengers. Epimetheus, though, doesn't listen to his brother. He falls for the gorgeous Pandora. The chest of presents is opened. Out of it flow all of the ailments of humankind, cancer, heart disease, jealousy, hatred, and so on. The calculation of all of this is mind-numbing. I am hoping that I am Prometheus but only insofar as having foresight, as we know the gods would do poor Prometheus bad, eventually," she shrugged and gave them both a grimace.

McAbee said, "There's an old blonde joke. Politically incorrect but it has parallels to what you just said. The blonde beauty is walking down the street. She sees a banana peel, 20 feet beyond. She stares at it and then says 'Oh no! Here I go again'."

Alexandra thought about it for a minute and then laughed. "A good joke. It could be said at the expense of anyone or any group. Universal appeal," she said. "Epimetheus, the dumb blonde."

He knew that Augusta had heard him tell that joke often, probably tired of it. He looked at her, she was shaking her head with a smile on her lips."

"So, Bertrand, the letter that you sent with Lena Dzik. Have you heard back?"

"No. Not yet."

"Do you think that she didn't deliver it to him?" Alexandra asked.

"I doubt that. My assumption is that she did. It was such that a response was almost of necessity. But that's my way of thinking. The Putin gang is another story."

"I am leaving tonight." She arose and went to her desk and came back, handing Bertrand a large stuffed folder. "Everything you need to know is in this. Also a phone number. Yours and Augusta's are keyed into this number. If, for some extraordinary reason you need to call me, just hear the buzz once and then hang up. I will call you, always from a different exchange but one that is in Canada. My disappearance will be complete, I hope."

Augusta said, "This is a sad ending for me. I found you to be incredible. You changed my perception of things."

"Well Augusta, you have special gifts. Try to find them but remember the price I had to pay for mine. And Bertrand. Your gifts lie in another direction. But they also are formidable."

He said, "Alexandra, one question. The powers? The gifts? Where do these come from?"

She looked at him for a bit, her hand holding the left side of her face. She said, "Bertrand, I know that you didn't preface your question with the phrase *the supposed*. You'll never truly believe. Augusta does, not you. Your skepticism is rigorously set in your mind. Regardless of that I answer this way, I don't know where or how I have them but *believe me* I do. How about some tea for us all?

When McAbee and Satin sat in his car they looked at each other, the sun just beginning to splinter the gray sky. He said, "Well, it's good to know that the leaves say we'll be friends forever."

She said, "Mistah, I could think of worse fates."

They both laughed. They kissed gently.

McAbee said, "Let's get the hell out of here before she finds some other tea leaves."

CHAPTER FIFTY-SIX

Putin sat across from Dimitri. "I wonder about this letter. It had to be penned during or right after Dzik's collapse. God knows what she disclosed to that bunch."

"I don't see any governmental interaction in all of this," Dimitri said into Putin's silence. "All appearances seem to indicate that Alexandra Speranskya has taken us to a draw. She doesn't want to associate with us. I imagine that the letter is the statement of a deal."

"I am hesitant to open it. So, this Boris? He just dies? All of a sudden just as he is about to disable Speranskya? Makes me even more curious about her. Rasputin on steroids? Dangerous possibilities. Well, here goes," Putin said as he slit the envelope's top. It was handwritten. Dimitri would have to unscramble the handwriting. Putin's command of English was mediocre at best. But his ability to handle actual handwriting was so poor that he didn't hesitate to have Dimitri read it. After all? Who else? He handed the four pages across to Dimitri, whose command of English was excellent.

Dimitri looked hurriedly at all four pages. On page four he found the author. Bertrand McAbee, ACJ Investigations.

That was not a surprise. The security apparatus had already determined the intervention of ACJ. He said to Vladimir, "The investigator McAbee has the handwriting of a monkey on cocaine, but I think that I can handle it." He read the following:

President Putin:

> You don't know me. At the end of this you will. You have demonstrated great interest in Alexandra Speranskya. Your methods are illegal and unseemly. This is an American citizen who has no desire for involvement with Russia. She never will. I speak for her. This letter will be seen by her before given over.

"That ends page one."

> You have associated her with her forebears. One of them is prominent in Russian history. No need to be explicit. Your agent, Lena Dzik, has been highly cooperative in sharing the nature of fixation that has among other things caused the death of a man called Boris.

Dimitri stopped. "Notice the word he used, 'caused'. Interesting. According to Dzik this McAbee was present when Boris died. In fact, he seems to be inside on much of this."

Your other behaviors, listening devices, U.N. staffers, are considered to be affronts by Alexandra.

"And page two ends with that sentence."

You are correct in your assumptions. She is gifted as a psychic and a healer. Actually your intervention into her life was foreseen by her months ago. I can assert that she appears to have these abilities. But she demonstrates them with only a few and only willingly. Force of any kind would not win out. Her proposal is simple, leave her be. The knowledge of this affair is limited to only a few. Her desire is to be hidden. The matter ends here.

"One more page," Dimitri said.

There is one other gift that she seems to possess. The death of Boris is the silent witness to such. Take this as something to heed. My personal information is enclosed in this envelope. I need some assurances from you that peace will exist between all. Alexandra will be unfindable from here on in. The account of this affair including our taped interview with Lena Dzik will be kept as leverage against any further actions from you.

Dimitri looked up from the pages. Putin's face was stony, jaw set tight. A card dropped out of the envelope onto the floor. He picked it up. It had the contact information for McAbee. Gently, he asked Putin, "What do you think?"

"For the moment we let things stand down. For how long I don't know. As a game of strategies and tactics we've been compromised for the moment. This man from the U.N., Ivan? How much does he know?"

Dimtri, perhaps sharing too much with his favorite, was caught off guard as some of his dealings with Ivan could be constituted as a betrayal of Putin. "He knows that there is more to this than three purported thefts from the Hermitage."

"Yes. I see. Lena Dzik turned out to be over her head."

Dimitri knew Putin no longer trusted the Ukrainian. "I can brief Ivan if you want him to visit McAbee. Ivan is very crafty, disarming. I can coach him if you will."

"Yes. For now, this is the only path. I need to be alone. Give me the letter."

When Dimitri left, Putin went to his private safe. He opened it. He read again, Rasputin's predictions, the note to the nun concerning Rasputin's son Alexei, and his note about that old man who had predicted his rise to power. He placed them back in the safe. Then he hurled in McAbee's letter with the words, "Sonofabitch."

CHAPTER FIFTY-SEVEN

Once again Ivan Brodsky found himself in the Holiday Inn Express at the Moline International Airport. He wondered how Moline, Illinois, had conjured up the word International for the small airport. He reviewed, yet again, his carefully given instructions by Dimitri. First off was the order, fly in, fly out. Don't meander. Use Uber while there, no need for a rental. Call ACJ, give his assistant your name, talk of urgency and meet with McAbee. Cut the deal! Know this, he knows who you are.

Ivan understood that he was not given the whole truth by Dimitri. He was glad of that as he sniffed involvement from Vladimir Putin. Unlike Icarus of legend he did not want to fly close to the sun with his waxen wings.

The information on McAbee was edited down to essentials. He had been a classics professor. He had a notorious brother who headed an international investigation agency. Brother Bill was dead and that agency was on life support. Bill talked Bertrand into leaving academia and opening his own investigation agency in Iowa. Bertrand had been in business for almost 25 years. Articles about him show his ability to handle daunting cases.

He has a team, some markedly nasty individuals. Girlfriend is Augusta Satin. A black woman. Both present at Dzik's betrayal of mission. The proffered offer that you will make is a one-time concession. Everything that can be learned about McAbee is that he will keep his word. *But* be careful of his words. May be tricky, a practitioner of linguistic ambiguities according to one knowledgeable source.

And so it was that a woman aide, having put Ivan on hold for a minute, came back on line and scheduled an appointment for the next morning. Ivan was apprehensive. He knew what had been done by them to Lena Dzik. That tough cow broke in short order. He wouldn't stand a chance if they came at him as with her.

The name on her desk was Pat Trump. He went to her and announced himself. She looked him up and down. Inspector General with marked foxlike features. She went to a closed door, entered and came back in a matter of seconds.

"He'll be with you shortly. Can I get you something? Coffee, tea, Coke?"

Coke would be good but not the kind she was offering. He said, "Black coffee would be gratefully accepted."

"Please sit," she pointed to a row of seats, "I'll have it for you in a minute."

He noticed that one of the seats was cut low as if for a child. That was odd. She brought the coffee in a thick paper cup circled by a piece of cardboard. He thanked her and waited as she went back to her seat.

Shortly after, a door opened and out came the man matching the sent photo, McAbee. Yes, he was surely into his seventies. Balding, high forehead, glasses, curious eyes – shifting colors between blue, gray, and green. Firm jaw and high cheekbones. He wore a blue sports coat, gray slacks, a collarless shirt – light blue and, of all things, he wore a pair of sneakers, black, blue, and gray.

Ivan arose. They were about the same height 5'10". Same weight too, about 165 pounds. But, blessedly, Ivan had 40 years on the American. But he was in shape. Moved well for his age, strong handshake, as he extended his hand and welcomed Ivan into his office.

McAbee said to Pat, "Pat, no interruptions, thanks."

His voice was clear, slight accent, East coast? One thing was for sure to Ivan. McAbee had psychologically stripped him and re-clothed him in that roughly 15 second interval.

He closed the door behind him and pointed to a chair around a small table. One seat was already occupied. She had to be Augusta Satin. McAbee introduced her. She was quite stern looking, unlike McAbee who showed some warmth.

After they sat, McAbee said, "Well, I'm listening. But before that I am aware of your visit to Alexandra Speranskya. Also your other Russian colleagues. What was said. She is a client to us. Augusta is a partner with me. She knows everything about this matter. If you're speaking with me you're speaking with her and vice versa."

Ivan was a polished diplomat. He had enough dealings in Russia and the U.N. with a variety of characters. They could be slotted. Then his innate charm would go to work. But he was not sure-footed around these two. An odd arrangement if he ever saw one.

But he proceeded into the winds. "I am not fully conversant about this entire matter. But let me say some things." He looked at McAbee whose eyes were moving around the room and while Satin's eyes were a black beam going right through him. "I was instructed to make a bargain concerning Alexandra Speranskya. Her connections biologically with *the* Rasputin were established. Scientific interest in her alleged gifts or abilities were high up in Russian scientific circles. My entire portfolio was to tell her what she could have if she came back to her origins, to Russia, that is. At no time did I threaten her. It is not in my manual of operations. I am a diplomat."

McAbee stated, "I have no reason to doubt you. But you travelled here with others, different intent and methods. You said as much to Alexandra."

"I said that as an alert to her, not as a threat. To prepare herself. I am not an advocate of rough stuff as you Americans say. And I know the outcome of the next day and what transpired with Lena Dzik. Alexandra took my warning, she prepared." He knew that there was a seed of truth to what he said but in no way was he trying to undermine the mission of the four of them. He noticed Augusta raise her head a few inches. She looked down upon him from a newly lofty angle. She didn't say anything. McAbee was tapping his fingers near his breastbone. Hard to read the two of them.

McAbee said, "So you went back to New York, the United Nations. Two others returned to Moscow. Dzik and Vasily. And poor Boris was dead. Dzik was broken down completely by us. This you know?"

"Yes. All this I have been briefed about."

"Then, only then, when a letter was sent with Dzik for these same higher-ups you were given the charge of coming here. Presumably with an offer?" McAbee remarked.

"This is all true. Higher-ups? I don't know how far," he lied.

Augusta leaned forward, "What did you infer from the death of your hood, Boris? Before you answer, he was never touched by anyone. Close to being so but never touched."

Ivan gasped for air. He took a sip of his cooling cup of coffee. "Personally? Or officially?"

"Both," she said still leaning across the table.

"Officially I infer nothing. The situation was quite stressful. It happened in what she called her Persian room. Very small. Also I understand that there was a mob in it? Heart attack is the guess. His body was not transported back to Russia. No autopsy. That's all I know. In what I have just said is also the official version. But personally? I think Speranskya murdered him. I think it is very likely that she has that ability."

Augusta leaned back in her chair, her head resting on her right hand. McAbee caught him with a hard stare before saying, "In the letter that I sent I indicated that Alexandra would be gone. You most likely will never find her. She has erased herself. And if what you said is true, why in God's name would you ever want to find her? There is only one deal. Tell me what you're offering."

"All matters go unresolved by all parties. We stop any further inquiries. It is a closed file. No effort will be made to track her. We wish her godspeed. The matter is to be a secret among the few with knowledge of it. That is my offer."

"Guarantees?" McAbee said.

"Well, you can release your entire files including the disclosures from Lena Dzik. That's your trump card. Ours? If you violate the agreement, every effort possible would be made to find her. If and when we do, the original offer I made to her stands. If she won't accept she will be dispatched. It is seen as a standoff with strong guarantees. There will be no written submissions, no records of our dealing. You have my word."

McAbee said, "Please step out of the room for a bit. I want to speak with my partner."

About ten minutes later Ivan, with a fresh cup of coffee, was asked back. McAbee came forward, "I accept on behalf of Lady Alexandra. It seems that Russians and Americans are very good at honoring this code – mutually insured destruction."

CHAPTER FIFTY-EIGHT

"There might be a right time for us. After all, we are quite good at the long game. We may yet have our chance at Alexandra Speranskya," Putin said.

"Yes. Of course. Ivan is back in New York at the U.N. He perceives two things. McAbee will keep his bargain and, two, he and his black woman are not easy marks. But as you say, it's a long game," Dimitri responded. "One other point. Vasily, the IT guy? He's safe but if you see different he'll be taken care of."

"No. Leave him be but keep an eye on him. Dzik though? What is the word defenestration?"

Dimitri winced. Lena had so many positives. He nodded, it would be done.

AFTERWORD

- Joanna's mother died shortly after Lady Alexandra disappeared. Peter Goodkind was diagnosed with dementia. He is in skilled care, in rapid decline. She is running the business and is remarkably happy.
- Everything planned by Lady Alexandra came to fruition. Maria cried when handed $50,000 in cash.
- Adam died several months after the Speranskya probes were halted, cirrhosis of the liver.
- Ivan Brodsky was promoted to Second in Command of the Russian delegation at the U.N., his career arc in ascent.
- Father Damien sits at St. Sergius shuffling papers, waiting for his chance.
- There was a cheer and a vodka toast at the Russian Embassy in Kiev when news came that Lena Dzik had committed suicide by throwing herself from the seventh story balcony of her hotel room in Moscow.
- Marta Verlovsky died in her sleep in her cold Kiev apartment. Her grandson said, 'finally'.
- Vladimir Putin removes from his safe almost daily the three pieces pertinent to his ascendency. But he

removes a fourth as well, from McAbee. This one hits a nerve; a sign of unfinished business.

- Augusta has taken to tea readings, sauntering around them with her eyes. She has not told Bertrand, yet.
- Bertrand McAbee shakes his head in dismay when he thinks about this case. He can detail his hardest case, most dangerous case, and so on. By far this was his strangest case. He wondered if it would ever end, when all was said and done.

Printed in the United States
by Baker & Taylor Publisher Services